SOUTH SEA TALES

JACK LONDON

SOUTH SEA TALES

Introduction by Tony Horwitz

Edited, with a Preface and Notes,
by Christopher Gair

THE MODERN LIBRARY

NEW YORK

2002 Modern Library Paperback Edition
Biographical note, reading group guide,
and note on the text copyright
© 2002 by Random House, Inc.
Introduction copyright © 2002 by Tony Horwitz
Editor's preface and notes copyright © 2002 by Christopher Gair

LIBRARY OF CONGRESS CATALOGING-IN-PUBLICATION DATA
London, Jack.
South Sea tales / Jack London; introduction by Tony Horwitz; edited, with a
preface and notes, by Christopher Gair.
p. cm.
ISBN 978-0-375-75929-1
1. Oceania—Fiction. I. Gair, Christopher. II. Title.
PS3523.O46 S76 2002   813'.52—dc21   2001056227

Modern Library website address:
www. modernlibrary.com

Printed in the United States of America

12 14 15 13 11

JACK LONDON

John Griffith London, the novelist, short story writer, essayist, and journalist whose own life proved as dramatic as his fiction, was born in San Francisco on January 12, 1876. He was the illegitimate son of Flora Wellman, a spiritualist and music teacher, and William Henry Chaney, an astrologer and itinerant lecturer. Renamed for his stepfather, Civil War veteran John London, he endured an impoverished childhood on various California farms and a succession of poorhouses in Oakland, where the family moved in 1886. London left school at the age of fourteen to work in a cannery. After a brief, dangerous stint as an oyster pirate on San Francisco Bay, he became a deputy for the California Fish Patrol, having adventures he later recalled in *The Cruise of the Dazzler* (1902) and *Tales of the Fish Patrol* (1905). In 1893 he boarded a sealing schooner headed for the Bering Sea. The seven-month voyage inspired "Story of a Typhoon Off the Coast of Japan" (1893), which was awarded first prize in a writing contest sponsored by a San Francisco newspaper, and *The Sea-Wolf* (1904), perhaps his best novel about the struggle of man against nature.

The following year London headed east by rail with other young hobos. He roamed across America as far as Niagara Falls, New York, where he was arrested for vagrancy. "I have often thought that to this training of my tramp days is due much of my success as a story writer," he reflected. "In order to get the food whereby I lived, I was compelled to tell tales that rang true. At the back door, out of inexorable necessity, is developed the convincingness and sincerity laid down by all authorities on the art of the short story." *The Road* (1907), a forerunner of the work of Dos Passos and Kerouac, recounts his experiences as a "road kid." Upon returning to California, London resumed his education by studying the works of Charles Darwin, Herbert Spencer, and Friedrich Nietzsche. He attended Oakland High School for a year and spent one semester at the University of California at Berkeley. During this time he became interested in Marxism and joined the Socialist Labor Party, gaining notoriety as the "Boy Socialist" of Oakland. The semi-autobiographical novel *Martin Eden* (1909) chronicles his dreams of literary fame that date from this period.

In the summer of 1897, London joined the Klondike gold rush, little realizing the wealth of material it would provide him as a writer. "It was in the Klondike I found myself," he later attested. "There you get your perspective. I got mine." He sold his first story, "To the Man on the Trail," to the *Overland Monthly* in 1899, and the *Atlantic Monthly* published "An Odyssey of the North" in January 1900. London's first book, *The Son of the Wolf* (1900), was a collection of Klondike tales that proved enormously popular. He quickly capitalized on its success with *The God of His Fathers* (1901) and *Children of the Frost* (1902). His other volumes of Klondike stories include *The Faith of Men* (1904), *Love of Life and Other Stories* (1907), *Lost Face* (1910), and *Smoke Bellew* (1912).

The Call of the Wild brought London international acclaim when it was published in 1903. Viewed by many as his symbolic autobiography, it recounts the story of the dog Buck, who learns to survive in the brutal Yukon wilderness. "No other popular writer of his time did any better writing than you will find in *The Call of the Wild*," noted H. L. Mencken. "Here, indeed, are all the elements of sound fiction." *White Fang*, which was conceived by London as "a complete antithesis and companion piece to *The Call of the Wild*," appeared in 1906. "The quintessential Jack London is in the on-rushing compulsiveness of his northern stories," noted James Dickey. "Few men have more convincingly examined the connection between the creative powers of the individual writer and the unconscious drive to breed and to survive, found in the natural world."

London next focused on social and political issues. He journeyed to England in 1902 to research *The People of the Abyss* (1903), a study of the appalling slum conditions in the East End of London. In 1904 he traveled to Korea and Manchuria to report on the Russo-Japanese War for the Hearst newspaper syndicate. The Russian Revolution of 1905 prompted London to give a series of socialist lectures subsequently compiled in *War of the Classes* (1905) and *Revolution and Other Essays* (1910). And in *The Iron Heel* (1908), an astonishing political fantasy judged by Leon Trotsky to be a work of genius, he imagined the rise of fascism in America.

In 1907 London sailed for the South Pacific. *The Cruise of the "Snark"* (1911) recounts the writer's grueling two-year journey through the islands of Polynesia and Melanesia in search of untouched civilizations. Forced to abandon his travels in Australia owing to illness, he returned to California in shattered health. Yet London soon produced *South Sea Tales* (1911), *The House of Pride and Other Tales of Hawaii* (1912), and *A Son of the Sun* (1912), works that attempt to reconcile his dream of an unfallen world with the harsh reality of twentieth-century materialism.

By 1913 London was the highest-paid writer in the world. In that year alone he published *The Night-Born*, a collection of stories; *The Valley of the Moon*, a novel of California ranch life; *The Abysmal Brute*, a fictional exposé of professional boxing; and *John Barleycorn*, a memoir about his struggles with alcoholism. In 1914 he traveled to Vera Cruz to cover the Mexican Revolution for *Collier's* magazine. Jack London's final years were spent at his ranch in the Sonoma Valley, where he died of uremic poisoning on November 22, 1916. His last works of fiction include *The Mutiny of the "Elsinore"* (1914), *The Strength of the Strong* (1914), *The Scarlet Plague* (1915), *The Star Rover* (1915), *The Little Lady of the Big House* (1916), *The Turtles of Tasman* (1916), *The Red One* (1918), and *Island Tales* (1920).

"Jack London was an instinctive artist of a high order," said H. L.

Mencken. "There was in him a vast delicacy of perception, a high feeling, a sensitiveness to beauty. And there was in him, too, under all his blatancies, a poignant sense of the infinite romance and mystery of human life." James Dickey wrote: "The key to London's effectiveness is to be found in his complete absorption in the world he evokes. The author is *in* and committed to his creations to a degree very nearly unparalleled in the composition of fiction." As E. L. Doctorow remarked on the front page of *The New York Times Book Review:* "To this day Jack London is the most widely read American writer in the world."

CONTENTS

FROM *ON THE MAKALOA MAT*

FROM *THE RED ONE*

INTRODUCTION

Tony Horwitz

In Jack London's fiction it's always fifty below. Sled dogs huff clouds. Saliva freezes and crackles mid-spit. Man and beast toil across borderless snow. Simply recalling the titles that I read as a schoolboy—*The Call of the Wild, White Fang,* "To Build a Fire"—sends a subzero blast through my window in Virginia and sets the wolves howling in my summery backyard.

It seems strange, then, to flip open *South Sea Tales* and find London writing about the sultry, Gauguin-hued Pacific. No one romanticizes the North Sea, except herring fishermen. But the South Seas! Swaying palms, sun-struck beaches, shimmying hips and shimmering moonlight. What in Buck's name is Jack London doing in Tahiti?

Much the same thing he was doing in the Yukon, it turns out. In *South Sea Tales,* London comes in from the cold but not from his cherished themes: man (and woman) against the elements, man in extremis, man's fragile hold on the planet. In "The House of Mapuhi," twelve hundred souls hug an atoll that is one hundred yards wide and three feet above sea level. When a typhoon swamps the island and rips out trees that people have climbed for refuge, only the fittest and craftiest survive, including a grandmother who lashes coconuts together as a life raft. Think "Old Woman and the Sea."

"The Seed of McCoy" pits sailors aboard a burning cargo vessel against the high winds, fierce currents, and deadly shoals of a place called the Dangerous Archipelago. London writes of the ship: "She was a shell, filled with a conflagration, and on the outside of the shell, clinging precariously, the little motes of men, by pull and haul, helped her in the battle." A mysterious, mesmerizing Pitcairner named McCoy, the descendant of a *Bounty* mutineer, arrives in a canoe. The desperate skipper asks if McCoy can pilot the flaming ship to shore. "I am as much a pilot as anybody. We are all pilots here, Captain," McCoy cryptically replies, before steering the vessel through the rest of this eerie, apocalyptic story.

But London's *South Sea Tales* are much more than a tropical recasting of his earlier and better known *Klondike Tales.* London's turn-of-the-century Pacific is a colonial universe of pearl traders, blackbirders, and plantation masters who ruthlessly exploit the islands and their people. In "Mauki," a Melanesian slave keeps running away until dispatched to a Polynesian Alcatraz ruled by a demonic German named Max Bunster. With characteristic tautness, London sets the stage for yet another duel, this one between man and man rather than man and nature: "Bunster was a degenerate brute. But Mauki was a primitive savage. While both had wills and ways of their own."

The phrase "primitive savage" jars twenty-first-century ears. So does London's periodic use of "pickaninny" and "monkey" to describe dark-skinned islanders. London was a man of his times, and the late-nineteenth and early-twentieth centuries were rank with racism and social Darwinism. But London was also a poorhouse-reared child who became a cannery worker, rail tramp, and committed socialist. His sympathy for underdogs, of all backgrounds, courses through *South Sea Tales,* as it does through much of his other writing. In London's fiction, brutes like Bunster rarely die peacefully in bed.

London also strips the South Sea of the myth and romance that have clouded the Pacific since James Cook introduced the ocean and its people to the West during three voyages of discovery in the eighteenth century. For the Enlightenment Europe of Cook's day, the Pacific seemed an Edenic realm of "noble savages," dwelling in a blessed state of nature. To the missionaries and imperialists who followed, these same natives became ignoble: naked heathens, destined to serve the white man and doomed by their inferior genes to perish. Then came steamships, package tours, and airplanes, transforming the Pacific of Western imagination into a hula-dancing, rum-soaked playground.

London, who saw the South Pacific for himself during a two-year voyage, paints a much more somber picture. The islanders in his stories aren't Rousseauian innocents; they're recognizable, flawed humans, struggling to survive the disease, drink, and dispossession brought on by Western contact. The narrator of "Good-bye, Jack" says of Hawaii: "The native women are sun-ripe Junos, the native men bronzed Apollos." But a few pages on, this idealized vision shatters when the narrator confronts Hawaiians hideously disfigured by leprosy.

Nor are Western churchmen and merchants the civilizing force they imagine themselves to be. In London's stories, most are greedy hypocrites who preach Christianity and submission—only to steal land and drive natives into near-extinction. "The missionary who came to give the bread of life remained to gobble up the whole heathen feast," London writes of Hawaii. The tropical landscape, as rendered by London, also defies advertising stereotype. Rain sheets down, monstrous centipedes crawl into women's hair, the jungle is a sea of "unrefreshing green," and a coral reef looms as "a bleak and perilous place over which the seas broke unceasingly." Of the Polynesian gulag to which the slave Mauki is exiled, London tells us: "Thomas Cook & Son do not sell tickets to it, and tourists do not dream of its existence."

The dark tone of many of these stories reflects, in part, London's disturbed state of mind and health. He first sailed to the South Pacific in 1907 on a ketch called the *Snark*, enduring a rough passage that ended in Tahiti. From there, London had to return to California to deal with his crumbling finances. Resuming his trip, he became so sick with illnesses such as yaws, a tropical disease causing ulcerated flesh, that he had to abandon the *Snark* once again and board a steamer to a hospital in Sydney. He later took refuge in Hawaii, immersed himself in the works of Jung and Freud, and wrote feverishly as both his health and the world unraveled. It seems forlornly appropriate that Jack London, who so potently evoked solitary combat against nature, died in 1916 at the age of forty, as millions of young men perished in the faceless trench warfare of the Western Front.

While the despair of London's last years infuses his writing about the Pacific, the stories in *South Sea Tales* are nonetheless rich with moments of exotic wonderment. Mauki, a Solomon Islander, has no need for pockets; he lodges a knife in his thick hair, puts a pipe in his pierced ear, and loops the handle of a cup through a ring dangling from his nose. During storms in Polynesia, sea spray strikes walls "like the rattle of musketry" and the ocean becomes "a checker-board of squalls." In Hawaii, even white businessmen "yield to the climate and the sun, and no matter how busy they may be, are prone to dance and sing and wear flowers behind their ears and in their hair."

In these and other sharply observed scenes, London the journalist emerges, filing vivid dispatches from afar, much as he did in his reporting from the East London slums and Russo-Japanese War. His is not the finely burnished prose of a writing school graduate, imagining the world from the confines of a library carrel or New York loft. London, an extreme adventurer, lived what he wrote: a large life of risk and challenge, ranging from the frigid goldfields of the Yukon to the torpid heat of the South Pacific. This immersion gives his stories a raw, headlong immediacy we associate today with nonfiction adventures such as Jon Krakauer's *Into Thin Air.*

When London's stories click, we are utterly there, at the edge of the world and the limit of human endurance. In "The Heathen," a pearl-buyer named Charley is trapped aboard an overcrowded, smallpox-ridden schooner. "There was nothing to do but rot and die," he says. Charley and his fellow pearl-buyers stay drunk until the whiskey gives out. Then a hurricane hits. Eighty-foot waves roll over the ship. "The bananas and cocoanuts [*sic*], the pigs and trade-boxes, the sick and the dying, were swept along in a solid, screeching, groaning mass." As the ship goes down, one man clings to a floating hatch-cover, kicking away another shipmate to keep the makeshift life raft to himself. And that's just the start. Before the story is done, Charley battles angry headhunters and circling sharks.

You don't stumble very often into this kind of adventure in the contemporary South Seas. I've spent most of the past two years traveling the Pacific, visiting many of the islands London wrote about. These days, you're more likely to be maimed by a speedboat than a shark. Descendants of the cannibals of old now gorge themselves on American junk food, and American junk culture. Colonial plantations have become gated golf communities. The Hawaiian island of Molokai, a leper colony in London's stories, has a website offering "Sunset Beach Weddings" and "Oceanfront Condos." When ships go down in Pacific storms, they're usually racing yachts, able to quickly alert rescue boats and helicopters.

Jack London's Pacific wasn't a better place, but it was certainly more exotic and elemental. We can't go back, and wouldn't if we could. But on a slow summer day, with the air conditioner thrumming, we can still open *South Sea Tales* and drift away, as the barometer plunges, sailors suck down quinine and "squareface" gin, and tattooed warriors step from the fringe of a mangrove swamp, their spears at the ready.

TONY HORWITZ is the author of *Baghdad Without a Map*, *Confederates in the Attic*, and an upcoming book on the voyages of Captain Cook.

EDITOR'S PREFACE

Christopher Gair

It is often said of Jack London that although he failed to find gold on his expedition to the Klondike during the gold rush of 1897–98, the material he gathered there provided the backdrop to his massively successful Northland tales and novels, such as *The Call of the Wild*, *White Fang*, and "To Build a Fire." With the publication of these works, London was swiftly transformed from penniless adventurer, fearful of slipping into the "abyss" of poverty and physical toil, into a celebrated bestselling author. Much of the same process can be seen with his experiences in the South Seas between 1907 and 1909. London's voyage could hardly be called a success: the construction of his schooner, the *Snark*, cost vastly more than he had anticipated; he had troubles with unreliable crew; and what had been planned as a round-the-world adventure was aborted in Australia owing to London's increasingly poor health and need to return to California to recuperate. Nevertheless, as with his Klondike experiences, the South Seas provided the author with new landscapes and cultures to write about. Thus, in addition to *The Cruise of the "Snark"* (the account of the trip), London produced novels (*Adventure*, *Jerry of the Islands*) and several collections of short stories based on what he had seen.

Typically, the quality of this work is highly variable. In part, this is a result of the cost of building the *Snark* and London's confession that he would write potboilers as a means of making quick cash. There is no doubt that he was rather better at earning money than using it wisely or saving it. In consequence, some of these works—for example, *Adventure* and several of the David Grief stories collected in *A Son of the Sun*—neatly transplant ideas developed in earlier novels and stories from the Klondike to the South Seas. Tapping into contemporary middle-class fears about a degenerate and overcivilized white elite being overwhelmed by the masses or by immigrants, London presents a series of alcoholic, cowardly, or crooked Euro-Americans, all ultimately taught the worth of key frontier values such as honesty and bravery. Grief himself is the model of the idealized Westerner. Hugely successful as a capitalist, worth "many millions," and with "holdings and ventures ... everywhere in the great South Pacific," Grief is also the supreme physical specimen, immune to the sun, to sickness, and to the alcoholism that is the fate of most white men in London's Pacific writings. Indeed, in "A Son of the Sun," London maps out Grief's exceptional nature and constitution in great detail, making clear that: "Unlike other white men in the tropics, he was there because he liked it.... One he was in ten thousand in the matter of sun-resistance." Grief epitomizes the Western individualist out to assert his "manhood":

> His was the golden touch, but he played the game, not for the gold, but for the game's sake. It was a man's game, the rough contacts and fierce give and take of the adventurers of his own blood and of half the bloods of Europe and the rest of the world, and it was a good game; but over and beyond was his love of all the other things that go to make up a South Seas rover's life—the smell of the reef; the infinite exquisiteness of the shoals of living coral in the mirror-surfaced lagoons; ... and even the howling savages of Melanesia, head-hunters and man-eaters, half-devil and all beast.

Although Grief does show a concern with and respect for native customs (and even has a blood brother called Mauriri with whom he converses in Polynesian), the descriptions of the land and its inhabitants largely serve as backdrops to the reconstruction of white identity, a process repeatedly undertaken via the application of the moral code to degenerates, under Grief's supervision. In contrast, many of London's other tales reject such implicit racial and cultural superiority and examine local cultures and landscapes as potential alternatives to the problems of modern life. As he recounts in *Cruise of the "Snark,"* London had been impressed by what he saw as the contrast between the natives and white settlers in Hawaii ("clean men... with their unsmirched souls") and the "panicky little merchants with rusty dollars for souls" that he had left behind him in San Francisco. Subsequently, the chapter on Tahiti is devoted to "The Nature Man," an American ex-teacher named Ernest Darling, whose response to his own failing physical and mental health is to take the classic American step into the wilderness to seek a cure for overcivilization. In the "brush," of course, Darling finds relief, "feeling that the sunshine was an elixir of health." He studies the robust, carefree animals, and concludes that they are "splendidly vigorous" because "they lived naturally, while he lived most unnaturally." By the time London meets him in Tahiti, and despite the efforts of insanity commissions to certify him for his dissidence, he is almost entirely self-sufficient and has imitated the natural world to such an extent that his health—considered ruined by the experts—is "perfect." As with Ralph Waldo Emerson's famous emphasis on the relative "manhood" of the American and the New Zealander in his essay "Self-Reliance," in which Emerson claimed that "the white man has lost his aboriginal strength," the "natural" is equated with the recovery of a masculinity perceived as being under threat from a "feminizing" modernity.

Such yearning for authenticity is played out in many of London's best Pacific tales. In "Koolau the Leper," for example, Koolau's empathy with the land and desire for freedom enable him to triumph over the "blue-eyed" American police, as London illustrates the injustices of disease and the natives' loss of their land. "The Heathen" traces the moral education of the American narrator, Charley, whose life is saved and then transformed by Otoo, the "heathen" whose physical and moral courage act as the model of good behavior. A similar pattern is enacted in "The House of Pride," in which the contrast between the overcivilized Percival Ford and his half-brother, the half-Kanaka Joe Garland reiterates London's enthusiasm for pleasure and hostility to the "righteous" New England Puritanism that (for him) continues to dictate a repressive and regimented lifestyle to too many of his countrymen.

London's late tales, mostly collected posthumously in *On the Makaloa Mat* (1919), go even further in their challenge to dominant American values. It is important to note not only the content of such stories—myths and detailed histories of the times before colonization, usually ignored by white chroniclers—but also their form. Tales like "The Bones of Kahekili" and "Shin-Bones" do more than analyze and record other cultures. Rather, they incorporate the native tradition of spoken storytelling within their structure, in a fusion of orality and literacy, traditional myth and literary professionalism.

At the end of "Shin-Bones," Prince Akuli, a figure located between the traditions of Hawaiian culture and the commercialism of modern life, comments that, "This is the twentieth century and we stink of gasoline." In many ways, Akuli represents London's attitude to life. The prince is part of an ancient dynasty and is fully conversant with its traditions. On the other hand, he has been educated in England, been an officer in the British army, and has a love of expensive automobiles. Akuli's embrace of the new, and knowledge of oral history point toward the dilemma apparent in so many of London's short stories about the Pacific. On the one hand, figures such as David Grief or Prince Akuli are adventurers and nature lovers, constantly testing themselves against the land and other men. On the other, they are in the vanguard of the colonization of that world and illustrate London's belief that such transformation is inevitable. As a result, their actions are instrumental in the destruction of the lifestyle that Grief epitomizes, and create a sense of pessimism in many of the tales. Although stories such as "The Heathen" do offer the possibility of self-transformation, London suggests that the spaces for such personal fulfillment are rapidly being eradicated. At the very moment when other cultures are seen to be disappearing in the face of industrialization and global capitalism, the sense of alienation felt by London's white American protagonists in their own society means that they must look toward and identify with the very Otherness they are simultaneously helping to destroy.

A NOTE ON THE TEXT

Jack London's stories were generally published first in magazines, whose editors altered them in order to appeal to their readership. However, London typically revised his stories for book publication, usually restoring them to their original state. Consequently, this edition uses the book versions of London's stories published in *House of Pride and Other Tales of Hawaii* (1912), *South Sea Tales* (1911), *A Son of the Sun* (1912), *On the Makaloa Mat* (1919) and *The Red One* (1918).

FROM *HOUSE OF PRIDE*
AND OTHER TALES OF HAWAII

The House of Pride

Percival Ford wondered why he had come. He did not dance. He did not care much for army people. Yet he knew them all—gliding and revolving there on the broad *lanai* of the Seaside, the officers in their fresh-starched uniforms of white, the civilians in white and black, and the women bare of shoulders and arms. After two years in Honolulu the Twentieth was departing to its new station in Alaska, and Percival Ford, as one of the big men of the Islands, could not help knowing the officers and their women.

But between knowing and liking was a vast gulf. The army women frightened him just a little. They were in ways quite different from the women he liked best—the elderly women, the spinsters and the bespectacled maidens, and the very serious women of all ages whom he met on church and library and kindergarten committees, who came meekly to him for contributions and advice. He ruled those women by virtue of his superior mentality, his great wealth, and the high place he occupied in the commercial baronage of Hawaii. And he was not afraid of them in the least. Sex, with them, was not obtrusive. Yes, that was it. There was in them something else, or more, than the assertive grossness of life. He was fastidious; he acknowledged that to himself; and these army women, with their bare shoulders and naked arms, their straight-looking eyes, their vitality and challenging femaleness, jarred upon his sensibilities.

Nor did he get on better with the army men, who took life lightly, drinking and smoking and swearing their way through life and asserting the essential grossness of flesh no less shamelessly than their women. He was always uncomfortable in the company of the army men. They seemed uncomfortable, too. And he felt, always, that they were laughing at him up their sleeves, or pitying him, or tolerating him. Then, too, they seemed, by mere contiguity, to emphasize a lack in him, to call attention to that in them which he did not possess and which he thanked God he did not possess. Faugh! They were like their women!

In fact, Percival Ford was no more a woman's man than he was a man's man. A glance at him told the reason. He had a good constitution, never was on intimate terms with sickness, nor even mild disorders; but he lacked vitality. His was a negative organism. No blood with a ferment in it could have nourished and shaped that long and narrow face, those thin lips, lean cheeks, and the small, sharp eyes. The thatch of hair, dust-coloured, straight and sparse, advertised the niggard soil, as did the nose, thin, delicately modelled, and just hinting the suggestion of a beak. His meagre blood had denied him much of life, and permitted him to be an extremist in one thing only, which thing was righteousness. Over right conduct he pondered and agonized, and that he should do right was as necessary to his nature as loving and being loved were necessary to commoner clay.

He was sitting under the algaroba trees between the *lanai* and the beach. His eyes wandered over the dancers and he turned his head away and gazed seaward across the mellow-sounding surf to the Southern Cross burning low on the horizon. He was irritated by the bare shoulders and arms of the women. If he had a daughter he would never permit it, never. But his hypothesis was the sheerest abstraction. The thought process had been accompanied by no inner vision of that daughter. He did not see a daughter with arms and shoulders. Instead, he smiled at the remote contingency of marriage. He was thirty-five, and, having had no personal experience of love, he looked upon it, not as mythical, but as bestial. Anybody could marry. The Japanese and Chinese coolies, toiling on the sugar plantations and in the rice-fields, married. They invariably married at the first opportunity. It was because they were so low in the scale of life. There was nothing else for them to do. They were like the army men and women. But for him there were other and higher things. He was different from them—from all of them. He was proud of how he happened to be. He had come of no petty love-match. He had come of lofty conception of duty and of devotion to a cause. His father had not married for love. Love was a madness that had never perturbed Isaac Ford. When he answered the call to go to the heathen with the message of life, he had had no thought and no desire for marriage. In this they were alike, his father and he. But the Board of Missions was economical. With New England thrift it weighed and measured and decided that married missionaries were less expensive per capita and more efficacious. So the Board commanded Isaac Ford to marry. Furthermore, it furnished him with a wife, another zealous soul with no thought of marriage, intent only on doing the Lord's work among the heathen. They saw each other for the first time in Boston. The Board brought them together, arranged everything, and by the end of the week they were married and started on the long voyage around the Horn.

Percival Ford was proud that he had come of such a union. He had been born high, and he thought of himself as a spiritual aristocrat. And he was proud of his father. It was a passion with him. The erect, austere figure of Isaac Ford had burned itself upon his pride. On his desk was a miniature of that soldier of the Lord. In his bedroom hung the portrait of Isaac Ford, painted at the time when he had served under the Monarchy as prime minister. Not that Isaac Ford had coveted place and worldly wealth, but that, as prime minister, and, later, as banker, he had been of greater service to the missionary cause. The German crowd, and the English crowd, and all the rest of the trading crowd, had sneered at Isaac Ford as a commercial soul-saver; but he, his son, knew different. When the natives, emerging abruptly from their feudal system, with no conception of the nature and significance of property in land, were letting their broad acres slip through their fingers, it was Isaac Ford who had stepped in between the trading crowd and its prey and taken possession of fat, vast holdings. Small wonder the trading crowd did not like his memory. But he had never looked upon his enormous wealth as his own. He had considered himself God's steward. Out of the revenues he had built schools, and hospitals, and churches. Nor was it his fault that sugar, after the slump, had paid forty per cent; that the bank he founded had prospered into a railroad; and that, among other things, fifty thousand acres of Oahu pasture land, which he had bought for a dollar an acre, grew eight tons of sugar to the acre every eighteen months. No, in all truth, Isaac Ford was an heroic figure, fit, so Percival Ford thought privately, to stand beside the statue of Kamehameha I. in front of the Judiciary Building. Isaac Ford was gone, but he, his son, carried on the good work at least as inflexibly if not as masterfully.

He turned his eyes back to the *lanai*. What was the difference, he asked himself, between the shameless, grass-girdled *hula* dances and the decolleté dances of the women of his own race? Was there an essential difference? or was it a matter of degree?

As he pondered the problem a hand rested on his shoulder.

"Hello, Ford, what are you doing here? Isn't this a bit festive?"

"I try to be lenient, Dr. Kennedy, even as I look on," Percival Ford answered gravely. "Won't you sit down?"

Dr. Kennedy sat down, clapping his palms sharply. A white-clad Japanese servant answered swiftly.

Scotch and soda was Kennedy's order; then, turning to the other, he said:—

"Of course, I don't ask you."

"But I will take something," Ford said firmly. The doctor's eyes showed surprise, and the servant waited. "Boy, a lemonade, please."

The doctor laughed at it heartily, as a joke on himself, and glanced at the musicians under the *hau* tree.

"Why, it's the Aloha Orchestra," he said. "I thought they were with the Hawaiian Hotel on Tuesday nights. Some rumpus, I guess."

His eyes paused for a moment, and dwelt upon the one who was playing a guitar and singing a Hawaiian song to the accompaniment of all the instruments. His face became grave as he looked at the singer, and it was still grave as he turned it to his companion.

"Look here, Ford, isn't it time you let up on Joe Garland? I understand you are in opposition to the Promotion Committee's sending him to the States on this surf-board proposition, and I've been wanting to speak to you about it. I should have thought you'd be glad to get him out of the country. It would be a good way to end your persecution of him."

"Persecution?" Percival Ford's eyebrows lifted interrogatively.

"Call it by any name you please," Kennedy went on. "You've hounded that poor devil for years. It's not his fault. Even you will admit that."

"Not his fault?" Percival Ford's thin lips drew tightly together for the moment. "Joe Garland is dissolute and idle. He has always been a wastrel, a profligate."

"But that's no reason you should keep on after him the way you do. I've watched you from the beginning. The first thing you did when you returned from college and found him working on the plantation as outside *luna* was to fire him—you with your millions, and he with his sixty dollars a month."

"Not the first thing," Percival Ford said judicially, in a tone he was accustomed to use in committee meetings. "I gave him his warning. The superintendent said he was a capable *luna*. I had no objection to him on that ground. It was what he did outside working hours. He undid my work faster than I could build it up. Of what use were the Sunday schools, the night schools, and the sewing classes, when in the evenings there was Joe Garland with his internal and eternal tum-tumming of guitar and *ukulele*, his strong drink, and his *hula* dancing? After I warned him, I came upon him—I shall never forget it—came upon him, down at the cabins. It was evening. I could hear the *hula* songs before I saw the scene. And when I did see it, there were the girls, shameless in the moonlight and dancing—the girls upon whom I had worked to teach clean living and right conduct. And there were three girls there, I remember, just graduated from the mission school. Of course I discharged Joe Garland. I know it was the same at Hilo. People said I went out of my way when I persuaded Mason and Fitch to discharge him. But it was the missionaries who requested me to do so. He was undoing their work by his reprehensible example."

"Afterwards, when he got on the railroad, your railroad, he was discharged without cause," Kennedy challenged.

"Not so," was the quick answer. "I had him into my private office and talked with him for half an hour."

"You discharged him for inefficiency?"

"For immoral living, if you please."

Dr. Kennedy laughed with a grating sound. "Who the devil gave it to you to be judge and jury? Does landlordism give you control of the immortal souls of those that toil for you? I have been your physician. Am I to expect to-morrow your ukase that I give up Scotch and soda or your patronage? Bah! Ford, you take life too seriously. Besides, when Joe got into that smuggling scrape (he wasn't in your employ, either), and he sent word to you, asked you to pay his fine, you left him to do his six months' hard labour on the reef. Don't forget, you left Joe Garland in the lurch that time. You threw him down, hard; and yet I remember the first day you came to school—we boarded, you were only a day scholar—you had to be initiated. Three times under in the swimming tank—you remember, it was the regular dose every new boy got. And you held back. You denied that you could swim. You were frightened, hysterical——"

"Yes, I know," Percival Ford said slowly. "I was frightened. And it was a lie, for I could swim.... And I was frightened."

"And you remember who fought for you? who lied for you harder than you could lie and swore he knew you couldn't swim? Who jumped into the tank and pulled you out after the first under and was nearly drowned for it by the other boys, who had discovered by that time that you *could* swim?"

"Of course I know," the other rejoined coldly. "But a generous act as a boy does not excuse a lifetime of wrong living."

"He has never done wrong to you?—personally and directly, I mean?"

"No," was Percival Ford's answer.

"That is what makes my position impregnable. I have no personal spite against him. He is bad, that is all. His life is bad——"

"Which is another way of saying that he does not agree with you in the way life should be lived," the doctor interrupted.

"Have it that way. It is immaterial. He is an idler——"

"With reason," was the interruption, "considering the jobs out of which you have knocked him."

"He is immoral——"

"Oh, hold on now, Ford. Don't go harping on that. You are pure New England stock. Joe Garland is half Kanaka. Your blood is thin. His is warm. Life is one thing to you, another thing to him. He laughs and sings and dances through life, genial, unselfish, childlike, everybody's friend. You go through life like a perambulating prayer-wheel, a friend of nobody but the righteous, and the righteous are those who agree with you as to what is right. And after all, who shall say? You live like an anchorite. Joe Garland lives like a good fellow. Who has extracted the most from life? We are paid to live, you know. When the wages are too meagre we throw up the job, which is the cause, believe me, of all rational suicide. Joe Garland would starve to death on the wages you get from life. You see, he is made differently. So would you starve on his wages, which are singing, and love——"

"Lust, if you will pardon me," was the interruption.

Dr. Kennedy smiled.

"Love, to you, is a word of four letters and a definition which you have extracted from the dictionary. But love, real love, dewy and palpitant and tender, you do not know. If God made you and me, and men and women, believe me He made love, too. But to come back. It's about time you quit hounding Joe Garland. It is not worthy of you, and it is cowardly. The thing for you to do is to reach out and lend him a hand."

"Why I, any more than you?" the other demanded. "Why don't you reach him a hand?"

"I have. I'm reaching him a hand now. I'm trying to get you not to down the Promotion Committee's proposition of sending him away. I got him the job at Hilo with Mason and Fitch. I've got him half a dozen jobs, out of every one of which you drove him. But never mind that. Don't forget one thing—and a little frankness won't hurt you—it is not fair play to saddle another's fault on Joe Garland; and you know that you, least of all, are the man to do it. Why, man, it's not good taste. It's positively indecent."

"Now I don't follow you," Percival Ford answered. "You're up in the air with some obscure scientific theory of heredity and personal irresponsibility. But how any theory can hold Joe Garland irresponsible for his wrongdoings and at the same time hold me personally responsible for them—more responsible than any one else, including Joe Garland—is beyond me."

"It's a matter of delicacy, I suppose, or of taste, that prevents you from following me," Dr. Kennedy snapped out. "It's all very well, for the sake of society, tacitly to ignore some things, but you do more than tacitly ignore."

"What is it, pray, that I tacitly ignore!"

Dr. Kennedy was angry. A deeper red than that of constitutional Scotch and soda suffused his face, as he answered:

"Your father's son."

"Now just what do you mean?"

"Damn it, man, you can't ask me to be plainer spoken than that. But if you will, all right—Isaac's Ford's son—Joe Garland—your brother."

Percival Ford sat quietly, an annoyed and shocked expression on his face. Kennedy looked at him curiously, then, as the slow minutes dragged by, became embarrassed and frightened.

"My God!" he cried finally, "you don't mean to tell me that you didn't know!"

As in answer, Percival Ford's cheeks turned slowly gray.

"It's a ghastly joke," he said; "a ghastly joke."

The doctor had got himself in hand.

"Everybody knows it," he said. "I thought you knew it. And since you don't know it, it's time you did, and I'm glad of the chance of setting you straight. Joe Garland and you are brothers—half-brothers."

"It's a lie," Ford cried. "You don't mean it. Joe Garland's mother was Eliza Kunilio." (Dr. Kennedy nodded.) "I remember her well, with her duck pond and *taro* patch. His father was Joseph Garland, the beachcomber." (Dr. Kennedy shook his head.) "He died only two or three years ago. He used to get drunk. There's where Joe got his dissoluteness. There's the heredity for you."

"And nobody told you," Kennedy said wonderingly, after a pause.

"Dr. Kennedy, you have said something terrible, which I cannot allow to pass. You must either prove or, or ..."

"Prove it yourself. Turn around and look at him. You've got him in profile. Look at his nose. That's Isaac Ford's. Yours is a thin edition of it. That's right. Look. The lines are fuller, but they are all there."

Percival Ford looked at the Kanaka half-breed who played under the *hau* tree, and it seemed, as by some illumination, that he was gazing on a wraith of himself. Feature after feature flashed up an unmistakable resemblance. Or, rather, it was he who was the wraith of that other full-muscled and generously moulded man. And his features, and that other man's features, were all reminiscent of Isaac Ford. And nobody had told him. Every line of Isaac Ford's face he knew. Miniatures, portraits, and photographs of his father were passing in review through his mind, and here and there, over and again, in the face before him, he caught resemblances and vague hints of likeness. It was devil's work that could reproduce the austere features of Isaac Ford in the loose and sensuous features before him. Once, the man turned, and for one flashing instant it seemed to Percival Ford that he saw his father, dead and gone, peering at him out of the face of Joe Garland.

"It's nothing at all," he could faintly hear Dr. Kennedy saying. "They were all mixed up in the old days. You know that. You've seen it all your life. Sailors married queens and begat princesses and all the rest of it. It was the usual thing in the Islands."

"But not with my father," Percival Ford interrupted.

"There you are." Kennedy shrugged his shoulders. "Cosmic sap and smoke of life. Old Isaac Ford was straitlaced and all the rest, and I know there's no explaining it, least of all to himself. He understood it no more than you do. Smoke of life, that's all. And don't forget one thing, Ford. There was a dab of unruly blood in old Isaac Ford, and Joe Garland inherited it—all of it, smoke of life and cosmic sap; while you inherited all of old Isaac's ascetic blood. And just because your blood is cold, well-ordered, and well-disciplined, is no reason that you should frown upon Joe Garland. When Joe Garland undoes the work you do, remember that it is only old Isaac Ford on both sides, undoing with one hand what he does with the other. You are Isaac Ford's right hand, let us say; Joe Garland is his left hand."

Percival Ford made no answer, and in the silence Dr. Kennedy finished his forgotten Scotch and soda. From across the grounds an automobile hooted imperatively.

"There's the machine," Dr. Kennedy said, rising. "I've got to run. I'm sorry I've shaken you up, and at the same time I'm glad. And know one thing, Isaac Ford's dab of unruly blood was remarkably small, and Joe Garland got it all. And one other thing. If your father's left hand offend you, don't smite it off. Besides, Joe is all right. Frankly, if I could choose between you and him to live with me on a desert isle, I'd choose Joe."

Little bare-legged children ran about him, playing, on the grass; but Percival Ford did not see them. He was gazing steadily at the singer under the *hau* tree. He even changed his position once, to get closer. The clerk of the Seaside went by, limping with age and dragging his reluctant feet. He had lived forty years on the Islands. Percival Ford beckoned to him, and the clerk came respectfully, and wondering that he should be noticed by Percival Ford.

"John," Ford said, "I want you to give me some information. Won't you sit down?"

The clerk sat down awkwardly, stunned by the unexpected honour. He blinked at the other and mumbled, "Yes, sir, thank you."

"John, who is Joe Garland?"

The clerk stared at him, blinked, cleared his throat, and said nothing.

"Go on," Percival Ford commanded. "Who is he?"

"You're joking me, sir," the other managed to articulate.

"I spoke to you seriously."

The clerk recoiled from him.

"You don't mean to say you don't know?" he questioned, his question in itself the answer.

"I want to know."

"Why, he's——" John broke off and looked about him helplessly. "Hadn't you better ask somebody else? Everybody thought you knew. We always thought..."

"Yes, go ahead."

"We always thought that that was why you had it in for him."

Photographs and miniatures of Isaac Ford were trooping through his son's brain, and ghosts of Isaac Ford seemed in the air about him. "I wish you good night, sir," he could hear the clerk saying, and he saw him beginning to limp away.

"John," he called abruptly.

John came back and stood near him, blinking and nervously moistening his lips.

"You haven't told me yet, you know."

"Oh, about Joe Garland?"

"Yes, about Joe Garland. Who is he?"

"He's your brother, sir, if I say it who shouldn't."

"Thank you, John. Good night."

"And you didn't know?" the old man queried, content to linger, now that the crucial point was past.

"Thank you, John. Good night," was the response.

"Yes, sir, thank you, sir. I think it's going to rain. Good night, sir."

Out of a clear sky, filled only with stars and moonlight, fell a rain so fine and attenuated as to resemble a vapour spray. Nobody minded it; the children played on, running bare-legged over the grass and leaping into the sand; and in a few minutes it was gone. In the southeast, Diamond Head, a black blot, sharply defined, silhouetted its crater-form against the stars. At sleepy intervals the surf flung its foam across the sands to the grass, and far out could be seen the black specks of swimmers under the moon. The voices of the singers, singing a waltz, died away; and in the silence, from somewhere under the trees, arose the laugh of a woman that was a love-cry. It startled Percival Ford, and it reminded him of Dr. Kennedy's phrase. Down by the outrigger canoes, where they lay hauled out on the sand, he saw men and women, Kanakas, reclining languorously, like lotus-eaters, the women in white *holokus;* and against one such *holoku* he saw the dark head of the steersman of the canoe resting upon the woman's shoulder. Farther down, where the strip of sand widened at the entrance to the lagoon, he saw a man and woman walking side by side. As they drew near the light *lanai,* he saw the woman's hand go down to her waist and disengage a girdling arm. And as they passed him, Percival Ford nodded to a captain he knew, and to a major's daughter. Smoke of life, that was it, an ample phrase. And again, from under the dark algaroba tree arose the laugh of a woman that was a love-cry; and past his chair, on the way to bed, a bare-legged youngster was led by a chiding Japanese nurse-maid. The voices of the singers broke softly and meltingly into an Hawaiian love-song, and officers and women, with encircling arms, were gliding and whirling on the *lanai;* and once again the woman laughed under the algaroba trees.

And Percival Ford knew only disapproval of it all. He was irritated by the love-laugh of the woman, by the steersman with pillowed head on the white *holoku,* by the couples that walked on the beach, by the officers and women that danced, and by the voices of the singers singing of love, and his brother singing there with them under the *hau* tree. The woman that laughed especially irritated him. A curious train of thought was aroused. He was Isaac Ford's son, and what had happened with Isaac Ford might happen with him. He felt in his cheeks the faint heat of a blush at the thought, and experienced a poignant sense of shame. He was appalled by what was in his blood. It was like learning suddenly that his father had been a leper and that his own blood might bear the taint of that dread disease. Isaac Ford, the austere soldier of the Lord—the old hypocrite! What difference between him and any beach-comber? The house of pride that Percival Ford had builded was tumbling about his ears.

The hours passed, the army people laughed and danced, the native orchestra played on, and Percival Ford wrestled with the abrupt and overwhelming problem that had been thrust upon him. He prayed quietly, his elbow on the table, his head bowed upon his hand, with all the appearance of any tired onlooker. Between the dances the army men and women and the civilians fluttered up to him and buzzed conventionally, and when they went back to the *lanai* he took up his wrestling where he had left it off.

He began to patch together his shattered ideal of Isaac Ford, and for cement he used a cunning and subtle logic. It was of the sort that is compounded in the brain laboratories of egotists, and it worked.

It was incontrovertible that his father had been made of finer clay than those about him; but still, old Isaac had been only in the process of becoming, while he, Percival Ford, had become. As proof of it, he rehabilitated his father and at the same time exalted himself. His lean little ego waxed to colossal proportions. He was great enough to forgive. He glowed at the thought of it. Isaac Ford had been great, but he was greater, for he could forgive Isaac Ford and even restore him to the holy place in his memory, though the place was not quite so holy as it had been. Also, he applauded Isaac Ford for having ignored the outcome of his one step aside. Very well, he, too, would ignore it.

The dance was breaking up. The orchestra had finished "Aloha Oe" and was preparing to go home. Percival Ford clapped his hands for the Japanese servant.

"You tell that man I want to see him," he said, pointing out Joe Garland. "Tell him come here, now."

Joe Garland approached and halted respectfully several paces away, nervously fingering the guitar which he still carried. The other did not ask him to sit down.

"You are my brother," he said.

"Why, everybody knows that," was the reply, in tones of wonderment.

"Yes, so I understand," Percival Ford said dryly. "But I did not know it till this evening."

The half-brother waited uncomfortably in the silence that followed, during which Percival Ford coolly considered his next utterance.

"You remember that first time I came to school and the boys ducked me?" he asked. "Why did you take my part?"

The half-brother smiled bashfully.

"Because you knew?"

"Yes, that was why."

"But I didn't know," Percival Ford said in the same dry fashion.

"Yes," the other said.

Another silence fell. Servants were beginning to put out the lights on the *lanai*.

"You know … now," the half-brother said simply.

Percival Ford frowned. Then he looked the other over with a considering eye.

"How much will you take to leave the Islands and never come back?" he demanded.

"And never come back?" Joe Garland faltered. "It is the only land I know. Other lands are cold. I do not know other lands. I have many friends here. In other lands there would not be one voice to say, '*Aloha,* Joe, my boy.' "

"I said never to come back," Percival Ford reiterated. "The *Alameda* sails to-morrow for San Francisco."

Joe Garland was bewildered.

"But why?" he asked. "You know now that we are brothers."

"That is why," was the retort. "As you said yourself, everybody knows. I will make it worth your while."

All awkwardness and embarrassment disappeared from Joe Garland. Birth and station were bridged and reversed.

"You want me to go?" he demanded.

"I want you to go and never to come back," Percival Ford answered.

And in that moment, flashing and fleeting, it was given him to see his brother tower above him like a mountain, and to feel himself dwindle and dwarf to microscopic insignificance. But it is not well for one to see himself truly, nor can one so see himself for long and live; and only for that flashing moment did Percival Ford see himself and his brother in true perspective. The next moment he was mastered by his meagre and insatiable ego.

"As I said, I will make it worth your while. You will not suffer. I will pay you well."

"All right," Joe Garland said. "I'll go."

He started to turn away.

"Joe," the other called. "You see my lawyer to-morrow morning. Five hundred down and two hundred a month as long as you stay away."

"You are very kind," Joe Garland answered softly. "You are too kind. And anyway, I guess I don't want your money. I go to-morrow on the *Alameda*."

He walked away, but did not say good-bye.

Percival Ford clapped his hands.

"Boy," he said to the Japanese, "a lemonade."

And over the lemonade he smiled long and contentedly to himself.

Koolau the Leper

"Because we are sick they take away our liberty. We have obeyed the law. We have done no wrong. And yet they would put us in prison. Molokai is a prison. That you know. Niuli, there, his sister was sent to Molokai seven years ago. He has not seen her since. Nor will he ever see her. She must stay there until she dies. This is not her will. It is not Niuli's will. It is the will of the white men who rule the land. And who are these white men?

"We know. We have it from our fathers and our fathers' fathers. They came like lambs, speaking softly. Well might they speak softly, for we were many and strong, and all the islands were ours. As I say, they spoke softly. They were of two kinds. The one kind asked our permission, our gracious permission, to preach to us the word of God. The other kind asked our permission, our gracious permission, to trade with us. That was the beginning. To-day all the islands are theirs, all the land, all the cattle—everything is theirs. They that preached the word of God and they that preached the word of Rum have foregathered and become great chiefs. They live like kings in houses of many rooms, with multitudes of servants to care for them. They who had nothing have everything, and if you, or I, or any Kanaka be hungry, they sneer and say, 'Well, why don't you work? There are the plantations.'"

Koolau paused. He raised one hand, and with gnarled and twisted fingers lifted up the blazing wreath of hibiscus that crowned his black hair. The moonlight bathed the scene in silver. It was a night of peace, though those who sat about him and listened had all the seeming of battle-wrecks. Their faces were leonine. Here a space yawned in a face where should have been a nose, and there an arm stump showed where a hand had rotted off. They were men and women beyond the pale, the thirty of them, for upon them had been placed the mark of the beast.

They sat, flower-garlanded, in the perfumed, luminous night, and their lips made uncouth noises and their throats rasped approval of Koolau's speech. They were creatures who once had been men and women. But they were men and women no longer. They were monsters—in face and form grotesque caricatures of everything human. They were hideously maimed and distorted, and had the seeming of creatures that had been racked in millenniums of hell. Their hands, when they possessed them, were like harpy claws. Their faces were the misfits and slips, crushed and bruised by some mad god at play in the machinery of life. Here and there were features which the mad god had smeared half away, and one woman wept scalding tears from twin pits of horror, where her eyes once had been. Some were in pain and groaned from their chests. Others coughed, making sounds like the tearing of tissue. Two were idiots, more like huge apes marred in the making, until even an ape were an angel. They mowed and gibbered in the moonlight, under crowns of drooping, golden blossoms. One, whose bloated ear-lobe flapped like a fan upon his shoulder, caught up a gorgeous flower of orange and scarlet and with it decorated the monstrous ear that flip-flapped with his every movement.

And over these things Koolau was king. And this was his kingdom,—a flower-throttled gorge, with beetling cliffs and crags, from which floated the blattings of wild goats. On three sides the grim walls rose, festooned in fantastic draperies of tropic vegetation and pierced by cave-entrances—the rocky lairs of Koolau's subjects. On the fourth side the earth fell away into a tremendous abyss, and, far below, could be seen the summits of lesser peaks and crags, at whose bases foamed and rumbled the Pacific surge. In fine weather a boat could land on the rocky beach that marked the entrance of Kalalau Valley, but the weather must be very fine. And a cool-headed mountaineer might climb from the beach to the head of Kalalau Valley, to this pocket among the peaks where Koolau ruled; but such a mountaineer must be very cool of head, and he must know the wild-goat trails as well. The marvel was that the mass of human wreckage that constituted Koolau's people should have been able to drag its helpless misery over the giddy goat-trails to this inaccessible spot.

"Brothers," Koolau began.

But one of the mowing, apelike travesties emitted a wild shriek of madness, and Koolau waited while the shrill cachination was tossed back and forth among the rocky walls and echoed distantly through the pulseless night.

"Brothers, is it not strange? Ours was the land, and behold, the land is not ours. What did these preachers of the word of God and the word of Rum give us for the land? Have you received one dollar, as much as one dollar, any one of you, for the land? Yet it is theirs, and in return they tell us we can go to work on the land, their land, and that what we produce by our toil shall be theirs. Yet in the old days we did not have to work. Also, when we are sick, they take away our freedom."

"Who brought the sickness, Koolau?" demanded Kiloliana, a lean and wiry man with a face so like a laughing faun's that one might expect to see the cloven hoofs under him. They were cloven, it was true, but the cleavages were great ulcers and livid putrefactions. Yet this was Kiloliana, the most daring climber of them all, the man who knew every goat-trail and who had led Koolau and his wretched followers into the recesses of Kalalau.

"Ay, well questioned," Koolau answered. "Because we would not work the miles of sugar-cane where once our horses pastured, they brought the Chinese slaves from over seas. And with them came the Chinese sickness—that which we suffer from and because of which they would imprison us on Molokai. We were born on Kauai. We have been to the other islands, some here and some there, to Oahu, to Maui, to Hawaii, to Honolulu. Yet always did we come back to Kauai. Why did we come back? There must be a reason. Because we love Kauai. We were born here. Here we have lived. And here shall we die—unless—unless—there be weak hearts amongst us. Such we do not want. They are fit for Molokai. And if there be such, let them not remain. To-morrow the soldiers land on the shore. Let the weak hearts go down to them. They will be sent swiftly to Molokai. As for us, we shall stay and fight. But know that we will not die. We have rifles. You know the narrow trails where men must creep, one by one. I, alone, Koolau, who was once a cowboy on Niihau, can hold the trail against a thousand men. Here is Kapalei, who was once a judge over men and a man with honour, but who is now a hunted rat, like you and me. Hear him. He is wise."

Kapalei arose. Once he had been a judge. He had gone to college at Punahou. He had sat at meat with lords and chiefs and the high representatives of alien powers who protected the interests of traders and missionaries. Such had been Kapalei. But now, as Koolau had said, he was a hunted rat, a creature outside the law, sunk so deep in the mire of human horror that he was above the law as well as beneath it. His face was featureless, save for gaping orifices and for the lidless eyes that burned under hairless brows.

"Let us not make trouble," he began. "We ask to be left alone. But if they do not leave us alone, then is the trouble theirs and the penalty. My fingers are gone, as you see." He held up his stumps of hands that all might see. "Yet have I the joint of one thumb left, and it can pull a trigger as firmly as did its lost neighbour in the old days. We love Kauia. Let us live here, or die here, but do not let us go to the prison of Molokai. The sickness is not ours. We have not sinned. The men who preached the word of God and the word of Rum brought the sickness with the coolie slaves who work the stolen land. I have been a judge. I know the law and the justice, and I say to you it is unjust to steal a man's land, to make that man sick with the Chinese sickness, and then to put that man in prison for life."

"Life is short, and the days are filled with pain," said Koolau. "Let us drink and dance and be happy as we can."

From one of the rocky lairs calabashes were produced and passed around. The calabashes were filled with the fierce distillation of the root of the *ti*-plant; and as the liquid fire coursed through them and mounted to their brains, they forgot that they had once been men and women, for they were men and women once more. The woman who wept scalding tears from open eye-pits was indeed a woman apulse with life as she plucked the strings of an *ukulele* and lifted her voice in a barbaric love-call such as might have come from the dark forest-depths of the primeval world. The air tingled with her cry, softly imperious and seductive. Upon a mat, timing his rhythm to the woman's song, Kiloliana danced. It was unmistakable. Love danced in all his movements, and, next, dancing with him on the mat, was a woman whose heavy hips and generous breast gave the lie to her disease-corroded face. It was a dance of the living dead, for in their disintegrating bodies life still loved and longed. Ever the woman whose sightless eyes ran scalding tears chanted her love-cry, ever the dancers of love danced in the warm night, and ever the calabashes went around till in all their brains were maggots crawling of memory and desire. And with the woman on the mat danced a slender maid whose face was beautiful and unmarred, but whose twisted arms that rose and fell marked the disease's ravage. And the two idiots, gibbering and mouthing strange noises, danced apart, grotesque, fantastic, travestying love as they themselves had been travestied by life.

But the woman's love-cry broke midway, the calabashes were lowered, and the dancers ceased, as all gazed into the abyss above the sea, where a rocket flared like a wan phantom through the moonlit air.

"It is the soldiers," said Koolau. "To-morrow there will be fighting. It is well to sleep and be prepared."

The lepers obeyed, crawling away to their lairs in the cliff, until only Koolau remained, sitting motionless in the moonlight, his rifle across his knees, as he gazed far down to the boats landing on the beach.

The far head of Kalalau Valley had been well chosen as a refuge. Except Kiloliana, who knew back-trails up the precipitous walls, no man could win to the gorge save by advancing across a knife-edged ridge. This passage was a hundred yards in length. At best, it was a scant twelve inches wide. On either side yawned the abyss. A slip, and to right or left the man would fall to his death. But once across he would find himself in an earthly paradise. A sea of vegetation laved the landscape, pouring its green billows from wall to wall, dripping from the cliff-lips in great vine-masses, and flinging a spray of ferns and air-plants in to the multitudinous crevices. During the many months of Koolau's rule, he and his followers had fought with this vegetable sea. The choking jungle, with its riot of blossoms, had been driven back from the bananas, oranges, and mangoes that grew wild. In little clear-ings grew the wild arrowroot; on stone terraces, filled with soil scrap-ings, were the *taro* patches and the melons; and in every open space where the sunshine penetrated were *papaia* trees burdened with their golden fruit.

Koolau had been driven to this refuge from the lower valley by the beach. And if he were driven from it in turn, he knew of gorges among the jumbled peaks of the inner fastnesses where he could lead his sub-jects and live. And now he lay with his rifle beside him, peering down through a tangled screen of foliage at the soldiers on the beach. He noted that they had large guns with them, from which the sunshine flashed as from mirrors. The knife-edged passage lay directly before him. Crawling upward along the trail that led to it he could see tiny specks of men. He knew they were not the soldiers, but the police. When they failed, then the soldiers would enter the game.

He affectionately rubbed a twisted hand along his rifle barrel and made sure that the sights were clean. He had learned to shoot as a wild cattle hunter on Niihau, and on that island his skill as a marks-man was unforgotten. As the toiling specks of men grew nearer and larger, he estimated the range, judged the deflection of the wind that swept at right angles across the line of fire, and calculated the chances of overshooting marks that were so far below his level. But he did not shoot. Not until they reached the beginning of the passage did he make his presence known. He did not disclose himself, but spoke from the thicket.

"What do you want?" he demanded.

"We want Koolau, the leper," answered the man who led the native police, himself a blue-eyed American.

"You must go back," Koolau said.

He knew the man, a deputy sheriff, for it was by him that he had been harried out of Niihau, across Kauai, to Kalalau Valley, and out of the valley to the gorge.

"Who are you?" the sheriff asked.

"I am Koolau, the leper," was the reply.

"Then come out. We want you. Dead or alive, there is a thousand dollars on your head. You cannot escape."

Koolau laughed aloud in the thicket.

"Come out!" the sheriff commanded, and was answered by silence.

He conferred with the police, and Koolau saw that they were preparing to rush him.

"Koolau," the sheriff called. "Koolau, I am coming across to get you."

"Then look first and well about you at the sun and sea and sky, for it will be the last time you behold them."

"That's all right, Koolau," the sheriff said soothingly. "I know you're a dead shot. But you won't shoot me. I have never done you any wrong."

Koolau grunted in the thicket.

"I say, you know, I've never done you any wrong, have I?" the sheriff persisted.

"You do me wrong when you try to put me in prison," was the reply. "And you do me wrong when you try for the thousand dollars on my head. If you will live, stay where you are."

"I've got to come across and get you. I'm sorry. But it is my duty."

"You will die before you get across."

The sheriff was no coward. Yet was he undecided. He gazed into the gulf on either side and ran his eyes along the knife-edge he must travel. Then he made up his mind.

"Koolau," he called.

But the thicket remained silent.

"Koolau, don't shoot. I am coming."

The sheriff turned, gave some orders to the police, then started on his perilous way. He advanced slowly. It was like walking a tight rope. He had nothing to lean upon but the air. The lava rock crumbled under his feet, and on either side the dislodged fragments pitched downward through the depths. The sun blazed upon him, and his face was wet with sweat. Still he advanced, until the halfway point was reached.

"Stop!" Koolau commanded from the thicket. "One more step and I shoot."

The sheriff halted, swaying for balance as he stood poised above the void. His face was pale, but his eyes were determined. He licked his dry lips before he spoke.

"Koolau, you won't shoot me. I know you won't."

He started once more. The bullet whirled him half about. On his face was an expression of querulous surprise as he reeled to the fall. He tried to save himself by throwing his body across the knife-edge; but at that moment he knew death. The next moment the knife-edge was vacant. Then came the rush, five policemen, in single file, with superb steadiness, running along the knife-edge. At the same instant the rest of the posse opened fire on the thicket. It was madness. Five times Koolau pulled the trigger, so rapidly that his shots constituted a rattle. Changing his position and crouching low under the bullets that were biting and singing through the bushes, he peered out. Four of the police had followed the sheriff. The fifth lay across the knife-edge still alive. On the farther side, no longer firing, were the surviving police. On the naked rock there was no hope for them. Before they could clamber down Koolau could have picked off the last man. But he did not fire, and, after a conference, one of them took off a white undershirt and waved it as a flag. Followed by another, he advanced along the knife-edge to their wounded comrade. Koolau gave no sign, but watched them slowly withdraw and become specks as they descended into the lower valley.

Two hours later, from another thicket, Koolau watched a body of police trying to make the ascent from the opposite side of the valley. He saw the wild goats flee before them as they climbed higher and higher, until he doubted his judgment and sent for Kiloliana, who crawled in beside him.

"No, there is no way," said Kiloliana.

"The goats?" Koolau questioned.

"They come over from the next valley, but they cannot pass to this.

There is no way. Those men are not wiser than goats. They may fall to their deaths. Let us watch."

"They are brave men," said Koolau. "Let us watch."

Side by side they lay among the morning-glories, with the yellow blossoms of the *hau* dropping upon them from overhead, watching the motes of men toil upward, till the thing happened, and three of them, slipping, rolling, sliding, dashed over a cliff-lip and fell sheer half a thousand feet.

Kiloliana chuckled.

"We will be bothered no more," he said.

"They have war guns," Koolau made answer. "The soldiers have not yet spoken."

In the drowsy afternoon, most of the lepers lay in their rock dens asleep. Koolau, his rifle on his knees, fresh-cleaned and ready, dozed in the entrance to his own den. The maid with the twisted arms lay below in the thicket and kept watch on the knife-edge passage. Suddenly Koolau was startled wide awake by the sound of an explosion on the beach. The next instant the atmosphere was incredibly rent asunder. The terrible sound frightened him. It was as if all the gods had caught the envelope of the sky in their hands and were ripping it apart as a woman rips apart a sheet of cotton cloth. But it was such an immense ripping, growing swiftly nearer. Koolau glanced up apprehensively, as if expecting to see the thing. Then high up on the cliff overhead the shell burst in a fountain of black smoke. The rock was shattered, the fragments falling to the foot of the cliff.

Koolau passed his hand across his sweaty brow. He was terribly shaken. He had had no experience with shell-fire, and this was more dreadful than anything he had imagined.

"One," said Kapahei, suddenly bethinking himself to keep count.

A second and a third shell flew screaming over the top of the wall, bursting beyond view. Kapahei methodically kept the count. The lepers crowded into the open space before the caves. At first they were frightened, but as the shells continued their flight overhead the leper folk became reassured and began to admire the spectacle. The two idiots shrieked with delight, prancing wild antics as each air-tormenting shell went by. Koolau began to recover his confidence. No damage was being done. Evidently they could not aim such large missiles at such long range with the precision of a rifle.

But a change came over the situation. The shells began to fall short. One burst below in the thicket by the knife-edge. Koolau remembered the maid who lay there on watch, and ran down to see. The smoke was still rising from the bushes when he crawled in. He was astounded. The branches were splintered and broken. Where the girl had lain was a hole in the ground. The girl herself was in shattered fragments. The shell had burst right on her.

First peering out to make sure no soldiers were attempting the passage, Koolau started back on the run for the caves. All the time the shells were moaning, whining, screaming by, and the valley was rumbling and reverberating with the explosions. As he came in sight of the caves, he saw the two idiots cavorting about, clutching each other's hands with their stumps of fingers. Even as he ran, Koolau saw a spout of black smoke rise from the ground, near to the idiots. They were flung apart bodily by the explosion. One lay motionless, but the other was dragging himself by his hands toward the cave. His legs trailed out helplessly behind him, while the blood was pouring from his body. He seemed bathed in blood, and as he crawled he cried like a little dog. The rest of the lepers, with the exception of Kapahei, had fled into the caves.

"Seventeen," said Kapahei. "Eighteen," he added.

This last shell had fairly entered into one of the caves. The explosion caused the caves to empty. But from the particular cave no one emerged. Koolau crept in through the pungent, acrid smoke. Four bodies, frightfully mangled, lay about. One of them was the sightless woman whose tears till now had never ceased.

Outside, Koolau found his people in a panic and already beginning to climb the goat-trail that led out of the gorge and on among the jumbled heights and chasms. The wounded idiot, whining feebly and dragging himself along on the ground by his hands, was trying to follow. But at the first pitch of the wall his helplessness overcame him and he fell back.

"It would be better to kill him," said Koolau to Kapahei, who still sat in the same place.

"Twenty-two," Kapahei answered. "Yes, it would be a wise thing to kill him. Twenty-three—twenty-four."

The idiot whined sharply when he saw the rifle levelled at him. Koolau hesitated, then lowered the gun.

"It is a hard thing to do," he said.

"You are a fool, twenty-six, twenty-seven," said Kapahei. "Let me show you."

He arose, and with a heavy fragment of rock in his hand, approached the wounded thing. As he lifted his arm to strike, a shell burst full upon him, relieving him of the necessity of the act and at the same time putting an end to his count.

Koolau was alone in the gorge. He watched the last of his people drag their crippled bodies over the brow of the height and disappear. Then he turned and went down to the thicket where the maid had been killed. The shell-fire still continued, but he remained; for far below he could see the soldiers climbing up. A shell burst twenty feet away. Flattening himself into the earth, he heard the rush of the fragments above his body. A shower of *hau* blossoms rained upon him. He lifted his head to peer down the trail, and sighed. He was very much afraid. Bullets from rifles would not have worried him, but this shell-fire was abominable. Each time a shell shrieked by he shivered and crouched; but each time he lifted his head again to watch the trail.

At last the shells ceased. This, he reasoned, was because the soldiers were drawing near. They crept along the trail in single file, and he tried to count them until he lost track. At any rate, there were a hundred or so of them—all come after Koolau the leper. He felt a fleeting prod of pride. With war guns and rifles, police and soldiers, they came for him, and he was only one man, a crippled wreck of a man at that. They offered a thousand dollars for him, dead or alive. In all his life he had never possessed that much money. The thought was a bitter one. Kapahei had been right. He, Koolau, had done no wrong. Because the *haoles* wanted labour with which to work the stolen land, they had brought in the Chinese coolies, and with them had come the sickness. And now, because he had caught the sickness, he was worth a thousand dollars—but not to himself. It was his worthless carcass, rotten with disease or dead from a bursting shell, that was worth all that money.

When the soldiers reached the knife-edged passage, he was prompted to warn them. But his gaze fell upon the body of the murdered maid, and he kept silent. When six had ventured on the knife-edge, he opened fire. Nor did he cease when the knife-edge was bare. He emptied his magazine, reloaded, and emptied it again. He kept on shooting. All his wrongs were blazing in his brain, and he was in a fury of vengeance. All down the goat-trail the soldiers were firing, and though they lay flat and sought to shelter themselves in the shallow inequalities of the surface, they were exposed marks to him. Bullets whistled and thudded about him, and an occasional ricochet sang sharply through the air. One bullet ploughed a crease through his scalp, and a second burned across his shoulder-blade without breaking the skin.

It was a massacre, in which one man did the killing. The soldiers began to retreat, helping along their wounded. As Koolau picked them off he became aware of the smell of burnt meat. He glanced about him at first, and then discovered that it was his own hands. The heat of the rifle was doing it. The leprosy had destroyed most of the nerves in his hands. Though his flesh burned and he smelled it, there was no sensation.

He lay in the thicket, smiling, until he remembered the war guns. Without doubt they would open upon him again, and this time upon the very thicket from which he had inflicted the danger. Scarcely had he changed his position to a nook behind a small shoulder of the wall where he had noted that no shells fell, than the bombardment recommenced. He counted the shells. Sixty more were thrown into the gorge before the war-guns ceased. The tiny area was pitted with their explosions, until it seemed impossible that any creature could have survived. So the soldiers thought, for, under the burning afternoon sun, they climbed the goat-trail again. And again the knife-edged passage was disputed, and again they fell back to the beach.

For two days longer Koolau held the passage, though the soldiers contented themselves with flinging shells into his retreat. Then Pahau, a leper boy, came to the top of the wall at the back of the gorge and shouted down to him that Kiloliana, hunting goats that they might eat, had been killed by a fall, and that the women were frightened and knew not what to do. Koolau called the boy down and left him with a spare gun with which to guard the passage. Koolau found his people disheartened. The majority of them were too helpless to forage food for themselves under such forbidding circumstances, and all were starving. He selected two women and a man who were not too far gone with the disease, and sent them back to the gorge to bring up food and mats. The rest he cheered and consoled until even the weakest took a hand in building rough shelters for themselves.

But those he had dispatched for food did not return, and he started back for the gorge. As he came out on the brow of the wall, half a dozen rifles cracked. A bullet tore through the fleshy part of his shoulder, and his cheek was cut by a sliver of rock where a second bullet smashed against the cliff. In the moment that this happened, and he leaped back, he saw that the gorge was alive with soldiers. His own people had betrayed him. The shell-fire had been too terrible, and they had preferred the prison of Molokai.

Koolau dropped back and unslung one of his heavy cartridge-belts. Lying among the rocks, he allowed the head and shoulders of the first soldier to rise clearly into view before pulling trigger. Twice this happened, and then, after some delay, in place of a head and shoulders a white flag was thrust above the edge of the wall.

"What do you want?" he demanded.

"I want you, if you are Koolau the leper," came the answer.

Koolau forgot where he was, forgot everything, as he lay and marvelled at the strange persistence of these *haoles* who would have their will though the sky fell in. Aye, they would have their will over all men and all things, even though they died in getting it. He could not but admire them, too, what of that will in them that was stronger than life and that bent all things to their bidding. He was convinced of the hopelessness of his struggle. There was no gainsaying that terrible will of the *haoles*. Though he killed a thousand, yet would they rise like the sands of the sea and come upon him, ever more and more. They never knew when they were beaten. That was their fault and their virtue. It was where his own kind lacked. He could see, now, how the handful of the preachers of God and the preachers of Rum had conquered the land. It was because—

"Well, what have you got to say? Will you come with me?"

It was the voice of the invisible man under the white flag. There he was, like any *haole*, driving straight toward the end determined.

"Let us talk," said Koolau.

The man's head and shoulders arose, then his whole body. He was a smooth-faced, blue-eyed youngster of twenty-five, slender and natty in his captain's uniform. He advanced until halted, then seated himself a dozen feet away:—

"You are a brave man," said Koolau wonderingly. "I could kill you like a fly."

"No, you couldn't," was the answer.

"Why not?"

"Because you are a man, Koolau, though a bad one. I know your story. You kill fairly."

Koolau grunted, but was secretly pleased.

"What have you done with my people?" he demanded. "The boy, the two women, and the man?"

"They gave themselves up, as I have now come for you to do."

Koolau laughed incredulously.

"I am a free man," he announced. "I have done no wrong. All I ask is to be left alone. I have lived free, and I shall die free. I will never give myself up."

"Then your people are wiser than you," answered the young captain. "Look—they are coming now."

Koolau turned and watched the remnant of his band approach. Groaning and sighing, a ghastly procession, it dragged its wretchedness past. It was given to Koolau to taste a deeper bitterness, for they hurled imprecations and insults at him as they went by; and the panting hag who brought up the rear halted, and with skinny, harpy-claws extended, shaking her snarling death's head from side to side, she laid a curse upon him. One by one they dropped over the lip-edge and surrendered to the hiding soldiers.

"You can go now," said Koolau to the captain. "I will never give myself up. That is my last word. Good-bye."

The captain slipped over the cliff to his soldiers. The next moment, and without a flag of truce, he hoisted his hat on his scabbard, and

Koolau's bullet tore through it. That afternoon they shelled him out from the beach, and as he retreated into the high inaccessible pockets beyond, the soldiers followed him.

For six weeks they hunted him from pocket to pocket, over the volcanic peaks and along the goat-trails. When he hid in the lantana jungle, they formed lines of beaters, and through lantana jungle and guava scrub they drove him like a rabbit. But ever he turned and doubled and eluded. There was no cornering him. When pressed too closely, his sure rifle held them back and they carried their wounded down the goat-trails to the beach. There were times when they did the shooting as his brown body showed for a moment through the underbrush. Once, five of them caught him on an exposed goat-trail between pockets. They emptied their rifles at him as he limped and climbed along his dizzy way. Afterwards they found blood-stains and knew that he was wounded. At the end of six weeks they gave up. The soldiers and police returned to Honolulu, and Kalalau Valley was left to him for his own, though head-hunters ventured after him from time to time and to their own undoing.

Two years later, and for the last time, Koolau crawled into a thicket and lay down among the *ti*-leaves and wild ginger blossoms. Free he had lived, and free he was dying. A slight drizzle of rain began to fall, and he drew a ragged blanket about the distorted wreck of his limbs. His body was covered with an oilskin coat. Across his chest he laid his Mauser rifle, lingering affectionately for a moment to wipe the dampness from the barrel. The hand with which he wiped had no fingers left upon it with which to pull the trigger.

He closed his eyes, for, from the weakness in his body and the fuzzy turmoil in his brain, he knew that his end was near. Like a wild animal he had crept into hiding to die. Half-conscious, aimless and wandering, he lived back in his life to his early manhood on Niihau. As life faded and the drip of the rain grew dim in his ears it seemed to him that he was once more in the thick of the horse-breaking, with raw colts rearing and bucking under him, his stirrups tied together beneath, or charging madly about the breaking corral and driving the helping cowboys over the rails. The next instant, and with seeming naturalness, he found himself pursuing the wild bulls of the upland pastures, roping them and leading them down to the valleys. Again the sweat and dust of the branding pen stung his eyes and bit his nostrils.

All his lusty, whole-bodied youth was his, until the sharp pangs of impending dissolution brought him back. He lifted his monstrous hands and gazed at them in wonder. But how? Why? Why should the wholeness of that wild youth of his change to this? Then he remembered, and once again, and for a moment, he was Koolau, the leper. His eyelids fluttered wearily down and the drip of the rain ceased in his ears. A prolonged trembling set up in his body. This, too, ceased. He half-lifted his head, but it fell back. Then his eyes opened, and did not close. His last thought was of his Mauser, and he pressed it against his chest with his folded, fingerless hands.

Good-bye, Jack

Hawaii is a queer place. Everything socially is what I may call topsy-turvy. Not but what things are correct. They are almost too much so. But still things are sort of upside down. The most ultra-exclusive set there is the "Missionary Crowd." It comes with rather a shock to learn that in Hawaii the obscure martyrdom-seeking missionary sits at the head of the table of the moneyed aristocracy. But it is true. The humble New Englanders who came out in the third decade of the nineteenth century, came for the lofty purpose of teaching the kanakas the true religion, the worship of the one only genuine and undeniable God. So well did they succeed in this, and also in civilizing the kanaka, that by the second or third generation he was practically extinct. This being the fruit of the seed of the Gospel, the fruit of the seed of the missionaries (the sons and the grandsons) was the possession of the islands themselves,—of the land, the ports, the town sites, and the sugar plantations. The missionary who came to give the bread of life remained to gobble up the whole heathen feast.

But that is not the Hawaiian queerness I started out to tell. Only one cannot speak of things Hawaiian without mentioning the missionaries.

There is Jack Kersdale, the man I wanted to tell about; he came of missionary stock. That is, on his grandmother's side. His grandfather was old Benjamin Kersdale, a Yankee trader, who got his start for a million in the old days by selling cheap whiskey and square-face gin. There's another queer thing. The old missionaries and old traders were mortal enemies. You see, their interests conflicted. But their children made it up by intermarrying and dividing the island between them.

Life in Hawaii is a song. That's the way Stoddard put it in his "Hawaii Noi":—

> "Thy life is music—Fate the notes prolong!
> Each isle a stanza, and the whole a song."

And he was right. Flesh is golden there. The native women are sun-ripe Junos, the native men bronzed Apollos. They sing, and dance, and all are flower-bejewelled and flower-crowned. And, outside the rigid "Missionary Crowd," the white men yield to the climate and the sun, and no matter how busy they may be, are prone to dance and sing and wear flowers behind their ears and in their hair. Jack Kersdale was one of these fellows. He was one of the busiest men I ever met. He was a several-times millionaire. He was a sugar king, a coffee planter, a rubber pioneer, a cattle rancher, and a promoter of three out of every four new enterprises launched in the islands. He was a society man, a club man, a yachtsman, a bachelor, and withal as handsome a man as was ever doted upon by mammas with marriageable daughters. Incidentally, he had finished his education at Yale, and his head was crammed fuller with vital statistics and scholarly information concerning Hawaii Nei than any other islander I ever encountered. He turned off an immense amount of work, and he sang and danced and put flowers in his hair as immensely as any of the idlers.

He had grit, and had fought two duels—both political—when he was no more than a raw youth essaying his first adventures in politics. In fact, he played a most creditable and courageous part in the last revolution, when the native dynasty was overthrown; and he could not have been over sixteen at the time. I am pointing out that he was no coward, in order that you may appreciate what happens later on. I've seen him in the breaking yard at the Haleakala Ranch, conquering a four-year-old brute that for two years had defied the pick of Von Tempsky's cow-boys. And I must tell of one other thing. It was down in Kona,—or up, rather, for the Kona people scorn to live at less than a thousand feet elevation. We were all on the *lanai* of Doctor Goodhue's bungalow. I was talking with Dottie Fairchild when it happened. A big centipede—it was seven inches, for we measured it afterward—fell from the rafters overhead squarely into her coiffure. I confess, the hideousness of it paralysed me. I couldn't move. My mind refused to work. There, within two feet of me, the ugly venomous devil was writhing in her hair. It threatened at any moment to fall down upon her exposed shoulders—we had just come out from dinner.

"What is it?" she asked, starting to raise her hand to her head.

"Don't!" I cried. "Don't!"

"But what is it?" she insisted, growing frightened by the fright she read in my eyes and on my stammering lips.

My exclamation attracted Kersdale's attention. He glanced our way carelessly, but in that glance took in everything. He came over to us, but without haste.

"Please don't move, Dottie," he said quietly.

He never hesitated, nor did he hurry and make a bungle of it.

"Allow me," he said.

And with one hand he caught her scarf and drew it tightly around her shoulders so that the centipede could not fall inside her bodice. With the other hand—the right—he reached into her hair, caught the repulsive abomination as near as he was able by the nape of the neck, and held it tightly between thumb and forefinger as he withdrew it from her hair. It was as horrible and heroic a sight as man could wish to see. It made my flesh crawl. The centipede, seven inches of squirming legs, writhed and twisted and dashed itself about his hand, the body twining around the fingers and the legs digging into the skin and scratching as the beast endeavoured to free itself. It bit him twice—I saw it—though he assured the ladies that he was not harmed as he dropped it upon the walk and stamped it into the gravel. But I saw him in the surgery five minutes afterward, with Doctor Goodhue scarifying the wounds and injecting permanganate of potash. The next morning

Kersdale's arm was as big as a barrel, and it was three weeks before the swelling went down.

All of which has nothing to do with my story, but which I could not avoid giving in order to show that Jack Kersdale was anything but a coward. It was the cleanest exhibition of grit I have ever seen. He never turned a hair. The smile never left his lips. And he dived with thumb and forefinger into Dottie Fairchild's hair as gaily as if it had been a box of salted almonds. Yet that was the man I was destined to see stricken with fear a thousand times more hideous even than the fear that was mine when I saw that writhing abomination in Dottie Fairchild's hair, dangling over her eyes and the trap of her bodice.

I was interested in leprosy, and upon that, as upon every other island subject, Kersdale had encyclopedic knowledge. In fact, leprosy was one of his hobbies. He was an ardent defender of the settlement at Molokai, where all the island lepers were segregated. There was much talk and feeling among the natives, fanned by the demagogues, concerning the cruelties of Molokai, where men and women, not alone banished from friends and family, were compelled to live in perpetual imprisonment until they died. There were no reprieves, no commutations of sentences. "Abandon hope" was written over the portal of Molokai.

"I tell you they are happy there," Kersdale insisted. "And they are infinitely better off than their friends and relatives outside who have nothing the matter with them. The horrors of Molokai are all poppycock. I can take you through any hospital or any slum in any of the great cities of the world and show you a thousand times worse horrors. The living death! The creatures that once were men! Bosh! You ought to see those living deaths racing horses on the Fourth of July. Some of them own boats. One has a gasoline launch. They have nothing to do but have a good time. Food, shelter, clothes, medical attendance, everything, is theirs. They are the wards of the Territory. They have a much finer climate than Honolulu, and the scenery is magnificent. I shouldn't mind going down there myself for the rest of my days. It is a lovely spot."

So Kersdale on the joyous leper. He was not afraid of leprosy. He said so himself, and that there wasn't one chance in a million for him or any other white man to catch it, though he confessed afterward that one of his school chums, Alfred Starter, had contracted it, gone to Molokai, and there died.

"You know, in the old days," Kersdale explained, "there was no certain test for leprosy. Anything unusual or abnormal was sufficient to send a fellow to Molokai. The result was that dozens were sent there who were no more lepers than you or I. But they don't make that mistake now. The Board of Health tests are infallible. The funny thing is that when the test was discovered they immediately went down to Molokai and applied it, and they found a number who were not lepers. These were immediately deported. Happy to get away? They wailed harder at leaving the settlement than when they left Honolulu to go to it. Some refused to leave, and really had to be forced out. One of them even married a leper woman in the last stages and then wrote pathetic letters to the Board of Health, protesting against his expulsion on the ground that no one was so well able as he to take care of his poor old wife."

"What is this infallible test?" I demanded.

"The bacteriological test. There is no getting away from it. Doctor Hervey—he's our expert, you know—was the first man to apply it here. He is a wizard. He knows more about leprosy than any living man, and if a cure is ever discovered, he'll be that discoverer. As for the test, it is very simple. They have succeeded in isolating the *bacillus leprae* and studying it. They know it now when they see it. All they do is to snip a bit of skin from the suspect and subject it to the bacteriological test. A man without any visible symptoms may be chock full of the leprosy bacilli."

"Then you or I, for all we know," I suggested, "may be full of it now."

Kersdale shrugged his shoulders and laughed.

"Who can say? It takes seven years for it to incubate. If you have any doubts go and see Doctor Hervey. He'll just snip out a piece of your skin and let you know in a jiffy."

Later on he introduced me to Dr. Hervey, who loaded me down with Board of Health reports and pamphlets on the subject, and took me out to Kalihi, the Honolulu receiving station, where suspects were examined and confirmed lepers were held for deportation to Molokai. These deportations occurred about once a month, when, the last good-byes said, the lepers were marched on board the little steamer, the *Noeau*, and carried down to the settlement.

One afternoon, writing letters at the club, Jack Kersdale dropped in on me.

"Just the man I want to see," was his greeting. "I'll show you the sad-dest aspect of the whole situation—the lepers wailing as they depart for Molokai. The *Noeau* will be taking them on board in a few minutes. But let me warn you not to let your feelings be harrowed. Real as their grief is, they'd wail a whole sight harder a year hence if the Board of Health tried to take them away from Molokai. We've just time for a whiskey and soda. I've a carriage outside. It won't take us five minutes to get down to the wharf."

To the wharf we drove. Some forty sad wretches, amid their mats, blankets, and luggage of various sorts, were squatting on the stringer piece. The *Noeau* had just arrived and was making fast to a lighter that lay between her and the wharf. A Mr. McVeigh, the superintendent of the settlement, was overseeing the embarkation, and to him I was in-troduced, also to Dr. Georges, one of the Board of Health physicians whom I had already met at Kalihi. The lepers were a woebegone lot. The faces of the majority were hideous—too horrible for me to de-scribe. But here and there I noticed fairly good-looking persons, with no apparent signs of the fell disease upon them. One, I noticed, a little white girl, not more than twelve, with blue eyes and golden hair. One cheek, however, showed the leprous bloat. On my remarking on the sadness of her alien situation among the brown-skinned afflicted ones, Doctor Georges replied:—

"Oh, I don't know. It's a happy day in her life. She comes from Kauai. Her father is a brute. And now that she has developed the dis-ease she is going to join her mother at the settlement. Her mother was sent down three years ago—a very bad case."

"You can't always tell from appearances," Mr. McVeigh explained. "That man there, that big chap, who looks the pink of condition, with nothing the matter with him, I happen to know has a perforating ulcer in his foot and another in his shoulder-blade. Then there are others—

there, see that girl's hand, the one who is smoking the cigarette. See her twisted fingers. That's the anæsthetic form. It attacks the nerves. You could cut her fingers off with a dull knife, or rub them off on a nutmeg-grater, and she would not experience the slightest sensation."

"Yes, but that fine-looking woman, there," I persisted; "surely, surely, there can't be anything the matter with her. She is too glorious and gorgeous altogether."

"A sad case," Mr. McVeigh answered over his shoulder, already turning away to walk down the wharf with Kersdale.

She was a beautiful woman, and she was pure Polynesian. From my meagre knowledge of the race and its types I could not but conclude that she had descended from old chief stock. She could not have been more than twenty-three or four. Her lines and proportions were magnificent, and she was just beginning to show the amplitude of the women of her race.

"It was a blow to all of us," Dr. Georges volunteered. "She gave herself up voluntarily, too. No one suspected. But somehow she had contracted the disease. It broke us all up, I assure you. We've kept it out of the papers, though. Nobody but us and her family knows what has become of her. In fact, if you were to ask any man in Honolulu, he'd tell you it was his impression that she was somewhere in Europe. It was at her request that we've been so quiet about it. Poor girl, she has a lot of pride."

"But who is she?" I asked. "Certainly, from the way you talk about her, she must be somebody."

"Did you ever hear of Lucy Mokunui?" he asked.

"Lucy Mokunui?" I repeated, haunted by some familiar association. I shook my head. "It seems to me I've heard the name, but I've forgotten it."

"Never heard of Lucy Mokunui! The Hawaiian nightingale! I beg your pardon. Of course you are a *malahini*, and could not be expected to know. Well, Lucy Mokunui was the best beloved of Honolulu—of all Hawaii, for that matter."

"You say *was*," I interrupted.

"And I mean it. She is finished." He shrugged his shoulders pityingly. "A dozen *haoles*—I beg your pardon, white men—have lost their hearts to her at one time or another. And I'm not counting in the ruck. The dozen I refer to were *haoles* of position and prominence.

"She could have married the son of the Chief Justice if she'd wanted to. You think she's beautiful, eh? But you should hear her sing. Finest native woman singer in Hawaii Nei. Her throat is pure silver and melted sunshine. We adored her. She toured America first with the Royal Hawaiian Band. After that she made two more trips on her own—concert work."

"Oh!" I cried. "I remember now. I heard her two years ago at the Boston Symphony. So that is she. I recognize her now."

I was oppressed by a heavy sadness. Life was a futile thing at best. A short two years and this magnificent creature, at the summit of her magnificent success, was one of the leper squad awaiting deportation to Molokai. Henley's lines came into my mind:

"The poor old tramp explains his poor old ulcers;
Life is, I think, a blunder and a shame."

I recoiled from my own future. If this awful fate fell to Lucy Mokunui, what might my lot not be?—or anybody's lot? I was thoroughly aware that in life we are in the midst of death—but to be in the midst of living death, to die and not be dead, to be one of that draft of creatures that once were men, aye, and women, like Lucy Mokunui, the epitome of all Polynesian charms, an artist as well, and well beloved of men—. I am afraid I must have betrayed my perturbation, for Doctor Georges hastened to assure me that they were very happy down in the settlement.

It was all too inconceivably monstrous. I could not bear to look at her. A short distance away, behind a stretched rope guarded by u po liceman, were the lepers' relatives and friends. They were not allowed to come near. There were no last embraces, no kisses of farewell. They called back and forth to one another—last messages, last words of love, last reiterated instructions. And those behind the rope looked with terrible intensity. It was the last time they would behold the faces of their loved ones, for they were the living dead, being carted away in the funeral ship to the graveyard of Molokai.

Doctor Georges gave the command, and the unhappy wretches dragged themselves to their feet and under their burdens of luggage began to stagger across the lighter and aboard the steamer. It was the funeral procession. At once the wailing started from those behind the rope. It was blood-curdling; it was heart-rending. I never heard such woe, and I hope never to again. Kersdale and McVeigh were still at the other end of the wharf, talking earnestly—politics, of course, for both were head-over-heels in that particular game. When Lucy Mokunui passed me, I stole a look at her. She *was* beautiful. She was beautiful by our standards, as well—one of those rare blossoms that occur but once in generations. And she, of all women, was doomed to Molokai. She walked like a queen, across the lighter, straight on board, and aft on the open deck where the lepers huddled by the rail, wailing now, to their dear ones on shore.

The lines were cast off, and the *Noeau* began to move away from the wharf. The wailing increased. Such grief and despair! I was just re-solving that never again would I be a witness to the sailing of the *Noeau,* when McVeigh and Kersdale returned. The latter's eyes were sparkling, and his lips could not quite hide the smile of delight that was his. Evidently the politics they had talked had been satisfactory. The rope had been flung aside, and the lamenting relatives now crowded the stringer piece on either side of us.

"That's her mother," Doctor Georges whispered, indicating an old woman next to me, who was rocking back and forth and gazing at the steamer rail out of tear-blinded eyes. I noticed that Lucy Mokunui was also wailing. She stopped abruptly and gazed at Kersdale. Then she stretched forth her arms in that adorable, sensuous way that Olga Nethersole has of embracing an audience. And with arms outspread, she cried:

"Good-bye, Jack! Good-bye!"

He heard the cry, and looked. Never was a man overtaken by more crushing fear. He reeled on the stringer piece, his face went white to the roots of his hair, and he seemed to shrink and wither away inside his clothes. He threw up his hands and groaned, "My God! My God!" Then he controlled himself by a great effort.

"Good-bye, Lucy! Good-bye!" he called.

And he stood there on the wharf, waving his hands to her till the *Noeau* was clear away and the faces lining her after-rail were vague and indistinct.

"I thought you knew," said McVeigh, who had been regarding him curiously. "You, of all men, should have known. I thought that was why you were here."

"I know now," Kersdale answered with immense gravity. "Where's the carriage?"

He walked rapidly—half-ran—to it. I had to half-run myself to keep up with him.

"Drive to Doctor Hervey's," he told the driver. "Drive as fast as you can."

He sank down in a seat, panting and gasping. The pallor of his face had increased. His lips were compressed and the sweat was standing out on his forehead and upper lip. He seemed in some horrible agony.

"For God's sake, Martin, make those horses go!" he broke out suddenly. "Lay the whip into them!—do you hear?—lay the whip into them!"

"They'll break, sir," the driver remonstrated.

"Let them break," Kersdale answered. "I'll pay your fine and square you with the police. Put it to them. That's right. Faster! Faster!"

"And I never knew, I never knew," he muttered, sinking back in the seat and with trembling hands wiping the sweat away.

The carriage was bouncing, swaying and lurching around corners at such a wild pace as to make conversation impossible. Besides, there was nothing to say. But I could hear him muttering over and over, "And I never knew. I never knew."

FROM *SOUTH SEA TALES*

THE SEED OF MCCOY

The *Pyrenees*, her iron sides pressed low in the water by her cargo of wheat, rolled sluggishly, and made it easy for the man who was climbing aboard from out a tiny outrigger canoe. As his eyes came level with the rail, so that he could see inboard, it seemed to him that he saw a dim, almost indiscernible haze. It was more like an illusion, like a blurring film that had spread abruptly over his eyes. He felt an inclination to brush it away, and the same instant he thought that he was growing old and that it was time to send to San Francisco for a pair of spectacles.

As he came over the rail he cast a glance aloft at the tall masts, and, next, at the pumps. They were not working. There seemed nothing the matter with the big ship, and he wondered why she had hoisted the signal of distress. He thought of his happy islanders, and hoped it was not disease. Perhaps the ship was short of water or provisions. He shook hands with the captain whose gaunt face and care-worn eyes made no secret of the trouble, whatever it was. At the same moment the newcomer was aware of a faint, indefinable smell. It seemed like that of burnt bread, but different.

He glanced curiously about him. Twenty feet away a weary-faced sailor was calking the deck. As his eyes lingered on the man, he saw suddenly arise from under his hands a faint spiral of haze that curled and twisted and was gone. By now he had reached the deck. His bare feet were pervaded by a dull warmth that quickly penetrated the thick calluses. He knew now the nature of the ship's distress. His eyes roved swiftly forward, where the full crew of weary-faced sailors regarded him eagerly. The glance from his liquid brown eyes swept over them like a benediction, soothing them, wrapping them about as in the mantle of a great peace. "How long has she been afire, Captain?" he asked in a voice so gentle and unperturbed that it was as the cooing of a dove.

At first the captain felt the peace and content of it stealing in upon him; then the consciousness of all that he had gone through and was going through smote him, and he was resentful. By what right did this ragged beachcomber, in dungaree trousers and a cotton shirt, suggest such a thing as peace and content to him and his overwrought, exhausted soul? The captain did not reason this; it was the unconscious process of emotion that caused his resentment.

"Fifteen days," he answered shortly. "Who are you?"

"My name is McCoy," came the answer in tones that breathed tenderness and compassion.

"I mean, are you the pilot?"

McCoy passed the benediction of his gaze over the tall, heavy-shouldered man with the haggard, unshaven face who had joined the captain.

"I am as much a pilot as anybody," was McCoy's answer. "We are all pilots here, Captain, and I know every inch of these waters."

But the captain was impatient.

"What I want is some of the authorities. I want to talk with them, and blame quick."

"Then I'll do just as well."

Again that insidious suggestion of peace, and his ship a raging furnace beneath his feet! The captain's eyebrows lifted impatiently and nervously, and his fist clenched as if he were about to strike a blow with it.

"Who in hell are you?" he demanded.

"I am the chief magistrate," was the reply in a voice that was still the softest and gentlest imaginable.

The tall, heavy-shouldered man broke out in a harsh laugh that was partly amusement, but mostly hysterical. Both he and the captain regarded McCoy with incredulity and amazement. That this barefooted beachcomber should possess such high-sounding dignity was inconceivable. His cotton shirt, unbuttoned, exposed a grizzled chest and the fact that there was no undershirt beneath.

A worn straw hat failed to hide the ragged gray hair. Halfway down his chest descended an untrimmed patriarchal beard. In any slop shop, two shillings would have outfitted him complete as he stood before them.

"Any relation to the McCoy of the *Bounty*?" the captain asked.

"He was my great-grandfather."

"Oh," the captain said, then bethought himself. "My name is Davenport, and this is my first mate, Mr. Konig."

They shook hands.

"And now to business." The captain spoke quickly, the urgency of a great haste pressing his speech. "We've been on fire for over two weeks. She's ready to break all hell loose any moment. That's why I held for Pitcairn. I want to beach her, or scuttle her, and save the hull."

"Then you made a mistake, Captain," said McCoy. "You should have slacked away for Mangareva. There's a beautiful beach there, in a lagoon where the water is like a mill pond."

"But we're here, ain't we?" the first mate demanded. "That's the point. We're here, and we've got to do something."

McCoy shook his head kindly.

"You can do nothing here. There is no beach. There isn't even anchorage."

"Gammon!" said the mate. "Gammon!" he repeated loudly, as the captain signaled him to be more soft spoken. "You can't tell me that sort of stuff. Where d'ye keep your own boats, hey—your schooner, or cutter, or whatever you have? Hey? Answer me that."

McCoy smiled as gently as he spoke. His smile was a caress, an embrace that surrounded the tired mate and sought to draw him into the quietude and rest of McCoy's tranquil soul.

"We have no schooner or cutter," he replied. "And we carry our canoes to the top of the cliff."

"You've got to show me," snorted the mate. "How d'ye get around to
the other islands, heh? Tell me that."

"We don't get around. As governor of Pitcairn, I sometimes go.
When I was younger, I was away a great deal—sometimes on the trading schooners, but mostly on the missionary brig. But she's gone now,
and we depend on passing vessels. Sometimes we have had as high as
six calls in one year. At other times, a year, and even longer, has gone
by without one passing ship. Yours is the first in seven months."

"And you mean to tell me—" the mate began.

But Captain Davenport interfered.

"Enough of this. We're losing time. What is to be done, Mr.
McCoy?"

The old man turned his brown eyes, sweet as a woman's, shoreward,
and both captain and mate followed his gaze around from the lonely
rock of Pitcairn to the crew clustering forward and waiting anxiously
for the announcement of a decision. McCoy did not hurry. He thought
smoothly and slowly, step by step, with the certitude of a mind that
was never vexed or outraged by life.

"The wind is light now," he said finally. "There is a heavy current
setting to the westward."

"That's what made us fetch to leeward," the captain interrupted,
desiring to vindicate his seamanship.

"Yes, that is what fetched you to leeward," McCoy went on. "Well,
you can't work up against this current today. And if you did, there is no
beach. Your ship will be a total loss."

He paused, and captain and mate looked despair at each other.

"But I will tell you what you can do. The breeze will freshen to-
night around midnight—see those tails of clouds and that thickness to
windward, beyond the point there? That's where she'll come from, out
of the southeast, hard. It is three hundred miles to Mangareva. Square
away for it. There is a beautiful bed for your ship there."

The mate shook his head.

"Come in to the cabin, and we'll look at the chart," said the captain.

McCoy found a stifling, poisonous atmosphere in the pent cabin.

Stray waftures of invisible gases bit his eyes and made them sting. The deck was hotter, almost unbearably hot to his bare feet. The sweat poured out of his body. He looked almost with apprehension about him. This malignant, internal heat was astounding. It was a marvel that the cabin did not burst into flames. He had a feeling as if of being in a huge bake oven where the heat might at any moment increase tremendously and shrivel him up like a blade of grass.

As he lifted one foot and rubbed the hot sole against the leg of his trousers, the mate laughed in a savage, snarling fashion.

"The anteroom of hell," he said. "Hell herself is right down there under your feet."

"It's hot!" McCoy cried involuntarily, mopping his face with a bandana handkerchief.

"Here's Mangareva," the captain said, bending over the table and pointing to a black speck in the midst of the white blankness of the chart. "And here, in between, is another island. Why not run for that?"

McCoy did not look at the chart.

"That's Crescent Island," he answered "It is uninhabited, and it is only two or three feet above water. Lagoon, but no entrance. No, Mangareva is the nearest place for your purpose."

"Mangareva it is, then," said Captain Davenport, interrupting the mate's growling objection. "Call the crew aft, Mr. Konig."

The sailors obeyed, shuffling wearily along the deck and painfully endeavoring to make haste. Exhaustion was evident in every movement. The cook came out of his galley to hear, and the cabin boy hung about near him.

When Captain Davenport had explained the situation and announced his intention of running for Mangareva, an uproar broke out. Against a background of throaty rumbling arose inarticulate cries of rage, with here and there a distinct curse, or word, or phase. A shrill Cockney voice soared and dominated for a moment, crying; "Gawd! After bein' in ell for fifteen days—an' now e wants us to sail this floatin' ell to sea again?"

The captain could not control them, but McCoy's gentle presence seemed to rebuke and calm them, and the muttering and cursing died away, until the full crew, save here and there an anxious face directed at the captain, yearned dumbly toward the green clad peaks and beetling coast of Pitcairn.

Soft as a spring zephyr was the voice of McCoy:

"Captain, I thought I heard some of them say they were starving."

"Ay," was the answer, "and so we are. I've had a sea biscuit and a spoonful of salmon in the last two days. We're on whack. You see, when we discovered the fire, we battened down immediately to suffocate the fire. And then we found how little food there was in the pantry. But it was too late. We didn't dare break out the lazarette. Hungry? I'm just as hungry as they are."

He spoke to the men again, and again the throat rumbling and cursing arose, their faces convulsed and animal-like with rage. The second and third mates had joined the captain, standing behind him at the break of the poop. Their faces were set and expressionless; they seemed bored, more than anything else, by this mutiny of the crew. Captain Davenport glanced questioningly at his first mate, and that person merely shrugged his shoulders in token of his helplessness.

"You see," the captain said to McCoy, "you can't compel sailors to leave the safe land and go to sea on a burning vessel. She has been their floating coffin for over two weeks now. They are worked out, and starved out, and they've got enough of her. We'll beat up for Pitcairn."

But the wind was light, the *Pyrenees'* bottom was foul, and she could not beat up against the strong westerly current. At the end of two hours she had lost three miles. The sailors worked eagerly, as if by main strength they could compel the *Pyrenees* against the adverse elements. But steadily, port tack and starboard tack, she sagged off to the westward. The captain paced restlessly up and down, pausing occasionally to survey the vagrant smoke wisps and to trace them back to the portions of the deck from which they sprang. The carpenter was engaged constantly in attempting to locate such places, and, when he succeeded, in calking them tighter and tighter.

"Well, what do you think?" the captain finally asked McCoy, who was watching the carpenter with all a child's interest and curiosity in his eyes.

McCoy looked shoreward, where the land was disappearing in the thickening haze.

"I think it would be better to square away for Mangareva. With that breeze that is coming, you'll be there tomorrow evening."

"But what if the fire breaks out? It is liable to do it any moment."

"Have your boats ready in the falls. The same breeze will carry your boats to Mangareva if the ship burns out from under."

Captain Davenport debated for a moment, and then McCoy heard the question he had not wanted to hear, but which he knew was surely coming.

"I have no chart of Mangareva. On the general chart it is only a fly speck. I would not know where to look for the entrance into the lagoon. Will you come along and pilot her in for me?"

McCoy's serenity was unbroken.

"Yes, Captain," he said, with the same quiet unconcern with which he would have accepted an invitation to dinner; "I'll go with you to Mangareva."

Again the crew was called aft, and the captain spoke to them from the break of the poop.

"We've tried to work her up, but you see how we've lost ground. She's setting off in a two-knot current. This gentleman is the Honorable McCoy, Chief Magistrate and Governor of Pitcairn Island. He will come along with us to Mangareva. So you see the situation is not so dangerous. He would not make such an offer if he thought he was going to lose his life. Besides, whatever risk there is, if he of his own free will come on board and take it, we can do no less. What do you say for Mangareva?"

This time there was no uproar. In McCoy's presence, the surety and calm that seemed to radiate from him, had had its effect. They conferred with one another in low voices. There was little urging. They were virtually unanimous, and they shoved the Cockney out as their spokesman. That worthy was overwhelmed with consciousness of the heroism of himself and his mates, and with flashing eyes he cried:

"By Gawd! If 'e will, we will!"

The crew mumbled its assent and started forward.

"One moment, Captain," McCoy said, as the other was turning to give orders to the mate. "I must go ashore first."

Mr. Konig was thunderstruck, staring at McCoy as if he were a madman.

"Go ashore!" the captain cried. "What for? It will take you three hours to get there in your canoe."

McCoy measured the distance of the land away, and nodded.

"Yes, it is six now. I won't get ashore till nine. The people cannot be assembled earlier than ten. As the breeze freshens up tonight, you can begin to work up against it, and pick me up at daylight tomorrow morning."

"In the name of reason and common sense," the captain burst forth, "what do you want to assemble the people for? Don't you realize that my ship is burning beneath me?"

McCoy was as placid as a summer sea, and the other's anger produced not the slightest ripple upon it.

"Yes, Captain," he cooed in his dove-like voice. "I do realize that your ship is burning. That is why I am going with you to Mangareva. But I must get permission to go with you. It is our custom. It is an important matter when the governor leaves the island. The people's interests are at stake, and so they have the right to vote their permission or refusal. But they will give it, I know that."

"Are you sure?"

"Quite sure."

"Then if you know they will give it, why bother with getting it? Think of the delay—a whole night."

"It is our custom," was the imperturbable reply. "Also, I am the governor, and I must make arrangements for the conduct of the island during my absence."

"But it is only a twenty-four-hour run to Mangareva," the captain objected. "Suppose it took you six times that long to return to windward; that would bring you back by the end of a week."

McCoy smiled his large, benevolent smile.

"Very few vessels come to Pitcairn, and when they do, they are usually from San Francisco or from around the Horn. I shall be fortunate if I get back in six months. I may be away a year, and I may have to go to San Francisco in order to find a vessel that will bring me back. My father once left Pitcairn to be gone three months, and two years passed before he could get back. Then, too, you are short of food. If you have to take to the boats, and the weather comes up bad, you may be days in reaching land. I can bring off two canoe loads of food in the morning. Dried bananas will be best. As the breeze freshens, you beat up against it. The nearer you are, the bigger loads I can bring off. Goodbye."

He held out his hand. The captain shook it, and was reluctant to let go. He seemed to cling to it as a drowning sailor clings to a life buoy.

"How do I know you will come back in the morning?" he asked.

"Yes, that's it!" cried the mate. "How do we know but what he's skinning out to save his own hide?"

McCoy did not speak. He looked at them sweetly and benignantly, and it seemed to them that they received a message from his tremendous certitude of soul.

The captain released his hand, and, with a last sweeping glance that embraced the crew in its benediction, McCoy went over the rail and descended into his canoe.

The wind freshened, and the *Pyrenees*, despite the foulness of her bottom, won half a dozen miles away from the westerly current. At daylight, with Pitcairn three miles to windward, Captain Davenport made out two canoes coming off to him. Again McCoy clambered up the side and dropped over the rail to the hot deck. He was followed by many packages of dried bananas, each package wrapped in dry leaves.

"Now, Captain," he said, "swing the yards and drive for dear life. You see, I am no navigator," he explained a few minutes later, as he stood by the captain aft, the latter with gaze wandering from aloft to overside as he estimated the *Pyrenees*' speed. "You must fetch her to Mangareva. When you have picked up the land, then I will pilot her in. What do you think she is making?"

"Eleven," Captain Davenport answered, with a final glance at the water rushing past.

"Eleven. Let me see, if she keeps up that gait, we'll sight Mangareva between eight and nine o'clock tomorrow morning. I'll have her on the beach by ten or by eleven at latest. And then your troubles will be all over."

It almost seemed to the captain that the blissful moment had already arrived, such was the persuasive convincingness of McCoy.

Captain Davenport had been under the fearful strain of navigating his burning ship for over two weeks, and he was beginning to feel that he had had enough.

A heavier flaw of wind struck the back of his neck and whistled by his ears. He measured the weight of it, and looked quickly overside.

"The wind is making all the time," he announced. "The old girl's doing nearer twelve than eleven right now. If this keeps up, we'll be shortening down tonight."

All day the *Pyrenees,* carrying her load of living fire, tore across the foaming sea. By nightfall, royals and topgallantsails were in, and she flew on into the darkness, with great, crested seas roaring after her. The auspicious wind had had its effect, and fore and aft a visible brightening was apparent. In the second dog-watch some careless soul started a song, and by eight bells the whole crew was singing.

Captain Davenport had his blankets brought up and spread on top the house.

"I've forgotten what sleep is," he explained to McCoy. "I'm all in. But give me a call at any time you think necessary."

At three in the morning he was aroused by a gentle tugging at his arm. He sat up quickly, bracing himself against the skylight, stupid yet from his heavy sleep. The wind was thrumming its war song in the rigging, and a wild sea was buffeting the *Pyrenees.* Amidships she was wallowing first one rail under and then the other, flooding the waist more often than not. McCoy was shouting something he could not hear. He reached out, clutched the other by the shoulder, and drew him close so that his own ear was close to the other's lips.

"It's three o'clock," came McCoy's voice, still retaining its dove-like quality, but curiously muffled, as if from a long way off. "We've run two hundred and fifty. Crescent Island is only thirty miles away, somewhere there dead ahead. There's no lights on it. If we keep running, we'll pile up, and lose ourselves as well as the ship."

"What d' ye think—heave to?"

"Yes; heave to till daylight. It will only put us back four hours."

So the *Pyrenees,* with her cargo of fire, was hove to, bitting the teeth of the gale and fighting and smashing the pounding seas. She was a shell, filled with a conflagration, and on the outside of the shell, clinging precariously, the little motes of men, by pull and haul, helped her in the battle.

"It is most unusual, this gale," McCoy told the captain, in the lee of the cabin. "By rights there should be no gale at this time of the year. But everything about the weather has been unusual. There has been a stoppage of the trades, and now it's howling right out of the trade quarter." He waved his hand into the darkness, as if his vision could dimly penetrate for hundreds of miles. "It is off to the westward. There is something big making off there somewhere— a hurricane or something. We're lucky to be so far to the eastward. But this is only a little blow," he added. "It can't last. I can tell you that much."

By daylight the gale had eased down to normal. But daylight revealed a new danger. It had come on thick. The sea was covered by a fog, or, rather, by a pearly mist that was fog-like in density, in so far as it obstructed vision, but that was no more than a film on the sea, for the sun shot it through and filled it with a glowing radiance.

The deck of the *Pyrenees* was making more smoke than on the preceding day, and the cheerfulness of officers and crew had vanished. In the lee of the galley the cabin boy could be heard whimpering. It was his first voyage, and the fear of death was at his heart. The captain wandered about like a lost soul, nervously chewing his mustache, scowling, unable to make up his mind what to do.

"What do you think?" he asked, pausing by the side of McCoy, who was making a breakfast off fried bananas and a mug of water.

McCoy finished the last banana, drained the mug, and looked slowly around. In his eyes was a smile of tenderness as he said:

"Well, Captain, we might as well drive as burn. Your decks are not going to hold out forever. They are hotter this morning. You haven't a pair of shoes I can wear? It is getting uncomfortable for my bare feet."

The *Pyrenees* shipped two heavy seas as she was swung off and put once more before it, and the first mate expressed a desire to have all that water down in the hold, if only it could be introduced without taking off the hatches. McCoy ducked his head into the binnacle and watched the course set.

"I'd hold her up some more, Captain," he said. "She's been making drift when hove to."

"I've set it to a point higher already," was the answer. "Isn't that enough?"

"I'd make it two points, Captain. This bit of a blow kicked that westerly current ahead faster than you imagine."

Captain Davenport compromised on a point and a half, and then went aloft, accompanied by McCoy and the first mate, to keep a lookout for land. Sail had been made, so that the *Pyrenees* was doing ten knots. The following sea was dying down rapidly. There was no break in the pearly fog, and by ten o'clock Captain Davenport was growing nervous. All hands were at their stations, ready, at the first warning of land ahead, to spring like fiends to the task of bringing the *Pyrenees* up on the wind. That land ahead, a surf-washed outer reef, would be perilously close when it revealed itself in such a fog.

Another hour passed. The three watchers aloft stared intently into the pearly radiance. "What if we miss Mangareva?" Captain Davenport asked abruptly.

McCoy, without shifting his gaze, answered softly:

"Why, let her drive, Captain. That is all we can do. All the Paumotus are before us. We can drive for a thousand miles through reefs and atolls. We are bound to fetch up somewhere."

"Then drive it is." Captain Davenport evidenced his intention of descending to the deck.

"We've missed Mangareva. God knows where the next land is. I wish I'd held her up that other half-point," he confessed a moment later. "This cursed current plays the devil with a navigator."

"The old navigators called the Paumotus the Dangerous Archipelago," McCoy said, when they had regained the poop. "This very current was partly responsible for that name."

"I was walking with a sailor chap in Sydney, once," said Mr. Konig. "He'd been trading in the Paumotus. He told me insurance was eighteen per cent. Is that right?"

McCoy smiled and nodded.

"Except that they don't insure," he explained. "The owners write off twenty per cent of the cost of their schooners each year."

"My God!" Captain Davenport groaned. "That makes the life of a schooner only five years!" He shook his head sadly, murmuring, "Bad waters! Bad waters!"

Again they went into the cabin to consult the big general chart; but the poisonous vapors drove them coughing and gasping on deck.

"Here is Moerenhout Island," Captain Davenport pointed it out on the chart, which he had spread on the house. "It can't be more than a hundred miles to leeward."

"A hundred and ten." McCoy shook his head doubtfully. "It might be done, but it is very difficult. I might beach her, and then again I might put her on the reef. A bad place, a very bad place."

"We'll take the chance," was Captain Davenport's decision, as he set about working out the course.

Sail was shortened early in the afternoon, to avoid running past in the night; and in the second dog-watch the crew manifested its regained cheerfulness. Land was so very near, and their troubles would be over in the morning.

But morning broke clear, with a blazing tropic sun. The southeast trade had swung around to the eastward, and was driving the *Pyrenees* through the water at an eight-knot clip. Captain Davenport worked up his dead reckoning, allowing generously for drift, and announced Moerenhout Island to be not more than ten miles off. The *Pyrenees* sailed the ten miles; she sailed ten miles more; and the lookouts at the three mastheads saw naught but the naked, sun-washed sea.

"But the land is there, I tell you," Captain Davenport shouted to them from the poop.

McCoy smiled soothingly, but the captain glared about him like a madman, fetched his sextant, and took a chronometer sight.

"I knew I was right," he almost shouted, when he had worked up the observation. "Twenty-one, fifty-five, south; one-thirty-six, two, west. There you are. We're eight miles to windward yet. What did you make it out, Mr. Konig?"

The first mate glanced at his own figures, and said in a low voice:

"Twenty-one, fifty-five all right; but my longitude's one-thirty-six, forty-eight. That puts us considerably to leeward—"

But Captain Davenport ignored his figures with so contemptuous a silence as to make Mr. Konig grit his teeth and curse savagely under his breath.

"Keep her off," the captain ordered the man at the wheel. "Three points—steady there, as she goes!"

Then he returned to his figures and worked them over. The sweat poured from his face. He chewed his mustache, his lips, and his pencil, staring at the figures as a man might at a ghost. Suddenly, with a fierce, muscular outburst, he crumpled the scribbled paper in his fist and crushed it under foot. Mr. Konig grinned vindictively and turned away, while Captain Davenport leaned against the cabin and for half an hour spoke no word, contenting himself with gazing to leeward with an expression of musing hopelessness on his face.

"Mr. McCoy," he broke silence abruptly. "The chart indicates a group of islands, but not how many, off there to the north'ard, or nor'-nor'westward, about forty miles—the Acteon Islands. What about them?"

"There are four, all low," McCoy answered. "First to the southeast is Matuerui—no people, no entrance to the lagoon. Then comes Tenarunga. There used to be about a dozen people there, but they may be all gone now. Anyway, there is no entrance for a ship—only a boat entrance, with a fathom of water. Vehauga and Teua-raro are the other two. No entrances, no people, very low. There is no bed for the *Pyrenees* in that group. She would be a total wreck."

"Listen to that!" Captain Davenport was frantic. "No people! No entrances! What in the devil are islands good for?

"Well, then," he barked suddenly, like an excited terrier, "the chart gives a whole mess of islands off to the nor'west. What about them? What one has an entrance where I can lay my ship?"

McCoy calmly considered. He did not refer to the chart. All these islands, reefs, shoals, lagoons, entrances, and distances were marked on the chart of his memory. He knew them as the city dweller knows his buildings, streets, and alleys.

"Papakena and Vanavana are off there to the westward, or west-nor'westward a hundred miles and a bit more," he said. "One is uninhabited, and I heard that the people on the other had gone off to

Cadmus Island. Anyway, neither lagoon has an entrance. Ahunui is another hundred miles on to the nor'west. No entrance, no people."

"Well, forty miles beyond them are two islands?" Captain Davenport queried, raising his head from the chart.

McCoy shook his head.

"Paros and Manuhungi—no entrances, no people. Nengo-Nengo is forty miles beyond them, in turn, and it has no people and no entrance. But there is Hao Island. It is just the place. The lagoon is thirty miles long and five miles wide. There are plenty of people. You can usually find water. And any ship in the world can go through the entrance."

He ceased and gazed solicitously at Captain Davenport, who, bending over the chart with a pair of dividers in hand, had just emitted a low groan.

"Is there any lagoon with an entrance anywhere nearer than Hao Island?" he asked.

"No, Captain; that is the nearest."

"Well, it's three hundred and forty miles." Captain Davenport was speaking very slowly, with decision. "I won't risk the responsibility of all these lives. I'll wreck her on the Acteons. And she's a good ship, too," he added regretfully, after altering the course, this time making more allowance than ever for the westerly current.

An hour later the sky was overcast. The southeast trade still held, but the ocean was a checker board of squalls.

"We'll be there by one o'clock," Captain Davenport announced confidently. "By two o'clock at the outside. McCoy, you put her ashore on the one where the people are."

The sun did not appear again, nor, at one o'clock, was any land to be seen. Captain Davenport looked astern at the *Pyrenees'* canting wake.

"Good Lord!" he cried. "An easterly current? Look at that!"

Mr. Konig was incredulous. McCoy was noncommittal, though he said that in the Paumotus there was no reason why it should not be an easterly current. A few minutes later a squall robbed the *Pyrenees* temporarily of all her wind, and she was left rolling heavily in the trough.

"Where's that deep lead? Over with it, you there!" Captain Davenport held the lead line and watched it sag off to the northeast. "There, look at that! Take hold of it for yourself."

McCoy and the mate tried it, and felt the line thrumming and vibrating savagely to the grip of the tidal stream.

"A four-knot current," said Mr. Konig.

"An easterly current instead of a westerly," said Captain Davenport, glaring accusingly at McCoy, as if to cast the blame for it upon him.

"That is one of the reasons, Captain, for insurance being eighteen per cent in these waters," McCoy answered cheerfully. "You can never tell. The currents are always changing. There was a man who wrote books, I forget his name, in the yacht *Casco*. He missed Takaroa by thirty miles and fetched Tikei, all because of the shifting currents. You are up to windward now, and you'd better keep off a few points."

"But how much has this current set me?" the captain demanded irately. "How am I to know how much to keep off?"

"I don't know, Captain," McCoy said with great gentleness. The wind returned, and the *Pyrenees,* her deck smoking and shimmering in the bright gray light, ran off dead to leeward. Then she worked back, port tack and starboard tack, crisscrossing her track, combing the sea for the Acteon Islands, which the masthead lookouts failed to sight.

Captain Davenport was beside himself. His rage took the form of sullen silence, and he spent the afternoon in pacing the poop or leaning against the weather shrouds. At nightfall, without even consulting McCoy, he squared away and headed into the northwest. Mr. Konig, surreptitiously consulting chart and binnacle, and McCoy, openly and innocently consulting the binnacle, knew that they were running for Hao Island. By midnight the squalls ceased, and the stars came out. Captain Davenport was cheered by the promise of a clear day.

"I'll get an observation in the morning," he told McCoy, "though what my latitude is, is a puzzler. But I'll use the Sumner method, and settle that. Do you know the Sumner line?"

And thereupon he explained it in detail to McCoy.

The day proved clear, the trade blew steadily out of the east, and the *Pyrenees* just as steadily logged her nine knots. Both the captain and mate worked out the position on a Sumner line, and agreed, and at noon agreed again, and verified the morning sights by the noon sights.

"Another twenty-four hours and we'll be there," Captain Davenport assured McCoy. "It's a miracle the way the old girl's decks hold out. But they can't last. They can't last. Look at them smoke, more and more every day. Yet it was a tight deck to begin with, fresh-calked in Frisco. I was surprised when the fire first broke out and we battened down. Look at that!"

He broke off to gaze with dropped jaw at a spiral of smoke that coiled and twisted in the lee of the mizzenmast twenty feet above the deck.

"Now, how did that get there?" he demanded indignantly.

Beneath it there was no smoke. Crawling up from the deck, sheltered from the wind by the mast, by some freak it took form and visibility at the height. It writhed away from the mast, and for a moment overhung the captain like some threatening portent. The next moment the wind whisked it away, and the captain's jaw returned to place.

"As I was saying, when we first battened down, I was surprised. It was a tight deck, yet it leaked smoke like a sieve. And we've calked and calked ever since. There must be tremendous pressure underneath to drive so much smoke through."

That afternoon the sky became overcast again, and squally, drizzly weather set in. The wind shifted back and forth between southeast and northeast, and at midnight the *Pyrenees* was caught aback by a sharp squall from the southwest, from which point the wind continued to blow intermittently.

"We won't make Hao until ten or eleven," Captain Davenport complained at seven in the morning, when the fleeting promise of the sun had been erased by hazy cloud masses in the eastern sky. And the next moment he was plaintively demanding, "And what are the currents doing?"

Lookouts at the mastheads could report no land, and the day passed in drizzling calms and violent squalls. By nightfall a heavy sea began to make from the west. The barometer had fallen to 29.50. There was no wind, and still the ominous sea continued to increase. Soon the *Pyre-*

nees was rolling madly in the huge waves that marched in an unending procession from out of the darkness of the west. Sail was shortened as fast as both watches could work, and, when the tired crew had finished, its grumbling and complaining voices, peculiarly animal-like and menacing, could be heard in the darkness. Once the starboard watch was called aft to lash down and make secure, and the men openly advertised their sullenness and unwillingness. Every slow movement was a protest and a threat. The atmosphere was moist and sticky like mucilage, and in the absence of wind all hands seemed to pant and gasp for air. The sweat stood out on faces and bare arms, and Captain Davenport for one, his face more gaunt and care-worn than ever, and his eyes troubled and staring, was oppressed by a feeling of impending calamity.

"It's off to the westward," McCoy said encouragingly. "At worst, we'll be only on the edge of it."

But Captain Davenport refused to be comforted, and by the light of a lantern read up the chapter in his *Epitome* that related to the strategy of shipmasters in cyclonic storms. From somewhere amidships the silence was broken by a low whimpering from the cabin boy.

"Oh, shut up!" Captain Davenport yelled suddenly and with such force as to startle every man on board and to frighten the offender into a wild wail of terror.

"Mr. Konig," the captain said in a voice that trembled with rage and nerves, "will you kindly step for'ard and stop that brat's mouth with a deck mop?"

But it was McCoy who went forward, and in a few minutes had the boy comforted and asleep.

Shortly before daybreak the first breath of air began to move from out the southeast, increasing swiftly to a stiff and stiffer breeze. All hands were on deck waiting for what might be behind it. "We're all right now, Captain," said McCoy, standing close to his shoulder. "The hurricane is to the west'ard, and we are south of it. This breeze is the insuck. It won't blow any harder. You can begin to put sail on her."

"But what's the good? Where shall I sail? This is the second day without observations, and we should have sighted Hao Island yesterday morning. Which way does it bear, north, south, east, or what? Tell me that, and I'll make sail in a jiffy."

"I am no navigator, Captain," McCoy said in his mild way.

"I used to think I was one," was the retort, "before I got into these Paumotus."

At midday the cry of "Breakers ahead!" was heard from the lookout. The *Pyrenees* was kept off, and sail after sail was loosed and sheeted home. The *Pyrenees* was sliding through the water and fighting a current that threatened to set her down upon the breakers. Officers and men were working like mad, cook and cabin boy, Captain Davenport himself, and McCoy all lending a hand. It was a close shave. It was a low shoal, a bleak and perilous place over which the seas broke unceasingly, where no man could live, and on which not even sea birds could rest. The *Pyrenees* was swept within a hundred yards of it before the wind carried her clear, and at this moment the panting crew, its work done, burst out in a torrent of curses upon the head of McCoy— of McCoy who had come on board, and proposed the run to Mangareva, and lured them all away from the safety of Pitcairn Island to certain destruction in this baffling and terrible stretch of sea. But McCoy's tranquil soul was undisturbed. He smiled at them with simple and gracious benevolence, and, somehow, the exalted goodness of him seemed to penetrate to their dark and somber souls, shaming them, and from very shame stilling the curses vibrating in their throats.

"Bad waters! Bad waters!" Captain Davenport was murmuring as his ship forged clear; but he broke off abruptly to gaze at the shoal which should have been dead astern, but which was already on the *Pyrenees'* weather-quarter and working up rapidly to windward.

He sat down and buried his face in his hands. And the first mate saw, and McCoy saw, and the crew saw, what he had seen. South of the shoal an easterly current had set them down upon it; north of the shoal an equally swift westerly current had clutched the ship and was sweeping her away.

"I've heard of these Paumotus before," the captain groaned, lifting his blanched face from his hands. "Captain Moyendale told me about them after losing his ship on them. And I laughed at him behind his back. God forgive me, I laughed at him. What shoal is that?" he broke off, to ask McCoy.

"I don't know, Captain."

"Why don't you know?"

"Because I never saw it before, and because I have never heard of it. I do know that it is not charted. These waters have never been thoroughly surveyed."

"Then you don't know where we are?"

"No more than you do," McCoy said gently.

At four in the afternoon cocoanut trees were sighted, apparently growing out of the water. A little later the low land of an atoll was raised above the sea.

"I know where we are now, Captain." McCoy lowered the glasses from his eyes. "That's Resolution Island. We are forty miles beyond Hao Island, and the wind is in our teeth."

"Get ready to beach her then. Where's the entrance?"

"There's only a canoe passage. But now that we know where we are, we can run for Barclay de Tolley. It is only one hundred and twenty miles from here, due nor'-nor'west. With this breeze we can be there by nine o'clock tomorrow morning."

Captain Davenport consulted the chart and debated with himself.

"If we wreck her here," McCoy added, "we'd have to make the run to Barclay de Tolley in the boats just the same."

The captain gave his orders, and once more the *Pyrenees* swung off for another run across the inhospitable sea.

And the middle of the next afternoon saw despair and mutiny on her smoking deck. The current had accelerated, the wind had slackened, and the *Pyrenees* had sagged off to the west. The lookout sighted Barclay de Tolley to the eastward, barely visible from the masthead, and vainly and for hours the *Pyrenees* tried to beat up to it. Ever, like a mirage, the cocoanut trees hovered on the horizon, visible only from the masthead. From the deck they were hidden by the bulge of the world.

Again Captain Davenport consulted McCoy and the chart. Makemo lay seventy-five miles to the southwest. Its lagoon was thirty miles long, and its entrance was excellent. When Captain Davenport gave his orders, the crew refused duty. They announced that they had had enough of hell fire under their feet. There was the land. What if the ship could not make it? They could make it in the boats. Let her burn, then. Their lives amounted to something to them. They had served faithfully the ship, now they were going to serve themselves.

They sprang to the boats, brushing the second and third mates out of the way, and proceeded to swing the boats out and to prepare to lower away. Captain Davenport and the first mate, revolvers in hand, were advancing to the break of the poop, when McCoy, who had climbed on top of the cabin, began to speak.

He spoke to the sailors, and at the first sound of his dove-like, cooing voice they paused to hear. He extended to them his own ineffable serenity and peace. His soft voice and simple thoughts flowed out to them in a magic stream, soothing them against their wills. Long forgotten things came back to them, and some remembered lullaby songs of childhood and the content and rest of the mother's arm at the end of the day. There was no more trouble, no more danger, no more irk, in all the world. Everything was as it should be, and it was only a matter of course that they should turn their backs upon the land and put to sea once more with hell fire hot beneath their feet.

McCoy spoke simply; but it was not what he spoke. It was his personality that spoke more eloquently than any word he could utter. It was an alchemy of soul occultly subtle and profoundly deep—a mysterious emanation of the spirit, seductive, sweetly humble, and terribly imperious. It was illumination in the dark crypts of their souls, a compulsion of purity and gentleness vastly greater than that which resided in the shining, death-spitting revolvers of the officers.

The men wavered reluctantly where they stood, and those who had loosed the turns made them fast again. Then one, and then another, and then all of them, began to sidle awkwardly away.

McCoy's face was beaming with childlike pleasure as he descended from the top of the cabin. There was no trouble. For that matter there had been no trouble averted. There never had been any trouble, for there was no place for such in the blissful world in which he lived.

"You hypnotized 'em," Mr. Konig grinned at him, speaking in a low voice.

"Those boys are good," was the answer. "Their hearts are good. They have had a hard time, and they have worked hard, and they will work hard to the end."

Mr. Konig had no time to reply. His voice was ringing out orders, the sailors were springing to obey, and the *Pyrenees* was paying slowly off from the wind until her bow should point in the direction of Makemo.

The wind was very light, and after sundown almost ceased. It was insufferably warm, and fore and aft men sought vainly to sleep. The deck was too hot to lie upon, and poisonous vapors, oozing through the seams, crept like evil spirits over the ship, stealing into the nostrils and windpipes of the unwary and causing fits of sneezing and coughing. The stars blinked lazily in the dim vault overhead; and the full moon, rising in the east, touched with its light the myriads of wisps and threads and spidery films of smoke that intertwined and writhed and twisted along the deck, over the rails, and up the masts and shrouds.

"Tell me," Captain Davenport said, rubbing his smarting eyes, "what happened with that *Bounty* crowd after they reached Pitcairn? The account I read said they burnt the *Bounty*, and that they were not discovered until many years later. But what happened in the meantime? I've always been curious to know. They were men with their necks in the rope. There were some native men, too. And then there were women. That made it look like trouble right from the jump."

"There was trouble," McCoy answered. "They were bad men. They quarreled about the women right away. One of the mutineers, Williams, lost his wife. All the women were Tahitian women. His wife fell from the cliffs when hunting sea birds. Then he took the wife of one of the native men away from him. All the native men were made very angry by this, and they killed off nearly all the mutineers. Then the mutineers that escaped killed off all the native men. The women helped. And the natives killed each other. Everybody killed everybody. They were terrible men.

"Timiti was killed by two other natives while they were combing his hair in friendship. The white men had sent them to do it. Then the white men killed them. The wife of Tullaloo killed him in a cave because she wanted a white man for husband. They were very wicked. God had hidden His face from them. At the end of two years all the native men were murdered, and all the white men except four. They were Young, John Adams, McCoy, who was my great-grandfather, and Quintal. He was a very bad man, too. Once, just because his wife did not catch enough fish for him, he bit off her ear."

"They were a bad lot!" Mr. Konig exclaimed.

"Yes, they were very bad," McCoy agreed and went on serenely cooing of the blood and lust of his iniquitous ancestry. "My great-grandfather escaped murder in order to die by his own hand. He made a still and manufactured alcohol from the roots of the ti-plant. Quintal was his chum, and they got drunk together all the time. At last McCoy got delirium tremens, tied a rock to his neck, and jumped into the sea.

"Quintal's wife, the one whose ear he bit off, also got killed by falling from the cliffs. Then Quintal went to Young and demanded his wife, and went to Adams and demanded his wife. Adams and Young were afraid of Quintal. They knew he would kill them. So they killed him, the two of them together, with a hatchet. Then Young died. And that was about all the trouble they had."

"I should say so," Captain Davenport snorted. "There was nobody left to kill."

"You see, God had hidden His face," McCoy said.

By morning no more than a faint air was blowing from the eastward, and, unable to make appreciable southing by it, Captain Davenport hauled up full-and-by on the port track. He was afraid of that terrible westerly current which had cheated him out of so many ports of refuge. All day the calm continued, and all night, while the sailors, on a short ration of dried banana, were grumbling. Also, they were growing weak and complaining of stomach pains caused by the straight banana diet. All day the current swept the *Pyrenees* to the westward, while there was no wind to bear her south. In the middle of the first dogwatch, cocoanut trees were sighted due south, their tufted heads rising above the water and marking the low-lying atoll beneath.

"That is Taenga Island," McCoy said. "We need a breeze tonight, or else we'll miss Makemo."

"What's become of the southeast trade?" the captain demanded. "Why don't it blow? What's the matter?"

"It is the evaporation from the big lagoons—there are so many of them," McCoy explained. "The evaporation upsets the whole system of trades. It even causes the wind to back up and blow gales from the southwest. This is the Dangerous Archipelago, Captain."

Captain Davenport faced the old man, opened his mouth, and was about to curse, but paused and refrained. McCoy's presence was a rebuke to the blasphemies that stirred in his brain and trembled in his larynx. McCoy's influence had been growing during the many days they had been together. Captain Davenport was an autocrat of the sea, fearing no man, never bridling his tongue, and now he found himself unable to curse in the presence of this old man with the feminine brown eyes and the voice of a dove. When he realized this, Captain Davenport experienced a distinct shock. This old man was merely the seed of McCoy, of McCoy of the *Bounty,* the mutineer fleeing from the hemp that waited him in England, the McCoy who was a power for evil in the early days of blood and lust and violent death on Pitcairn Island.

Captain Davenport was not religious, yet in that moment he felt a mad impulse to cast himself at the other's feet—and to say he knew not what. It was an emotion that so deeply stirred him, rather than a coherent thought, and he was aware in some vague way of his own unworthiness and smallness in the presence of this other man who possessed the simplicity of a child and the gentleness of a woman.

Of course he could not so humble himself before the eyes of his officers and men. And yet the anger that had prompted the blasphemy still raged in him. He suddenly smote the cabin with his clenched hand and cried:

"Look here, old man, I won't be beaten. These Paumotus have cheated and tricked me and made a fool of me. I refuse to be beaten. I am going to drive this ship, and drive and drive and drive clear through the Paumotus to China but what I find a bed for her. If every man deserts, I'll stay by her. I'll show the Paumotus. They can't fool me.

She's a good girl, and I'll stick by her as long as there's a plank to stand on. You hear me?"

"And I'll stay with you, Captain," McCoy said.

During the night, light, baffling airs blew out of the south, and the frantic captain, with his cargo of fire, watched and measured his westward drift and went off by himself at times to curse softly so that McCoy should not hear.

Daylight showed more palms growing out of the water to the south. "That's the leeward point of Makemo," McCoy said. "Katiu is only a few miles to the west. We may make that."

But the current, sucking between the two islands, swept them to the northwest, and at one in the afternoon they saw the palms of Katiu rise above the sea and sink back into the sea again.

A few minutes later, just as the captain had discovered that a new current from the northeast had gripped the *Pyrenees,* the masthead lookouts raised cocoanut palms in the northwest.

"It is Raraka," said McCoy. "We won't make it without wind. The current is drawing us down to the southwest. But we must watch out. A few miles farther on a current flows north and turns in a circle to the northwest. This will sweep us away from Fakarava, and Fakarava is the place for the *Pyrenees* to find her bed."

"They can sweep all they da— all they well please," Captain Davenport remarked with heat. "We'll find a bed for her somewhere just the same." But the situation on the *Pyrenees* was reaching a culmination. The deck was so hot that it seemed an increase of a few degrees would cause it to burst into flames. In many places even the heavy-soled shoes of the men were no protection, and they were compelled to step lively to avoid scorching their feet. The smoke had increased and grown more acrid. Every man on board was suffering from inflamed eyes, and they coughed and strangled like a crew of tuberculo sis patients. In the afternoon the boats were swung out and equipped. The last several packages of dried bananas were stored in them, as well as the instruments of the officers. Captain Davenport even put the chronometer into the longboat, fearing the blowing up of the deck at any moment.

All night this apprehension weighed heavily on all, and in the first morning light, with hollow eyes and ghastly faces, they stared at one another as if in surprise that the *Pyrenees* still held together and that they still were alive.

Walking rapidly at times, and even occasionally breaking into an undignified hop-skip-and-run, Captain Davenport inspected his ship's deck.

"It is a matter of hours now, if not of minutes," he announced on his return to the poop.

The cry of land came down from the masthead. From the deck the land was invisible, and McCoy went aloft, while the captain took advantage of the opportunity to curse some of the bitterness out of his heart. But the cursing was suddenly stopped by a dark line on the water which he sighted to the northeast. It was not a squall, but a regular breeze—the disrupted trade wind, eight points out of its direction but resuming business once more.

"Hold her up, Captain," McCoy said as soon as he reached the poop. "That's the easterly point of Fakarava, and we'll go in through the passage full-tilt, the wind abeam, and every sail drawing."

At the end of an hour, the cocoanut trees and the low-lying land were visible from the deck. The feeling that the end of the *Pyrenees'* resistance was imminent weighed heavily on everybody. Captain Davenport had the three boats lowered and dropped short astern, a man in each to keep them apart. The *Pyrenees* closely skirted the shore, the surf-whitened atoll a bare two cable lengths away.

And a minute later the land parted, exposing a narrow passage and the lagoon beyond, a great mirror, thirty miles in length and a third as broad.

"Now, Captain."

For the last time the yards of the *Pyrenees* swung around as she obeyed the wheel and headed into the passage. The turns had scarcely been made, and nothing had been coiled down, when the men and mates swept back to the poop in panic terror. Nothing had happened, yet they averred that something was going to happen. They could not tell why. They merely knew that it was about to happen. McCoy started forward to take up his position on the bow in order to con the vessel in; but the captain gripped his arm and whirled him around.

"Do it from here," he said. "That deck's not safe. What's the matter?" he demanded the next instant. "We're standing still."

McCoy smiled.

"You are bucking a seven-knot current, Captain," he said. "That is the way the full ebb runs out of this passage."

At the end of another hour the *Pyrenees* had scarcely gained her length, but the wind freshened and she began to forge ahead.

"Better get into the boats, some of you," Captain Davenport commanded.

His voice was still ringing, and the men were just beginning to move in obedience, when the amidship deck of the *Pyrenees*, in a mass of flame and smoke, was flung upward into the sails and rigging, part of it remaining there and the rest falling into the sea. The wind being abeam, was what had saved the men crowded aft. They made a blind rush to gain the boats, but McCoy's voice, carrying its convincing message of vast calm and endless time, stopped them.

"Take it easy," he was saying. "Everything is all right. Pass that boy down somebody, please."

The man at the wheel had forsaken it in a funk, and Captain Davenport had leaped and caught the spokes in time to prevent the ship from yawing in the current and going ashore.

"Better take charge of the boats," he said to Mr. Konig. "Tow one of them short, right under the quarter.... When I go over, it'll be on the jump."

Mr. Konig hesitated, then went over the rail and lowered himself into the boat.

"Keep her off half a point, Captain."

Captain Davenport gave a start. He had thought he had the ship to himself.

"Ay, ay; half a point it is," he answered.

Amidships the *Pyrenees* was an open flaming furnace, out of which poured an immense volume of smoke which rose high above the masts and completely hid the forward part of the ship. McCoy, in the shelter of the mizzen-shrouds, continued his difficult task of conning the ship through the intricate channel. The fire was working aft along the deck from the seat of explosion, while the soaring tower of canvas on the mainmast went up and vanished in a sheet of flame. Forward, though they could not see them, they knew that the head-sails were still drawing.

"If only she don't burn all her canvas off before she makes inside," the captain groaned.

"She'll make it," McCoy assured him with supreme confidence. "There is plenty of time. She is bound to make it. And once inside, we'll put her before it; that will keep the smoke away from us and hold back the fire from working aft."

A tongue of flame sprang up the mizzen, reached hungrily for the lowest tier of canvas, missed it, and vanished. From aloft a burning shred of rope stuff fell square on the back of Captain Davenport's neck. He acted with the celerity of one stung by a bee as he reached up and brushed the offending fire from his skin.

"How is she heading, Captain?"

"Nor'west by west."

"Keep her west-nor'west."

Captain Davenport put the wheel up and steadied her.

"West by north, Captain."

"West by north she is."

"And now west."

Slowly, point by point, as she entered the lagoon, the *Pyrenees* described the circle that put her before the wind; and point by point, with all the calm certitude of a thousand years of time to spare, McCoy chanted the changing course.

"Another point, Captain."

"A point it is."

Captain Davenport whirled several spokes over, suddenly reversing and coming back one to check her.

"Steady."

"Steady she is—right on it."

Despite the fact that the wind was now astern, the heat was so intense that Captain Davenport was compelled to steal sidelong glances into the binnacle, letting go the wheel now with one hand, now with the other, to rub or shield his blistering cheeks.

McCoy's beard was crinkling and shriveling and the smell of it, strong in the other's nostrils, compelled him to look toward McCoy with sudden solicitude. Captain Davenport was letting go the spokes alternately with his hands in order to rub their blistering backs against his trousers. Every sail on the mizzenmast vanished in a rush of flame, compelling the two men to crouch and shield their faces.

"Now," said McCoy, stealing a glance ahead at the low shore, "four points up, Captain, and let her drive."

Shreds and patches of burning rope and canvas were falling about them and upon them. The tarry smoke from a smouldering piece of rope at the captain's feet set him off into a violent coughing fit, during which he still clung to the spokes.

The *Pyrenees* struck, her bow lifted, and she ground ahead gently to a stop. A shower of burning fragments, dislodged by the shock, fell about them. The ship moved ahead again and struck a second time. She crushed the fragile coral under her keel, drove on, and struck a third time.

"Hard over," said McCoy. "Hard over?" he questioned gently, a minute later.

"She won't answer," was the reply.

"All right. She is swinging around." McCoy peered over the side. "Soft, white sand. Couldn't ask better. A beautiful bed."

As the *Pyrenees* swung around her stern away from the wind, a fearful blast of smoke and flame poured aft. Captain Davenport deserted the wheel in blistering agony. He reached the painter of the boat that lay under the quarter, then looked for McCoy, who was standing aside to let him go down.

"You first," the captain cried, gripping him by the shoulder and almost throwing him over the rail. But the flame and smoke were too terrible, and he followed hard after McCoy, both men wriggling on the rope and sliding down into the boat together. A sailor in the bow, without waiting for orders, slashed the painter through with his sheath knife. The oars, poised in readiness, bit into the water, and the boat shot away.

"A beautiful bed, Captain," McCoy murmured, looking back.

"Ay, a beautiful bed, and all thanks to you," was the answer.

The three boats pulled away for the white beach of pounded coral, beyond which, on the edge of a cocoanut grove, could be seen a half dozen grass houses and a score or more of excited natives, gazing wide-eyed at the conflagration that had come to land.

The boats grounded and they stepped out on the white beach.

"And now," said McCoy, "I must see about getting back to Pitcairn."

The House of Mapuhi

Despite the heavy clumsiness of her lines, the *Aorai* handled easily in the light breeze, and her captain ran her well in before he hove to just outside the suck of the surf. The atoll of Hikueru lay low on the water, a circle of pounded coral sand a hundred yards wide, twenty miles in circumference, and from three to five feet above high-water mark. On the bottom of the huge and glassy lagoon was much pearl shell, and from the deck of the schooner, across the slender ring of the atoll, the divers could be seen at work. But the lagoon had no entrance for even a trading schooner. With a favoring breeze cutters could win in through the tortuous and shallow channel, but the schooners lay off and on outside and sent in their small boats.

The *Aorai* swung out a boat smartly, into which sprang half a dozen brown-skinned sailors clad only in scarlet loincloths. They took the oars, while in the stern sheets, at the steering sweep, stood a young man garbed in the tropic white that marks the European. The golden strain of Polynesia betrayed itself in the sun-gilt of his fair skin and cast up golden sheens and lights through the glimmering blue of his eyes. Raoul he was, Alexandre Raoul, youngest son of Marie Raoul, the wealthy quarter-caste, who owned and managed half a dozen trading schooners similar to the *Aorai*. Across an eddy just outside the entrance, and in and through and over a boiling tide-rip, the boat fought its way to the mirrored calm of the lagoon. Young Raoul leaped out upon the white sand and shook hands with a tall native. The man's chest and shoulders were magnificent, but the stump of a right arm, beyond the flesh of which the age-whitened bone projected several inches, attested the encounter with a shark that had put an end to his diving days and made him a fawner and an intriguer for small favors.

"Have you heard, Alec?" were his first words. "Mapuhi has found a pearl—such a pearl. Never was there one like it ever fished up in Hikueru, nor in all the Paumotus, nor in all the world. Buy it from him. He has it now. And remember that I told you first. He is a fool and you can get it cheap. Have you any tobacco?"

Straight up the beach to a shack under a pandanus tree Raoul headed. He was his mother's supercargo, and his business was to comb all the Paumotus for the wealth of copra, shell, and pearls that they yielded up.

He was a young supercargo, it was his second voyage in such capacity, and he suffered much secret worry from his lack of experience in pricing pearls. But when Mapuhi exposed the pearl to his sight he managed to suppress the startle it gave him, and to maintain a careless, commercial expression on his face.

For the pearl had struck him a blow. It was large as a pigeon egg, a perfect sphere, of a whiteness that reflected opalescent lights from all colors about it. It was alive. Never had he seen anything like it. When Mapuhi dropped it into his hand he was surprised by the weight of it. That showed that it was a good pearl. He examined it closely, through a pocket magnifying glass. It was without flaw or blemish. The purity of it seemed almost to melt into the atmosphere out of his hand. In the shade it was softly luminous, gleaming like a tender moon. So translucently white was it, that when he dropped it into a glass of water he had difficulty in finding it. So straight and swiftly had it sunk to the bottom that he knew its weight was excellent.

"Well, what do you want for it?" he asked, with a fine assumption of nonchalance.

"I want—" Mapuhi began, and behind him, framing his own dark face, the dark faces of two women and a girl nodded concurrence in what he wanted. Their heads were bent forward, they were animated by a suppressed eagerness, their eyes flashed avariciously.

"I want a house," Mapuhi went on. "It must have a roof of galvanized iron and an octagon-drop-clock. It must be six fathoms long with a porch all around. A big room must be in the centre, with a round table in the middle of it and the octagon-drop-clock on the wall. There must be four bedrooms, two on each side of the big room, and in each bedroom must be an iron bed, two chairs, and a washstand. And back of the house must be a kitchen, a good kitchen, with pots and pans and a stove. And you must build the house on my island, which is Fakarava."

"Is that all?" Raoul asked incredulously.

"There must be a sewing machine," spoke up Tefara, Mapuhi's wife.

"Not forgetting the octagon-drop-clock," added Nauri, Mapuhi's mother.

"Yes, that is all," said Mapuhi.

Young Raoul laughed. He laughed long and heartily. But while he laughed he secretly performed problems in mental arithmetic. He had never built a house in his life, and his notions concerning house building were hazy. While he laughed, he calculated the cost of the voyage to Tahiti for materials, of the materials themselves, of the voyage back again to Fakarava, and the cost of landing the materials and of building the house. It would come to four thousand French dollars, allowing a margin for safety—four thousand French dollars were equivalent to twenty thousand francs. It was impossible. How was he to know the value of such a pearl? Twenty thousand francs was a lot of money—and of his mother's money at that.

"Mapuhi," he said, "you are a big fool. Set a money price."

But Mapuhi shook his head, and the three heads behind him shook with his.

"I want the house," he said. "It must be six fathoms long with a porch all around—"

"Yes, yes," Raoul interrupted. "I know all about your house, but it won't do. I'll give you a thousand Chili dollars."

The four heads chorused a silent negative.

"And a hundred Chili dollars in trade."

"I want the house," Mapuhi began.

"What good will the house do you?" Raoul demanded. "The first hurricane that comes along will wash it away. You ought to know. Captain Raffy says it looks like a hurricane right now."

"Not on Fakarava," said Mapuhi. "The land is much higher there. On this island, yes. Any hurricane can sweep Hikueru. I will have the house on Fakarava. It must be six fathoms long with a porch all around—"

And Raoul listened again to the tale of the house. Several hours he spent in the endeavor to hammer the house obsession out of Mapuhi's mind; but Mapuhi's mother and wife, and Ngakura, Mapuhi's daughter, bolstered him in his resolve for the house. Through the open doorway, while he listened for the twentieth time to the detailed description of the house that was wanted, Raoul saw his schooner's second boat draw up on the beach. The sailors rested on the oars, advertising haste to be gone. The first mate of the *Aorai* sprang ashore, exchanged a word with the one-armed native, then hurried toward Raoul. The day grew suddenly dark, as a squall obscured the face of the sun. Across the lagoon Raoul could see approaching the ominous line of the puff of wind.

"Captain Raffy says you've got to get to hell outa here," was the mate's greeting. "If there's any shell, we've got to run the risk of picking it up later on—so he says. The barometer's dropped to twenty-nine-seventy."

The gust of wind struck the pandanus tree overhead and tore through the palms beyond, flinging half a dozen ripe cocoanuts with heavy thuds to the ground.

Then came the rain out of the distance, advancing with the roar of a gale of wind and causing the water of the lagoon to smoke in driven windrows. The sharp rattle of the first drops was on the leaves when Raoul sprang to his feet.

"A thousand Chili dollars, cash down, Mapuhi," he said. "And two hundred Chili dollars in trade."

"I want a house—" the other began.

"Mapuhi!" Raoul yelled, in order to make himself heard. "You are a fool!"

He flung out of the house, and, side by side with the mate, fought his way down the beach toward the boat. They could not see the boat. The tropic rain sheeted about them so that they could see only the beach under their feet and the spiteful little waves from the lagoon that snapped and bit at the sand. A figure appeared through the deluge. It was Huru-Huru, the man with the one arm.

"Did you get the pearl?" he yelled in Raoul's ear.

"Mapuhi is a fool!" was the answering yell, and the next moment they were lost to each other in the descending water.

Half an hour later, Huru-Huru, watching from the seaward side of the atoll, saw the two boats hoisted in and the *Aorai* pointing her nose out to sea. And near her, just come in from the sea on the wings of the squall, he saw another schooner hove to and dropping a boat into the water. He knew her. It was the *Orohena,* owned by Toriki, the half-caste trader, who served as his own supercargo and who doubtlessly was even then in the stern sheets of the boat. Huru-Huru chuckled. He knew that Mapuhi owed Toriki for trade goods advanced the year before.

The squall had passed. The hot sun was blazing down, and the lagoon was once more a mirror. But the air was sticky like mucilage, and the weight of it seemed to burden the lungs and make breathing difficult.

"Have you heard the news, Toriki?" Huru-Huru asked. "Mapuhi has found a pearl. Never was there a pearl like it ever fished up in Hikueru, nor anywhere in the Paumotus, nor anywhere in all the world. Mapuhi is a fool. Besides, he owes you money. Remember that I told you first. Have you any tobacco?"

And to the grass shack of Mapuhi went Toriki. He was a masterful man, withal a fairly stupid one. Carelessly he glanced at the wonderful pearl—glanced for a moment only; and carelessly he dropped it into his pocket.

"You are lucky," he said. "It is a nice pearl. I will give you credit on the books."

"I want a house," Mapuhi began, in consternation. "It must be six fathoms—"

"Six fathoms your grandmother!" was the trader's retort. "You want to pay up your debts, that's what you want. You owed me twelve hundred dollars Chili. Very well; you owe them no longer. The amount is squared. Besides, I will give you credit for two hundred Chili. If, when I get to Tahiti, the pearl sells well, I will give you credit for another hundred—that will make three hundred. But mind, only if the pearl sells well. I may even lose money on it."

Mapuhi folded his arms in sorrow and sat with bowed head. He had been robbed of his pearl. In place of the house, he had paid a debt. There was nothing to show for the pearl.

"You are a fool," said Tefara.

"You are a fool," said Nauri, his mother. "Why did you let the pearl into his hand?"

"What was I to do?" Mapuhi protested. "I owed him the money. He knew I had the pearl. You heard him yourself ask to see it. I had not told him. He knew. Somebody else told him. And I owed him the money."

"Mapuhi is a fool," mimicked Ngakura.

She was twelve years old and did not know any better. Mapuhi relieved his feelings by sending her reeling from a box on the ear; while Tefara and Nauri burst into tears and continued to upbraid him after the manner of women.

Huru-Huru, watching on the beach, saw a third schooner that he knew heave to outside the entrance and drop a boat. It was the *Hira,* well named, for she was owned by Levy, the German Jew, the greatest pearl buyer of them all, and, as was well known, Hira was the Tahitian god of fishermen and thieves.

"Have you heard the news?" Huru-Huru asked, as Levy, a fat man with massive asymmetrical features, stepped out upon the beach. "Mapuhi has found a pearl. There was never a pearl like it in Hikueru, in all the Paumotus, in all the world. Mapuhi is a fool. He has sold it to Toriki for fourteen hundred Chili—I listened outside and heard. Toriki is likewise a fool. You can buy it from him cheap. Remember that I told you first. Have you any tobacco?"

"Where is Toriki?"

"In the house of Captain Lynch, drinking absinthe. He has been there an hour."

And while Levy and Toriki drank absinthe and chaffered over the pearl, Huru-Huru listened and heard the stupendous price of twenty-five thousand francs agreed upon.

It was at this time that both the *Orohena* and the *Hira,* running in close to the shore, began firing guns and signalling frantically. The three men stepped outside in time to see the two schooners go hastily about and head off shore, dropping mainsails and flying jibs on the run in the teeth of the squall that heeled them far over on the whitened water. Then the rain blotted them out.

"They'll be back after it's over," said Toriki. "We'd better be getting out of here."

"I reckon the glass has fallen some more," said Captain Lynch.

He was a white-bearded sea-captain, too old for service, who had learned that the only way to live on comfortable terms with his asthma was on Hikueru. He went inside to look at the barometer.

"Great God!" they heard him exclaim, and rushed in to join him at staring at a dial, which marked twenty-nine-twenty.

Again they came out, this time anxiously to consult sea and sky. The squall had cleared away, but the sky remained overcast. The two schooners, under all sail and joined by a third, could be seen making back. A veer in the wind induced them to slack off sheets, and five minutes afterward a sudden veer from the opposite quarter caught all three schooners aback, and those on shore could see the boom-tackles being slacked away or cast off on the jump. The sound of the surf was loud, hollow, and menacing, and a heavy swell was setting in. A terrible sheet of lightning burst before their eyes, illuminating the dark day, and the thunder rolled wildly about them.

Toriki and Levy broke into a run for their boats, the latter ambling along like a panic-stricken hippopotamus. As their two boats swept out the entrance, they passed the boat of the *Aorai* coming in. In the stern sheets, encouraging the rowers, was Raoul. Unable to shake the vision of the pearl from his mind, he was returning to accept Mapuhi's price of a house.

He landed on the beach in the midst of a driving thunder squall that was so dense that he collided with Huru-Huru before he saw him.

"Too late," yelled Huru-Huru. "Mapuhi sold it to Toriki for fourteen hundred Chili, and Toriki sold it to Levy for twenty-five thousand francs. And Levy will sell it in France for a hundred thousand francs. Have you any tobacco?"

Raoul felt relieved. His troubles about the pearl were over. He need not worry any more, even if he had not got the pearl. But he did not believe Huru-Huru. Mapuhi might well have sold it for fourteen hundred Chili, but that Levy, who knew pearls, should have paid twenty-five thousand francs was too wide a stretch. Raoul decided to interview Captain Lynch on the subject, but when he arrived at that ancient mariner's house, he found him looking wide-eyed at the barometer.

"What do you read it?" Captain Lynch asked anxiously, rubbing his spectacles and staring again at the instrument.

"Twenty-nine-ten," said Raoul. "I have never seen it so low before."

"I should say not!" snorted the captain. "Fifty years boy and man on all the seas, and I've never seen it go down to that. Listen!"

They stood for a moment, while the surf rumbled and shook the house. Then they went outside. The squall had passed. They could see the *Aorai* lying becalmed a mile away and pitching and tossing madly in the tremendous seas that rolled in stately procession down out of the northeast and flung themselves furiously upon the coral shore. One of the sailors from the boat pointed at the mouth of the passage and shook his head. Raoul looked and saw a white anarchy of foam and surge.

"I guess I'll stay with you tonight, Captain," he said; then turned to the sailor and told him to haul the boat out and to find shelter for himself and fellows.

"Twenty-nine flat," Captain Lynch reported, coming out from another look at the barometer, a chair in his hand.

He sat down and stared at the spectacle of the sea. The sun came out, increasing the sultriness of the day, while the dead calm still held. The seas continued to increase in magnitude.

"What makes that sea is what gets me," Raoul muttered petulantly.

"There is no wind, yet look at it, look at that fellow there!"

Miles in length, carrying tens of thousands of tons in weight, its impact shook the frail atoll like an earthquake. Captain Lynch was startled.

"Gracious!" he bellowed, half rising from his chair, then sinking back. "But there is no wind," Raoul persisted. "I could understand it if there was wind along with it."

"You'll get the wind soon enough without worryin' for it," was the grim reply.

The two men sat on in silence. The sweat stood out on their skin in myriads of tiny drops that ran together, forming blotches of moisture, which, in turn, coalesced into rivulets that dripped to the ground. They panted for breath, the old man's efforts being especially painful. A sea swept up the beach, licking around the trunks of the cocoanuts and subsiding almost at their feet.

"Way past high water mark," Captain Lynch remarked; "and I've been here eleven years." He looked at his watch. "It is three o'clock."

A man and woman, at their heels a motley following of brats and curs, trailed disconsolately by. They came to a halt beyond the house, and, after much irresolution, sat down in the sand. A few minutes later another family trailed in from the opposite direction, the men and women carrying a heterogeneous assortment of possessions. And soon several hundred persons of all ages and sexes were congregated about the captain's dwelling. He called to one new arrival, a woman with a nursing babe in her arms, and in answer received the information that her house had just been swept into the lagoon.

This was the highest spot of land in miles, and already, in many places on either hand, the great seas were making a clean breach of the slender ring of the atoll and surging into the lagoon. Twenty miles around stretched the ring of the atoll, and in no place was it more than fifty fathoms wide. It was the height of the diving season, and from all the islands around, even as far as Tahiti, the natives had gathered.

"There are twelve hundred men, women, and children here," said Captain Lynch. "I wonder how many will be here tomorrow morning."

"But why don't it blow?—that's what I want to know," Raoul demanded.

"Don't worry, young man, don't worry; you'll get your troubles fast enough."

Even as Captain Lynch spoke, a great watery mass smote the atoll. The sea water churned about them three inches deep under the chairs. A low wail of fear went up from the many women. The children, with clasped hands, stared at the immense rollers and cried piteously. Chickens and cats, wading perturbedly in the water, as by common consent, with flight and scramble took refuge on the roof of the captain's house. A Paumotan, with a litter of new-born puppies in a basket, climbed into a cocoanut tree and twenty feet above the ground made the basket fast. The mother floundered about in the water beneath, whining and yelping.

And still the sun shone brightly and the dead calm continued. They sat and watched the seas and the insane pitching of the *Aorai*. Captain Lynch gazed at the huge mountains of water sweeping in until he could gaze no more. He covered his face with his hands to shut out the sight; then went into the house.

"Twenty-eight-sixty," he said quietly when he returned.

In his arm was a coil of small rope. He cut it into two-fathom lengths, giving one to Raoul and, retaining one for himself, distributed the remainder among the women with the advice to pick out a tree and climb.

A light air began to blow out of the northeast, and the fan of it on his cheek seemed to cheer Raoul up. He could see the *Aorai* trimming her sheets and heading off shore, and he regretted that he was not on her. She would get away at any rate, but as for the atoll—A sea breached across, almost sweeping him off his feet, and he selected a tree. Then he remembered the barometer and ran back to the house. He encountered Captain Lynch on the same errand and together they went in.

"Twenty-eight-twenty," said the old mariner. "It's going to be fair hell around here—what was that?"

The air seemed filled with the rush of something. The house quivered and vibrated, and they heard the thrumming of a mighty note of sound. The windows rattled. Two panes crashed; a draught of wind tore in, striking them and making them stagger. The door opposite banged shut, shattering the latch. The white door knob crumbled in fragments to the floor. The room's walls bulged like a gas balloon in the process of sudden inflation. Then came a new sound like the rattle of musketry, as the spray from a sea struck the wall of the house. Captain Lynch looked at his watch. It was four o'clock. He put on a coat of pilot cloth, unhooked the barometer, and stowed it away in a capacious pocket. Again a sea struck the house, with a heavy thud, and the light building tilted, twisted, quarter around on its foundation, and sank down, its floor at an angle of ten degrees.

Raoul went out first. The wind caught him and whirled him away. He noted that it had hauled around to the east. With a great effort he threw himself on the sand, crouching and holding his own. Captain Lynch, driven like a wisp of straw, sprawled over him. Two of the *Aorai*'s sailors, leaving a cocoanut tree to which they had been clinging, came to their aid, leaning against the wind at impossible angles and fighting and clawing every inch of the way.

The old man's joints were stiff and he could not climb, so the sailors, by means of short ends of rope tied together, hoisted him up the trunk, a few feet at a time, till they could make him fast, at the top of the tree, fifty feet from the ground. Raoul passed his length of rope around the base of an adjacent tree and stood looking on. The wind was frightful. He had never dreamed it could blow so hard. A sea breached across the atoll, wetting him to the knees ere it subsided into the lagoon. The sun had disappeared, and a lead-colored twilight settled down. A few drops of rain, driving horizontally, struck him. The impact was like that of leaden pellets. A splash of salt spray struck his face. It was like the slap of a man's hand. His cheeks stung, and involuntary tears of pain were in his smarting eyes. Several hundred natives had taken to the trees, and he could have laughed at the bunches of human fruit clustering in the tops. Then, being Tahitian-born, he doubled his body at the waist, clasped the trunk of his tree with his hands, pressed the soles of his feet against the near surface of the trunk, and began to walk up the tree. At the top he found two women, two children, and a man. One little girl clasped a housecat in her arms.

From his eyrie he waved his hand to Captain Lynch, and that

doughty patriarch waved back. Raoul was appalled at the sky. It had approached much nearer—in fact, it seemed just over his head; and it had turned from lead to black. Many people were still on the ground grouped about the bases of the trees and holding on. Several such clusters were praying, and in one the Mormon missionary was exhorting. A weird sound, rhythmical, faint as the faintest chirp of a far cricket, enduring but for a moment, but in the moment suggesting to him vaguely the thought of heaven and celestial music, came to his ear. He glanced about him and saw, at the base of another tree, a large cluster of people holding on by ropes and by one another. He could see their faces working and their lips moving in unison. No sound came to him, but he knew that they were singing hymns.

Still the wind continued to blow harder. By no conscious process could he measure it, for it had long since passed beyond all his experience of wind; but he knew somehow, nevertheless, that it was blowing harder. Not far away a tree was uprooted, flinging its load of human beings to the ground. A sea washed across the strip of sand, and they were gone. Things were happening quickly. He saw a brown shoulder and a black head silhouetted against the churning white of the lagoon. The next instant that, too, had vanished. Other trees were going, falling and criss-crossing like matches. He was amazed at the power of the wind. His own tree was swaying perilously, one woman was wailing and clutching the little girl, who in turn still hung on to the cat. The man, holding the other child, touched Raoul's arm and pointed. He looked and saw the Mormon church careering drunkenly a hundred feet away. It had been torn from its foundations, and wind and sea were heaving and shoving it toward the lagoon. A frightful wall of water caught it, tilted it, and flung it against half a dozen cocoanut trees. The bunches of human fruit fell like ripe cocoanuts. The subsiding wave showed them on the ground, some lying motionless, others squirming and writhing. They reminded him strangely of ants. He was not shocked. He had risen above horror. Quite as a matter of course he noted the succeeding wave sweep the sand clean of the human wreckage. A third wave, more colossal than any he had yet seen, hurled the church into the lagoon, where it floated off into the obscurity to leeward, half-submerged, reminding him for all the world of a Noah's ark.

He looked for Captain Lynch's house, and was surprised to find it gone. Things certainly were happening quickly. He noticed that many of the people in the trees that still held had descended to the ground. The wind had yet again increased. His own tree showed that. It no longer swayed or bent over and back. Instead, it remained practically stationary, curved in a rigid angle from the wind and merely vibrating. But the vibration was sickening. It was like that of a tuning-fork or the tongue of a jew's-harp. It was the rapidity of the vibration that made it so bad. Even though its roots held, it could not stand the strain for long Something would have to break.

Ah, there was one that had gone. He had not seen it go, but there it stood, the remnant, broken off half-way up the trunk. One did not know what happened unless he saw it. The mere crashing of trees and wails of human despair occupied no place in that mighty volume of sound. He chanced to be looking in Captain Lynch's direction when it happened. He saw the trunk of the tree, half-way up, splinter and part without noise. The head of the tree, with three sailors of the *Aorai* and the old captain, sailed off over the lagoon. It did not fall to the ground, but drove through the air like a piece of chaff. For a hundred yards he followed its flight, when it struck the water. He strained his eyes, and was sure that he saw Captain Lynch wave farewell.

Raoul did not wait for anything more. He touched the native and made signs to descend to the ground. The man was willing, but his women were paralyzed from terror, and he elected to remain with them. Raoul passed his rope around the tree and slid down. A rush of salt water went over his head. He held his breath and clung desperately to the rope. The water subsided, and in the shelter of the trunk he breathed once more. He fastened the rope more securely, and then was put under by another sea. One of the women slid down and joined him, the native remaining by the other woman, the two children, and the cat.

The supercargo had noticed how the groups clinging at the bases of the other trees continually diminished. Now he saw the process work out alongside him. It required all his strength to hold on, and the woman who had joined him was growing weaker. Each time he emerged from a sea he was surprised to find himself still there, and next, surprised to find the woman still there. At last he emerged to find himself alone. He looked up. The top of the tree had gone as well. At half its original height, a splintered end vibrated. He was safe. The roots still held, while the tree had been shorn of its windage. He began to climb up. He was so weak that he went slowly, and sea after sea caught him before he was above them. Then he tied himself to the trunk and stiffened his soul to face the night and he knew not what.

He felt very lonely in the darkness. At times it seemed to him that it was the end of the world and that he was the last one left alive. Still the wind increased. Hour after hour it increased. By what he calculated was eleven o'clock, the wind had become unbelievable. It was a horrible, monstrous thing, a screaming fury, a wall that smote and passed on but that continued to smite and pass on—a wall without end. It seemed to him that he had become light and ethereal; that it was he that was in motion; that he was being driven with inconceivable velocity through unending solidness. The wind was no longer air in motion. It had become substantial as water or quicksilver. He had a feeling that he could reach into it and tear it out in chunks as one might do with the meat in the carcass of a steer; that he could seize hold of the wind and hang on to it as a man might hang on to the face of a cliff.

The wind strangled him. He could not face it and breathe, for it rushed in through his mouth and nostrils, distending his lungs like bladders. At such moments it seemed to him that his body was being packed and swollen with solid earth. Only by pressing his lips to the trunk of the tree could he breathe. Also, the ceaseless impact of the wind exhausted him. Body and brain became wearied. He no longer observed, no longer thought, and was but semiconscious. One idea constituted his consciousness: *So this was a hurricane.* That one idea persisted irregularly. It was like a feeble flame that flickered occasionally. From a state of stupor he would return to it—*So this was a hurricane.* Then he would go off into another stupor.

The height of the hurricane endured from eleven at night till three in the morning, and it was at eleven that the tree in which clung Mapuhi and his women snapped off. Mapuhi rose to the surface of the lagoon, still clutching his daughter Ngakura. Only a South Sea islander could have lived in such a driving smother. The pandanus tree, to which he attached himself, turned over and over in the froth and churn; and it was only by holding on at times and waiting, and at other times shifting his grips rapidly, that he was able to get his head and Ngakura's to the surface at intervals sufficiently near together to keep the breath in them. But the air was mostly water, what with flying spray and sheeted rain that poured along at right angles to the perpendicular.

It was ten miles across the lagoon to the farther ring of sand. Here, tossing tree trunks, timbers, wrecks of cutters, and wreckage of houses, killed nine out of ten of the miserable beings who survived the passage of the lagoon. Half drowned, exhausted, they were hurled into this mad mortar of the elements and battered into formless flesh. But Mapuhi was fortunate. His chance was the one in ten; it fell to him by the freakage of fate. He emerged upon the sand, bleeding from a score of wounds.

Ngakura's left arm was broken; the fingers of her right hand were crushed; and cheek and forehead were laid open to the bone. He clutched a tree that yet stood, and clung on, holding the girl and sobbing for air, while the waters of the lagoon washed by knee-high and at times waist-high.

At three in the morning the backbone of the hurricane broke. By five no more than a stiff breeze was blowing. And by six it was dead calm and the sun was shining. The sea had gone down. On the yet restless edge of the lagoon, Mapuhi saw the broken bodies of those that had failed in the landing. Undoubtedly Tetara and Nauri were among them. He went along the beach examining them, and came upon his wife, lying half in and half out of the water. He sat down and wept, making harsh animal noises after the manner of primitive grief. Then she stirred uneasily, and groaned. He looked more closely. Not only was she alive, but she was uninjured. She was merely sleeping. Hers also had been the one chance in ten.

Of the twelve hundred alive the night before but three hundred remained. The Mormon missionary and a gendarme made the census. The lagoon was cluttered with corpses. Not a house nor a hut was standing. In the whole atoll not two stones remained one upon another. One in fifty of the cocoanut palms still stood, and they were wrecks, while on not one of them remained a single nut.

There was no fresh water. The shallow wells that caught the surface seepage of the rain were filled with salt. Out of the lagoon a few soaked bags of flour were recovered. The survivors cut the hearts out of the fallen cocoanut trees and ate them. Here and there they crawled into tiny hutches, made by hollowing out the sand and covering over with fragments of metal roofing. The missionary made a crude still, but he could not distill water for three hundred persons. By the end of the second day, Raoul, taking a bath in the lagoon, discovered that his thirst was somewhat relieved. He cried out the news, and there upon three hundred men, women, and children could have been seen, standing up to their necks in the lagoon and trying to drink water in through their skins. Their dead floated about them, or were stepped upon where they still lay upon the bottom. On the third day the people buried their dead and sat down to wait for the rescue steamers.

In the meantime, Nauri, torn from her family by the hurricane, had been swept away on an adventure of her own. Clinging to a rough plank that wounded and bruised her and that filled her body with splinters, she was thrown clear over the atoll and carried away to sea. Here, under the amazing buffets of mountains of water, she lost her plank. She was an old woman nearly sixty; but she was Paumotan-born, and she had never been out of sight of the sea in her life. Swimming in the darkness, strangling, suffocating, fighting for air, she was struck a heavy blow on the shoulder by a cocoanut. On the instant her plan was formed, and she seized the nut. In the next hour she captured seven more. Tied together, they formed a life-buoy that preserved her life while at the same time it threatened to pound her to a jelly. She was a fat woman, and she bruised easily; but she had had experience of hurricanes, and while she prayed to her shark god for protection from sharks, she waited for the wind to break. But at three o'clock she was in such a stupor that she did not know. Nor did she know at six o'clock when the dead calm settled down. She was shocked into consciousness when she was thrown upon the sand. She dug in with raw and bleeding hands and feet and clawed against the backwash until she was beyond the reach of the waves.

She knew where she was. This land could be no other than the tiny islet of Takokota. It had no lagoon. No one lived upon it.

Hikueru was fifteen miles away. She could not see Hikueru, but she knew that it lay to the south. The days went by, and she lived on the cocoanuts that had kept her afloat. They supplied her with drinking water and with food. But she did not drink all she wanted, nor eat all she wanted. Rescue was problematical. She saw the smoke of the rescue steamers on the horizon, but what steamer could be expected to come to lonely, uninhabited Takokota?

From the first she was tormented by corpses. The sea persisted in flinging them upon her bit of sand, and she persisted, until her strength failed, in thrusting them back into the sea where the sharks tore at them and devoured them. When her strength failed, the bodies festooned her beach with ghastly horror, and she withdrew from them as far as she could, which was not far.

By the tenth day her last cocoanut was gone, and she was shrivelling from thirst. She dragged herself along the sand, looking for cocoanuts. It was strange that so many bodies floated up, and no nuts. Surely, there were more cocoanuts afloat than dead men! She gave up at last, and lay exhausted. The end had come. Nothing remained but to wait for death.

Coming out of a stupor, she became slowly aware that she was gazing at a patch of sandy-red hair on the head of a corpse. The sea flung the body toward her, then drew it back. It turned over, and she saw that it had no face. Yet there was something familiar about that patch of sandy-red hair. An hour passed. She did not exert herself to make the identification. She was waiting to die, and it mattered little to her what man that thing of horror once might have been. But at the end of the hour she sat up slowly and stared at the corpse. An unusually large wave had thrown it beyond the reach of the lesser waves. Yes, she was right; that patch of red hair could belong to but one man in the Paumotus. It was Levy, the German Jew, the man who had bought the pearl and carried it away on the *Hira*. Well, one thing was evident: The *Hira* had been lost. The pearl buyer's god of fishermen and thieves had gone back on him.

She crawled down to the dead man. His shirt had been torn away, and she could see the leather money belt about his waist. She held her breath and tugged at the buckles. They gave easier than she had expected, and she crawled hurriedly away across the sand, dragging the belt after her. Pocket after pocket she unbuckled in the belt and found empty. Where could he have put it? In the last pocket of all she found it, the first and only pearl he had bought on the voyage. She crawled a few feet farther, to escape the pestilence of the belt, and examined the pearl. It was the one Mapuhi had found and been robbed of by Toriki. She weighed it in her hand and rolled it back and forth caressingly. But in it she saw no intrinsic beauty. What she did see was the house Mapuhi and Tefara and she had builded so carefully in their minds. Each time she looked at the pearl she saw the house in all its details, including the octagon-drop-clock on the wall. That was something to live for.

She tore a strip from her ahu and tied the pearl securely about her neck. Then she went on along the beach, panting and groaning, but resolutely seeking for cocoanuts. Quickly she found one, and, as she glanced around, a second. She broke one, drinking its water, which was mildewy, and eating the last particle of the meat. A little later she found a shattered dugout. Its outrigger was gone, but she was hopeful, and, before the day was out, she found the outrigger. Every find was an augury. The pearl was a talisman. Late in the afternoon she saw a wooden box floating low in the water. When she dragged it out on the beach its contents rattled, and inside she found ten tins of salmon. She opened one by hammering it on the canoe. When a leak was started, she drained the tin. After that she spent several hours in extracting the salmon, hammering and squeezing it out a morsel at a time.

Eight days longer she waited for rescue. In the meantime she fastened the outrigger back on the canoe, using for lashings all the cocoanut fibre she could find, and also what remained of her ahu. The canoe was badly cracked, and she could not make it water-tight; but a calabash made from a cocoanut she stored on board for a bailer. She was hard put for a paddle. With a piece of tin she sawed off all her hair close to the scalp. Out of the hair she braided a cord; and by means of the cord she lashed a three-foot piece of broom handle to a board from the salmon case.

She gnawed wedges with her teeth and with them wedged the lashing.

On the eighteenth day, at midnight, she launched the canoe through the surf and started back for Hikueru. She was an old woman. Hardship had stripped her fat from her till scarcely more than bones and skin and a few stringy muscles remained. The canoe was large and should have been paddled by three strong men.

But she did it alone, with a make-shift paddle. Also, the canoe leaked badly, and one-third of her time was devoted to bailing. By clear daylight she looked vainly for Hikueru. Astern, Takokota had sunk beneath the sea rim. The sun blazed down on her nakedness, compelling her body to surrender its moisture. Two tins of salmon were left, and in the course of the day she battered holes in them and drained the liquid. She had no time to waste in extracting the meat. A current was setting to the westward, she made westing whether she made southing or not.

In the eary afternoon, standing upright in the canoe, she sighted Hikueru. Its wealth of cocoanut palms was gone. Only here and there, at wide intervals, could she see the ragged remnants of trees. The sight cheered her. She was nearer than she had thought. The current was setting her to the westward. She bore up against it and paddled on. The wedges in the paddle lashing worked loose, and she lost much time, at frequent intervals, in driving them tight. Then there was the bailing. One hour in three she had to cease paddling in order to bail. And all the time she drifted to the westward.

By sunset Hikueru bore southeast from her, three miles away. There was a full moon, and by eight o'clock the land was due east and two miles away. She struggled on for another hour, but the land was as far away as ever. She was in the main grip of the current; the canoe was too large; the paddle was too inadequate; and too much of her time and strength was wasted in bailing. Besides, she was very weak and growing weaker. Despite her efforts, the canoe was drifting off to the westward.

She breathed a prayer to her shark god, slipped over the side, and began to swim. She was actually refreshed by the water, and quickly left the canoe astern. At the end of an hour the land was perceptibly nearer. Then came her fright. Right before her eyes, not twenty feet away, a large fin cut the water. She swam steadily toward it, and slowly it glided away, curving off toward the right and circling around her. She kept her eyes on the fin and swam on. When the fin disappeared, she lay face downward in the water and watched. When the fin reappeared she resumed her swimming. The monster was lazy—she could see that. Without doubt he had been well fed since the hurricane. Had he been very hungry, she knew he would not have hesitated from making a dash for her. He was fifteen feet long, and one bite, she knew, could cut her in half.

But she did not have any time to waste on him. Whether she swam or not, the current drew away from the land just the same. A half hour went by, and the shark began to grow bolder. Seeing no harm in her he drew closer, in narrowing circles, cocking his eyes at her impudently as he slid past. Sooner or later, she knew well enough, he would get up sufficient courage to dash at her. She resolved to play first. It was a desperate act she meditated. She was an old woman, alone in the sea and weak from starvation and hardship; and yet she, in the face of this sea tiger, must anticipate his dash by herself dashing at him. She swam on, waiting her chance. At last he passed languidly by, barely eight feet away. She rushed at him suddenly, feigning that she was attacking him. He gave a wild flirt of his tail as he fled away, and his sandpaper hide, striking her, took off her skin from elbow to shoulder. He swam rapidly, in a widening circle, and at last disappeared.

In the hole in the sand, covered over by fragments of metal roofing, Mapuhi and Tefara lay disputing.

"If you had done as I said," charged Tefara, for the thousandth time, "and hidden the pearl and told no one, you would have it now."

"But Huru-Huru was with me when I opened the shell—have I not told you so times and times and times without end?"

"And now we shall have no house. Raoul told me today that if you had not sold the pearl to Toriki—"

"I did not sell it. Toriki robbed me."

"—that if you had not sold the pearl, he would give you five thousand French dollars, which is ten thousand Chili."

"He has been talking to his mother," Mapuhi explained. "She has an eye for a pearl."

"And now the pearl is lost," Tefara complained.

"It paid my debt with Toriki. That is twelve hundred I have made, anyway."

"Toriki is dead," she cried. "They have heard no word of his schooner. She was lost along with the *Aorai* and the *Hira.* Will Toriki pay you the three hundred credit he promised? No, because Toriki is dead. And had you found no pearl, would you today owe Toriki the twelve hundred? No, because Toriki is dead, and you cannot pay dead men."

"But Levy did not pay Toriki," Mapuhi said. "He gave him a piece of paper that was good for the money in Papeete; and now Levy is dead and cannot pay; and Toriki is dead and the paper lost with him, and the pearl is lost with Levy. You are right, Tefara. I have lost the pearl, and got nothing for it. Now let us sleep."

He held up his hand suddenly and listened. From without came a noise, as of one who breathed heavily and with pain. A hand fumbled against the mat that served for a door.

"Who is there?" Mapuhi cried.

"Nauri," came the answer. "Can you tell me where is my son, Mapuhi?"

Tefara screamed and gripped her husband's arm.

"A ghost! she chattered. "A ghost!"

Mapuhi's face was a ghastly yellow. He clung weakly to his wife.

"Good woman," he said in faltering tones, striving to disguise his voice, "I know your son well. He is living on the east side of the lagoon."

From without came the sound of a sigh. Mapuhi began to feel elated. He had fooled the ghost.

"But where do you come from, old woman?" he asked.

"From the sea," was the dejected answer.

"I knew it! I knew it!" screamed Tefara, rocking to and fro.

"Since when has Tefara bedded in a strange house?" came Nauri's voice through the matting.

Mapuhi looked fear and reproach at his wife. It was her voice that had betrayed them.

"And since when has Mapuhi, my son, denied his old mother?" the voice went on.

"No, no, I have not—Mapuhi has not denied you," he cried. "I am not Mapuhi. He is on the east end of the lagoon, I tell you."

Ngakura sat up in bed and began to cry. The matting started to shake.

"What are you doing?" Mapuhi demanded.

"I am coming in," said the voice of Nauri.

One end of the matting lifted. Tefara tried to dive under the blankets, but Mapuhi held on to her. He had to hold on to something. Together, struggling with each other, with shivering bodies and chattering teeth, they gazed with protruding eyes at the lifting mat. They saw Nauri, dripping with sea water, without her ahu, creep in. They rolled over backward from her and fought for Ngakura's blanket with which to cover their heads.

"You might give your old mother a drink of water," the ghost said plaintively.

"Give her a drink of water," Tefara commanded in a shaking voice.

"Give her a drink of water," Mapuhi passed on the command to Ngakura.

And together they kicked out Ngakura from under the blanket. A minute later, peeping, Mapuhi saw the ghost drinking. When it reached out a shaking hand and laid it on his, he felt the weight of it and was convinced that it was no ghost. Then he emerged, dragging Tefara after him, and in a few minutes all were listening to Nauri's tale. And when she told of Levy, and dropped the pearl into Tefara's hand, even she was reconciled to the reality of her mother-in-law.

"In the morning," said Tefara, "you will sell the pearl to Raoul for five thousand French."

"The house?" objected Nauri.

"He will build the house," Tefara answered. "He says it will cost four thousand French. Also will he give one thousand French in credit, which is two thousand Chili."

"And it will be six fathoms long?" Nauri queried.

"Ay," answered Mapuhi, "six fathoms."

"And in the middle room will be the octagon-drop-clock?"

"Ay, and the round table as well."

"Then give me something to eat, for I am hungry," said Nauri, complacently. "And after that we will sleep, for I am weary. And tomorrow we will have more talk about the house before we sell the pearl. It will be better if we take the thousand French in cash. Money is ever better than credit in buying goods from the traders."

THE HEATHEN

I met him first in a hurricane. And though we had been through the hurricane on the same schooner, it was not until the schooner had gone to pieces under us that I first laid eyes on him. Without doubt I had seen him with the rest of the Kanaka crew on board, but I had not consciously been aware of his existence, for the *Petite Jeanne* was rather overcrowded. In addition to her eight or ten Kanaka sea men, her white captain, mate, and supercargo, and her six cabin passengers, she sailed from Rangiroa with something like eighty-five deck passengers—Paumotuans and Tahitians, men, women, and children, each with a trade-box, to say nothing of sleeping-mats, blankets, and clothes-bundles.

The pearling season in the Paumotus was over, and all hands were returning to Tahiti. The six of us cabin passengers were pearl-buyers. Two were Americans, one was Ah Choon, the whitest Chinese I have ever known, one was a German, one was a Polish Jew, and I completed the half-dozen. It had been a prosperous season. Not one of us had cause for complaint, nor one of the eighty-five deck passengers either. All had done well, and all were looking forward to a rest-off and a good time in Papeete. Of course the *Petite Jeanne* was overloaded. She was only seventy tons, and she had no right to carry a tithe of the mob she had on board. Beneath her hatches she was crammed and jammed with pearl shell and copra. Even the trade-room was packed full of shell. It was a miracle that the sailors could work her. There was no moving about the decks. They simply climbed back and forth along the rails. In the night-time they walked upon the sleepers, who carpeted the deck, two deep, I'll swear. Oh, and there were pigs and chickens on deck, and sacks of yams, while every conceivable place was festooned with strings of drinking cocoanuts and bunches of bananas. On both sides, between the fore and main shrouds, guys had been stretched, just low enough for the fore-boom to swing clear; and from each of these guys at least fifty bunches of bananas were suspended.

It promised to be a messy passage, even if we did make it in the two or three days that would have been required if the southeast trades had been blowing fresh. But they weren't blowing fresh. After the first five hours, the trade died away in a dozen gasping fans. The calm continued all that night and the next day—one of those glaring, glossy calms when the very thought of opening one's eyes to look at it is sufficient to cause a headache. The second day a man died, an Easter Islander, one of the best divers that season in the lagoon. Smallpox, that is what it was, though how smallpox could come on board when there had been no known cases ashore when we left Rangiroa is beyond me. There it was, though, smallpox, a man dead, and three others down on their backs. There was nothing to be done. We could not segregate the sick, nor could we care for them. We were packed like sardines. There was nothing to do but die—that is, there was nothing to do after the night that followed the first death. On that night, the mate, the supercargo, the Polish Jew, and four native divers sneaked away in the large whaleboat. They were never heard of again. In the morning the captain promptly scuttled the remaining boats, and there we were.

That day there were two deaths; the following day three; then it jumped to eight. It was curious to see how we took it. The natives, for instance, fell into a condition of dumb, stolid fear. The captain—Oudouse, his name was, a Frenchman—became very nervous and voluble. The German, the two Americans, and myself bought up all the

Scotch whisky and proceeded to drink. The theory was beautiful—namely, if we kept ourselves soaked in alcohol, every smallpox germ that came into contact with us would immediately be scorched to a cinder. And the theory worked, though I must confess that neither Captain Oudouse nor Ah Choon was attacked by the disease either. The Frenchman did not drink at all, while Ah Choon restricted himself to one drink daily.

We had a week of it, and then the whisky gave out. It was just as well, or I shouldn't be alive now. It took a sober man to pull through what followed, as you will agree when I mention the little fact that only two men did pull through. The other man was the Heathen—at least that was what I heard Captain Oudouse call him at the moment I first became aware of the Heathen's existence.

But to come back. It was at the end of the week that I happened to glance at the barometer that hung in the cabin companion-way. Its normal register in the Paumotus was 29.90, and it was quite customary to see it vacillate between 29.85 and 30.00, or even 30.05; but to see it, as I saw it, down to 29.62, was sufficient to chill the blood of any pearl-buyer in Oceania.

I called Captain Oudouse's attention to it, only to be informed that he had watched it going down for several hours. There was little to do, but that little he did very well, considering the circumstances. He took off the light sails, shortened right down to storm canvas, spread life-lines, and waited for the wind. His mistake lay in what he did after the wind came. He hove to on the port tack, which was the right thing to do south of the Equator, *if*—and there was the rub—*if* one were *not* in the direct path of the hurricane. We were in the direct path. I could see that by the steady increase of the wind and the equally steady fall of the barometer. I wanted to turn and run with the wind on the port quarter until the barometer ceased falling, and then to heave to. We argued till he was reduced to hysteria, but budge he would not. The worst of it was that I could not get the rest of the pearl-buyers to back me up. Who was I, anyway, to know more about the sea and its ways than a properly qualified captain?

Of course, the sea rose with the wind, frightfully, and I shall never forget the first three seas the *Petite Jeanne* shipped. She had fallen off, as vessels do when hove to, and the first sea made a clean breach. The lifelines were only for the strong and well, and little good were they even for these when the women and children, the bananas and cocoanuts, the pigs and trade-boxes, the sick and the dying, were swept along in a solid, screeching, groaning mass.

The second sea filled the *Petite Jeanne*'s decks flush with the rails, and, as her stern sank down and her bow tossed skyward, all the miserable dunnage of life and luggage poured aft. It was a human torrent. They came head-first, feet-first, sidewise, rolling over and over, twisting, squirming, writhing, and crumpling up. Now and again one or another caught a grip on a stanchion or a rope, but the weight of the bodies behind tore such grips loose. I saw what was coming, sprang on top of the cabin, and from there into the mainsail itself. Ah Choon and one of the Americans tried to follow me, but I was one jump ahead of them. The American was swept away and over the stern like a piece of chaff. Ah Choon caught a spoke of the wheel and swung in behind it. But a strapping Raiotonga vahine—she must have weighed two hundred and fifty—brought up against him and got an arm around his neck. He clutched the Kanaka steersman with his other hand. And just at that moment the schooner flung down to starboard. The rush of bodies and the sea that was coming along the port runway between the cabin and the rail, turned abruptly and poured to starboard. Away they went, vahine, Ah Choon, and steersman; and I swear I saw Ah Choon grin at me with philosophic resignation as he cleared the rail and went under.

The third sea—the biggest of the three—did not do so much damage. By the time it arrived, nearly everybody was in the rigging. On deck perhaps a dozen gasping, half-drowned, and half-stunned wretches were rolling about or attempting to crawl into safety. They went by the board, as did the wreckage of the two remaining boats. The other pearl-buyers and myself, between seas, managed to get about fifteen women and children into the cabin and battened down. Little good it did the poor creatures in the end.

Wind? Out of all my experiences I could not have believed it possible for the wind to blow as it did. There is no describing it. How can one describe a nightmare? It was the same way with that wind. It tore the clothes off our bodies. I say *tore them off,* and I mean it. I am not asking you to believe it. I am merely telling something that I saw and felt. There are times when I do not believe it myself. I went through it, and that is enough. One could not face that wind and live. It was a monstrous thing, and the most monstrous thing about it was that it increased and continued to increase. Imagine countless millions and billions of tons of sand. Imagine this sand tearing along at ninety, a hundred, a hundred and twenty, or any other number of miles per hour. Imagine, further, this sand to be invisible, impalpable, yet to retain all the weight and density of sand. Do all this, and you may get a vague inkling of what that wind was like. Perhaps sand is not the right comparison. Consider it mud, invisible, impalpable, but heavy as mud. Nay, it goes beyond that. Consider every molecule of air to be a mud-bank in itself. Then try to imagine the multitudinous impact of mud-banks—no, it is beyond me. Language may be adequate to express the ordinary conditions of life, but it cannot possibly express any of the conditions of so enormous a blast of wind. It would have been better had I stuck by my original intention of not attempting a description.

I will say this much: The sea, which had risen at first, was beaten down by that wind. More—it seemed as if the whole ocean had been sucked up in the maw of the hurricane and hurled on through that portion of space which previously had been occupied by the air. Of course, our canvas had gone long before. But Captain Oudouse had on the *Petite Jeanne* something I had never before seen on a South Sea schooner—a sea-anchor. It was a conical canvas bag, the mouth of which was kept open by a huge hoop of iron. The sea-anchor was bridled something like a kite, so that it bit into the water as a kite bites into the air—but with a difference. The sea-anchor remained just under the surface of the ocean, in a perpendicular position. A long line, in turn, connected it with the schooner. As a result, the *Petite Jeanne* rode bow-on to the wind and to what little sea there was.

The situation really would have been favorable, had we not been in the path of the storm. True, the wind itself tore our canvas out of the gaskets, jerked out our topmasts, and made a raffle of our running gear; but still we would have come through nicely had we not been square in front of the advancing storm-center. That was what fixed us. I was in a state of stunned, numbed, paralyzed collapse from enduring the impact of the wind, and I think I was just about ready to give up and die when the center smote us. The blow we received was an absolute lull. There was not a breath of air. The effect on one was sickening. Remember that for hours we had been at terrific muscular tension, withstanding the awful pressure of that wind. And then, suddenly, the pressure was removed. I know that I felt as though I were about to expand, to fly apart in all directions. It seemed as if every atom composing my body was repelling every other atom, and was on the verge of rushing off irresistibly into space. But that lasted only for a moment. Destruction was upon us.

In the absence of the wind and its pressure, the sea rose. It jumped, it leaped, it soared straight toward the clouds. Remember, from every point of the compass that inconceivable wind was blowing in toward the center of calm. The result was that the seas sprang up from every point of the compass. There was no wind to check them. They popped up like corks released from the bottom of a pail of water. There was no system to them, no stability. They were hollow, maniacal seas. They were eighty feet high at the least. They were not seas at all. They resembled no sea a man had ever seen. They were splashes, monstrous splashes, that is all, splashes that were eighty feet high. Eighty! They were more than eighty. They went over our mastheads. They were spouts, explosions. They were drunken. They fell anywhere, anyhow. They jostled one another, they collided. They rushed together and collapsed upon one another, or fell apart like a thousand waterfalls all at once. It was no ocean any man ever dreamed of, that hurricane-center. It was confusion thrice confounded. It was anarchy. It was a hell-pit of sea water gone mad.

The *Petite Jeanne?* I don't know. The Heathen told me afterward that he did not know. She was literally torn apart, ripped wide open, beaten into a pulp, smashed into kindling wood, annihilated. When I came to, I was in the water, swimming automatically, though I was about two-thirds drowned. How I got there I had no recollection. I remembered seeing the *Petite Jeanne* fly to pieces at what must have been the instant that my own consciousness was buffeted out of me. But there I was, with nothing to do but make the best of it, and in that best there was little promise. The wind was blowing again, the sea was much smaller and more regular, and I knew that I had passed through the center. Fortunately, there were no sharks about. The hurricane had dissipated the ravenous horde that had surrounded the death ship.

It was about midday when the *Petite Jeanne* went to pieces, and it must have been two hours afterward when I picked up with one of her hatch-covers. Thick rain was driving at the time, and it was the merest chance that flung me and the hatch-cover together. A short length of line was trailing from the rope handle, and I knew that I was good for a day at least, if the sharks did not return. Three hours later, possibly a little longer, sticking close to the cover and, with closed eyes, concentrating my whole soul upon the task of breathing in enough air to keep me going and, at the same time, to avoid breathing in enough water to drown me, it seemed to me that I heard voices. The rain had ceased, and wind and sea were easing marvelously. Not twenty feet away from me, on another hatch-cover, were Captain Oudouse and the Heathen. They were fighting over the possession of the cover—at least the Frenchman was.

"Païen noir!" I heard him scream, and at the same time I saw him kick the Kanaka.

Now, Captain Oudouse had lost all his clothes except his shoes, and they were heavy brogans. It was a cruel blow, for it caught the Heathen on the mouth and the point of the chin, half-stunning him. I looked for him to retaliate, but he contented himself with swimming about forlornly, a safe ten feet away. Whenever a fling of the sea threw him closer, the Frenchman, hanging on with his hands, kicked out at him with both feet. Also, at the moment of delivering each kick, he called the Kanaka a black heathen.

"For two centimes I'd come over there and drown you, you white beast!" I yelled.

The only reason I did not go was that I felt too tired. The very thought of the effort to swim over was nauseating. So I called to the Kanaka to come to me, and proceeded to share the hatch-cover with him. Otoo, he told me his name was (pronounced *O'm-to'm-o'm*); also he told me that he was a native of Bora Bora, the most westerly of the Society Group. As I learned afterward, he had got the hatch-cover first, and, after some time, encountering Captain Oudouse, had offered to share it with him, and had been kicked off for his pains.

And that was how Otoo and I first came together. He was no fighter. He was all sweetness and gentleness, a love-creature though he stood nearly six feet tall and was muscled like a gladiator. He was no fighter, but he was also no coward. He had the heart of a lion, and in the years that followed I have seen him run risks that I would never dream of taking. What I mean is that, while he was no fighter, and while he always avoided precipitating a row, he never ran away from trouble when it started. And it was " 'Ware shoal!" when once Otoo went into action. I shall never forget what he did to Bill King. It occurred in German Samoa. Bill King was hailed the champion heavyweight of the American navy. He was a big brute of a man, a veritable gorilla, one of those hard hitting, rough-housing chaps, and clever with his fists as well. He picked the quarrel, and he kicked Otoo twice and struck him once before Otoo felt it to be necessary to fight. I don't think it lasted four minutes, at the end of which time Bill King was the unhappy possessor of four broken ribs, a broken fore-arm, and a dislocated shoulder-blade. Otoo knew nothing of scientific boxing. He was merely a man-handler, and Bill King was something like three months in recovering from the bit of man-handling he received that afternoon on Apia beach.

But I am running ahead of my yarn. We shared the hatch-cover between us. We took turn and turn about, one lying flat on the cover and resting, while the other, submerged to the neck, merely held on with his hands. For three days and nights, spell and spell, on the cover and in the water, we drifted over the ocean. Toward the last I was delirious most of the time, and there were times, too, when I heard Otoo babbling and raving in his native tongue. Our continuous immersion prevented us from dying of thirst, though the sea water and the sunshine gave us the prettiest imaginable combination of salt pickle and sunburn. In the end, Otoo saved *my* life; for I came to, lying on the beach twenty feet from the water, sheltered from the sun by a couple of cocoanut leaves. No one but Otoo could have dragged me there and stuck up the leaves for shade. He was lying beside me. I went off again, and the next time I came around it was cool and starry night and Otoo was pressing a drinking cocoanut to my lips.

We were the sole survivors of the *Petite Jeanne*. Captain Oudouse must have succumbed to exhaustion, for several days later his hatch-cover drifted ashore without him. Otoo and I lived with the natives of the atoll for a week, when we were rescued by a French cruiser and taken to Tahiti. In the meantime, however, we had performed the ceremony of exchanging names. In the South Seas such a ceremony binds two men closer together than blood-brothership. The initiative had been mine, and Otoo was rapturously delighted when I suggested it.

"It is well," he said, in Tahitian. "For we have been mates together for three days on the lips of Death."

"But Death stuttered," I smiled.

"It was a brave deed you did, master," he replied, "and Death was not vile enough to speak."

"Why do you 'master' me?" I demanded, with a show of hurt feelings. "We have exchanged names. To you I am Otoo. To me you are Charley. And between you and me, forever and forever, you shall be Charley and I shall be Otoo. It is the way of the custom. And when we die, if it does happen that we live again, somewhere beyond the stars and the sky, still shall you be Charley to me and I Otoo to you."

"Yes, master," he answered, his eyes luminous and soft with joy.

"There you go!" I cried indignantly.

"What does it matter what my lips utter?" he argued. "They are only my lips. But I shall think *Otoo* always. Whenever I think of myself I shall think of you. Whenever men call me by name I shall think of you. And beyond the sky and beyond the stars always and forever you shall be Otoo to me. Is it well, master?"

I hid my smile and answered that it was well.

We parted at Papeete. I remained ashore to recuperate, and he went on in a cutter to his own island, Bora Bora. Six weeks later he was back. I was surprised, for he had told me of his wife and said that he was returning to her and would give over sailing on far voyages.

"Where do you go, master?" he asked, after our first greetings.

I shrugged my shoulders. It was a hard question. "To all the world," was my answer. "All the world, all the sea, and all the islands that are in the sea."

"I will go with you," he said simply. "My wife is dead."

I never had a brother, but from what I have seen of other men's brothers I doubt if any man ever had one who was to him what Otoo was to me. He was brother, and father and mother as well. And this I know—I lived a straighter and a better man because of Otoo. I had to live straight in Otoo's eyes. Because of him I dared not tarnish myself. He made me his ideal, compounding me, I fear, chiefly out of his own love and worship; and there were times when I stood close to the steep pitch of hell and would have taken the plunge had not the thought of Otoo restrained me. His pride in me entered into me until it became one of the major rules in my personal code to do nothing that would diminish that pride of his. Naturally, I did not learn right away what his feelings were toward me. He never criticised, never censured, and slowly the exalted place I held in his eyes dawned upon me, and slowly I grew to comprehend the hurt I could inflict upon him by being anything less than my best.

For seventeen years we were together. For seventeen years he was at my shoulder, watching while I slept, nursing me through fever and wounds, aye, and receiving wounds in fighting for me. He signed on the same ships with me, and together we ranged the Pacific from Hawaii to Sydney Head and from Torres Strait to the Galapagos. We blackbirded from the New Hebrides and the Line Islands over to the westward, clear through the Louisiades, New Britain, New Ireland, and New Hanover.

We were wrecked three times—in the Gilberts, in the Santa Cruz group, and in the Fijis. And we traded and salved wherever a dollar promised in the way of pearl and pearl shell, copra, beche de mer, hawkbill turtle shell, and stranded wrecks.

It began in Papeete, immediately after his announcement that he was going with me over all the sea and the islands in the midst thereof. There was a club in those days in Papeete, where the pearlers, traders, captains, and South Sea adventurers foregathered. The play ran high and the drink ran high, and I am very much afraid that I kept later hours than were becoming or proper. No matter what the hour was when I left the club, there was Otoo waiting to see me safely home. At first I smiled. Next I chided him. Then I told him flatly I stood in need of no wet-nursing. After that I did not see him when I came out of the club. Quite by accident, a week or so later, I discovered that he still saw me home, lurking across the street among the shadows of the mango trees. What could I do? I know what I did do. Insensibly I began to keep better hours. On wet and stormy nights, in the thick of the folly and the fun, the thought would come to me of Otoo keeping his dreary vigil under the dripping mangoes. Truly, he made me a better man.

Yet he was not strait-laced. And he knew nothing of common Christian morality. All the people on Bora Bora were Christians. But he was a heathen, the only unbeliever on the island, a gross materialist who believed that when he died he was dead. He believed merely in fair play and square-dealing. Petty meanness, in his code, was almost as serious as wanton homicide, and I am sure that he respected a murderer more than a man given to small practices. Concerning me, personally, he objected to my doing anything that was hurtful to me. Gambling was all right. He was an ardent gambler himself. But late hours, he explained, were bad for one's health. He had seen men who did not take care of themselves die of fever. He was no teetotaler, and welcomed a stiff nip any time when it was wet work in the boats. On the other hand, he believed in liquor in moderation. He had seen many men killed or disgraced by squareface or Scotch.

Otoo had my welfare always at heart. He thought ahead for me, weighed my plans and took a greater interest in them than I did myself. At first, when I was unaware of this interest of his in my affairs, he had to divine my intentions, as, for instance, at Papeete, when I contemplated going partners with a knavish fellow countryman on a guano venture. I did not know he was a knave. Nor did any white man in Papeete. Neither did Otoo know; but he saw how thick we were getting and found out for me, and that without my asking. Native sailors from the ends of the seas knock about on the beach in Tahiti, and Otoo, suspicious merely, went among them till he had gathered sufficient data to justify his suspicions. Oh, it was a nice history, that of Randolph Waters! I couldn't believe it when Otoo first narrated it, but when I sheeted it home to Waters he gave in without a murmur and got away on the first steamer to Auckland.

At first, I am free to confess, I resented Otoo's poking his nose into my business. But I knew that he was wholly unselfish, and soon I had to acknowledge his wisdom and discretion. He had his eyes open always to my main chance, and he was both keen-sighted and far-sighted. In time he became my counselor, until he knew more of my business than I did myself. He really had my interest at heart more than I did. Mine was the magnificent carelessness of youth, for I preferred romance to dollars, and adventure to a comfortable billet with all night in. So it was well that I had some one to look out for me. I know that if it had not been for Otoo, I should not be here to-day.

Of numerous instances, let me give one. I had had some experience in blackbirding before I went pearling in the Paumotus. Otoo and I were on the beach in Samoa—we really were on the beach and hard aground—when my chance came to go as a recruiter on a blackbird brig. Otoo signed on before the mast, and for the next half-dozen years, in as many ships, we knocked about the wildest portions of Melanesia. Otoo saw to it that he always pulled stroke-oar in my boat. Our custom, in recruiting labor, was to land the recruiter on the beach. The covering boat always lay on its oars several hundred feet off shore, while the recruiter's boat, also lying on its oars, kept afloat on the edge of the beach. When I landed with my trade goods, leaving my steering sweep apeak, Otoo left his stroke position and came into the stern sheets, where a Winchester lay ready to hand under a flap of canvas. The boat's crew was also armed, the Sniders concealed under canvas flaps that ran the length of the gunwales. While I was busy arguing and persuading the woolly-headed cannibals to come and labor on the Queensland plantations Otoo kept watch. And often and often his low voice warned me of suspicious actions and impending treachery. Sometimes it was the quick shot from his rifle, knocking a nigger over, that was the first warning I received. And in my rush to the boat his hand was always there to jerk me flying aboard.

Once, I remember, on Santa Anna, the boat grounded just as the trouble began. The covering boat was dashing to our assistance, but the several score of savages would have wiped us out before it arrived.

Otoo took a flying leap ashore, dug both hands into the trade goods, and scattered tobacco, beads, tomahawks, knives, and calicoes in all directions. This was too much for the woolly heads. While they scrambled for the treasures, the boat was shoved clear and we were aboard and forty feet away. And I got thirty recruits off that very beach in the next four hours.

The particular instance I have in mind was on Malaita, the most savage island in the easterly Solomons. The natives had been remarkably friendly; and how were we to know that the whole village had been taking up a collection for over two years with which to buy a white man's head? The beggars are all head-hunters, and they especially esteem that of a white man. The fellow who captured the head would receive the whole collection. As I say, they appeared very friendly, and this day I was fully a hundred yards down the beach from the boat. Otoo had cautioned me, and, as usual when I did not heed him, I came to grief. The first thing I knew a cloud of spears sailed out of the mangrove swamp at me. At least a dozen were sticking into me. I started to run, but tripped over one that was fast in my calf and went down. The woolly heads made a run for me, each with a long-handled, fantail tomahawk with which to hack off my head. They were so eager for the prize that they got in one another's way. In the confusion I avoided several hacks by throwing myself right and left on the sand. Then Otoo arrived—Otoo the man-handler. In some way he had got hold of a heavy war-club, and at close quarters it was a far more efficient weapon than a rifle. He was right in the thick of them, so that they could not spear him, while their tomahawks seemed worse than useless. He was fighting for me, and he was in a true Berserker rage. The way he handled that club was amazing. Their skulls squashed like overripe oranges. It was not until he had driven them back, picked me up in his arms, and started to run, that he received his first wounds. He arrived in the boat with four spear-thrusts, got his Winchester, and with it got a man for every shot. Then we pulled aboard the schooner and doctored up.

Seventeen years we were together. He made me. I should to-day be a supercargo, a recruiter, or a memory, if it had not been for him.

"You spend your money, and you go out and get more," he said, one day. "It is easy to get money, now. But when you get old, your money will be spent and you will not be able to go out and get more. I know, master. I have studied the way of white men. On the beaches are many old men who were young once and who could get money just like you. Now they are old, and they have nothing, and they wait about for the young men like you to come ashore and buy drinks for them.

"The black boy is a slave on the plantations. He gets twenty dollars a year. He works hard. The overseer does not work hard. He rides a horse and watches the black boy work. He gets twelve hundred dollars a year. I am a sailor on the schooner. I get fifteen dollars a month. That is because I am a good sailor. I work hard. The captain has a double awning and drinks beer out of long bottles. I have never seen him haul a rope or pull an oar. He gets one hundred and fifty dollars a month. I am a sailor. He is a navigator. Master, I think it would be very good for you to know navigation."

Otoo spurred me on to it. He sailed with me as second mate on my first schooner, and he was far prouder of my command than was I myself. Later on it was:

"The captain is well paid, master, but the ship is in his keeping and he is never free from the burden. It is the owner who is better paid, the owner who sits ashore with many servants and turns his money over."

"True, but a schooner costs five thousand dollars—an old schooner at that," I objected. "I should be an old man before I saved five thousand dollars."

"There be short ways for white men to make money," he went on, pointing ashore at the cocoanut-fringed beach.

We were in the Solomons at the time, picking up a cargo of ivory-nuts along the east coast of Guadalcanar.

"Between this river mouth and the next it is two miles," he said. "The flat land runs far back. It is worth nothing now. Next year—who knows!—or the year after—men will pay much money for that land. The anchorage is good. Big steamers can lie close up. You can buy the land four miles deep from the old chief for ten thousand sticks of tobacco, ten bottles of squareface, and a Snider, which will cost you maybe one hundred dollars. Then you place the deed with the commissioner, and the next year, or the year after, you sell and become the owner of a ship."

I followed his lead, and his words came true, though in three years instead of two. Next came the grass-lands deal on Guadalcanar—twenty thousand acres on a governmental nine hundred and ninety-nine years' lease at a nominal sum. I owned the lease for precisely ninety days, when I sold it to the Moonlight Soap crowd for half a fortune. Always it was Otoo who looked ahead and saw the opportunity. He was responsible for the salving of the *Doncaster*—bought in at auction for five hundred dollars and clearing fifteen thousand after every expense was paid. He led me into the Savaii plantation and the cocoa venture on Upolu.

We did not go seafaring so much as in the old days now. I was too well off. I married and my standard of living rose; but Otoo remained the same old-time Otoo, moving about the house or trailing through the office, his wooden pipe in his mouth, a shilling undershirt on his back, and a four-shilling lava-lava about his loins. I could not get him to spend money. There was no way of repaying him except with love, and God knows he got that in full measure from all of us. The children worshiped him, and if he had been spoilable my wife would surely have been his undoing.

The children! He really was the one who showed them the way of their feet in the world practical. He began by teaching them to walk. He sat up with them when they were sick. One by one, when they were scarcely toddlers, he took them down to the lagoon and made them into amphibians. He taught them more than I ever knew of the habits of fish and the ways of catching them. In the bush it was the same thing. At seven, Tom knew more woodcraft than I ever dreamed existed. At six, Mary went over the Sliding Rock without a quiver—and I have seen strong men balk at that feat. And when Frank had just turned six he could bring up shillings from the bottom in three fathoms.

"My people in Bora Bora do not like heathen; they are all Christians; and I do not like Bora Bora Christians," he said one day, when I, with the idea of getting him to spend some of the money that was rightfully his, had been trying to persuade him to make a visit to his own island in one of our schooners—a special voyage that I had hoped to make a record-breaker in the matter of prodigal expense.

I say one of *our* schooners, though legally, at the time, they belonged to me. I struggled long with him to enter into partnership.

"We have been partners from the day the *Petite Jeanne* went down," he said at last. "But if your heart so wishes, then shall we become partners by the law. I have no work to do, yet are my expenses large. I drink and eat and smoke in plenty—it costs much, I know. I do not pay for the playing of billiards, for I play on your table; but still the money goes. Fishing on the reef is only a rich man's pleasure. It is shocking, the cost of hooks and cotton line. Yes, it is necessary that we be partners by the law. I need the money. I shall get it from the head clerk in the office."

So the papers were made out and recorded. A year later I was compelled to complain.

"Charley," said I, "you are a wicked old fraud, a miserly skinflint, a miserable land-crab. Behold, your share for the year in all our partnership has been thousands of dollars. The head clerk has given me this paper. It says that during the year you have drawn just eighty-seven dollars and twenty cents."

"Is there any owing me?" he asked anxiously.

"I tell you thousands and thousands," I answered.

His face brightened as with an immense relief.

"It is well," he said. "See that the head-clerk keeps good account of it. When I want it, I shall want it, and there must not be a cent missing. If there is," he added fiercely, after a pause, "it must come out of the clerk's wages."

And all the time, as I afterward learned, his will, drawn up by Carruthers and making me sole beneficiary, lay in the American consul's safe.

But the end came as the end must come to all human associations. It occurred in the Solomons, where our wildest work had been done in the wild young days, and where we were once more—principally on a holiday, incidentally to look after our holdings on Florida Island and to look over the pearling possibilities of the Mboli Pass. We were lying at Savo, having run in to trade for curios. Now Savo is alive with sharks. The custom of the woolly heads of burying their dead in the sea did not tend to discourage the sharks from making the adjacent waters a hang-out. It was my luck to be coming aboard in a tiny, overloaded, native canoe, when the thing capsized. There were four woolly heads and myself in it, or rather, hanging to it. The schooner was a hundred yards away. I was just hailing for a boat when one of the woolly heads began to scream. Holding on to the end of the canoe, both he and that portion of the canoe were dragged under several times. Then he loosed his clutch and disappeared. A shark had got him.

The three remaining niggers tried to climb out of the water upon the bottom of the canoe. I yelled and cursed and struck at the nearest with my fist, but it was no use. They were in a blind funk. The canoe could barely have supported one of them. Under the three it up-ended and rolled sidewise, throwing them back into the water.

I abandoned the canoe and started to swim toward the schooner, expecting to be picked up by the boat before I got there. One of the niggers elected to come with me, and we swam along silently, side by side, now and again putting our faces into the water and peering about for sharks. The screams of the men who stayed by the canoe informed us that they were taken. I was peering into the water when I saw a big shark pass directly beneath me. He was fully sixteen feet in length. I saw the whole thing. He got the woolly head by the middle and away he went, the poor devil, head, shoulders, and arms out of water all the time, screeching in a heart-rending way. He was carried along in this fashion for several hundred feet, when he was dragged beneath the surface.

I swam doggedly on, hoping that that was the last unattached shark. But there was another. Whether it was one that had attacked the natives earlier, or whether it was one that had made a good meal elsewhere, I do not know. At any rate, he was not in such haste as the others. I could not swim so rapidly now, for a large part of my effort was devoted to keeping track of him. I was watching him when he made his first attack. By good luck I got both hands on his nose, and, though his momentum nearly shoved me under, I managed to keep him off. He veered clear and began circling about again. A second time I escaped him by the same maneuver. The third rush was a miss on both sides. He sheered at the moment my hands should have landed on his nose, but his sandpaper hide—I had on a sleeveless undershirt—scraped the skin off one arm from elbow to shoulder.

By this time I was played out and gave up hope. The schooner was still two hundred feet away. My face was in the water and I was watching him maneuver for another attempt, when I saw a brown body pass between us. It was Otoo.

"Swim for the schooner, master," he said, and he spoke gayly, as though the affair was a mere lark. "I know sharks. The shark is my brother."

I obeyed, swimming slowly on, while Otoo swam about me, keeping always between me and the shark, foiling his rushes and encouraging me.

"The davit-tackle carried away, and they are rigging the falls," he explained a minute or so later, and then went under to head off another attack.

By the time the schooner was thirty feet away I was about done for. I could scarcely move. They were heaving lines at us from on board, but these continually fell short. The shark, finding that it was receiving no hurt, had become bolder. Several times it nearly got me, but each time Otoo was there just the moment before it was too late. Of course Otoo could have saved himself any time. But he stuck by me.

"Good by, Charley, I'm finished," I just managed to gasp.

I knew that the end had come and that the next moment I should throw up my hands and go down.

But Otoo laughed in my face, saying:

"I will show you a new trick. I will make that shark damn sick."

He dropped in behind me, where the shark was preparing to come at me.

"A little more to the left," he next called out. "There is a line there on the water. To the left, master, to the left."

I changed my course and struck out blindly. I was by that time barely conscious. As my hand closed on the line I heard an exclamation from on board. I turned and looked. There was no sign of Otoo. The next instant he broke surface. Both hands were off at the wrist, the stumps spouting blood.

"Otoo," he called softly, and I could see in his gaze the love that thrilled in his voice. Then, and then only, at the very last of all our years, he called me by that name.

"Good by, Otoo," he called.

Then he was dragged under, and I was hauled aboard, where I fainted in the captain's arms.

And so passed Otoo, who saved me and made me a man, and who saved me in the end. We met in the maw of a hurricane and parted in the maw of a shark, with seventeen intervening years of comradeship the like of which I dare to assert have never befallen two men, the one brown and the other white. If Jehovah be from his high place watching every sparrow fall, not least in His Kingdom shall be Otoo, the one heathen of Bora Bora. And if there be no place for him in that Kingdom, then will I have none of it.

MAUKI

He weighed one hundred and ten pounds. His hair was kinky and negroid, and he was black. He was peculiarly black. He was neither blue-black nor purple-black, but plum-black. His name was Mauki, and he was the son of a chief. He had three *tambos*. *Tambo* is Melanesian for *tahoo*, and is first cousin to that Polynesian word. Mauki's three *tambos* were as follows: first, he must never shake hands with a woman, nor have a woman's hand touch him or any of his personal belongings; secondly, he must never eat clams nor any food from a fire in which clams had been cooked; thirdly, he must never touch a crocodile, nor travel in a canoe that carried any part of a crocodile even if as large as a tooth.

Of a different black were his teeth, which were deep black, or, perhaps better, *lamp*-black. They had been made so in a single night, by his mother, who had compressed about them a powdered mineral which was dug from the landslide back of Port Adams. Port Adams is a salt-water village on Malaita, and Malaita is the most savage island in the Solomons—so savage that no traders nor planters have yet gained a foothold on it; while, from the time of the earliest bêche-de-mer fishers and sandalwood traders down to the latest labor recruiters equipped with automatic rifles and gasolene engines, scores of white adventurers have been passed out by tomahawks and soft-nosed Snider bullets. So Malaita remains to-day, in the twentieth century, the stamping ground of the labor recruiters, who farm its coasts for laborers who engage and contract themselves to toil on the plantations of the neighboring and more civilized islands for a wage of thirty dollars a year. The natives of those neighboring and more civilized islands have themselves become too civilized to work on plantations.

Mauki's ears were pierced, not in one place, nor two places, but in a couple of dozen places. In one of the smaller holes he carried a clay pipe. The larger holes were too large for such use. The bowl of the pipe would have fallen through. In fact, in the largest hole in each ear he habitually wore round wooden plugs that were an even four inches in diameter. Roughly speaking, the circumference of said holes was twelve and one-half inches. Mauki was catholic in his tastes. In the various smaller holes he carried such things as empty rifle cartridges, horseshoe nails, copper screws, pieces of string, braids of sennit, strips of green leaf, and, in the cool of the day, scarlet hibiscus flowers. From which it will be seen that pockets were not necessary to his well-being. Besides, pockets were impossible, for his only wearing apparel consisted of a piece of calico several inches wide. A pocket knife he wore in his hair, the blade snapped down on a kinky lock. His most prized possession was the handle of a china cup, which he suspended from a ring of turtle-shell, which, in turn, was passed through the partition-cartilage of his nose.

But in spite of embellishments, Mauki had a nice face. It was really a pretty face, viewed by any standard, and for a Melanesian it was a remarkably good-looking face. Its one fault was its lack of strength. It was softly effeminate, almost girlish. The features were small, regular, and delicate. The chin was weak, and the mouth was weak. There was no strength nor character in the jaws, forehead, and nose. In the eyes only could be caught any hint of the unknown quantities that were so large a part of his make-up and that other persons could not understand. These unknown quantities were pluck, pertinacity, fearlessness, imagination, and cunning; and when they found expression in some consistent and striking action, those about him were astounded.

Mauki's father was chief over the village at Port Adams, and thus, by birth a salt-water man, Mauki was half amphibian. He knew the way of the fishes and oysters, and the reef was an open book to him. Canoes, also, he knew. He learned to swim when he was a year old. At seven years he could hold his breath a full minute and swim straight down to bottom through thirty feet of water. And at seven years he was stolen by the bushmen, who cannot even swim and who are afraid of salt water. Thereafter Mauki saw the sea only from a distance, through rifts in the jungle and from open spaces on the high mountain sides. He became the slave of old Fanfoa, head chief over a score of scattered bush-villages on the range-lips of Malaita, the smoke of which, on calm mornings, is about the only evidence the seafaring white men have of the teeming interior population. For the whites do not penetrate Malaita. They tried it once, in the days when the search was on for gold, but they always left their heads behind to grin from the smoky rafters of the bushmen's huts.

When Mauki was a young man of seventeen, Fanfoa got out of tobacco. He got dreadfully out of tobacco. It was hard times in all his villages. He had been guilty of a mistake. Suo was a harbor so small that a large schooner could not swing at anchor in it. It was surrounded by mangroves that overhung the deep water. It was a trap, and into the trap sailed two white men in a small ketch. They were after recruits, and they possessed much tobacco and trade-goods, to say nothing of three rifles and plenty of ammunition. Now there were no salt-water men living at Suo, and it was there that the bushmen could come down to the sea. The ketch did a splendid traffic. It signed on twenty recruits the first day. Even old Fanfoa signed on. And that same day the score of new recruits chopped off the two white men's heads, killed the boat's crew, and burned the ketch. Thereafter, and for three months, there was tobacco and trade-goods in plenty and to spare in all the bush-villages. Then came the man-of-war that threw shells for miles into the hills, frightening the people out of their villages and into the deeper bush. Next the man-of-war sent landing parties ashore. The villages were all burned, along with the tobacco and trade-stuff. The cocoanuts and bananas were chopped down, the taro gardens uprooted, and the pigs and chickens killed.

It taught Fanfoa a lesson, but in the meantime he was out of tobacco. Also, his young men were too frightened to sign on with the recruiting vessels. That was why Fanfoa ordered his slave, Mauki, to be carried down and signed on for half a case of tobacco advance, along with knives, axes, calico, and beads, which he would pay for with his toil on the plantations. Mauki was sorely frightened when they brought him on board the schooner. He was a lamb led to the slaughter. White men were ferocious creatures. They had to be, or else they would not make a practice of venturing along the Malaita coast and into all harbors, two on a schooner, when each schooner carried from fifteen to twenty blacks as boat's crew, and often as high as sixty or seventy black recruits. In addition to this, there was always the danger of the shore population, the sudden attack and the cutting off of the schooner and all hands. Truly, white men must be terrible. Besides, they were possessed of such devil-devils—rifles that shot very rapidly many times, things of iron and brass that made the schooners go when there was no wind, and boxes that talked and laughed just as men talked and laughed. Ay, and he had heard of one white man whose particular devil-devil was so powerful that he could take out all his teeth and put them back at will.

Down into the cabin they took Mauki. On deck, the one white man kept guard with two revolvers in his belt. In the cabin the other white man sat with a book before him, in which he inscribed strange marks and lines. He looked at Mauki as though he had been a pig or a fowl, glanced under the hollows of his arms, and wrote in the book. Then he held out the writing stick and Mauki just barely touched it with his hand, in so doing pledging himself to toil for three years on the plantations of the Moongleam Soap Company. It was not explained to him that the will of the ferocious white men would be used to enforce the pledge, and that, behind all, for the same use, was all the power and all the warships of Great Britain.

Other blacks there were on board, from unheard-of far places, and when the white man spoke to them, they tore the long feather from Mauki's hair, cut that same hair short, and wrapped about his waist a lava-lava of bright yellow calico.

After many days on the schooner, and after beholding more land and islands than he had ever dreamed of, he was landed on New Georgia, and put to work in the field clearing jungle and cutting cane grass. For the first time he knew what work was. Even as a slave to Fanfoa he had not worked like this. And he did not like work. It was up at dawn and in at dark, on two meals a day. And the food was tiresome. For weeks at a time they were given nothing but sweet potatoes to eat, and for weeks at a time it would be nothing but rice. He cut out the cocoanut from the shells day after day; and for long days and weeks he fed the fires that smoked the copra, till his eyes got sore and he was set to felling trees. He was a good axe-man, and later he was put in the bridge-building gang. Once, he was punished by being put in the road-building gang. At times he served as boat's crew in the whale-boats, when they brought in copra from distant beaches or when the white men went out to dynamite fish.

Among other things he learned *bêche-de-mer* English, with which he could talk with all white men, and with all recruits who otherwise would have talked in a thousand different dialects. Also, he learned certain things about the white men, principally that they kept their word. If they told a boy he was going to receive a stick of tobacco, he got it. If they told a boy they would knock seven bells out of him if he did a certain thing, when he did that thing seven bells invariably were knocked out of him. Mauki did not know what seven bells were, but they occurred in bêche-de-mer, and he imagined them to be the blood and teeth that sometimes accompanied the process of knocking out seven bells. One other thing he learned: no boy was struck or punished unless he did wrong. Even when the white men were drunk, as they were frequently, they never struck unless a rule had been broken.

Mauki did not like the plantation. He hated work, and he was the son of a chief. Furthermore, it was ten years since he had been stolen from Port Adams by Fanfoa, and he was homesick. He was even homesick for the slavery under Fanfoa. So he ran away. He struck back into the bush, with the idea of working southward to the beach and stealing a canoe in which to go home to Port Adams. But the fever got him, and he was captured and brought back more dead than alive.

A second time he ran away, in the company of two Malaita boys. They got down the coast twenty miles, and were hidden in the hut of a Malaita freeman, who dwelt in that village. But in the dead of night two white men came, who were not afraid of all the village people and who knocked seven bells out of the three runaways, tied them like pigs, and tossed them into the whale-boat. But the man in whose house they had hidden—seven times seven bells must have been knocked out of him from the way the hair, skin, and teeth flew, and he was discouraged for the rest of his natural life from harboring runaway laborers.

For a year Mauki toiled on. Then he was made a house-boy, and had good food and easy times, with light work in keeping the house clean and serving the white men with whiskey and beer at all hours of the day and most hours of the night. He liked it, but he liked Port Adams more. He had two years longer to serve, but two years were too long for him in the throes of homesickness. He had grown wiser with his year of service, and, being now a house-boy, he had opportunity. He had the cleaning of the rifles, and he knew where the key to the store-room was hung. He planned the escape, and one night ten Malaita boys and one boy from San Cristoval sneaked from the barracks and dragged one of the whale-boats down to the beach. It was Mauki who supplied the key that opened the padlock on the boat, and it was Mauki who equipped the boat with a dozen Winchesters, an immense amount of ammunition, a case of dynamite with detonators and fuse, and ten cases of tobacco.

The northwest monsoon was blowing, and they fled south in the night-time, hiding by day on detached and uninhabited islets, or dragging their whale-boat into the bush on the large islands. Thus they gained Guadalcanar, skirted halfway along it, and crossed the Indispensable Straits to Florida Island. It was here that they killed the San Cristoval boy, saving his head and cooking and eating the rest of him. The Malaita coast was only twenty miles away, but the last night a strong current and baffling winds prevented them from gaining across. Daylight found them still several miles from their goal. But daylight brought a cutter, in which were two white men, who were not afraid of eleven Malaita men armed with twelve rifles. Mauki and his companions were carried back to Tulagi, where lived the great white master of all the white men. And the great white master held a court, after which, one by one, the runaways were tied up and given twenty lashes each, and sentenced to a fine of fifteen dollars. Then they were sent back to New Georgia, where the white men knocked seven bells out of them all around and put them to work. But Mauki was no longer house-boy. He was put in the road-making gang. The fine of fifteen dollars had been paid by the white men from whom he had run away, and he was told that he would have to work it out, which meant six months' additional toil. Further, his share of the stolen tobacco earned him another year of toil.

Port Adams was now three years and a half away, so he stole a canoe one night, hid on the islets in Manning Straits, passed through the Straits, and began working along the eastern coast of Ysabel, only to be captured, two-thirds of the way along, by the white men on Meringe Lagoon. After a week, he escaped from them and took to the bush. There were no bush natives on Ysabel, only salt-water men, who were all Christians. The white men put up a reward of five hundred sticks of tobacco, and every time Mauki ventured down to the sea to steal a canoe he was chased by the salt-water men. Four months of this passed, when, the reward having been raised to a thousand sticks, he was caught and sent back to New Georgia and the road-building gang. Now a thousand sticks are worth fifty dollars, and Mauki had to pay the reward himself, which required a year and eight months' labor. So Port Adams was now five years away.

His homesickness was greater than ever, and it did not appeal to him to settle down and be good, work out his four years, and go home. The next time, he was caught in the very act of running away. His case was brought before Mr. Haveby, the island manager of the Moongleam Soap Company, who adjudged him an incorrigible. The Company had plantations on the Santa Cruz Islands, hundreds of miles across the sea, and there it sent its Solomon Islands' incorrigibles. And there Mauki was sent, though he never arrived. The schooner stopped at Santa Anna, and in the night Mauki swam ashore, where he stole two rifles and a case of tobacco from the trader and got away in a canoe to Cristoval. Malaita was now to the north, fifty or sixty miles away. But when he attempted the passage, he was caught by a light gale and driven back to Santa Anna, where the trader clapped him in irons and held him against the return of the schooner from Santa Cruz. The two rifles the trader recovered, but the case of tobacco was charged up to

Mauki at the rate of another year. The sum of years he now owed the Company was six.

On the way back to New Georgia, the schooner dropped anchor in Marau Sound, which lies at the southeastern extremity of Guadalcanar. Mauki swam ashore with handcuffs on his wrists and got away to the bush. The schooner went on, but the Moongleam trader ashore offered a thousand sticks, and to him Mauki was brought by the bushmen with a year and eight months tacked on to his account. Again, and before the schooner called in, he got away, this time in a whale-boat accompanied by a case of the trader's tobacco. But a northwest gale wrecked him upon Ugi, where the Christian natives stole his tobacco and turned him over to the Moongleam trader who resided there. The tobacco the natives stole meant another year for him, and the tale was now eight years and a half.

"We'll send him to Lord Howe," said Mr. Haveby. "Bunster is there, and we'll let them settle it between them. It will be a case, imagine, of Mauki getting Bunster, or Bunster getting Mauki, and good riddance in either event."

If one leaves Meringe Lagoon, on Ysabel, and steers a course due north, magnetic, at the end of one hundred and fifty miles he will lift the pounded coral beaches of Lord Howe above the sea. Lord Howe is a ring of land some one hundred and fifty miles in circumference, several hundred yards wide at its widest, and towering in places to a height of ten feet above sea-level. Inside this ring of sand is a mighty lagoon studded with coral patches. Lord Howe belongs to the Solomons neither geographically nor ethnologically. It is an atoll, while the Solomons are high islands; and its people and language are Polynesian, while the inhabitants of the Solomons are Melanesian. Lord Howe has been populated by the westward Polynesian drift which continues to this day, big outrigger canoes being washed upon its beaches by the southeast trade. That there has been a slight Melanesian drift in the period of the northwest monsoon, is also evident.

Nobody ever comes to Lord Howe, or Ontong-Java as it is sometimes called. Thomas Cook & Son do not sell tickets to it, and tourists do not dream of its existence. Not even a white missionary has landed on its shore. Its five thousand natives are as peaceable as they are primitive. Yet they were not always peaceable. The *Sailing Directions* speak of them as hostile and treacherous. But the men who compile the *Sailing Directions* have never heard of the change that was worked in the hearts of the inhabitants, who, not many years ago, cut off a big bark and killed all hands with the exception of the second mate. This survivor carried the news to his brothers. The captains of three trading schooners returned with him to Lord Howe. They sailed their vessels right into the lagoon and proceeded to preach the white man's gospel that only white men shall kill white men and that the lesser breeds must keep hands off. The schooners sailed up and down the lagoon, harrying and destroying. There was no escape from the narrow sand-circle, no bush to which to flee. The men were shot down at sight, and there was no avoiding being sighted. The villages were burned, the canoes smashed, the chickens and pigs killed, and the precious cocoanut-trees chopped down. For a month this continued, when the schooners sailed away; but the fear of the white man had been seared into the souls of the islanders and never again were they rash enough to harm one.

Max Bunster was the one white man on Lord Howe, trading in the pay of the ubiquitous Moongleam Soap Company. And the Company billeted him on Lord Howe, because, next to getting rid of him, it was the most out-of-the-way place to be found. That the Company did not get rid of him was due to the difficulty of finding another man to take his place. He was a strapping big German, with something wrong in his brain. Semi-madness would be a charitable statement of his condition. He was a bully and a coward, and a thrice-bigger savage than any savage on the island. Being a coward, his brutality was of the cowardly order. When he first went into the Company's employ, he was stationed on Savo. When a consumptive colonial was sent to take his place, he beat him up with his fists and sent him off a wreck in the schooner that brought him.

Mr. Haveby next selected a young Yorkshire giant to relieve Bunster. The Yorkshire man had a reputation as a bruiser and preferred fighting to eating. But Bunster wouldn't fight. He was a regular little lamb—for ten days, at the end of which time the Yorkshire man was prostrated by a combined attack of dysentery and fever. Then Bunster went for him, among other things getting him down and jumping on him a score or so of times. Afraid of what would happen when his victim recovered, Bunster fled away in a cutter to Guvutu, where he signalized himself by beating up a young Englishman already crippled by a Boer bullet through both hips.

Then it was that Mr. Haveby sent Bunster to Lord Howe, the falling-off place. He celebrated his landing by mopping up half a case of gin and by thrashing the elderly and wheezy mate of the schooner which had brought him. When the schooner departed, he called the kanakas down to the beach and challenged them to throw him in a wrestling bout, promising a case of tobacco to the one who succeeded. Three kanakas he threw, but was promptly thrown by a fourth, who, instead of receiving the tobacco, got a bullet through his lungs.

And so began Bunster's reign on Lord Howe. Three thousand people lived in the principal village; but it was deserted, even in broad day, when he passed through. Men, women, and children fled before him. Even the dogs and pigs got out of the way, while the king was not above hiding under a mat. The two prime ministers lived in terror of Bunster, who never discussed any moot subject, but struck out with his fists instead.

And to Lord Howe came Mauki, to toil for Bunster for eight long years and a half. There was no escaping from Lord Howe. For better or worse, Bunster and he were tied together. Bunster weighed two hundred pounds. Mauki weighed one hundred and ten. Bunster was a degenerate brute. But Mauki was a primitive savage. While both had wills and ways of their own.

Mauki had no idea of the sort of master he was to work for. He had had no warnings, and he had concluded as a matter of course that Bunster would be like other white men, a drinker of much whiskey, a ruler and a lawgiver who always kept his word and who never struck a boy undeserved. Bunster had the advantage. He knew all about Mauki, and gloated over the coming into possession of him. The last cook was suffering from a broken arm and a dislocated shoulder, so Bunster made Mauki cook and general house-boy.

And Mauki soon learned that there were white men and white men.

On the very day the schooner departed he was ordered to buy a chicken from Samisee, the native Tongan missionary. But Samisee had sailed across the lagoon and would not be back for three days. Mauki returned with the information. He climbed the steep stairway (the house stood on piles twelve feet above the sand), and entered the living-room to report. The trader demanded the chicken. Mauki opened his mouth to explain the missionary's absence. But Bunster did not care for explanations. He struck out with his fist. The blow caught Mauki on the mouth and lifted him into the air. Clear through the doorway he flew, across the narrow veranda, breaking the top railing, and down to the ground. His lips were a contused, shapeless mass, and his mouth was full of blood and broken teeth.

"That'll teach you that back talk don't go with me," the trader shouted, purple with rage, peering down at him over the broken railing.

Mauki had never met a white man like this, and he resolved to walk small and never offend. He saw the boat-boys knocked about, and one of them put in irons for three days with nothing to eat for the crime of breaking a rowlock while pulling. Then, too, he heard the gossip of the village and learned why Bunster had taken a third wife—by force, as was well known. The first and second wives lay in the graveyard, under the white coral sand, with slabs of coral rock at head and feet. They had died, it was said, from beatings he had given them. The third wife was certainly ill-used, as Mauki could see for himself.

But there was no way by which to avoid offending the white man, who seemed offended with life. When Mauki kept silent, he was struck and called a sullen brute. When he spoke, he was struck for giving back talk. When he was grave, Bunster accused him of plotting and gave him a thrashing in advance; and when he strove to be cheerful and to smile, he was charged with sneering at his lord and master and given a taste of stick. Bunster was a devil. The village would have done for him, had it not remembered the lesson of the three schooners. It might have done for him anyway, if there had been a bush to which to flee. As it was, the murder of the white men, of any white man, would bring a man-of-war that would kill the offenders and chop down the precious cocoanut-trees. Then there were the boat-boys, with minds fully made up to drown him by accident at the first opportunity to capsize the cutter. Only Bunster saw to it that the boat did not capsize.

Mauki was of a different breed, and, escape being impossible while Bunster lived, he was resolved to get the white man. The trouble was that he could never find a chance. Bunster was always on guard. Day and night his revolvers were ready to hand. He permitted nobody to pass behind his back, as Mauki learned after having been knocked down several times. Bunster knew that he had more to fear from the good-natured, even sweet-faced, Malaita boy than from the entire population of Lord Howe; and it gave added zest to the programme of torment he was carrying out. And Mauki walked small, accepted his punishments, and waited.

All other white men had respected his *tambos*, but not so Bunster. Mauki's weekly allowance of tobacco was two sticks. Bunster passed them to his woman and ordered Mauki to receive them from her hand. But this could not be, and Mauki went without his tobacco. In the same way he was made to miss many a meal, and to go hungry many a day. He was ordered to make chowder out of the big clams that grew in the lagoon. This he could not do, for clams were *tambo*. Six times in succession he refused to touch the clams, and six times he was knocked senseless. Bunster knew that the boy would die first, but called his refusal mutiny, and would have killed him had there been another cook to take his place.

One of the trader's favorite tricks was to catch Mauki's kinky locks and bat his head against the wall. Another trick was to catch Mauki unawares and thrust the live end of a cigar against his flesh. This Bunster called vaccination, and Mauki was vaccinated a number of times a week. Once, in a rage, Bunster ripped the cup handle from Mauki's nose, tearing the hole clear out of the cartilage.

"Oh, what a mug!" was his comment, when he surveyed the damage he had wrought.

The skin of a shark is like sandpaper, but the skin of a ray fish is like a rasp. In the South Seas the natives use it as a wood file in smoothing down canoes and paddles. Bunster had a mitten made of ray fish skin. The first time he tried it on Mauki, with one sweep of the hand it fetched the skin off his back from neck to armpit. Bunster was delighted. He gave his wife a taste of the mitten, and tried it out thoroughly on the boat-boys. The prime ministers came in for a stroke each, and they had to grin and take it for a joke.

"Laugh, damn you, laugh!" was the cue he gave.

Mauki came in for the largest share of the mitten. Never a day passed without a caress from it. There were times when the loss of so much cuticle kept him awake at night, and often the half-healed surface was raked raw afresh by the facetious Mr. Bunster. Mauki continued his patient wait, secure in the knowledge that sooner or later his time would come. And he knew just what he was going to do, down to the smallest detail, when the time did come.

One morning Bunster got up in a mood for knocking seven bells out of the universe. He began on Mauki, and wound up on Mauki, in the interval knocking down his wife and hammering all the boat-boys. At breakfast he called the coffee slops and threw the scalding contents of the cup into Mauki's face. By ten o'clock Bunster was shivering with ague, and half an hour later he was burning with fever. It was no ordinary attack. It quickly became pernicious, and developed into blackwater fever. The days passed, and he grew weaker and weaker, never leaving his bed. Mauki waited and watched, the while his skin grew intact once more. He ordered the boys to beach the cutter, scrub her bottom, and give her a general overhauling. They thought the order emanated from Bunster, and they obeyed. But Bunster at the time was lying unconscious and giving no orders. This was Mauki's chance, but still he waited.

When the worst was past, and Bunster lay convalescent and conscious, but weak as a baby, Mauki packed his few trinkets, including the china cup handle, into his trade box. Then he went over to the village and interviewed the king and his two prime ministers.

"This fella Bunster, him good fella you like too much?" he asked.

They explained in one voice that they liked the trader not at all. The ministers poured forth a recital of all the indignities and wrongs that had been heaped upon them. The king broke down and wept. Mauki interrupted rudely.

"You savve me—me big fella marster my country. You no like 'm this fella white marster. Me no like 'm. Plenty good you put hundred cocoanut, two hundred cocoanut, three hundred cocoanut along cutter. Him finish, you go sleep 'm good fella. Altogether kanaka sleep 'm good fella. Bime by big fella noise along house, you no savve hear 'm that fella noise. You altogether sleep strong fella too much."

In like manner Mauki interviewed the boat-boys. Then he ordered Bunster's wife to return to her family house. Had she refused, he would have been in a quandary, for his *tambo* would not have permitted him to lay hands on her.

The house deserted, he entered the sleeping-room, where the trader lay in a doze. Mauki first removed the revolvers, then placed the ray fish mitten on his hand. Bunster's first warning was a stroke of the mitten that removed the skin the full length of his nose.

"Good fella, eh?" Mauki grinned, between two strokes, one of which swept the forehead bare and the other of which cleaned off one side of his face. "Laugh, damn you, laugh."

Mauki did his work thoroughly, and the kanakas, hiding in their houses, heard the "big fella noise" that Bunster made and continued to make for an hour or more.

When Mauki was done, he carried the boat compass and all the rifles and ammunition down to the cutter, which he proceeded to ballast with cases of tobacco. It was while engaged in this that a hideous, skinless thing came out of the house and ran screaming down the beach till it fell in the sand and mowed and gibbered under the scorching sun. Mauki looked toward it and hesitated. Then he went over and removed the head, which he wrapped in a mat and stowed in the stern-locker of the cutter.

So soundly did the kanakas sleep through that long hot day that they did not see the cutter run out through the passage and head south, close-hauled on the southeast trade. Nor was the cutter ever sighted on that long tack to the shores of Ysabel, and during the tedious head-beat from there to Malaita. He landed at Port Adams with a wealth of rifles and tobacco such as no one man had ever possessed before. But he did not stop there. He had taken a white man's head, and only the bush could shelter him. So back he went to the bush-villages, where he shot old Fanfoa and half a dozen of the chief men, and made himself the chief over all the villages. When his father died, Mauki's brother ruled in Port Adams, and, joined together, salt-water men and bush-men, the resulting combination was the strongest of the ten score fighting tribes of Malaita.

More than his fear of the British government was Mauki's fear of the all-powerful Moongleam Soap Company; and one day a message came up to him in the bush, reminding him that he owed the Company eight and one-half years of labor. He sent back a favorable answer, and then appeared the inevitable white man, the captain of the schooner, the only white man during Mauki's reign who ventured the bush and came out alive. This man not only came out, but he brought with him seven hundred and fifty dollars in gold sovereigns—the money price of eight years and a half of labor plus the cost price of certain rifles and cases of tobacco.

Mauki no longer weighs one hundred and ten pounds. His stomach is three times its former girth, and he has four wives. He has many other things—rifles and revolvers, the handle of a china cup, and an excellent collection of bushmen's heads. But more precious than the entire collection is another head, perfectly dried and cured, with sandy hair and a yellowish beard, which is kept wrapped in the finest of fibre lava-lavas. When Mauki goes to war with villages beyond his realm, he invariably gets out this head, and, alone in his grass palace, contemplates it long and solemnly. At such times the hush of death falls on the village, and not even a pickaninny dares make a noise. The head is esteemed the most powerful devil-devil on Malaita, and to the possession of it is ascribed all of Mauki's greatness.

FROM *A SON OF THE SUN*

A Son of the Sun

I

The *Willi-Waw* lay in the passage between the shore-reef and the outer-reef. From the latter came the low murmur of a lazy surf, but the sheltered stretch of water, not more than a hundred yards across to the white beach of pounded coral sand, was of glass-like smoothness. Narrow as was the passage, and anchored as she was in the shoalest place that gave room to swing, the *Willi-Waw*'s chain rode up-and-down a clean hundred feet. Its course could be traced over the bottom of living coral. Like some monstrous snake, the rusty chain's slack wandered over the ocean floor, crossing and recrossing itself several times and fetching up finally at the idle anchor. Big rock-cod, dun and mottled, played warily in and out of the coral. Other fish, grotesque of form and colour, were brazenly indifferent, even when a big fish-shark drifted sluggishly along and sent the rock-cod scuttling for their favourite crevices.

On deck, for'ard, a dozen blacks pottered clumsily at scraping the teak rail. They were as inexpert at their work as so many monkeys. In fact they looked very much like monkeys of some enlarged and pre-historic type. Their eyes had in them the querulous plaintiveness of the monkey, their faces were even less symmetrical than the monkey's, and, hairless of body, they were far more ungarmented than any monkey, for clothes they had none. Decorated they were as no monkey ever was. In holes in their ears they carried short clay pipes, rings of turtle shell, huge plugs of wood, rusty wire nails, and empty rifle cartridges. The calibre of a Winchester rifle was the smallest hole an ear bore; some of the largest holes were inches in diameter, and any single ear averaged from three to half a dozen holes. Spikes and bodkins of polished bone or petrified shell were thrust through their noses. On the chest of one hung a white door-knob, on the chest of another the handle of a china cup, on the chest of a third the brass cog-wheel of an alarm clock. They chattered in queer, falsetto voices, and, combined, did no more work than a single white sailor.

Aft, under an awning, were two white men. Each was clad in a six-penny undershirt and wrapped about the loins with a strip of cloth. Belted about the middle of each was a revolver and tobacco pouch. The sweat stood out on their skin in myriads of globules. Here and there the globules coalesced in tiny streams that dripped to the heated deck and almost immediately evaporated. The lean, dark-eyed man wiped his fingers wet with a stinging stream from his forehead and flung it from him with a weary curse. Wearily, and without hope, he gazed seaward across the outer-reef, and at the tops of the palms along the beach.

"Eight o'clock, an' hell don't get hot till noon," he complained. "Wisht to God for a breeze. Ain't we never goin' to get away?"

The other man, a slender German of five and twenty, with the massive forehead of a scholar and the tumble-home chin of a degenerate, did not trouble to reply. He was busy emptying powdered quinine into a cigarette paper. Rolling what was approximately fifty grains of the drug into a tight wad, he tossed it into his mouth and gulped it down without the aid of water.

"Wisht I had some whiskey," the first man panted, after a fifteen-minute interval of silence.

Another equal period elapsed ere the German enounced, relevant of nothing:

"I'm rotten with fever. I'm going to quit you, Griffiths, when we get to Sydney. No more tropics for me. I ought to known better when I signed on with you."

"You ain't been much of a mate," Griffiths replied, too hot himself to speak heatedly. "When the beach at Guvutu heard I'd shipped you, they all laughed. 'What? Jacobsen?' they said. 'You can't hide a square face of trade gin or sulphuric acid that he won't smell out!' You've certainly lived up to your reputation. I ain't had a drink for a fortnight, what of your snoopin' my supply."

"If the fever was as rotten in you as me, you'd understand," the mate whimpered.

"I ain't kickin'," Griffiths answered. "I only wisht God'd send me a drink, or a breeze of wind, or something. I'm ripe for my next chill tomorrow."

The mate proffered him the quinine. Rolling a fifty-grain dose, he popped the wad into his mouth and swallowed it dry.

"God! God!" he moaned. "I dream of a land somewheres where they ain't no quinine. Damned stuff of hell! I've scoffed tons of it in my time."

Again he quested seaward for signs of wind. The usual trade-wind clouds were absent, and the sun, still low in its climb to meridian, turned all the sky to heated brass. One seemed to see as well as feel this heat, and Griffiths sought vain relief by gazing shoreward. The white beach was a searing ache to his eyeballs. The palm trees, absolutely still, outlined flatly against the unrefreshing green of the packed jungle, seemed so much cardboard scenery. The little black boys, playing naked in the dazzle of sand and sun, were an affront and a hurt to the sun-sick man. He felt a sort of relief when one, running, tripped and fell on all-fours in the tepid sea-water.

An exclamation from the blacks for'ard sent both men glancing seaward. Around the near point of land, a quarter of a mile away and skirting the reef, a long black canoe paddled into sight.

"Gooma boys from the next bight," was the mate's verdict.

One of the blacks came aft, treading the hot deck with the unconcern of one whose bare feet felt no heat. This, too, was a hurt to Grif-fiths, and he closed his eyes. But the next moment they were open wide.

"White fella marster stop along Gooma boy," the black said.

Both men were on their feet and gazing at the canoe. Aft could be seen the unmistakable sombrero of a white man. Quick alarm showed itself on the face of the mate.

"It's Grief," he said.

Griffiths satisfied himself by a long look, then ripped out a wrathful oath.

"What's he doing up here?" he demanded...of the mate, of the aching sea and sky, of the merciless blaze of sun, and of the whole superheated and implacable universe with which his fate was entan-gled.

The mate began to chuckle.

"I told you you couldn't get away with it," he said.

But Griffiths was not listening.

"With all his money, coming around like a rent collector," he chanted his outrage, almost in an ecstasy of anger. "He's loaded with money, he's stuffed with money, he's busting with money. I know for a fact he sold his Yringa plantations for three hundred thousand pounds. Bell told me so himself last time we were drunk at Guvutu. Worth millions and millions, and Shylocking me for what he wouldn't light his pipe with." He whirled on the mate. "Of course you told me so. Go on and say it, and keep on saying it. Now just what was it you did tell me so?"

"I told you you didn't know him, if you thought you could clear the Solomons without paying him. That man Grief is a devil, but he's straight. I know. I told you he'd throw a thousand quid away for the fun of it, and for sixpence fight like a shark for a rusty tin. I tell you I know. Didn't he give his *Balakula* to the Queensland Mission when they lost their *Evening Star* on San Cristobal?—and the *Balakula* worth three thousand pounds if she was worth a penny? And didn't he beat up Strothers till he lay abed a fortnight, all because of a difference of two pound ten in the account, and because Strothers got fresh and tried to make the gouge go through?"

"God strike me blind!" Griffiths cried in impotency of rage.

The mate went on with his exposition.

"I tell you only a straight man can buck a straight man like him, and the man's never hit the Solomons that could do it. Men like you and me can't buck him. We're too rotten, too rotten all the way through. You've got plenty more than twelve hundred quid below. Pay him, and get it over with."

But Griffiths gritted his teeth and drew his thin lips tightly across them.

"I'll buck him," he muttered—more to himself and the brazen ball of sun than to the mate. He turned and half started to go below, then turned back again. "Look here, Jacobsen. He won't be here for quarter of an hour. Are you with me? Will you stand by me?"

"Of course I'll stand by you. I've drunk all your whiskey, haven't I? What are you going to do?"

"I'm not going to kill him if I can help it. But I'm not going to pay. Take that flat."

Jacobsen shrugged his shoulders in calm acquiescence to fate, and Griffiths stepped to the companionway and went below.

II

Jacobsen watched the canoe across the low reef as it came abreast and passed on to the entrance of the passage. Griffiths, with ink-marks on right thumb and forefinger, returned on deck. Fifteen minutes later the canoe came alongside. The man with the sombrero stood up.

"Hello, Griffiths!" he said. "Hello, Jacobsen!" With his hand on the rail he turned to his dusky crew. "You fella boy stop along canoe altogether."

As he swung over the rail and stepped on deck a hint of catlike litheness showed in the apparently heavy body. Like the other two, he was scantily clad. The cheap undershirt and white loin-cloth did not serve to hide the well put up body. Heavy muscled he was, but he was not lumped and hummocked by muscles. They were softly rounded, and, when they did move, slid softly and silkily under the smooth, tanned skin. Ardent suns had likewise tanned his face till it was swarthy as a Spaniard's. The yellow moustache appeared incongruous in the midst of such swarthiness, while the clear blue of the eyes produced a feeling of shock on the beholder. It was difficult to realize that the skin of this man had once been fair.

"Where did you blow in from?" Griffiths asked, as they shook hands. "I thought you were over in the Santa Cruz."

"I was," the newcomer answered. "But we made a quick passage. The *Wonder*'s just around in the bight at Gooma, waiting for wind. Some of the bushmen reported a ketch here, and I just dropped around to see. Well, how goes it?"

"Nothing much. Copra sheds mostly empty, and not half a dozen tons of ivory nuts. The women all got rotten with fever and quit, and the men can't chase them back into the swamps. They're a sick crowd. I'd ask you to have a drink, but the mate finished off my last bottle. I wisht to God for a breeze of wind."

Grief, glancing with keen carelessness from one to the other, laughed.

"I'm glad the calm held," he said. "It enabled me to get around to see you. My supercargo dug up that little note of yours, and I brought it along."

The mate edged politely away, leaving his skipper to face his trouble.

"I'm sorry, Grief, damned sorry," Griffiths said, "but I ain't got it. You'll have to give me a little more time."

Grief leaned up against the companionway, surprise and pain depicted on his face.

"It does beat hell," he communed, "how men learn to lie in the Solomons. The truth's not in them. Now take Captain Jensen. I'd sworn by his truthfulness. Why, he told me only five days ago—do you want to know what he told me?"

Griffiths licked his lips.

"Go on."

"Why, he told me that you'd sold out—sold out everything, cleaned up, and was pulling out for the New Hebrides."

"He's a damned liar!" Griffiths cried hotly.

Grief nodded.

"I should say so. He even had the nerve to tell me that he'd bought two of your stations from you—Mauri and Kahula. Said he paid you seventeen hundred gold sovereigns, lock, stock and barrel, good will, trade-goods, credit, and copra."

Griffiths's eyes narrowed and glinted. The action was involuntary, and Grief noted it with a lazy sweep of his eyes.

"And Parsons, your trader at Hickimavi, told me that the Fulcrum Company had bought that station from you. Now what did he want to lie for?"

Griffiths, overwrought by sun and sickness, exploded. All his bitterness of spirit rose up in his face and twisted his mouth into a snarl.

"Look here, Grief, what's the good of playing with me that way? You know, and I know you know. Let it go at that. I *have* sold out, and I *am* getting away. And what are you going to do about it?"

Grief shrugged his shoulders, and no hint of resolve shadowed itself in his own face. His expression was as of one in a quandary.

"There's no law here," Griffiths pressed home his advantage. "Tulagi is a hundred and fifty miles away. I've got my clearance papers, and I'm on my own boat. There's nothing to stop me from sailing. You've got no right to stop me just because I owe you a little money. And by God! you can't stop me. Put that in your pipe."

The look of pained surprise on Grief's face deepened.

"You mean you're going to cheat me out of that twelve hundred, Griffiths?"

"That's just about the size of it, old man. And calling hard names won't help any. There's the wind coming. You'd better get overside before I pull out, or I'll tow your canoe under."

"Really, Griffiths, you sound almost right. I can't stop you." Grief fumbled in the pouch that hung on his revolver-belt and pulled out a crumpled official-looking paper. "But maybe this will stop you. And it's something for *your* pipe. Smoke up."

"What is it?"

"An admiralty warrant. Running to the New Hebrides won't save you. It can be served anywhere."

Griffiths hesitated and swallowed, when he had finished glancing at the document. With knit brows he pondered this new phase of the situation. Then, abruptly, as he looked up, his face relaxed into all frankness.

"You were cleverer than I thought, old man," he said. "You've got me hip and thigh. I ought to have known better than to try and beat you. Jacobsen told me I couldn't, and I wouldn't listen to him. But he was right, and so are you. I've got the money below. Come on down and we'll settle."

He started to go down, then stepped aside to let his visitor precede him, at the same time glancing seaward to where the dark flaw of wind was quickening the water.

"Heave short," he told the mate. "Get up sail and stand ready to break out."

As Grief sat down on the edge of the mate's bunk, close against and facing the tiny table, he noticed the butt of a revolver just projecting from under the pillow. On the table, which hung on hinges from the for'ard bulkhead, were pen and ink, also a battered log-book.

"Oh, I don't mind being caught in a dirty trick," Griffiths was saying defiantly. "I've been in the tropics too long. I'm a sick man, a damn sick man. And the whiskey, and the sun, and the fever have made me sick in morals, too. Nothing's too mean and low for me now, and I can understand why the niggers eat each other, and take heads, and such things. I could do it myself. So I call trying to do you out of that small account a pretty mild trick. Wisht I could offer you a drink."

Grief made no reply, and the other busied himself in attempting to unlock a large and much-dented cash-box. From on deck came falsetto cries and the creak and rattle of blocks as the black crew swung up mainsail and driver. Grief watched a large cockroach crawling over the greasy paintwork. Griffiths, with an oath of irritation, carried the cash-box to the companion-steps for better light. Here, on his feet, and bending over the box, his back to his visitor, his hands shot out to the rifle that stood beside the steps, and at the same moment he whirled about.

"Now don't you move a muscle," he commanded.

Grief smiled, elevated his eyebrows quizzically, and obeyed. His left hand rested on the bunk beside him; his right hand lay on the table.

His revolver hung on his right hip in plain sight. But in his mind was recollection of the other revolver under the pillow.

"Huh!" Griffiths sneered. "You've got everybody in the Solomons hypnotized, but let me tell you you ain't got me. Now I'm going to throw you off my vessel, along with your admiralty warrant, but first you've got to do something. Lift up that log-book."

The other glanced curiously at the log-book, but did not move.

"I tell you I'm a sick man, Grief; and I'd as soon shoot you as smash a cockroach. Lift up that log-book, I say."

Sick he did look, his lean face working nervously with the rage that possessed him. Grief lifted the book and set it aside. Beneath lay a written sheet of tablet paper.

"Read it," Griffiths commanded. "Read it aloud."

Grief obeyed; but while he read, the fingers of his left hand began an infinitely slow and patient crawl toward the butt of the weapon under the pillow.

"*On board the ketch* Willi-Waw, *Bombi Bight, Island of Anna, Solomon Islands,*" he read. "*Know all men by these presents that I do hereby sign off and release in full, for due value received, all debts whatsoever owing to me by Harrison J. Griffiths, who has this day paid to me twelve hundred pounds sterling.*"

"With that receipt in my hands," Griffiths grinned, "your admiralty warrant's not worth the paper it's written on. Sign it."

"It won't do any good, Griffiths," Grief said. "A document signed under compulsion won't hold before the law."

"In that case, what objection have you to signing it then?"

"Oh, none at all, only that I might save you heaps of trouble by not signing it."

Grief's fingers had gained the revolver, and, while he talked, with his right hand he played with the pen and with his left began slowly and imperceptibly drawing the weapon to his side. As his hand finally closed upon it, second finger on trigger and forefinger laid past the cylinder and along the barrel, he wondered what luck he would have at left-handed snap-shooting.

"Don't consider me," Griffiths gibed. "And just remember Jacobsen will testify that he saw me pay the money over. Now sign, sign in full, at the bottom, David Grief, and date it."

From on deck came the jar of sheet-blocks and the rat-tat-tat of the reef-points against the canvas. In the cabin they could feel the *Willi-Waw* heel, swing into the wind, and right. David Grief still hesitated. From for'ard came the jerking rattle of headsail halyards through the sheaves. The little vessel heeled, and through the cabin walls came the gurgle and wash of water.

"Get a move on!" Griffiths cried. "The anchor's out."

The muzzle of the rifle, four feet away, was bearing directly on him, when Grief resolved to act. The rifle wavered as Griffiths kept his balance in the uncertain puffs of the first of the wind. Grief took advantage of the wavering, made as if to sign the paper, and at the same instant, like a cat, exploded into swift and intricate action. As he ducked low and leaped forward with his body, his left hand flashed from under the screen of the table, and so accurately timed was the single stiff pull on the self-cocking trigger that the cartridge discharged as the muzzle came forward. Not a whit behind was Griffiths. The muzzle of his weapon dropped to meet the ducking body, and, shot at snap direction, rifle and revolver went off simultaneously.

Grief felt the sting and sear of a bullet across the skin of his shoulder, and knew that his own shot had missed. His forward rush carried him to Griffiths before another shot could be fired, both of whose arms, still holding the rifle, he locked with a low tackle about the body. He shoved the revolver muzzle, still in his left hand, deep into the other's abdomen. Under the press of his anger and the sting of his abraded skin, Grief's finger was lifting the hammer, when the wave of anger passed and he recollected himself. Down the companionway came indignant cries from the Gooma boys in his canoe.

Everything was happening in seconds. There was apparently no pause in his actions as he gathered Griffiths in his arms and carried him up the steep steps in a sweeping rush. Out into the blinding glare of sunshine he came. A black stood grinning at the wheel, and the *Willi-Waw*, heeled over from the wind, was foaming along. Rapidly dropping astern was his Gooma canoe. Grief turned his head. From amidships, revolver in hand, the mate was springing toward him. With two jumps, still holding the helpless Griffiths, Grief leaped to the rail and overboard.

Both men were grappled together as they went down; but Grief, with a quick updraw of his knees to the other's chest, broke the grip and forced him down. With both feet on Griffiths's shoulder, he forced him still deeper, at the same time driving himself to the surface. Scarcely had his head broken into the sunshine when two splashes of water, in quick succession and within a foot of his face, advertised that Jacobsen knew how to handle a revolver. There was a chance for no third shot, for Grief, filling his lungs with air, sank down. Under water he struck out, nor did he come up till he saw the canoe and the bubbling paddles overhead. As he climbed aboard, the *Willi-Waw* went into the wind to come about.

"Washee-washee!" Grief cried to his boys. "You fella make-um beach quick fella time!"

In all shamelessness, he turned his back on the battle and ran for cover. The *Willi-Waw*, compelled to deaden way in order to pick up its captain, gave Grief his chance for a lead. The canoe struck the beach full-tilt, with every paddle driving, and they leaped out and ran across the sand for the trees. But before they gained the shelter, three times the sand kicked into puffs ahead of them. Then they drove into the green safety of the jungle.

Grief watched the *Willi-Waw* haul up close, go out the passage, then slack its sheets as it headed south with the wind abeam. As it went out of sight past the point he could see the top-sail being broken out. One of the Gooma boys, a black, nearly fifty years of age, hideously marred and scarred by skin diseases and old wounds, looked up into his face and grinned.

"My word," the boy commented, "that fella skipper too much, cross along you."

Grief laughed, and led the way back across the sand to the canoe.

III

How many millions David Grief was worth no man in the Solomons knew, for his holdings and ventures were everywhere in the great South Pacific. From Samoa to New Guinea and even to the north of

the Line his plantations were scattered. He possessed pearling conces-
sions in the Paumotus. Though his name did not appear, he was in
truth the German company that traded in the French Marquesas. His
trading stations were in strings in all the groups, and his vessels that
operated them were many. He owned atolls so remote and tiny that his
smallest schooners and ketches visited the solitary agents but once a
year.

In Sydney, on Castlereagh Street, his offices occupied three floors.
But he was rarely in those offices. He preferred always to be on the go
amongst the islands, nosing out new investments, inspecting and shaking up old ones, and rubbing shoulders with fun and adventure in a
thousand strange guises. He bought the wreck of the great steamship
Gavonne for a song, and in salving it achieved the impossible and
cleaned up a quarter of a million. In the Louisiades he planted the
first commercial rubber, and in Bora-Bora he ripped out the South
Sea cotton and put the jolly islanders at the work of planting cacao. It
was he who took the deserted island of Lallu-Ka, colonized it with
Polynesians from the Ontong-Java Atoll, and planted four thousand
acres to cocoanuts. And it was he who reconciled the warring chief-
stocks of Tahiti and swung the great deal of the phosphate island of
Hikihu.

His own vessels recruited his contract labour. They brought Santa
Cruz boys to the New Hebrides, New Hebrides boys to the Banks, and
the head-hunting cannibals of Malaita to the plantations of New
Georgia. From Tonga to the Gilberts and on to the far Louisiades his
recruiters combed the islands for labour. His keels ploughed all ocean
stretches. He owned three steamers on regular island runs, though he
rarely elected to travel in them, preferring the wilder and more primitive way of wind and sail.

At least forty years of age, he looked no more than thirty. Yet beach-
combers remembered his advent among the islands a score of years
before, at which time the yellow moustache was already budding silkily on his lip. Unlike other white men in the tropics, he was there because he liked it. His protective skin pigmentation was excellent. He
had been born to the sun. One he was in ten thousand in the matter
of sun-resistance. The invisible and high-velocity light waves failed

to bore into him. Other white men were pervious. The sun drove through their skins, ripping and smashing tissues and nerves, till they became sick in mind and body, tossed most of the Decalogue overboard, descended to beastliness, drank themselves into quick graves, or survived so savagely that war vessels were sometimes sent to curb their licence.

But David Grief was a true son of the sun, and he flourished in all its ways. He merely became browner with the passing of the years, though in the brown was the hint of golden tint that glows in the skin of the Polynesian. Yet his blue eyes retained their blue, his moustache its yellow, and the lines of his face were those which had persisted through the centuries in his English race. English he was in blood, yet those that thought they knew contended he was at least American born. Unlike them, he had not come out to the South Seas seeking hearth and saddle of his own. In fact, he had brought hearth and saddle with him. His advent had been in the Paumotus. He arrived on board a tiny schooner yacht, master and owner, a youth questing romance and adventure along the sun-washed path of the tropics. He also arrived in a hurricane, the giant waves of which deposited him and yacht and all in the thick of a cocoanut grove three hundred yards beyond the surf. Six months later he was rescued by a pearling cutter. But the sun had got into his blood. At Tahiti, instead of taking a steamer home, he bought a schooner, outfitted her with trade-goods and divers, and went for a cruise through the Dangerous Archipelago.

As the golden tint burned into his face it poured molten out of the ends of his fingers. His was the golden touch, but he played the game, not for the gold, but for the game's sake. It was a man's game, the rough contacts and fierce give and take of the adventurers of his own blood and of half the bloods of Europe and the rest of the world, and it was a good game; but over and beyond was his love of all the other things that go to make up a South Seas rover's life—the smell of the reef; the infinite exquisiteness of the shoals of living coral in the mirror-surfaced lagoons; the crashing sunrises of raw colours spread with lawless cunning; the palm-tufted islets set in turquoise deeps; the tonic wine of the trade-winds; the heave and send of the orderly, crested seas; the moving deck beneath his feet, the straining canvas overhead; the flower-garlanded, golden-glowing men and maids of Polynesia, half-children and half-gods; and even the howling savages of Melanesia, head-hunters and man-eaters, half-devil and all beast.

And so, favoured child of the sun, out of munificence of energy and sheer joy of living, he, the man of many millions, forbore on his far way to play the game with Harrison J. Griffiths for a paltry sum. It was his whim, his desire, his expression of self and of the sun-warmth that poured through him. It was fun, a joke, a problem, a bit of play on which life was lightly hazarded for the joy of the playing.

IV

The early morning found the *Wonder* lying close-hauled along the coast of Guadalcanar. She moved lazily through the water under the dying breath of the land breeze. To the east, heavy masses of clouds promised a renewal of the south-east trades, accompanied by sharp puffs and rain squalls. Ahead, lying along the coast on the same course as the *Wonder*, and being slowly overtaken, was a small ketch. It was not the *Willi-Waw*, however, and Captain Ward, on the *Wonder*, putting down his glasses, named it the *Kauri*.

Grief, just on deck from below, sighed regretfully.

"If it had only been the *Willi-Waw*," he said.

"You do hate to be beaten," Denby, the supercargo, remarked sympathetically.

"I certainly do." Grief paused and laughed with genuine mirth. "It's my firm conviction that Griffiths is a rogue, and that he treated me quite scurvily yesterday. 'Sign,' he says, 'sign in full, at the bottom, and date it.' And Jacobsen, the little rat, stood in with him. It was rank piracy, the days of Bully Hayes all over again."

"If you weren't my employer, Mr. Grief, I'd like to give you a piece of my mind," Captain Ward broke in.

"Go on and spit it out," Grief encouraged.

"Well, then——" The captain hesitated and cleared his throat.

"With all the money you've got, only a fool would take the risk you did with those two curs. What do you do it for?"

"Honestly, I don't know, Captain. I just want to, I suppose. And can you give any better reason for anything you do?"

"You'll get your bally head shot off some fine day," Captain Ward growled in answer, as he stepped to the binnacle and took the bearing of a peak which had just thrust its head through the clouds that covered Guadalcanar.

The land breeze strengthened in a last effort, and the *Wonder*, slipping swiftly through the water, ranged alongside the *Kauri* and began to go by. Greetings flew back and forth, then David Grief called out:

"Seen anything of the *Willi-Waw?*"

The captain, slouch-hatted and barelegged, with a rolling twist hitched the faded blue *lava-lava* tighter around his waist and spat tobacco juice overside.

"Sure," he answered. "Griffiths lay at Savo last night, taking on pigs and yams and filling his water-tanks. Looked like he was going for a long cruise, but he said no. Why? Did you want to see him?"

"Yes; but if you see him first don't tell him you've seen me."

The captain nodded and considered, and walked for'ard on his own deck to keep abreast of the faster vessel.

"Say!" he called. "Jacobsen told me they were coming down this afternoon to Gabera. Said they were going to lie there tonight and take on sweet potatoes."

"Gabera has the only leading lights in the Solomons," Grief said, when his schooner had drawn well ahead. "Is that right, Captain Ward?"

The captain nodded.

"And the little bight just around the point on this side, it's a rotten anchorage, isn't it?"

"No anchorage. All coral patches and shoals, and a bad surf. That's where the *Molly* went to pieces three years ago."

Grief stared straight before him with lustreless eyes for a full minute, as if summoning some vision to his inner sight. Then the corners of his eyes wrinkled and the ends of his yellow moustache lifted in a smile.

"We'll anchor at Gabera," he said. "And run in close to the little bight this side. I want you to drop me in a whaleboat as you go by. Also, give me six boys, and serve out rifles. I'll be back on board before morning."

The captain's face took on an expression of suspicion, which swiftly slid into one of reproach.

"Oh, just a little fun, skipper," Grief protested with the apologetic air of a schoolboy caught in mischief by an elder.

Captain Ward grunted, but Denby was all alertness.

"I'd like to go along, Mr. Grief," he said.

Grief nodded consent.

"Bring some axes and bush-knives," he said. "And, oh, by the way, a couple of bright lanterns. See they've got oil in them."

V

An hour before sunset the *Wonder* tore by the little bight. The wind had freshened, and a lively sea was beginning to make. The shoals toward the beach were already white with the churn of water, while those farther out as yet showed no more sign than of discoloured water. As the schooner went into the wind and backed her jib and staysail the whaleboat was swung out. Into it leaped six breech-clouted Santa Cruz boys, each armed with a rifle. Denby, carrying the lanterns, dropped into the stern-sheets. Grief, following, paused on the rail.

"Pray for a dark night, skipper," he pleaded.

"You'll get it," Captain Ward answered. "There's no moon, anyway, and there won't be any sky. She'll be a bit squally, too."

The forecast sent a radiance into Grief's face, making more pronounced the golden tint of his sunburn. He leaped down beside the supercargo.

"Cast off!" Captain Ward ordered. "Draw the headsails! Put your wheel over! There! Steady! Take that course!"

The *Wonder* filled away and ran on around the point for Gabera, while the whaleboat, pulling six oars and steered by Grief, headed for the beach. With superb boatmanship he threaded the narrow, tortuous channel which no craft larger than a whaleboat could negotiate, until the shoals and patches showed seaward and they grounded on the quiet, rippling beach.

The next hour was filled with work. Moving about among the wild cocoanuts and jungle brush, Grief selected the trees.

"Chop this fella tree; chop that fella tree," he told his blacks. "No chop that other fella," he said, with a shake of head.

In the end, a wedge-shaped segment of jungle was cleared. Near to the beach remained one long palm. At the apex of the wedge stood another. Darkness was falling as the lanterns were lighted, carried up the two trees, and made fast.

"That outer lantern is too high." David Grief studied it critically. "Put it down about ten feet, Denby."

VI

The *Willi-Waw* was tearing through the water with a bone in her teeth, for the breath of the passing squall was still strong. The blacks were swinging up the big mainsail, which had been lowered on the run when the puff was at its height. Jacobsen, superintending the operation, ordered them to throw the halyards down on deck and stand by, then went for'ard on the lee-bow and joined Griffiths. Both men stared with wide-strained eyes at the blank wall of darkness through which they were flying, their ears tense for the sound of surf on the invisible shore. It was by this sound that they were for the moment steering.

The wind fell lighter, the scud of clouds thinned and broke, and in the dim glimmer of starlight loomed the jungle-clad coast. Ahead, and well on the lee-bow, appeared a jagged rock-point. Both men strained to it.

"Amboy Point," Griffiths announced. "Plenty of water close up. Take the wheel, Jacobsen, till we set a course. Get a move on!"

Running aft, barefooted and barelegged, the rainwater dripping from his scant clothing, the mate displaced the black at the wheel.

"How's she heading?" Griffiths called.

"South-a-half-west!"

"Let her come up south-by-west! Got it?"

"Right on it!"

Griffiths considered the changed relation of Amboy Point to the *Willi-Waw*'s course.

"And a-half-west!" he cried.

"And a-half-west!" came the answer. "Right on it!"

"Steady! That'll do!"

"Steady she is!" Jacobsen turned the wheel over to the savage. "You steer good fella, savve?" he warned. "No good fella, I knock your damn black head off."

Again he went for'ard and joined the other, and again the cloud-scud thickened, the star-glimmer vanished, and the wind rose and screamed in another squall.

"Watch that mainsail!" Griffiths yelled in the mate's ear, at the same time studying the ketch's behaviour.

Over she pressed, and lee-rail under, while he measured the weight of the wind and quested its easement. The tepid sea-water, with here and there tiny globules of phosphorescence, washed about his ankles and knees. The wind screamed a higher note, and every shroud and stay sharply chorused an answer as the *Willi-Waw* pressed farther over and down.

"Down mainsail!" Griffiths yelled, springing to the peak-halyards, thrusting away the black who held on, and casting off the turn.

Jacobsen, at the throat-halyards, was performing the like office. The big sail rattled down, and the blacks, with shouts and yells, threw themselves on the battling canvas. The mate, finding one skulking in the darkness, flung his bunched knuckles into the creature's face and drove him to his work.

The squall held at its high pitch, and under her small canvas the *Willi-Waw* still foamed along. Again the two men stood for'ard and vainly watched in the horizontal drive of rain.

"We're all right," Griffiths said. "This rain won't last. We can hold this course till we pick up the lights. Anchor in thirteen fathoms. You'd better overhaul forty-five on a night like this. After that get the gaskets on the mainsail. We won't need it."

Half an hour afterward his weary eyes were rewarded by a glimpse of two lights.

"There they are, Jacobsen. I'll take the wheel. Run down the fore-staysail and stand by to let go. Make the niggers jump."

Aft, the spokes of the wheel in his hands, Griffiths held the course till the two lights came in line, when he abruptly altered and headed directly in for them. He heard the tumble and roar of the surf, but decided it was farther away—as it should be, at Gabera.

He heard the frightened cry of the mate, and was grinding the wheel down with all his might, when the *Willi-Waw* struck. At the same instant her mainmast crashed over the bow. Five wild minutes followed. All hands held on while the hull upheaved and smashed down on the brittle coral and the warm seas swept over them. Grinding and crunching, the *Willi-Waw* worked itself clear over the shoal patch and came solidly to rest in the comparatively smooth and shallow channel beyond.

Griffiths sat down on the edge of the cabin, head bowed on chest, in silent wrath and bitterness. Once he lifted his face to glare at the two white lights, one above the other and perfectly in line.

"There they are," he said. "And this isn't Gabera. Then what the hell is it?"

Though the surf still roared and across the shoal flung its spray and upper wash over them, the wind died down and the stars came out. Shoreward came the sound of oars.

"What have you had?—an earthquake?" Griffiths called out. "The bottom's all changed. I've anchored here a hundred times in thirteen fathoms. Is that you, Wilson?"

A whaleboat came alongside, and a man climbed over the rail. In the faint light Griffiths found an automatic Colt's thrust into his face, and, looking up, saw David Grief.

"No, you never anchored here before," Grief laughed. "Gabera's just around the point, where I'll be as soon as I've collected that little sum of twelve hundred pounds. We won't bother for the receipt. I've your note here, and I'll just return it."

"You did this!" Griffiths cried, springing to his feet in a sudden gust of rage. "You faked those leading lights! You've wrecked me, and by——"

"Steady! Steady!" Grief's voice was cool and menacing. "I'll trouble you for that twelve hundred, please."

To Griffiths, a vast impotence seemed to descend upon him. He was overwhelmed by a profound disgust—disgust for the sunlands and the sun-sickness, for the futility of all his endeavour, for this blue-eyed, golden-tinted, superior man who defeated him on all his ways.

"Jacobsen," he said, "will you open the cash-box and pay this—this bloodsucker—twelve hundred pounds?"

THE DEVILS OF FUATINO

I

Of his many schooners, ketches and cutters that nosed about among the coral isles of the South Seas, David Grief loved most the *Rattler*— a yacht-like schooner of ninety tons with so swift a pair of heels that she had made herself famous, in the old days, opium-smuggling from San Diego to Puget Sound, raiding the seal-rookeries of Bering Sea, and running arms in the Far East. A stench and an abomination to government officials, she had been the joy of all sailormen, and the pride of the shipwrights who built her. Even now, after forty years of driving, she was still the same old *Rattler*, fore-reaching in the same marvellous manner that compelled sailors to see in order to believe and that punctuated many an angry discussion with words and blows on the beaches of all the ports from Valparaiso to Manila Bay.

On this night, close-hauled, her big mainsail preposterously flattened down, her luffs pulsing emptily on the lift of each smooth swell, she was sliding an easy four knots through the water on the veriest whisper of a breeze. For an hour David Grief had been leaning on the rail at the lee fore-rigging, gazing overside at the steady phosphores-cence of her gait. The faint back-draught from the headsails fanned his cheek and chest with a wine of coolness, and he was in an ecstasy of appreciation of the schooner's qualities.

"Eh!—she's a beauty, Taute, a beauty," he said to the Kanaka look-out, at the same time stroking the teak of the rail with an affectionate hand.

"Ay, skipper," the Kanaka answered in the rich, big-chested tones of Polynesia. "Thirty years I know ships, but never like this. On Raiatea we call her *Fanauao.*"

"The Dayborn," Grief translated the love-phrase. "Who named her so?"

About to answer, Taute peered ahead with sudden intensity. Grief joined him in the gaze.

"Land," said Taute.

"Yes; Fuatino," Grief agreed, his eyes still fixed on the spot where the star-luminous horizon was gouged by a blot of blackness. "It's all right. I'll tell the captain."

The *Rattler* slid along until the loom of the island could be seen as well as sensed, until the sleepy roar of breakers and the blatting of goats could be heard, until the wind, off the land, was flower-drenched with perfume.

"If it wasn't a crevice, she could run the passage a night like this," Captain Glass remarked regretfully, as he watched the wheel lashed hard down by the steersman.

The *Rattler*, run off shore a mile, had been hove to to wait until daylight ere she attempted the perilous entrance to Fuatino. It was a perfect tropic night, with no hint of rain or squall. For'ard, wherever their tasks left them, the Raiatea sailors sank down to sleep on deck. Aft, the captain and mate and Grief spread their beds with simi-lar languid unconcern. They lay on their blankets, smoking and mur-muring sleepy conjectures about Mataara, the Queen of Fuatino, and about the love-affair between her daughter, Naumoo, and Motu-aro.

"They're certainly a romantic lot," Brown, the mate, said. "As ro-mantic as we whites."

"As romantic as Pilsach," Grief laughed, "and that is going some. How long ago was it, Captain, that he jumped you?"

"Eleven years," Captain Glass grunted resentfully.

"Tell me about it," Brown pleaded. "They say he's never left Fuatino since. Is that right?"

"Right O," the captain rumbled. "He's in love with his wife—the little hussy! Stole him from me, and as good a sailorman as the trade has ever seen—if he is a Dutchman."

"German," Grief corrected.

"It's all the same," was the retort. "The sea was robbed of a good man that night he went ashore and Notutu took one look at him. I reckon they looked good to each other. Before you could say skat, she'd put a wreath of some kind of white flowers on his head, and in five minutes they were off down the beach, like a couple of kids, holding hands and laughing. I hope he's blown that big coral patch out of the channel. I always start a sheet or two of copper warping past."

"Go on with the story," Brown urged.

"That's all. He was finished right there. Got married that night. Never came on board again. I looked him up next day. Found him in a straw house in the bush, barelegged, a white savage, all mixed up with flowers and things and playing a guitar. Looked like a bally ass. Told me to send his things ashore. I told him I'd see him damned first. And that's all. You'll see her to-morrow. They've got three kiddies now—wonderful little rascals. I've a phonograph down below for him, and about a million records."

"And then you made him trader?" the mate inquired of Grief.

"What else could I do? Fuatino is a love island, and Pilsach is a lover. He knows the native, too—one of the best traders I've got, or ever had. He's responsible. You'll see him to-morrow."

"Look here, young man," Captain Glass rumbled threateningly at his mate. "Are you romantic? Because if you are, on board you stay. Fuatino's the island of romantic insanity. Everybody's in love with somebody. They live on love. It's in the milk of the cocoanuts, or the air, or the sea. The history of the island for the last ten thousand years is nothing but love-affairs. I know. I've talked with the old men. And if I catch you starting down the beach hand in hand——"

His sudden cessation caused both the other men to look at him. They followed his gaze, which passed across them to the main rigging, and saw what he saw, a brown hand and arm, muscular and wet, being joined from overside by a second brown hand and arm. A head followed, thatched with long elfin locks, and then a face, with roguish black eyes, lined with the marks of wild-wood's laughter.

"My God!" Brown breathed. "It's a faun—a sea-faun."

"It's the Goat Man," said Glass.

"It is Mauriri," said Grief. "He is my own blood brother by sacred plight of native custom. His name is mine, and mine is his."

Broad brown shoulders and a magnificent chest rose above the rail, and, with what seemed effortless ease, the whole grand body followed over the rail and noiselessly trod the deck. Brown, who might have been other things than the mate of an island schooner, was enchanted. All that he had ever gleaned from the books proclaimed indubitably the faun-likeness of this visitant of the deep. "But a sad faun," was the young man's judgment, as the golden-brown woods god strode forward to where David Grief sat up with outstretched hand.

"David," said David Grief.

"Mauriri, Big Brother," said Mauriri.

And thereafter, in the custom of men who have pledged blood brotherhood, each called the other, not by the other's name, but by his own. Also, they talked in the Polynesian tongue of Fuatino, and Brown could only sit and guess.

"A long swim to say *talofa*," Grief said, as the other sat and streamed water on the deck.

"Many days and nights have I watched for your coming, Big Brother," Mauriri replied. "I have sat on the Big Rock, where the dynamite is kept, of which I have been made keeper. I saw you come up to the entrance and run back into darkness. I knew you waited till morning, and I followed. Great trouble has come upon us. Mataara has cried these many days for your coming. She is an old woman, and Motuaro is dead, and she is sad."

"Did he marry Naumoo?" Grief asked, after he had shaken his head and sighed by the custom.

"Yes. In the end they ran to live with the goats, till Mataara forgave, when they returned to live with her in the Big House. But he is now dead, and Naumoo soon will die. Great is our trouble, Big Brother. Tori is dead, and Tati-Tori, and Petoo, and Nari, and Pilsach, and others."

"Pilsach, too!" Grief exclaimed. "Has there been a sickness?"

"There has been much killing. Listen, Big Brother. Three weeks ago a strange schooner came. From the Big Rock I saw her topsails above the sea. She towed in with her boats, but they did not warp by the big patch, and she pounded many times. She is now on the beach, where they are strengthening the broken timbers. There are eight white men on board. They have women from some island far to the east. The women talk a language in many ways like ours, only different. But we can understand. They say they were stolen by the men on the schooner. We do not know, but they sing and dance and are happy."

"And the men?" Grief interrupted.

"They talk French. I know, for there was a mate on your schooner who talked French long ago. There are two chief men, and they do not look like the others. They have blue eyes like you, and they are devils. One is a bigger devil than the other. The other six are also devils. They do not pay us for our yams, and taro, and bread-fruit. They take everything from us, and if we complain they kill us. Thus was killed Tori, and Tati-Tori, and Petoo, and others. We cannot fight, for we have no guns—only two or three old guns.

"They ill-treat our women. Thus was killed Motuaro, who made defence of Naumoo, whom they have now taken on board their schooner. It was because of this that Pilsach was killed. Him the chief of the two chief men, the Big Devil, shot once in his whaleboat, and twice when he tried to crawl up the sand of the beach. Pilsach was a brave man, and Notutu now sits in the house and cries without end. Many of the people are afraid, and have run to live with the goats. But there is not food for all in the high mountains. And the men will not go out and fish, and they work no more in the gardens because of the devils who take all they have. And we are ready to fight.

"Big Brother, we need guns, and much ammunition. I sent word before I swam out to you, and the men are waiting. The strange white men do not know you are come. Give me a boat, and the guns, and I will go back before the sun. And when you come to-morrow we will be ready for the word from you to kill the strange white men. They must be killed. Big Brother, you have ever been of the blood with us, and the men and women have prayed to many gods for your coming. And you are come."

"I will go in the boat with you," Grief said.

"No, Big Brother," was Mauriri's reply. "You must be with the schooner. The strange white men will fear the schooner, not us. We will have the guns, and they will not know. It is only when they see your schooner come that they will be alarmed. Send the young man there with the boat."

So it was that Brown, thrilling with all the romance and adventure he had read and guessed and never lived, took his place in the stern-sheets of a whaleboat, loaded with rifles and cartridges, rowed by four Raiatea sailors, steered by a golden-brown, sea-swimming faun, and directed through the warm tropic darkness toward the half-mythical love island of Fuatino, which had been invaded by twentieth-century pirates.

II

If a line be drawn between Jaluit, in the Marshall Group, and Bougainville in the Solomons, and if this line be bisected at two degrees south of the equator by a line drawn from Ukuor, in the Carolines, the high island of Fuatina will be raised in that sun-washed stretch of lonely sea. Inhabited by a stock kindred to the Hawaiian, the Samoan, the Tahitian, and the Maori, Fuatino becomes the apex of the wedge driven by Polynesia far to the west and in between Melanesia and Micronesia. And it was Fuatino that David Grief raised next morning, two miles to the east and in direct line with the rising sun. The same whisper of a breeze held, and the *Rattler* slid through the smooth sea at a rate that would have been eminently proper for an island schooner had the breeze been thrice as strong.

Fuatino was nothing else than an ancient crater, thrust upward from the sea-bottom by some primordial cataclysm. The western portion, broken and crumbled to sea level, was the entrance to the crater itself, which constituted the harbour. Thus, Fuatino was like a rugged horseshoe, the heel pointing to the west. And into the opening at the heel the *Rattler* steered. Captain Glass, binoculars in hand and peering at the chart made by himself, which was spread on top the cabin, straightened up with an expression on his face that was half alarm, half resignation.

"It's coming," he said. "Fever. It wasn't due till to-morrow. It always hits me hard, Mr. Grief. In five minutes I'll be off my head. You'll have to con the schooner in. Boy! Get my bunk ready! Plenty of blankets! Fill that hot-water bottle! It's so calm, Mr. Grief, that I think you can pass the big patch without warping. Take the leading wind and shoot her. She's the only craft in the South Pacific that can do it, and I know you know the trick. You can scrape the Big Rock by just watching out for the main boom."

He had talked rapidly, almost like a drunken man, as his reeling brain battled with the rising shock of the malarial stroke. When he stumbled toward the companionway, his face was purpling and mottling as if attacked by some monstrous inflammation or decay. His eyes were setting in a glassy bulge, his hands shaking, his teeth clicking in the spasms of chill.

"Two hours to get the sweat," he chattered with a ghastly grin. "And a couple more and I'll be all right. I know the damned thing to the last minute it runs its course. Y-y-you t-t-take ch-ch-ch-ch———"

His voice faded away in a weak stutter as he collapsed down into the cabin and his employer took charge. The *Rattler* was just entering the passage. The heels of the horseshoe island were two huge mountains of rock a thousand feet high, each almost broken off from the mainland and connected with it by a low and narrow peninsula. Between the heels was a half-mile stretch, all but blocked by a reef of coral extending across from the south heel. The passage, which Captain Glass had called a crevice, twisted into this reef, curved directly to the north heel, and ran along the base of the perpendicular rock. At this point, with the main-boom almost grazing the rock on the port side, Grief, peering down on the starboard side, could see bottom less than two fathoms beneath and shoaling steeply. With a whaleboat towing for steerage and as a precaution against back-draughts from the cliff, and taking advantage of a fan of breeze, he shook the *Rattler* full into it and glided by the big coral patch without warping. As it was, he just scraped, but so softly as not to start the copper.

The harbour of Fuatino opened before him. It was a circular sheet of water, five miles in diameter, rimmed with white coral beaches, from which the verdure-clad slopes rose swiftly to the frowning crater walls. The crests of the walls were saw-toothed, volcanic peaks, capped and halo'd with captive trade-wind clouds. Every nook and crevice of the disintegrating lava gave foothold to creeping, climbing vines and trees—a green foam of vegetation. Thin streams of water, that were mere films of mist, swayed and undulated downward in sheer descents of hundreds of feet. And to complete the magic of the place, the warm, moist air was heavy with the perfume of the yellow-blossomed *cassi*.

Fanning along against light, vagrant airs, the *Rattler* worked in. Calling the whaleboat on board, Grief searched out the shore with his binoculars. There was no life. In the hot blaze of tropic sun the place slept. There was no sign of welcome. Up the beach, on the north shore, where the fringe of cocoanut palms concealed the village, he could see the black bows of the canoes in the canoe-houses. On the beach, on even keel, rested the strange schooner. Nothing moved on board of her or around her. Not until the beach lay fifty yards away did Grief let go the anchor in forty fathoms. Out in the middle, long years before, he had sounded three hundred fathoms without reaching bottom, which was to be expected of a healthy crater-pit like Fuatino. As the chain roared and surged through the hawse-pipe he noticed a number of native women, lusciously large as only those of Polynesia are, in flowing *ahus*, flower-crowned, stream out on the deck of the schooner on the beach. Also, and what they did not see, he saw from the galley the squat figure of a man steal for'ard, drop to the sand, and dive into the green screen of bush.

While the sails were furled and gasketed, awnings stretched, and sheets and tackles coiled harbour fashion, David Grief paced the deck and looked vainly for a flutter of life elsewhere than on the strange schooner. Once, beyond any doubt, he heard the distant crack of a rifle in the direction of the Big Rock. There were no further shots, and he thought of it as some hunter shooting a wild goat.

At the end of another hour Captain Glass, under a mountain of blankets, had ceased shivering and was in the inferno of a profound sweat.

"I'll be all right in half an hour," he said weakly.

"Very well," Grief answered. "The place is dead, and I'm going ashore to see Mataara and find out the situation."

"It's a tough bunch; keep your eyes open," the captain warned him. "If you're not back in an hour, send word off."

Grief took the steering-sweep, and four of his Raiatea men bent to the oars. As they landed on the beach he looked curiously at the women under the schooner's awning. He waved his hand tentatively, and they, after giggling, waved back.

"*Talofa!*" he called.

They understood the greeting, but replied "*Iorana,*" and he knew they came from the Society Group.

"Huahine," one of his sailors unhesitatingly named their island. Grief asked them whence they came, and with giggles and laughter they replied "Huahine."

"It looks like old Dupuy's schooner," Grief said, in Tahitian, speaking in a low voice. "Don't look too hard. What do you think, eh? Isn't it the *Valetta?*"

As the men climbed out and lifted the whaleboat slightly up the beach they stole careless glances at the vessel.

"It is the *Valetta,*" Taute said. "She carried her topmast away seven years ago. At Papeete they rigged a new one. It was ten feet shorter. That is the one."

"Go over and talk with the women, you boys. You can almost see Huahine from Raiatea, and you'll be sure to know some of them. Find out all you can. And if any of the white men show up, don't start a row."

An army of hermit crabs scuttled and rustled away before him as he advanced up the beach, but under the palms no pigs rooted and grunted. The cocoanuts lay where they had fallen, and at the copra-sheds there were no signs of curing. Industry and tidiness had vanished. Grass house after grass house he found deserted. Once he came upon an old man, blind, toothless, prodigiously wrinkled, who sat in the shade and babbled with fear when he spoke to him. It was as if the place had been struck with the plague, was Grief's thought, as he finally approached the Big House. All was desolation and disarray. There were no flower-crowned men and maidens, no brown babies rolling in the shade of the avocado trees. In the doorway, crouched and rocking back and forth, sat Mataara, the old Queen. She wept afresh at sight of him, divided between the tale of her woe and regret that no follower was left to dispense to him her hospitality.

"And so they have taken Naumoo," she finished. "Motuaro is dead. My people have fled and are starving with the goats. And there is no one to open for you even a drinking cocoanut. O Brother, your white brothers be devils."

"They are no brothers of mine, Mataara," Grief consoled. "They are robbers and pigs, and I shall clean the island of them——"

He broke off to whirl half around, his hand flashing to his waist and back again, the big Colt's levelled at the figure of a man, bent double, that rushed at him from out of the trees. He did not pull the trigger, nor did the man pause till he had flung himself headlong at Grief's feet and begun to pour forth a stream of uncouth and awful noises. He recognized the creature as the one he had seen steal from the *Valetta* and dive into the bush; but not until he raised him up and watched the contortions of the hare-lipped mouth could he understand what he uttered.

"Save me, master, save me!" the man yammered, in English, though he was unmistakably a South Sea native. "I know you! Save me!"

And thereat he broke into a wild outpour of incoherence that did not cease until Grief seized him by the shoulders and shook him into silence.

"I know you," Grief said. "You were cook in the French hotel at Papeete two years ago. Everybody called you 'Hare-Lip.'"

The man nodded violently.

"I am now cook of the *Valetta*," he spat and spluttered, his mouth writhing in a fearful struggle with its defect. "I know you. I saw you at the hotel. I saw you at Lavina's. I saw you on the *Kittiwake*. I saw you at the *Mariposa* wharf. You are Captain Grief, and you will save me. Those men are devils. They killed Captain Dupuy. Me they made kill half the crew. Two they shot from the cross-trees. The rest they shot in the water. I knew them all. They stole the girls from Huahine. They added to their strength with jail-men from Noumea. They robbed the traders in the New Hebrides. They killed the trader at Vanikori, and stole two women there. They——"

But Grief no longer heard. Through the trees, from the direction of the harbour, came a rattle of rifles, and he started on the run for the beach. Pirates from Tahiti and convicts from New Caledonia! A pretty bunch of desperadoes that even now was attacking his schooner. Hare-Lip followed, still spluttering and spitting his tale of the white devils' doings.

The rifle-firing ceased as abruptly as it had begun, but Grief ran on, perplexed by ominous conjectures, until, in a turn of the path, he encountered Mauriri running toward him from the beach.

"Big Brother," the Goat Man panted, "I was too late. They have taken your schooner. Come! For now they will seek for you."

He started back up the path away from the beach.

"Where is Brown?" Grief demanded.

"On the Big Rock. I will tell you afterward. Come now!"

"But my men in the whaleboat?"

Mauriri was in an agony of apprehension.

"They are with the women on the strange schooner. They will not be killed. I tell you true. The devils want sailors. But you they will kill. Listen!" From the water, in a cracked tenor voice, came a French hunting song. "They are landing on the beach. They have taken your schooner—that I saw. Come!"

III

Careless of his own life and skin, nevertheless David Grief was possessed of no false hardihood. He knew when to fight and when to run, and that this was the time for running he had no doubt. Up the path, past the old men sitting in the shade, past Mataara crouched in the doorway of the Big House, he followed at the heels of Mauriri. At his own heels, dog-like, plodded Hare-Lip. From behind came the cries of the hunters, but the pace Mauriri led them was heartbreaking. The broad path narrowed, swung to the right, and pitched upward. The last grass house was left, and through high thickets of *cassi* and swarms of great golden wasps the way rose steeply until it became a goat-track. Pointing upward to a bare shoulder of volcanic rock, Mauriri indicated the trail across its face.

"Past that we are safe, Big Brother," he said. "The white devils never dare it, for there are rocks we roll down on their heads, and there is no other path. Always do they stop here and shoot when we cross the rock. Come!"

A quarter of an hour later they paused where the trail went naked on the face of the rock.

"Wait, and when you come, come quickly," Mauriri cautioned.

He sprang into the blaze of sunlight, and from below several rifles pumped rapidly. Bullets smacked about him, and puffs of stone-dust flew out, but he won safely across. Grief followed, and so near did one bullet come that the dust of its impact stung his cheek. Nor was Hare-Lip struck, though he essayed the passage more slowly.

For the rest of the day, on the greater heights, they lay in a lava glen where terraced taro and *papaia* grew. And here Grief made his plans and learned the fulness of the situation.

"It was ill luck," Mauriri said. "Of all nights this one night was selected by the white devils to go fishing. It was dark as we came through the passage. They were in boats and canoes. Always do they have their rifles with them. One Raiatea man they shot. Brown was very brave. We tried to get by to the top of the bay, but they headed us off, and we were driven in between the Big Rock and the village. We saved the guns and all the ammunition, but they got the boat. Thus they learned of your coming. Brown is now on this side of the Big Rock with the guns and the ammunition."

"But why didn't he go over the top of the Big Rock and give me warning as I came in from the sea?" Grief criticized.

"They knew not the way. Only the goats and I know the way. And this I forgot, for I crept through the bush to gain the water and swim to you. But the devils were in the bush shooting at Brown and the Raiatea men; and me they hunted till daylight, and through the morning they hunted me there in the low-lying land. Then you came in your schooner, and they watched till you went ashore, and I got away through the bush, but you were already ashore."

"You fired that shot?"

"Yes; to warn you. But they were wise and would not shoot back, and it was my last cartridge."

"Now you, Hare-Lip?" Grief said to the *Valetta's* cook.

His tale was long and painfully detailed. For a year he had been sailing out of Tahiti and through the Paumotus on the *Valetta*. Old Dupuy was owner and captain. On his last cruise he had shipped two strangers in Tahiti as mate and supercargo. Also, another stranger he carried to be his agent on Fanriki. Raoul Van Asveld and Carl Lepsius were the names of the mate and supercargo.

"They are brothers, I know, for I have heard them talk in the dark, on deck, when they thought no one listened," Hare-Lip explained.

The *Valetta* cruised through the Low Islands, picking up shell and pearls at Dupuy's stations. Frans Amundson, the third stranger, relieved Pierre Gollard at Fanriki. Pierre Gollard came on board to go back to Tahiti. The natives of Fanriki said he had a quart of pearls to turn over to Dupuy. The first night out from Fanriki there was shooting in the cabin. Then the bodies of Dupuy and Pierre Gollard were thrown overboard. The Tahitian sailors fled to the forecastle. For two days, with nothing to eat and the *Valetta* hove to, they remained below. Then Raoul Van Asveld put poison in the meal he made Hare-Lip cook and carry for'ard. Half the sailors died.

"He had a rifle pointed at me, master; what could I do?" Hare-Lip whimpered. "Of the rest, two went up the rigging and were shot. Fanriki was ten miles away. The others went overboard to swim. They were shot as they swam. I, only, lived, and the two devils; for me they wanted to cook for them. That day, with the breeze, they went back to Fanriki and took on Frans Amundson, for he was one of them."

Then followed Hare-Lip's nightmare experiences as the schooner wandered on the long reaches to the westward. He was the one living witness and knew they would have killed him had he not been the cook. At Noumea five convicts had joined them. Hare-Lip was never permitted ashore at any of the islands, and Grief was the first outsider to whom he had spoken.

"And now they will kill me," Hare-Lip spluttered, "for they will know I have told you. Yet am I not all a coward, and I will stay with you, master, and die with you."

The Goat Man shook his head and stood up.

"Lie here and rest," he said to Grief. "It will be a long swim tonight. As for this cook-man, I will take him now to the higher places where my brothers live with the goats."

IV

"It is well that you swim as a man should, Big Brother," Mauriri whispered.

From the lava glen they had descended to the head of the bay and taken to the water. They swam softly, without splash, Mauriri in the lead. The black walls of the crater rose about them till it seemed they swam on the bottom of a great bowl. Above was the sky of faintly luminous star-dust. Ahead they could see the light which marked the *Rattler,* and from her deck, softened by distance, came a gospel hymn played on the phonograph intended for Pilsach.

The two swimmers bore to the left, away from the captured schooner. Laughter and song followed on board after the hymn, then the phonograph started again. Grief grinned to himself at the appositeness of it as "Lead, Kindly Light" floated out over the dark water.

"We must take the passage and land on the Big Rock," Mauriri whispered. "The devils are holding the low land. Listen!"

Half a dozen rifle shots, at irregular intervals, attested that Brown still held the Rock and that the pirates had invested the narrow peninsula.

At the end of another hour they swam under the frowning loom of the Big Rock. Mauriri, feeling his way, led the landing in a crevice, up which for a hundred feet they climbed to a narrow ledge.

"Stay here," said Mauriri. "I go to Brown. In the morning I shall return."

"I will go with you, Brother," Grief said.

Mauriri laughed in the darkness.

"Even you, Big Brother, cannot do this thing. I am the Goat Man, and I only, of all Fuatino, can go over the Big Rock in the night. Furthermore, it will be the first time that even I have done it. Put out your hand. You feel it? That is where Pilsach's dynamite is kept. Lie close beside the wall and you may sleep without falling. I go now."

And high above the sounding surf, on a narrow shelf beside a ton of dynamite, David Grief planned his campaign, then rested his cheek on his arm and slept.

In the morning, when Mauriri led him over the summit of the Big Rock, David Grief understood why he could not have done it in the night. Despite the accustomed nerve of a sailor for height and precarious clinging, he marvelled that he was able to do it in the broad light of day. There were places, always under minute direction of Mauriri, that he leaned forward, falling, across hundred-foot-deep crevices, until his outstretched hands struck a grip on the opposing wall and his legs could then be drawn across after. Once, there was a ten-foot leap, above half a thousand feet of yawning emptiness and down a fathom's length to a meagre foothold. And he, despite his cool head, lost it another time on a shelf, a scant twelve inches wide, where all hand-holds seemed to fail him. And Mauriri, seeing him sway, swung his own body far out and over the gulf and passed him, at the same time striking him sharply on the back to brace his reeling brain. Then it was, and for ever after, that he fully knew why Mauriri had been named the Goat Man.

V

The defence of the Big Rock had its good points and its defects. Impregnable to assault, two men could hold it against ten thousand. Also, it guarded the passage to open sea. The two schooners, Raoul Van Asveld, and his cut-throat following were bottled up. Grief, with the ton of dynamite, which he had removed higher up the Rock, was master. This he demonstrated, one morning, when the schooners attempted to put to sea. The *Valetta* led, the whaleboat towing her manned by captured Fuatino men. Grief and the Goat Man peered straight down from a safe rock-shelter, three hundred feet above. Their rifles were beside them, also a glowing fire-stick and a big bundle of dynamite sticks with fuses and detonators attached. As the whaleboat came beneath, Mauriri shook his head.

"They are our brothers. We cannot shoot."

For'ard, on the *Valetta,* were several of Grief's own Raiatea sailors. Aft stood another at the wheel. The pirates were below, or on the other schooner, with the exception of one who stood, rifle in hand, amidships. For protection he held Naumoo, the Queen's daughter, close to him.

"That is the chief devil," Mauriri whispered, "and his eyes are blue like yours. He is a terrible man. See! He holds Naumoo that we may not shoot him."

A light air and a slight tide were making into the passage, and the schooner's progress was slow.

"Do you speak English?" Grief called down.

The man started, half lifted his rifle to the perpendicular, and looked up. There was something quick and catlike in his movements, and in his burned blond face a fighting eagerness. It was the face of a killer.

"Yes," he answered. "What do you want?"

"Turn back, or I'll blow your schooner up," Grief warned. He blew on the fire-stick and whispered, "Tell Naumoo to break away from him and run aft."

From the *Rattler,* close astern, rifles cracked, and bullets spatted against the Rock. Van Asveld laughed defiantly, and Mauriri called down in the native tongue to the woman. When directly beneath, Grief, watching, saw her jerk away from the man. On the instant Grief touched the fire-stick to the match-head in the split end of the short fuse, sprang into view on the face of the Rock, and dropped the dynamite. Van Asveld had managed to catch the girl and was struggling with her. The Goat Man held a rifle on him and waited a chance. The dynamite struck the deck in a compact package, bounded, and rolled into the port scupper. Van Asveld saw it and hesitated, then he and the girl ran aft for their lives. The Goat Man fired, but splintered the corner of the galley. The spattering of bullets from the *Rattler* increased, and the two on the Rock crouched low for shelter and waited. Mauriri tried to see what was happening below, but Grief held him back.

"The fuse was too long," he said. "I'll know better next time."

It was half a minute before the explosion came. What happened afterward, for some little time, they could not tell, for the *Rattler*'s marksmen had got the range and were maintaining a steady fire. Once, fanned by a couple of bullets, Grief risked a peep. The *Valetta,* her port deck and rail torn away, was listing and sinking as she drifted back into the harbour. Climbing on board the *Rattler* were the men and the Huahine women who had been hidden in the *Valetta*'s cabin and who had swum for it under the protecting fire. The Fuatino men who had been towing in the whaleboat had cast off the line, dashed back through the passage, and were rowing wildly for the south shore.

From the shore of the peninsula the discharges of four rifles announced that Brown and his men had worked through the jungle to the beach and were taking a hand. The bullets ceased coming, and Grief and Mauriri joined in with their rifles. But they could do no damage, for the men of the *Rattler* were firing from the shelter of the deckhouses, while the wind and tide carried the schooner farther in. There was no sign of the *Valetta,* which had sunk in the deep water of the crater.

Two things Raoul Van Asveld did that showed his keenness and coolness and that elicited Grief's admiration. Under the *Rattler*'s rifle fire Raoul compelled the fleeing Fuatino men to come in and surrender. And at the same time, dispatching half his cut-throats in the *Rattler*'s boat, he threw them ashore and across the peninsula, preventing Brown from getting away to the main part of the island. And for the rest of the morning the intermittent shooting told to Grief how Brown was being driven to the other side of the Big Rock. The situation was unchanged, with the exception of the loss of the *Valetta.*

VI

The defects of the position on the Big Rock were vital. There was neither food nor water. For several nights, accompanied by one of the Raiatea men, Mauriri swam to the head of the bay for supplies. Then came the night when lights flared on the water and shots were fired. After that the water-side of the Big Rock was invested as well.

"It's a funny situation," Brown remarked, who was getting all the adventure he had been led to believe resided in the South Seas. "We've got hold and can't let go, and Raoul has hold and can't let go. He can't get away, and we're liable to starve to death holding him."

"If the rain came, the rock-basins would fill," said Mauriri. It was their first twenty-four hours without water. "Big Brother, to-night you and I will get water. It is the work of strong men."

That night, with cocoanut calabashes, each of quart capacity and tightly stoppered, he led Grief down to the water from the peninsula side of the Big Rock. They swam out not more than a hundred feet. Beyond, they could hear the occasional click of an oar or the knock of a paddle against a canoe, and sometimes they saw the flare of matches as the men in the guarding boats lighted cigarettes or pipes.

"Wait here," whispered Mauriri, "and hold the calabashes."

Turning over, he swam down. Grief, face downward, watched his phosphorescent track glimmer, and dim, and vanish. A long minute afterward Mauriri broke surface noiselessly at Grief's side.

"Here! Drink!"

The calabash was full, and Grief drank sweet fresh water which had come up from the depths of the salt.

"It flows out from the land," said Mauriri.

"On the bottom?"

"No. The bottom is as far below as the mountains are above. Fifty feet down it flows. Swim down until you feel its coolness."

Several times filling and emptying his lungs in diver fashion, Grief turned over and went down through the water. Salt it was to his lips, and warm to his flesh; but at last, deep down, it perceptibly chilled and tasted brackish. Then, suddenly, his body entered the cold, subterranean stream. He removed the small stopper from the calabash, and, as the sweet water gurgled into it, he saw the phosphorescent glimmer of a big fish, like a sea-ghost, drift sluggishly by.

Thereafter, holding the growing weight of the calabashes, he remained on the surface, while Mauriri took them down, one by one, and filled them.

"There are sharks," Grief said, as they swam back to shore.

"Pooh!" was the answer. "They are fish sharks. We of Fuatino are brothers to the fish sharks."

"But the tiger sharks? I have seen them here."

"When they come, Big Brother, we will have no more water to drink—unless it rains."

VII

A week later Mauriri and a Raiatea man swam back with empty calabashes. The tiger sharks had arrived in the harbour. The next day they thirsted on the Big Rock.

"We must take our chance," said Grief. "To-night I shall go after water with Mautau. To-morrow night, Brother, you will go with Tehaa."

Three quarts only did Grief get, when the tiger sharks appeared and drove them in. There were six of them on the Rock, and a pint a day, in the sweltering heat of the mid-tropics, is not sufficient moisture for a man's body. The next night Mauriri and Tehaa returned with no water. And the day following Brown learned the full connotation of thirst, when the lips crack to bleeding, the mouth is coated with granular slime, and the swollen tongue finds the mouth too small for residence.

Grief swam out in the darkness with Mautau. Turn by turn, they went down through the salt, to the cool sweet stream, drinking their fill while the calabashes were filling. It was Mautau's turn to descend with the last calabash, and Grief, peering down from the surface, saw the glimmer of sea-ghosts and all the phosphorescent display of the struggle. He swam back alone, but without relinquishing the precious burden of full calabashes.

Of food they had little. Nothing grew on the Rock, and its sides, covered with shellfish at sea level where the surf thundered in, were too precipitous for access. Here and there, where crevices permitted, a few rank shellfish and sea urchins were gleaned. Sometimes frigate birds and other sea birds were snared. Once, with a piece of frigate bird, they succeeded in hooking a shark. After that, with jealously guarded shark-meat for bait, they managed on occasion to catch more sharks.

But water remained their direst need. Mauriri prayed to the Goat God for rain. Taute prayed to the Missionary God, and his two fellow islanders, backsliding, invoked the deities of their old heathen days. Grief grinned and considered. But Brown, wild-eyed, with protruding blackened tongue, cursed. Especially he cursed the phonograph that in the cool twilights ground out gospel hymns from the deck of the *Rattler*. One hymn in particular, "Beyond the Smiling and the Weeping," drove him to madness. It seemed a favourite on board the schooner, for it was played most of all. Brown, hungry and thirsty, half out of his head from weakness and suffering, could lie among the rocks with equanimity and listen to the tinkling of ukulélés and guitars, and the hulas and himines of the Huahine women. But when the voices of the Trinity Choir floated over the water he was beside himself. One evening the cracked tenor took up the song with the machine:

> "Beyond the smiling and the weeping,
> I shall be soon.
> Beyond the waking and the sleeping,
> Beyond the sowing and the reaping,
> I shall be soon,
> I shall be soon."

Then it was that Brown rose up. Again and again, blindly, he emptied his rifle at the schooner. Laughter floated up from the men and women, and from the peninsula came a splattering of return bullets; but the cracked tenor sang on, and Brown continued to fire, until the hymn was played out.

It was that night that Grief and Mauriri came back with but one calabash of water. A patch of skin six inches long was missing from Grief's shoulder in token of the scrape of the sandpaper hide of a shark whose dash he had eluded.

VIII

In the early morning of another day, before the sun-blaze had gained its full strength, came an offer of a parley from Raoul Van Asveld.

Brown brought the word in from the outpost among the rocks a hundred yards away. Grief was squatted over a small fire, broiling a strip of shark-flesh. The last twenty-four hours had been lucky. Seaweed and sea urchins had been gathered. Tehaa had caught a shark, and Mauriri had captured a fair-sized octopus at the base of the crevice where the dynamite was stored. Then, too, in the darkness they had made two successful swims for water before the tiger sharks had nosed them out.

"Said he'd like to come in and talk with you," Brown said. "But I know what the brute is after. Wants to see how near starved to death we are."

"Bring him in," Grief said.

"And then we will kill him," the Goat Man cried joyously.

Grief shook his head.

"But he is a killer of men, Big Brother, a beast and a devil," the Goat Man protested.

"He must not be killed, Brother. It is our way not to break our word."

"It is a foolish way."

"Still it is our way," Grief answered gravely, turning the strip of shark meat over on the coals and noting the hungry sniff and look of Tehaa. "Don't do that, Tehaa, when the Big Devil comes. Look as if you and hunger were strangers. Here, cook those sea urchins, you, and you, Big Brother, cook the squid. We will have the Big Devil to feast with us. Spare nothing. Cook all."

And, still broiling meat, Grief arose as Raoul Van Asveld, followed by a large Irish terrier, strode into camp. Raoul did not make the mistake of holding out his hand.

"Hello!" he said. "I've heard of you."

"I wish I'd never heard of you," Grief answered.

"Same here," was the response. "At first, before I knew who it was, I thought I had to deal with an ordinary trading captain. That's why you've got me bottled up."

"And I am ashamed to say that I underrated you," Grief smiled. "I took you for a thieving beachcomber, and not for a really intelligent pirate and murderer. Hence, the loss of my schooner. Honours are even, I fancy, on that score."

Raoul flushed angrily under his sunburn, but he contained himself. His eyes roved over the supply of food and the full water-calabashes, though he concealed the incredulous surprise he felt. His was a tall, slender, well-knit figure, and Grief, studying him, estimated his character from his face. The eyes were keen and strong, but a bit too close together—not pinched, however, but just a trifle near to balance the broad forehead, the strong chin and jaw, and the cheekbones wide apart. Strength! His face was filled with it, and yet Grief sensed in it the intangible something the man lacked.

"We are both strong men," Raoul said, with a bow. "We might have been fighting for empires a hundred years ago."

It was Grief's turn to bow.

"As it is, we are squalidly scrapping over the enforcement of the colonial laws of those empires whose destinies we might possibly have determined a hundred years ago."

"It all comes to dust," Raoul remarked sententiously, sitting down. "Go ahead with your meal. Don't let me interrupt."

"Won't you join us?" was Grief's invitation.

The other looked at him with sharp steadiness, then accepted.

"I'm sticky with sweat," he said. "Can I wash?"

Grief nodded and ordered Mauriri to bring a calabash. Raoul looked into the Goat Man's eyes, but saw nothing save languid uninterest as the precious quart of water was wasted on the ground.

"The dog is thirsty," Raoul said.

Grief nodded, and another calabash was presented to the animal.

Again Raoul searched the eyes of the natives and learned nothing.

"Sorry we have no coffee," Grief apologized. "You'll have to drink plain water. A calabash, Tehaa. Try some of this shark. There is squid to follow, and sea urchins and a seaweed salad. I'm sorry we haven't any frigate bird. The boys were lazy yesterday, and did not try to catch any."

With an appetite that would not have stopped at wire nails dipped in lard, Grief ate perfunctorily, and tossed the scraps to the dog.

"I'm afraid I haven't got down to the primitive diet yet," he sighed, as he sat back. "The tinned goods on the *Rattler*, now I could make a hearty meal off of them, but this muck——" He took a half-pound strip of broiled shark and flung it to the dog. "I suppose I'll come to it if you don't surrender pretty soon."

Raoul laughed unpleasantly.

"I came to offer terms," he said pointedly.

Grief shook his head.

"There aren't any terms. I've got you where the hair is short, and I'm not going to let go."

"You think you can hold me in this hole!" Raoul cried.

"You'll never leave it alive, except in double irons." Grief surveyed his guest with an air of consideration. "I've handled your kind before. We've pretty well cleaned it out of the South Seas. But you are a—how shall I say?—a sort of an anachronism. You're a throwback, and we've got to get rid of you. Personally, I would advise you to go back to the schooner and blow your brains out. It is the only way to escape what you've got coming to you."

The parley, so far as Raoul was concerned, proved fruitless, and he went back into his own lines convinced that the men on the Big Rock could hold out for years, though he would have been swiftly unconvinced could he have observed Tehaa and the Raiateans, the moment his back was turned and he was out of sight, crawling over the rocks and sucking and crunching the scraps his dog had left uneaten.

IX

"We hunger now, Brother," Grief said, "but it is better than to hunger for many days to come. The Big Devil, after feasting and drinking good water with us in plenty, will not stay long in Fuatino. Even tomorrow may he try to leave. To night you and I sleep over the top of the Rock, and Tehaa, who shoots well, will sleep with us if he can dare the Rock."

Tehaa, alone among the Raiateans, was cragsman enough to venture the perilous way, and dawn found him in a rock-barricaded nook, a hundred yards to the right of Grief and Mauriri.

The first warning was the firing of rifles from the peninsula, where Brown and his two Raiateans signalled the retreat and followed the besiegers through the jungle to the beach. From the eyrie on the face of the Rock Grief could see nothing for another hour, when the *Rattler* appeared, making for the passage. As before, the captive Fuatino men towed in the whaleboat. Mauriri, under direction of Grief, called down instructions to them as they passed slowly beneath. By Grief's side lay several bundles of dynamite sticks, well lashed together and with extremely short fuses.

The deck of the *Rattler* was populous. For'ard, rifle in hand, among the Raiatean sailors, stood a desperado whom Mauriri announced was Raoul's brother. Aft, by the helmsman, stood another. Attached to him, tied waist to waist, with slack, was Mataara, the old Queen. On the other side of the helmsman, his arm in a sling, was Captain Glass. Amidships, as before, was Raoul, and with him, lashed waist to waist, was Naumoo.

"Good morning, Mister David Grief," Raoul called up.

"And yet I warned you that only in double irons would you leave the island," Grief murmured down with a sad inflection.

"You can't kill all your people I have on board," was the answer.

The schooner, moving slowly, jerk by jerk, as the men pulled in the whaleboat, was almost directly beneath. The rowers, without ceasing, slacked on their oars, and were immediately threatened with the rifle of the man who stood for'ard.

"Throw, Big Brother!" Naumoo called up in the Fuatino tongue. "I am filled with sorrow and am willed to die. His knife is ready with which to cut the rope, but I shall hold him tight. Be not afraid, Big Brother. Throw, and throw straight, and good-bye."

Grief hesitated, then lowered the fire-stick which he had been blowing bright.

"Throw!" the Goat Man urged.

Still Grief hesitated.

"If they get to sea, Big Brother, Naumoo dies just the same. And there are all the others. What is her life against the many?"

"If you drop any dynamite, or fire a single shot, we'll kill all on board," Raoul cried up to them. "I've got you, David Grief. You can't kill these people, and I can. Shut up, you!"

This last was addressed to Naumoo, who was calling up in her native tongue and whom Raoul seized by the neck with one hand to choke to silence. In turn, she locked both arms about him and looked up beseechingly to Grief.

"Throw it, Mr. Grief, and be damned to them," Captain Glass rumbled in his deep voice. "They're bloody murderers, and the cabin's full of them."

The desperado who was fastened to the old Queen swung half about to menace Captain Glass with his rifle, when Tehaa, from his position farther along the Rock, pulled trigger on him. The rifle dropped from the man's hand, and on his face was an expression of intense surprise as his legs crumpled under him and he sank down on deck, dragging the Queen with him.

"Port! Hard a port!" Grief cried.

Captain Glass and the Kanaka whirled the wheel over, and the bow of the *Rattler* headed in for the Rock. Amidships Raoul still struggled with Naumoo. His brother ran from for'ard to his aid, being missed by the fusillade of quick shots from Tehaa and the Goat Man. As Raoul's brother placed the muzzle of his rifle to Naumoo's side Grief touched the fire-stick to the match-head in the split end of the fuse. Even as with both hands he tossed the big bundle of dynamite, the rifle went off, and Naumoo's fall to the deck was simultaneous with the fall of the dynamite. This time the fuse was short enough. The explosion occurred at the instant the deck was reached, and that portion of the *Rattler*, along with Raoul, his brother, and Naumoo, for ever disappeared.

The schooner's side was shattered, and she began immediately to settle. For'ard, every Raiatean sailor dived overboard. Captain Glass met the first man springing up the companionway from the cabin, with a kick full in the face, but was overborne and trampled on by the rush. Following the desperadoes came the Huahine women, and as they went overboard, the *Rattler* sank on an even keel close to the base of the Rock. Her cross-trees still stuck out when she reached bottom.

Looking down, Grief could see all that occurred beneath the surface. He saw Mataara, a fathom deep, unfasten herself from the dead pirate and swim upward. As her head emerged she saw Captain Glass, who could not swim, sinking several yards away. The Queen, old woman that she was, but an islander, turned over, swam down to him, and held him up as she struck out for the unsubmerged cross-trees.

Five heads, blond and brown, were mingled with the dark heads of

Polynesia that dotted the surface. Grief, rifle in hand, watched for a chance to shoot. The Goat Man, after a minute, was successful, and they saw the body of one man sink sluggishly. But to the Raiatean sailors, big and brawny, half fish, was the vengeance given. Swimming swiftly, they singled out the blond heads and the brown. Those from above watched the four surviving desperadoes, clutched and locked, dragged far down beneath and drowned like curs.

In ten minutes everything was over. The Huahine women, laughing and giggling, were holding on to the sides of the whaleboat which had done the towing. The Raiatean sailors, waiting for orders, were about the cross-tree to which Captain Glass and Mataara clung.

"The poor old *Rattler!*" Captain Glass lamented.

"Nothing of the sort," Grief answered. "In a week we'll have her raised, new timbers amidships, and we'll be on our way." And to the Queen, "How is it with you, Sister?"

"Naumoo is gone, and Motuaro, Brother, but Fuatino is ours again. The day is young. Word shall be sent to all my people in the high places with the goats. And to-night, once again, and as never before, we shall feast and rejoice in the Big House."

"She's been needing new timbers abaft the beam there for years," quoth Captain Glass. "But the chronometers will be out of commission for the rest of the cruise."

THE FEATHERS OF THE SUN

I

It was the island of Fitu-Iva—the last independent Polynesian strong-
hold in the South Seas. Three factors conduced to Fitu-Iva's indepen-
dence. The first and second were its isolation and the warlikeness of its
population. But these would not have saved it in the end had it not
been for the fact that Japan, France, Great Britain, Germany, and the
United States discovered its desirableness simultaneously. It was like
gamins scrambling for a penny. They got in one another's way. The war
vessels of the five Powers cluttered Fitu-Iva's one small harbour. There
were rumours of war and threats of war. Over its morning toast all the
world read columns about Fitu-Iva. As a Yankee bluejacket epitomized
it at the time, they all got their feet in the trough at once.

So it was that Fitu-Iva escaped even a joint protectorate, and King
Tulifau, otherwise Tui Tulifau, continued to dispense the high justice
and the low in the frame-house palace built for him by a Sydney trader
out of California redwood. Not only was Tui Tulifau every inch a
king, but he was every second a king. When he had ruled fifty-eight

years and five months, he was only fifty-eight years and three months old. That is to say, he had ruled over five million seconds more than he had breathed, having been crowned two months before he was born.

He was a kingly king, a royal figure of a man, standing six feet and a half, and, without being excessively fat, weighing three hundred and twenty pounds. But this was not unusual for Polynesian "chief stock." Sepeli, his queen, was six feet three inches, and weighed two hundred and sixty, while her brother, Uiliami, who commanded the army in the intervals of resignation from the premiership, topped her by an inch and notched her an even half-hundred-weight. Tui Tulifau was a merry soul, a great feaster and drinker. So were all his people merry souls, save in anger, when, on occasion, they could be guilty even of throwing dead pigs at those who made them wroth. Nevertheless, on occasion, they could fight like Maoris, as piratical sandalwood traders and Blackbirders in the old days learned to their cost.

II

Grief's schooner, the *Cantani,* had passed the Pillar Rocks at the entrance two hours before and crept up the harbour to the whispering flutters of a breeze that could not make up its mind to blow. It was a cool, starlight evening, and they lolled about the poop waiting till their snail's pace would bring them to the anchorage. Willie Smee, the supercargo, emerged from the cabin, conspicuous in his shore clothes. The mate glanced at his shirt, of the finest and whitest silk, and giggled significantly.

"Dance, to-night, I suppose?" Grief observed.

"No," said the mate. "It's Taitua. Willie's stuck on her."

"Catch me," the supercargo disclaimed.

"Then she's stuck on you, and it's all the same," the mate went on. "You won't be ashore half an hour before you'll have a flower behind your ear, a wreath on your head, and your arm around Taitua."

"Simple jealousy," Willie Smee sniffed. "You'd like to have her yourself, only you can't."

"I can't find shirts like that, that's why. I'll bet you half a crown you won't sail from Fitu-Iva with that shirt."

"And if Taitua doesn't get it, it's an even break Tui Tulifau does," Grief warned. "Better not let him spot that shirt, or it's all day with it."

"That's right," Captain Boig agreed, turning his head from watching the house lights on the shore. "Last voyage he fined one of my Kanakas out of a fancy belt and sheath-knife." He turned to the mate. "You can let go any time, Mr. Mash. Don't give too much slack. There's no sign of wind, and in the morning we may shift opposite the copra-sheds."

A minute later the anchor rumbled down. The whaleboat, already hoisted out, lay alongside, and the shore-going party dropped into it. Save for the Kanakas, who were all bent for shore, only Grief and the supercargo were in the boat. At the head of the little coral-stone pier Willie Smee, with an apologetic gurgle, separated from his employer and disappeared down an avenue of palms. Grief turned in the opposite direction past the front of the old mission church. Here, among the graves on the beach, lightly clad in *ahus* and *lava-lavas*, flower-crowned and garlanded, with great phosphorescent hibiscus blossoms in their hair, youths and maidens were dancing. Farther on, Grief passed the long, grass-built *himine* house, where a few score of the elders sat in long rows chanting the old hymns taught them by forgotten missionaries. He passed also the palace of Tui Tulifau, where, by the lights and sounds, he knew the customary revelry was going on. For of the happy South Sea isles, Fitu Iva was the happiest. They feasted and frolicked at births and deaths, and the dead and the unborn were likewise feasted.

Grief held steadily along the Broom Road which curved and twisted through a lush growth of flowers and fern-like algarobas. The warm air was rich with perfume, and overhead, outlined against the stars, were fruit-burdened mangoes, stately avocado trees, and slender tufted palms. Every here and there were grass houses. Voices and laughter rippled through the darkness. Out on the water flickering lights and soft-voiced choruses marked the fishers returning from the reef.

At last Grief stepped aside from the road, stumbling over a pig that grunted indignantly. Looking through an open door, he saw a stout and elderly native sitting on a heap of mats a dozen deep. From time to time, automatically, he brushed his naked legs with a cocoanut-fibre fly-flicker. He wore glasses, and was reading methodically in what Grief knew to be an English Bible. For this was Ieremia, his trader, so named from the prophet Jeremiah.

Ieremia was lighter-skinned than the Fitu-Ivans, as was natural in a full-blooded Samoan. Educated by the missionaries, as lay teacher he had served their cause well over in the cannibal atolls to the westward. As a reward, he had been sent to the paradise of Fitu-Iva, where all were or had been good converts, to gather in the backsliders. Unfortunately, Ieremia had become too well educated. A stray volume of Darwin, a nagging wife, and a pretty Fitu-Ivan widow had driven him into the ranks of the backsliders. It was not a case of apostasy. The effect of Darwin had been one of intellectual fatigue. What was the use of trying to understand this vastly complicated and enigmatical world, especially when one was married to a nagging woman? As Ieremia slackened in his labours, the mission board threatened louder and louder to send him back to the atolls, while his wife's tongue grew correspondingly sharper. Tui Tulifau was a sympathetic monarch, whose queen, on occasions when he was particularly drunk, was known to beat him. For political reasons—the queen belonging to as royal stock as himself, and her brother commanding the army—Tui Tulifau could not divorce her, but he could and did divorce Ieremia, who promptly took up with commercial life and the lady of his choice. As an independent trader he had failed, chiefly because of the disastrous patronage of Tui Tulifau. To refuse credit to that merry monarch was to invite confiscation; to grant him credit was certain bankruptcy. After a year's idleness on the beach, Ieremia had become David Grief's trader, and for a dozen years his service had been honourable and efficient, for Grief had proven the first man who successfully refused credit to the king or who collected when it had been accorded.

Ieremia looked gravely over the rims of his glasses when his employer entered, gravely marked the place in the Bible and set it aside, and gravely shook hands.

"I am glad you came in person," he said.

"How else could I come?" Grief laughed.

But Ieremia had no sense of humour, and he ignored the remark.

"The commercial situation on the island is damn bad," he said with great solemnity and an unctuous mouthing of the many-syllabled words. "My ledger account is shocking."

"Trade bad?"

"On the contrary. It has been excellent. The shelves are empty, exceedingly empty. But——" His eyes glistened proudly. "But there are many goods remaining in the storehouse; I have kept it carefully locked."

"Been allowing Tui Tulifau too much credit?"

"On the contrary. There has been no credit at all. And every old account has been settled up."

"I don't follow you, Ieremia," Grief confessed. "What's the joke?—shelves empty, no credit, old accounts all square, storehouse carefully locked—what's the answer?"

Ieremia did not reply immediately. Reaching under the rear corner of the mats, he drew forth a large cash-box. Grief noted and wondered that it was not locked. The Samoan had always been fastidiously cautious in guarding cash. The box seemed filled with paper money. He skinned off the top note and passed it over.

"There is an answer."

Grief glanced at a fairly well executed banknote. "*The First Royal Bank of Fitu-Iva will pay to bearer on demand one pound sterling,*" he read. In the centre was the smudged likeness of a native face. At the bottom was the signature of Tui Tulifau, and the signature of Fulualea, with the printed information appended, "*Chancellor of the Exchequer.*"

"Who the deuce is Fulualea?" Grief demanded. "It's Fijian, isn't it?—meaning the feathers of the sun?"

"Just so. It means the feathers of the sun. Thus does this base interloper caption himself. He has come up from Fiji to turn Fitu-Iva upside down—that is, commercially."

"Some one of those smart Levuka boys, I suppose?"

Ieremia shook his head sadly. "No, this low fellow is a white man and a scoundrel. He has taken a noble and high-sounding Fijian name and dragged it in the dirt to suit his nefarious purposes. He has made Tui Tulifau drunk. He has made him very drunk. He has kept him very drunk all the time. In return, he has been made Chancellor of the Exchequer and other things. He has issued this false paper and compelled the people to receive it. He has levied a store tax, a copra tax, and a tobacco tax. There are harbour dues and regulations, and other taxes. But the people are not taxed—only the traders. When the copra tax was levied, I lowered the purchasing price accordingly. Then the people began to grumble, and Feathers of the Sun passed a new law, setting the old price back and forbidding any man to lower it. Me he fined two pounds and five pigs, it being well known that I possessed five pigs. You will find them entered in the ledger. Hawkins, who is trader for the Fulcrum Company, was fined first pigs, then gin, and, because he continued to make loud conversation, the army came and burned his store. When I declined to sell, this Feathers of the Sun fined me once more and promised to burn the store if again I offended. So I sold all that was on the shelves, and there is the box full of worthless paper. I shall be chagrined if you pay me my salary in paper, but it would be just, no more than just. Now, what is to be done?"

Grief shrugged his shoulders. "I must first see this Feathers of the Sun and size up the situation."

"Then you must see him soon," Ieremia advised. "Else he will have an accumulation of many fines against you. Thus does he absorb all the coin of the realm. He has it all now, save what has been buried in the ground."

III

On his way back along the Broom Road, under the lighted lamps that marked the entrance to the palace grounds, Grief encountered a short, rotund gentleman, in unstarched ducks, smooth-shaven and of florid complexion, who was just emerging. Something about his tentative, saturated gait was familiar. Grief knew it on the instant. On the beaches of a dozen South Sea ports had he seen it before.

"Of all men, Cornelius Deasy!" he cried.

"If it ain't Grief himself, the old devil," was the return greeting, as they shook hands.

"If you'll come on board I've some choice smoky Irish," Grief invited.

Cornelius threw back his shoulders and stiffened.

"Nothing doin', Mr. Grief. 'Tis Fulualea I am now. No blarneyin' of old times for me. Also, and by the leave of his gracious Majesty King Tulifau, 'tis Chancellor of the Exchequer I am, an' Chief Justice I am, save in moments of royal sport when the king himself chooses to toy with the wheels of justice."

Grief whistled in amazement. "So you're Feathers of the Sun!"

"I prefer the native idiom," was the correction. "Fulualea, an' it please you. Not forgettin' old times, Mr. Grief, it sorrows the heart of me to break you the news. You'll have to pay your legitimate import duties same as any other trader with mind intent on robbin' the gentle Polynesian savage on coral isles implanted—— Where was I? Ah! I remember. You've violated the regulations. With malice intent have you entered the port of Fitu-Iva after sunset without sidelights burnin'. Don't interrupt. With my own eyes did I see you. For which offence are you fined the sum of five pounds. Have you any gin? 'Tis a serious offence. Not lightly are the lives of the mariners of our commodious port to be risked for the savin' of a penny'orth of oil. Did I ask: have you any gin? 'Tis the harbour-master that asks."

"You've taken a lot on your shoulders," Grief grinned.

" 'Tis the white man's burden. These rapscallion traders have been puttin' it all over poor Tui Tulifau, the best-hearted old monarch that ever sat a South Sea throne an' mopped grog-root from the imperial calabash. 'Tis I, Cornelius—Fulualea, rather—that am here to see justice done. Much as I dislike the doin' of it, as harbour-master 'tis my duty to find you guilty of breach of quarantine."

"Quarantine?"

" 'Tis the rulin' of the port doctor. No intercourse with the shore till the ship is passed. What dire calamity to the confidin' native if chicken pox or whoopin' cough was aboard of you! Who is there to protect the gentle, confidin' Polynesian? I, Fulualea, the Feathers of the Sun, on my high mission."

"Who in hell is the port doctor?" Grief queried.

" 'Tis me, Fulualea. Your offence is serious. Consider yourself fined five cases of first-quality Holland gin."

Grief laughed heartily. "We'll compromise, Cornelius. Come aboard and have a drink."

The Feathers of the Sun waved the proffer aside grandly. " 'Tis bribery. I'll have none of it—me faithful to my salt. And wherefore did you not present your ship's papers? As chief of the custom house you are fined five pounds and two more cases of gin."

"Look here, Cornelius. A joke's a joke, but this one has gone far enough. This is not Levuka. I've half a mind to pull your nose for you. You can't buck me."

The Feathers of the Sun retreated unsteadily and in alarm.

"Lay no violence on me," he threatened. "You're right. This is not Levuka. And by the same token, with Tui Tulifau and the royal army behind me, buck you is just the thing I can and will. You'll pay them fines promptly, or I'll confiscate your vessel. You're not the first. What does that Chink pearl-buyer, Peter Gee, do but slip into harbour, violatin' all regulations an' makin' rough house for the matter of a few paltry fines. No; he wouldn't pay 'em, and he's on the beach now thinkin' it over."

"You don't mean to say——"

"Sure an' I do. In the high exercise of office I seized his schooner. A fifth of the loyal army is now in charge on board of her. She'll be sold this day week. Some ten tons of shell in the hold, and I'm wonderin' if I can trade it to you for gin. I can promise you a rare bargain. How much gin did you say you had?"

"Still more gin, eh?"

"An' why not? 'Tis a royal souse is Tui Tulifau. Sure it keeps my wits workin' overtime to supply him, he's that amazin' liberal with it. The whole gang of hanger-on-chiefs is perpetually loaded to the guards. It's disgraceful. Are you goin' to pay them fines, Mr. Grief, or is it to harsher measures I'll be forced?"

Grief turned impatiently on his heel.

"Cornelius, you're drunk. Think it over and come to your senses. The old rollicking South Sea days are gone. You can't play tricks like that now."

"If you think you're goin' on board, Mr. Grief, I'll save you the trouble. I know your kind. I foresaw your stiff-necked stubbornness. An' it's forestalled you are. 'Tis on the beach you'll find your crew. The vessel's seized."

Grief turned back on him in the half-belief still that he was joking.

Fulualea again retreated in alarm. The form of a large man loomed beside him in the darkness.

"Is it you, Uiliami?" Fulualea crooned. "Here is another sea pirate. Stand by me with the strength of thy arm, O herculean brother."

"Greeting, Uiliami," Grief said. "Since when has Fitu-Iva come to be run by a Levuka beachcomber? He says my schooner has been seized. Is it true?"

"It is true," Uiliami boomed from his deep chest. "Have you any more silk shirts like Willie Smee's? Tui Tulifau would like such a shirt. He has heard of it."

"'Tis all the same," Fulualea interrupted. "Shirts or schooners, the king shall have them."

"Rather high-handed, Cornelius," Grief murmured. "It's rank piracy. You seized my vessel without giving me a chance."

"A chance is it? As we stood here, not five minutes gone, didn't you refuse to pay your fines?"

"But she was already seized."

"Sure, an' why not? Didn't I know you'd refuse? 'Tis all fair, an' no injustice done—Justice, the bright, particular star at whose shining altar Cornelius Deasy—or Fulualea, 'tis the same thing—ever worships. Get thee gone, Mr. Trader, or I'll set the palace guards on you. Uiliami, 'tis a desperate character, this trader man. Call the guards."

Uiliami blew the whistle suspended on his broad bare chest by a cord of cocoanut sennit. Grief reached out an angry hand for Cornelius, who titubated into safety behind Uiliami's massive bulk. A dozen strapping Polynesians, not one under six feet, ran down the palace walk and ranged behind their commander.

"Get thee gone, Mr. Trader," Cornelius ordered. "The interview is terminated. We'll try your several cases in the mornin'. Appear promptly at the palace at ten o'clock to answer to the followin' charges, to wit: breach of the peace; seditious and treasonable utterance; violent assault on the chief magistrate with intent to cut, wound, maim, an' bruise; breach of quarantine; violation of harbour regulations; and gross breakage of custom house rules. In the mornin', fellow, in the mornin', justice shall be done while the bread-fruit falls. And the Lord have mercy on your soul."

IV

Before the hour set for the trial Grief, accompanied by Peter Gee, won access to Tui Tulifau. The king, surrounded by half a dozen chiefs, lay on mats under the shade of the avocados in the palace compound. Early as was the hour, palace maids were industriously serving squarefaces of gin. The king was glad to see his old friend Davida, and regretful that he had run foul of the new regulations. Beyond that he steadfastly avoided discussion of the matter in hand. All protests of the expropriated traders were washed away in proffers of gin. "Have a drink," was his invariable reply, though once he unbosomed himself enough to say that Feathers of the Sun was a wonderful man. Never had palace affairs been so prosperous. Never had there been so much money in the treasury, nor so much gin in circulation. "Well pleased am I with Fulualea," he concluded. "Have a drink."

"We've got to get out of this *pronto*," Grief whispered to Peter Gee a few minutes later, "or we'll be a pair of boiled owls. Also, I am to be tried for arson, or heresy, or leprosy, or something, in a few minutes, and I must control my wits."

As they withdrew from the royal presence, Grief caught a glimpse of Sepeli, the queen. She was peering out at her royal spouse and his fellow tipplers, and the frown on her face gave Grief his cue. Whatever was to be accomplished must be through her.

In another shady corner of the big compound Cornelius was holding court. He had been at it early, for when Grief arrived the case of Willie Smee was being settled. The entire royal army, save that portion in charge of the seized vessels, was in attendance.

"Let the defendant stand up," said Cornelius, "and receive the just and merciful sentence of the Court for licentious and disgraceful conduct unbecomin' a supercargo. The defendant says he has no money. Very well. The Court regrets it has no calaboose. In lieu thereof, and in view of the impoverished condition of the defendant, the Court fines said defendant one white silk shirt of the same kind, make and quality at present worn by defendant."

Cornelius nodded to several of the soldiers, who led the supercargo away behind an avocado tree. A minute later he emerged, minus the garment in question, and sat down beside Grief.

"What have you been up to?" Grief asked.

"Blessed if I know. What crimes have you committed?"

"Next case," said Cornelius in his most extra-legal tones. "David Grief, defendant, stand up. The Court has considered the evidence in the case, or cases, and renders the following judgment, to wit:—Shut up!" he thundered at Grief, who had attempted to interrupt. "I tell you the evidence has been considered, deeply considered. It is no wish of the Court to lay additional hardship on the defendant, and the Court takes this opportunity to warn the defendant that he is liable for contempt. For open and wanton violation of harbour rules and regulations, breach of quarantine, and disregard of shipping laws, his schooner, the *Cantani,* is hereby declared confiscated to the Government of Fitu-Iva, to be sold at public auction, ten days from date, with all appurtenances, fittings, and cargo thereunto pertaining. For the personal crimes of the defendant, consisting of violent and turbulent conduct and notorious disregard of the laws of the realm, he is fined in the sum of one hundred pounds sterling and fifteen cases of gin. I will not ask you if you have anything to say. But will you pay? That is the question."

Grief shook his head.

"In the meantime," Cornelius went on, "consider yourself a prisoner at large. There is no calaboose in which to confine you. And finally, it has come to the knowledge of the Court, that at an early hour of this morning, the defendant did wilfully and deliberately send Kanakas in his employ out on the reef to catch fish for breakfast. This is distinctly an infringement of the rights of the fisherfolk of Fitu-Iva. Home industries must be protected. This conduct of the defendant is severely reprehended by the Court, and on any repetition of the offence the offender and offenders, all and sundry, shall be immediately put to hard labour on the improvement of the Broom Road. The Court is dismissed."

As they left the compound, Peter Gee nudged Grief to look where Tui Tulifau reclined on the mats. The supercargo's shirt, stretched and bulged, already encased the royal fat.

V

"The thing is clear," said Peter Gee, at a conference in Ieremia's house. "Deasy has about gathered in all the coin. In the meantime he keeps the king going on the gin he's captured on our vessels. As soon as he can manoeuvre it he'll take the cash and skin out on your craft or mine."

"He is a low fellow," Ieremia declared, pausing in the polishing of his spectacles. "He is a scoundrel and a blackguard. He should be struck by a dead pig, by a particularly dead pig."

"The very thing," said Grief. "He shall be struck by a dead pig. Ieremia, I should not be surprised if you were the man to strike him with a dead pig. Be sure and select a particularly dead one. Tui Tulifau is down at the boat-house broaching a case of my Scotch. I'm going up to the palace to work kitchen politics with the queen. In the meantime you get a few things on your shelves from the storeroom. I'll lend you some, Hawkins. And you, Peter, see the German store. Start in all of you, selling for paper. Remember, I'll back the losses. If I'm not mistaken, in three days we'll have a national council or a revolution. You, Ieremia, start messengers around the island to the fishers and farmers, everywhere, even to the mountain goat-hunters. Tell them to assemble at the palace three days from now."

"But the soldiers," Ieremia objected.

"I'll take care of them. They haven't been paid for two months. Besides, Uiliami is the queen's brother. Don't have too much on your shelves at a time. As soon as the soldiers show up with paper, stop selling."

"Then will they burn the stores," said Ieremia.

"Let them. King Tulifau will pay for it if they do."

"Will he pay for my shirt?" Willie Smee demanded.

"That is purely a personal and private matter between you and Tui Tulifau," Grief answered.

"It's beginning to split up the back," the supercargo lamented. "I noticed that much this morning when he hadn't had it on ten minutes. It cost me thirty shillings and I only wore it once."

"Where shall I get a dead pig?" Ieremia asked.

"Kill one, of course," said Grief. "Kill a small one."

"A small one is worth ten shillings."

"Then enter it in your ledger under operating expenses." Grief paused a moment. "If you want it particularly dead, it would be well to kill it at once."

VI

"You have spoken well, Davida," said Queen Sepeli. "This Fulualea has brought a madness with him, and Tui Tulifau is drowned in gin. If he does not grant the big council, I shall give him a beating. He is easy to beat when he is in drink."

She doubled up her fist, and such were her Amazonian proportions and the determination in her face that Grief knew the council would be called. So akin was the Fitu-Ivan tongue to the Samoan that he spoke it like a native.

"And you, Uiliami," he said, "have pointed out that the soldiers have demanded coin and refused the paper Fulualea has offered them. Tell them to take the paper and see that they be paid to-morrow."

"Why trouble?" Uiliami objected. "The king remains happily drunk. There is much money in the treasury. And I am content. In my house are two cases of gin and much goods from Hawkins's store."

"Excellent pig, O my brother!" Sepeli erupted. "Has not Davida spoken? Have you no ears? When the gin and the goods in your house are gone, and no more traders come with gin and goods, and Feathers of the Sun has run away to Levuka with all the cash money of Fitu-Iva, what then will you do? Cash money is silver and gold, but paper is only paper. I tell you the people are grumbling. There is no fish in the palace. Yams and sweet potatoes seem to have fled from the soil, for they come not. The mountain dwellers have sent no wild goat in a week. Though Feathers of the Sun compels the traders to buy copra at the old price, the people sell not, for they will have none of the paper money. Only to-day have I sent messengers to twenty houses. There are no eggs. Has Feathers of the Sun put a blight upon the hens? I do not know. All I know is that there are no eggs. Well it is that those who drink much eat little, else would there be a palace famine. Tell your soldiers to receive their pay. Let it be in his paper money."

"And remember," Grief warned, "though there be selling in the stores, when the soldiers come with their paper it will be refused. And in three days will be the council, and Feathers of the Sun will be as dead as a dead pig."

VII

The day of the council found the population of the island crowded into the capital. By canoe and whaleboat, on foot and donkey-back, the five thousand inhabitants of Fitu-Iva had trooped in. The three intervening days had had their share of excitement. At first there had been much selling from the sparse shelves of the traders. But when the soldiers appeared, their patronage was declined, and they were told to go to Fulualea for coin. "Says it not so on the face of the paper," the traders demanded, "that for the asking the coin will be given in exchange?"

Only the strong authority of Uiliami had prevented the burning of the traders' houses. As it was, one of Grief's copra-sheds went up in smoke and was duly charged by Ieremia to the king's account. Ieremia himself had been abused and mocked, and his spectacles broken. The skin was off Willie Smee's knuckles. This had been caused by three boisterous soldiers who violently struck their jaws thereon in quick succession. Captain Boig was similarly injured. Peter Gee had come off undamaged, because it chanced that it was bread-baskets and not jaws that struck him on the fists.

Tui Tulifau, with Sepeli at his side and surrounded by his convival chiefs, sat at the head of the council in the big compound. His right eye and jaw were swollen as if he too had engaged in assaulting somebody's fist. It was palace gossip that morning that Sepeli had administered a conjugal beating. At any rate, her spouse was sober, and his fat bulged spiritlessly through the rips in Willie Smee's silk shirt. His thirst was prodigious and he was continually served with young drinking nuts. Outside the compound, held back by the army, was the mass of the common people. Only the lesser chiefs, village maids, village beaux, and talking men with their staffs of office were permitted inside. Cornelius Deasy, as befitted a high and favoured official, sat near to the right hand of the king. On the left of the queen, opposite Cornelius and surrounded by the white traders he was to represent, sat Ieremia. Bereft of his spectacles, he peered short-sightedly across at the Chancellor of the Exchequer.

In turn, the talking man of the windward coast, the talking man of the leeward coast, and the talking man of the mountain villages, each backed by his group of lesser talking men and chiefs, arose and made oration. What they said was much the same. They grumbled about the paper money. Affairs were not prosperous. No more copra was being smoked. The people were suspicious. To such a pass had things come that all people wanted to pay their debts and no one wanted to be paid. Creditors made a practice of running away from debtors. The money was cheap. Prices were going up and commodities were getting scarce. It cost three times the ordinary price to buy a fowl, and then it was tough and like to die of old age if not immediately sold. The outlook was gloomy. There were signs and omens. There was a plague of rats in some districts. The crops were bad. The custard apples were small. The best-bearing avocado on the windward coast had mysteriously shed all its leaves. The taste had gone from the mangoes. The plantains were eaten by a worm. The fish had forsaken the ocean and vast numbers of tiger-sharks appeared. The wild goats had fled to inaccessible summits. The poi in the poi-pits had turned bitter. There were rumblings in the mountains, night-walking of spirits; a woman of Punta-Puna had been struck speechless, and a five-legged she-goat had been born in the village of Eiho. And that all was due to the strange money of Fulualea was the firm conviction of the elders in the village councils assembled.

Uiliami spoke for the army. His men were discontented and mutinous. Though by royal decree the traders were bidden accept the money, yet did they refuse it. He would not say, but it looked as if the strange money of Fulualea had something to do with it.

Ieremia, as talking man of the traders, next spoke. When he arose, it was noticeable that he stood with legs spraddled over a large grass basket. He dwelt upon the cloth of the traders, its variety and beauty and durability, which so exceeded the Fitu-Iva wet-pounded tapa, fragile and coarse. No one wore tapa any more. Yet all had worn tapa, and nothing but tapa, before the traders came. There was the mosquito-netting, sold for a song, that the cleverest Fitu-Ivan net-weaver could not duplicate in a thousand years. He enlarged on the incomparable virtues of rifles, axes, and steel fish-hooks, down through needles, thread and cotton fish-lines to white flour and kerosene oil.

He expounded at length, with firstlies and secondlies and all minor subdivisions of argument, on organization, and order, and civilization. He contended that the trader was the bearer of civilization, and that the trader must be protected in his trade else he would not come. Over to the westward were islands which would not protect the traders. What was the result? The traders would not come, and the people were like wild animals. They wore no clothes, no silk shirts (here he peered and blinked significantly at the king), and they ate one another.

The queer paper of the Feathers of the Sun was not money. The traders knew what money was, and they would not receive it. If Fitu-Iva persisted in trying to make them receive it they would go away and never come back. And then the Fitu-Ivans, who had forgotten how to make tapa, would run around naked and eat one another.

Much more he said, talking a solid hour, and always coming back to what their dire condition would be when the traders came no more. "And in that day," he perorated, "how will the Fitu-Ivan be known in the great world? *Kai-kanak* will men call him. *'Kai-kanak! Kai-kanak!'*"

Tui Tulifau spoke briefly. The case had been presented, he said, for the people, the army, and the traders. It was now time for Feathers of the Sun to present his side. It could not be denied that he had wrought wonders with his financial system. "Many times has he explained to me the working of the system," Tui Tulifau concluded. "It is very simple. And now he will explain it to you."

It was a conspiracy of the white traders, Cornelius contended. Ieremia was right so far as concerned the manifold blessings of white flour and kerosene oil. Fitu-Iva did not want to become *kai-kanak*.

Fitu-Iva wanted civilization; it wanted more and more civilization. Now that was the very point, and they must follow him closely. Paper money was an earmark of higher civilization. That was why he, the Feathers of the Sun, had introduced it. And that was why the traders opposed it. They did not want to see Fitu-Iva civilized. Why did they come across the far ocean stretches with their goods to Fitu-Iva? He, the Feathers of the Sun, would tell them why, to their faces, in grand council assembled. In their own countries men were too civilized to let the traders make the immense profits that they made out of the Fitu-Ivans. If the Fitu-Ivans became properly civilized, the trade of the traders would be gone. In that day every Fitu-Ivan could become a trader if he pleased.

That was why the white traders fought the system of paper money, that he, the Feathers of the Sun, had brought. Why was he called the Feathers of the Sun? Because he was the Light-Bringer from the World Beyond the Sky. The paper money was the light. The robbing white traders could not flourish in the light. Therefore they fought the light.

He would prove it to the good people of Fitu-Iva, and he would prove it out of the mouths of his enemies. It was a well-known fact that all highly civilized countries had paper-money systems. He would ask Ieremia if this was not so.

Ieremia did not answer.

"You see," Cornelius went on, "he makes no answer. He cannot deny what is true. England, France, Germany, America, all the great *Papalangi* countries, have the paper-money system. It works. From century to century it works. I challenge you, Ieremia, as an honest man, as one who was once a zealous worker in the Lord's vineyard, I challenge you to deny that in the great *Papalangi* countries the system works."

Ieremia could not deny, and his fingers played nervously with the fastening of the basket on his knees.

"You see, it is as I have said," Cornelius continued. "Ieremia agrees that it is so. Therefore, I ask you, all good people of Fitu-Iva, if a system is good for the *Papalangi* countries, why is it not good for Fitu-Iva?"

"It is not the same!" Ieremia cried. "The paper of the Feathers of the Sun is different from the paper of the great countries."

That Cornelius had been prepared for this was evident. He held up a Fitu-Ivan note that was recognized by all.

"What is that?" he demanded.

"Paper, mere paper," was Ieremia's reply.

"And that?"

This time Cornelius held up a Bank of England note.

"It is the paper money of the English," he explained to the council, at the same time extending it for Ieremia to examine. "Is it not true, Ieremia, that it is paper money of the English?"

Ieremia nodded reluctantly.

"You have said that the paper money of Fitu-Iva was paper, now how about this of the English? What is it?...You must answer like a true man.... All wait for your answer, Ieremia."

"It is—it is——" the puzzled Ieremia began, then spluttered help-lessly, the fallacy beyond his penetration.

"Paper, mere paper," Cornelius concluded for him, imitating his halting utterance.

Conviction sat on the faces of all. The king clapped his hands ad-miringly and murmured, "It is most clear, very clear."

"You see, he himself acknowledges it." Assured triumph was in Deasy's voice and bearing. "He knows of no difference. There is no difference. 'Tis the very image of money. 'Tis money itself."

In the meantime Grief was whispering in Ieremia's ear, who nodded and began to speak.

"But it is well known to all the *Papalangi* that the English Govern-ment will pay coin money for the paper."

Deasy's victory was now absolute. He held aloft a Fitu-Ivan note.

"Is it not so written on this paper as well?"

Again Grief whispered.

"That Fitu-Iva will pay coin money?" asked Ieremia.

"It is so written."

A third time Grief prompted.

"On demand?" asked Ieremia.

"On demand," Cornelius assured him.

"Then I demand coin money now," said Ieremia, drawing a small package of notes from the pouch at his girdle.

Cornelius scanned the package with a quick, estimating eye.

"Very well," he agreed. "I shall give you the coin money now. How much?"

"And we will see the system work," the king proclaimed, partaking in his Chancellor's triumph.

"You have heard!—He will give coin money now!" Ieremia cried in a loud voice to the assemblage.

At the same time he plunged both hands in the basket and drew forth many packages of Fitu-Ivan notes. It was noticed that a peculiar odour was adrift about the council.

"I have here," Ieremia announced, "one thousand and twenty-eight pounds twelve shillings and sixpence. Here is a sack to put the coin money in."

Cornelius recoiled. He had not expected such a sum, and everywhere about the council his uneasy eyes showed him chiefs and talking men drawing out bundles of notes. The army, its two months' pay in its hands, pressed forward to the edge of the council, while behind it the populace, with more money, invaded the compound.

" 'Tis a run on the bank you've precipitated," he said reproachfully to Grief.

"Here is the sack to put the coin money in," Ieremia urged.

"It must be postponed," Cornelius said desperately. " 'Tis not in banking hours."

Ieremia flourished a package of money. "Nothing of banking hours is written here. It says on demand, and I now demand."

"Let them come to-morrow, O Tui Tulifau," Cornelius appealed to the king. "They shall be paid to-morrow."

Tui Tulifau hesitated, but his spouse glared at him, her brawny arm tensing as the fist doubled into a redoubtable knot. Tui Tulifau tried to look away, but failed. He cleared his throat nervously.

"We will see the system work," he decreed. "The people have come far."

" 'Tis good money you're asking me to pay out," Deasy muttered in a low voice to the king.

Sepeli caught what he said, and grunted so savagely as to startle the king, who involuntarily shrank away from her.

"Forget not the pig," Grief whispered to Ieremia, who immediately stood up.

With a sweeping gesture he stilled the babel of voices that was beginning to rise.

"It was an ancient and honourable custom of Fitu-Iva," he said, "that when a man was proved a notorious evildoer his joints were broken with a club and he was staked out at low water to be fed upon alive by the sharks. Unfortunately, that day is past. Nevertheless another ancient and honourable custom remains with us. You all know what it is. When a man is a proven thief and liar he shall be struck with a dead pig."

His right hand went into the basket, and, despite the lack of his spectacles, the dead pig that came into view landed accurately on Deasy's neck. With such force was it thrown that the Chancellor, in his sitting position, toppled over sidewise. Before he could recover, Sepeli, with an agility unexpected of a woman who weighed two hundred and sixty pounds, had sprung across to him. One hand clutched his shirt collar, the other hand brandished the pig, and amid the vast uproar of a delighted kingdom she royally swatted him.

There remained nothing for Tui Tulifau but to put a good face on his favourite's disgrace, and his mountainous fat lay back on the mats and shook in a gale of Gargantuan laughter.

When Sepeli dropped both pig and Chancellor, a talking man from the windward coast picked up the carcass. Cornelius was on his feet and running, when the pig caught him on the legs and tripped him. The people and the army, with shouts and laughter, joined in the sport. Twist and dodge as he would, everywhere the ex-Chancellor of the Exchequer was met or overtaken by the flying pig. He scuttled like a frightened rabbit in and out among the avocados and the palms. No hand was laid upon him, and his tormentors made way before him, but ever they pursued, and ever the pig flew as fast as hands could pick it up.

As the chase died away down the Broom Road, Grief led the traders to the royal treasury, and the day was well over ere the last Fitu-Ivan banknote had been redeemed with coin.

VIII

Through the mellow cool of twilight a man paddled out from a clump of jungle to the *Cantani*. It was a leaky and abandoned dugout, and he paddled slowly, desisting from time to time in order to bale. The Kanaka sailors giggled gleefully as he came alongside and painfully drew himself over the rail. He was bedraggled and filthy, and seemed half dazed.

"Could I speak a word with you, Mr. Grief?" he asked sadly and humbly.

"Sit to leeward and farther away," Grief answered. "A little farther away. That's better."

Cornelius sat down on the rail and held his head in both his hands.

"'Tis right," he said. "I'm as fragrant as a recent battlefield. My head aches to burstin'. My neck is fair broken. The teeth are loose in my jaws. There's nests of hornets buzzin' in my ears. My medulla oblongata is dislocated. I've been through earthquake and pestilence, and the heavens have rained pigs." He paused with a sigh that ended in a groan. "'Tis a vision of terrible death. One that the poets never dreamed. To be eaten by rats, or boiled in oil, or pulled apart by wild horses—that would be unpleasant. But to be beaten to death with a dead pig!" He shuddered at the awfulness of it. "Sure it transcends the human imagination."

Captain Boig sniffed audibly, moved his canvas chair farther to windward, and sat down again.

"I hear you're runnin' over to Yap, Mr. Grief," Cornelius went on. "An' two things I'm wantin' to beg of you: a passage an' a nip of the old smoky I refused the night you landed."

Grief clapped his hands for the black steward and ordered soap and towels.

"Go for'ard, Cornelius, and take a scrub first," he said. "The boy will bring you a pair of dungarees and a shirt. And by the way, before you go, how was it we found more coin in the treasury than paper you had issued?"

"'Twas the stake of my own I'd brought with me for the adventure."

"We've decided to charge the demurrage and other expenses and loss to Tui Tulifau," Grief said. "So the balance we found will be turned over to you. But ten shillings must be deducted."

"For what?"

"Do you think dead pigs grow on trees? The sum of ten shillings for that pig is entered in the accounts."

Cornelius bowed his assent with a shudder.

"Sure it's grateful I am it wasn't a fifteen-shilling pig or a twenty-shilling one."

FROM *ON THE MAKALOA MAT*

On the Makaloa Mat

Unlike the women of most warm races, those of Hawaii age well and nobly. With no pretence of make-up or cunning concealment of time's inroads, the woman who sat under the hau tree might have been permitted as much as fifty years by a judge competent anywhere over the world save in Hawaii. Yet her children and her grandchildren, and Roscoe Scandwell who had been her husband for forty years, knew that she was sixty-four and would be sixty-five come the next twenty-second day of June. But she did not look it, despite the fact that she thrust reading glasses on her nose as she read her magazine and took them off when her gaze desired to wander in the direction of the half-dozen children playing on the lawn.

It was a noble situation—noble as the ancient hau tree, the size of a house, where she sat as if in a house, so spaciously and comfortably house-like was its shade furnished; noble as the lawn that stretched away landward its plush of green at an appraisement of two hundred dollars a front foot to a bungalow equally dignified, noble, and costly. Seaward, glimpsed through a fringe of hundred-foot coconut palms, was the ocean; beyond the reef a dark blue that grew indigo blue to the horizon, within the reef all the silken gamut of jade and emerald and tourmaline.

And this was but one house of the half-dozen houses belonging to Martha Scandwell. Her town-house, a few miles away in Honolulu, on Nuuanu Drive between the first and second "showers," was a palace. Hosts of guests had known the comfort and joy of her mountain house on Tantalus, and of her volcano house, her *mauka* (mountainward) house, and her *makai* (seaward) house on the big island of Hawaii. Yet this Waikiki house stressed no less than the rest in beauty, in dignity, and in expensiveness of upkeep. Two Japanese yard-boys were trimming hibiscus, a third was engaged expertly with the long hedge of night-blooming cereus that was shortly expectant of unfolding in its mysterious night-bloom. In immaculate ducks, a house Japanese brought out the tea-things, followed by a Japanese maid, pretty as a butterfly in the distinctive garb of her race, and fluttery as a butterfly to attend on her mistress. Another Japanese maid, an array of Turkish towels on her arm, crossed the lawn well to the right in the direction of the bath-houses, from which the children, in swimming suits, were beginning to emerge. Beyond, under the palms at the edge of the sea, two Chinese nursemaids, in their pretty native costume of white *yee-shon* and straight-lined trousers, their black braids of hair down their backs, attended each on a baby in a perambulator.

And all these—servants, and nurses, and grandchildren—were Martha Scandwell's. So likewise was the colour of the skin of the grandchildren—the unmistakable Hawaiian colour, tinted beyond shadow of mistake by exposure to the Hawaiian sun. One-eighth and one-sixteenth Hawaiian were they, which meant that seven-eighths or fifteen-sixteenths white blood informed that skin yet failed to obliterate the modicum of golden tawny brown of Polynesia. But in this, again, only a trained observer would have known that the frolicking children were aught but pure-blooded white. Roscoe Scandwell, grandfather, was pure white; Martha three-quarters white; the many sons and daughters of them seven-eighths white; the grandchildren graded up to fifteen-sixteenths white, or, in the cases when their seven-eighths fathers and mothers had married seven-eighths, themselves fourteen-sixteenths or seven-eighths white. On both sides the stock was good, Roscoe straight descended from the New England Puritans, Martha no less straight descended from the royal chief-stocks of Hawaii whose genealogies were chanted in *meles* a thousand years before written speech was acquired.

In the distance a machine stopped and deposited a woman whose utmost years might have been guessed as sixty, who walked across the lawn as lightly as a well-cared-for woman of forty, and whose actual calendar age was sixty-eight. Martha rose from her seat to greet her, in the hearty Hawaiian way, arms about, lips on lips, faces eloquent and bodies no less eloquent with sincereness and frank excessiveness of emotion. And it was "Sister Bella," and "Sister Martha," back and forth, intermingled with almost incoherent inquiries about each other, and about Uncle This and Brother That and Aunt Some One Else, until, the first tremulousness of meeting over, eyes moist with tenderness of love, they sat gazing at each other across their teacups. Apparently, they had not seen nor embraced for years. In truth, two months marked the interval of their separation. And one sixty-four, the other sixty-eight. But the thorough comprehension resided in the fact that in each of them one-fourth of them was the sun-warm, love-warm heart of Hawaii.

The children flooded about Aunt Bella like a rising tide and were capaciously hugged and kissed ere they departed with their nurses to the swimming beach.

"I thought I'd run out to the beach for several days—the trades had stopped blowing," Martha explained.

"You've been here two weeks already," Bella smiled fondly at her younger sister. "Brother Edward told me. He met me at the steamer and insisted on running me out first of all to see Louise and Dorothy and that first grandchild of his. He's as mad as a silly hatter about it."

"Mercy!" Martha exclaimed. "Two weeks! I had not thought it that long."

"Where's Annie?—and Margaret?" Bella asked.

Martha shrugged her voluminous shoulders with voluminous and forgiving affection for her wayward, matronly daughters who left their children in her care for the afternoon.

"Margaret's at a meeting of the Out-door Circle—they're planning the planting of trees and hibiscus all along both sides of Kalakaua Avenue," she said. "And Annie's wearing out eighty dollars' worth of tyres to collect seventy-five dollars for the British Red Cross—this is their tag day, you know."

"Roscoe must be very proud," Bella said, and observed the bright glow of pride that appeared in her sister's eyes. "I got the news in San Francisco of Ho-o-la-a's first dividend. Remember when I put a thousand in it at seventy-five cents for poor Abbie's children, and said I'd sell when it went to ten dollars?"

"And everybody laughed at you, and at anybody who bought a share," Martha nodded. "But Roscoe knew. It's selling to-day at twenty-four."

"I sold mine from the steamer by wireless—at twenty even," Bella continued. "And now Abbie's wildly dressmaking. She's going with May and Tootsie to Paris."

"And Carl?" Martha queried.

"Oh, he'll finish Yale all right—"

"Which he would have done anyway, and you *know* it," Martha charged, lapsing charmingly into twentieth-century slang.

Bella affirmed her guilt of intention of paying the way of her school friend's son through college, and added complacently:

"Just the same it was nicer to have Ho-o-la-a pay for it. In a way, you see, Roscoe is doing it, because it was his judgment I trusted to when I made the investment." She gazed slowly about her, her eyes taking in, not merely the beauty and comfort and repose of all they rested on, but the immensity of beauty and comfort and repose represented by them, scattered in similar oases all over the islands. She sighed pleasantly and observed: "All our husbands have done well by us with what we brought them."

"And happily . . ." Martha agreed, then suspended her utterance with suspicious abruptness.

"And happily, all of us, except Sister Bella," Bella forgivingly completed the thought for her.

"It was too bad, that marriage," Martha murmured, all softness of sympathy. "You were so young. Uncle Robert should never have made you."

"I was only nineteen," Bella nodded. "But it was not George Castner's fault. And look what he, out of the grave, has done for me. Uncle Robert was wise. He knew George had the far-away vision of far ahead, the energy, and the steadiness. He saw, even then, and that's fifty years ago, the value of the Nahala water-rights which nobody else valued then. They thought he was struggling to buy the cattle range. He struggled to buy the future of the water—and how well he succeeded you know. I'm almost ashamed to think of my income sometimes. No; whatever else, the unhappiness of our marriage was not due to George. I could have lived happily with him, I know, even to this day, had he lived." She shook her head slowly. "No; it was not his fault. Nor anybody's. Not even mine. If it was anybody's fault—" The wistful fondness of her smile took the sting out of what she was about to say. "If it was anybody's fault it was Uncle John's."

"Uncle John's!" Martha cried with sharp surprise. "If it had to be one or the other, I should have said Uncle Robert. But Uncle John!"

Bella smiled with slow positiveness.

"But it was Uncle Robert who made you marry George Castner," her sister urged.

"That is true," Bella nodded corroboration. "But it was not the matter of a husband, but of a horse. I wanted to borrow a horse from Uncle John, and Uncle John said yes. That is how it all happened."

A silence fell, pregnant and cryptic, and, while the voices of the children and the soft mandatory protests of the Asiatic maids drew from the beach, Martha Scandwell felt herself vibrant and tremulous with sudden resolve of daring. She waved the children away.

"Run along, dears, run along, Grandma and Aunt Bella want to talk."

And as the shrill, sweet treble of child voices ebbed away across the lawn, Martha, with scrutiny of the heart, observed the sadness of the lines graven by secret woe for half a century in her sister's face. For nearly fifty years had she watched those lines. She steeled all the melting softness of the Hawaiian of her to break the half-century of silence.

"Bella," she said. "We never knew. You never spoke. But we wondered, oh, often and often—"

"And never asked," Bella murmured gratefully.

"But I am asking now, at the last. This is our twilight. Listen to them! Sometimes it almost frightens me to think that they are grandchildren, *my* grandchildren—*I*, who only the other day, it would seem, was as heart-free, leg-free, care-free a girl as ever bestrode a horse, or swam in the big surf, or gathered *opihis* at low tide, or laughed at a dozen lovers. And here in our twilight let us forget everything save that I am your dear sister as you are mine."

The eyes of both were dewy moist. Bella palpably trembled to utterance.

"We thought it was George Castner," Martha went on; "and we could guess the details. He was a cold man. You were warm Hawaiian. He must have been cruel. Brother Walcott always insisted he must have beaten you—"

"No! No!" Bella broke in. "George Castner was never a brute, a beast. Almost have I wished, often, that he had been. He never laid hand on me. He never raised hand to me. He never raised his voice to me. Never—oh, can you believe it?—do, please, sister, believe it—did we have a high word nor a cross word. But that house of his, of ours, at Nahala, was grey. All the colour of it was grey and cool, and chill, while I was bright with all colours of sun, and earth, and blood, and birth. It was very cold, grey cold, with that cold grey husband of mine at Nahala. You know he was grey, Martha. Grey like those portraits of Emerson we used to see at school. His skin was grey. Sun and weather and all hours in the saddle could never tan it. And he was grey inside as out.

"And I was only nineteen when Uncle Robert decided on the marriage. How was I to know? Uncle Robert talked to me. He pointed out how the wealth and property of Hawaii was already beginning to pass into the hands of the *haoles*. The Hawaiian chiefs let their possessions slip away from them. The Hawaiian chiefesses, who married haoles, had their possessions, under the management of their haole husbands, increase prodigiously. He pointed back to the original Grandfather Roger Wilton, who had taken Grandmother Wilton's poor *mauka* lands and added to them and built up about them the Kilohana Ranch—"

"Even then it was second only to the Parker Ranch," Martha interrupted proudly.

"—And he told me that had our father, before he died, been as far-seeing as grandfather, half the then Parker holdings would have been added to Kilohana, making Kilohana first. And he said that never, for ever and ever, would beef be cheaper. And he said that the big future of Hawaii would be in sugar. That was fifty years ago, and he has been more than proved right. And he said that the young haole, George Castner, saw far, and would go far, and that there were many girls of us, and that the Kilohana lands ought by rights to go to the boys, and that if I married George my future was assured in the biggest way.

"I was only nineteen. Just back from the Royal Chief School—that was before our girls went to the States for their education. You were among the first, Sister Martha, who got their education on the mainland. And what did I know of love and lovers, much less of marriage? All women married. It was their business in life. Mother and grandmother, all the way back they had married. It was my business in life to marry George Castner. Uncle Robert said so in his wisdom, and I knew he was very wise. And I went to live with my husband in the grey house at Nahala.

"You remember it. No trees, only the rolling grass lands, the high mountains behind, the sea beneath, and the wind!—the Waimea and Nahala winds, we got them both, and the kona wind as well. Yet little would I have minded them, any more than we minded them at Kilohana, or than they minded them at Mana, had not Nahala itself been so grey, and husband George so grey. We were alone. He was managing Nahala for the Glenns, who had gone back to Scotland. Eighteen hundred a year, plus beef, horses, cowboy service, and the ranch house, was what he received—"

"It was a high salary in those days," Martha said.

"And for George Castner, and the service he gave, it was very cheap," Bella defended. "I lived with him for three years. There was never a morning that he was out of his bed later than half-past four. He was the soul of devotion to his employers. Honest to a penny in his accounts, he gave them full measure and more of his time and energy. Perhaps that was what helped make our life so grey. But listen, Martha. Out of his eighteen hundred, he laid aside sixteen hundred each year. Think of it! The two of us lived on two hundred a year. Luckily he did not drink or smoke. Also, we dressed out of it as well. I made my own dresses. You can imagine them. Outside of the cowboys who chored the firewood, I did the work. I cooked, and baked, and scrubbed—"

"You who had never known anything but servants from the time you were born!" Martha pitied. "Never less than a regiment of them at Kilohana."

"Oh, but it was in the bare, naked, pinching meagreness of it!" Bella cried out. "How far I was compelled to make a pound of coffee go! A broom worn down to nothing before a new one was bought! And beef! Fresh beef and jerky, morning, noon, and night! And porridge! Never since have I eaten porridge or any breakfast food."

She arose suddenly and walked a dozen steps away to gaze a moment with unseeing eyes at the colour-lavish reef while she composed herself. And she returned to her seat with the splendid, sure, gracious, high-breasted, noble-headed port of which no out-breeding can ever rob the Hawaiian woman. Very haole was Bella Castner, fair-skinned, fine-textured. Yet, as she returned, the high pose of head, the level-lidded gaze of her long brown eyes under royal arches of eyebrows, the softly set lines of her small mouth that fairly sang sweetness of kisses after sixty-eight years—all made her the very picture of a chiefess of old Hawaii full-bursting through her ampleness of haole blood. Taller she was than her sister Martha, if anything more queenly.

"You know we were notorious as poor feeders," Bella laughed lightly enough. "It was many a mile on either side from Nahala to the next roof. Belated travellers, or storm-bound ones, would, on occasion, stop with us overnight. And you know the lavishness of the big ranches, then and now. How we were the laughing-stock! 'What do we care!' George would say. 'They live to-day and now. Twenty years from now will be our turn, Bella. They will be where they are now, and they will eat out of our hand. We will be compelled to feed them, they will need to be fed, and we will feed them well; for we will be rich, Bella, so rich that I am afraid to tell you. But I know what I know, and you must have faith in me.'

"George was right. Twenty years afterward, though he did not live to see it, my income was a thousand a month. Goodness! I do not know what it is to-day. But I was only nineteen, and I would say to George: 'Now! now! We live now. We may not be alive twenty years from now.

I do want a new broom. And there is a third-rate coffee that is only two cents a pound more than the awful stuff we are using. Why couldn't I fry eggs in butter—now? I should dearly love at least one new table-cloth. Our linen! I'm ashamed to put a guest between the sheets, though heaven knows they dare come seldom enough.'

"'Be patient, Bella,' he would reply. 'In a little while, in only a few years, those that scorn to sit at our table now, or sleep between our sheets, will be proud of an invitation—those of them who will not be dead. You remember how Stevens passed out last year—free-living and easy, everybody's friend but his own. The Kohala crowd had to bury him, for he left nothing but debts. Watch the others going the same pace. There's your brother Hal. He can't keep it up and live five years, and ho'o breaking his uncles' hearts. And there's Prince Lilolilo. Dashes by me with half a hundred mounted, able-bodied, roystering kanakas in his train who would be better at hard work and looking after their future, for he will never be king of Hawaii. He will not live to be king of Hawaii.'

"George was right. Brother Hal died. So did Prince Lilolilo. But George was not *all* right. He, who neither drank nor smoked, who never wasted the weight of his arms in an embrace, nor the touch of his lips a second longer than the most perfunctory of kisses, who was in-variably up before cockcrow and asleep ere the kerosene lamp had a tenth emptied itself, and who never thought to die, was dead even more quickly than Brother Hal and Prince Lilolilo.

"'Be patient, Bella,' Uncle Robert would say to me. 'George Cast-ner is a coming man. I have chosen well for you. Your hardships now are the hardships on the way to the promised land. Not always will the Hawaiians rule in Hawaii. Just as they let their wealth slip out of their hands, so will their rule slip out of their hands. Political power and the land always go together. There will be great changes, revolutions no one knows how many nor of what sort, save that in the end the haole will possess the land and the rule. And in that day you may well be first lady of Hawaii, just as surely as George Castner will be ruler of Hawaii. It is written in the books. It is ever so where the haole conflicts with the easier races. I, your Uncle Robert, who am half-Hawaiian and half-haole, know whereof I speak. Be patient, Bella, be patient.'

" 'Dear Bella,' Uncle John would say; and I knew his heart was tender for me. Thank God, he never told me to be patient. He knew. He was very wise. He was warm human, and, therefore, wiser than Uncle Robert and George Castner, who sought the thing, not the spirit, who kept records in ledgers rather than numbers of heart-beats breast to breast, who added columns of figures rather than remembered embraces and endearments of look and speech and touch. 'Dear Bella,' Uncle John would say. He knew. You have heard always how he was the lover of the Princess Naomi. He was a true lover. He loved but the once. After her death they said he was eccentric. He was. He was the one lover, once and always. Remember that taboo inner room of his at Kilohana that we entered only after his death and found it his shrine to her. 'Dear Bella,' it was all he ever said to me, but I knew he knew.

"And I was nineteen, and sun-warm Hawaiian in spite of my three-quarters haole blood, and I knew nothing save my girlhood splendours at Kilohana and my Honolulu education at the Royal Chief School, and my grey husband at Nahala with his grey preachments and practices of sobriety and thrift, and those two childless uncles of mine, the one with far, cold vision, the other the broken-hearted, for-ever-dreaming lover of a dead princess.

"Think of that grey house! I, who had known the ease and the delights and the ever-laughing joys of Kilohana, and of the Parkers at old Mana, and of Puuwaawaa! You remember. We did live in feudal spaciousness in those days. Would you, can you, believe it, Martha—at Nahala the only sewing machine I had was one of those the early missionaries brought, a tiny, crazy thing that one cranked around by hand!

"Robert and John had each given Husband George five thousand dollars at my marriage. But he had asked for it to be kept secret. Only the four of us knew. And while I sewed my cheap *holokus* on that crazy machine, he bought land with the money—the upper Nahala lands, you know—a bit at a time, each purchase a hard-driven bargain, his face the very face of poverty. To-day the Nahala Ditch alone pays me forty thousand a year.

"But was it worth it? I starved. If only once, madly, he had crushed me in his arms! If only once he could have lingered with me five minutes from his own business or from his fidelity to his employers! Sometimes I could have screamed, or showered the eternal bowl of hot porridge into his face, or smashed the sewing machine upon the floor and danced a hula on it, just to make him burst out and lose his temper and be human, be a brute, be a man of some sort instead of a grey, frozen demi-god."

Bella's tragic expression vanished, and she laughed outright in sheer genuineness of mirthful recollection.

"And when I was in such moods he would gravely look me over, gravely feel my pulse, examine my tongue, gravely dose me with castor oil, and gravely put me to bed early with hot stove-lids, and assure me that I'd feel better in the morning. Early to bed! Our wildest sitting up was nine o'clock. Eight o'clock was our regular bed-time. It saved kerosene. We did not eat dinner at Nahala—remember the great table at Kilohana where we did have dinner? But Husband George and I had supper. And then he would sit close to the lamp on one side the table and read old borrowed magazines for an hour, while I sat on the other side and darned his socks and underclothing. He always wore such cheap, shoddy stuff. And when he went to bed, I went to bed. No wastage of kerosene with only one to benefit by it. And he went to bed always the same way, winding up his watch, entering the day's weather in his diary, and taking off his shoes, right foot first invariably, left foot second, and placing them just so, side by side, on the floor, at the foot of the bed, on his side.

"He was the cleanest man I ever knew. He never wore the same undergarment a second time. I did the washing. He was so clean it hurt. He shaved twice a day. He used more water on his body than any kanaka. He did more work than any two haoles. And he saw the future of the Nahala water."

"And he made you wealthy, but did not make you happy," Martha observed.

Bella sighed and nodded.

"What is wealth after all, Sister Martha? My new Pierce-Arrow came down on the steamer with me. My third in two years. But oh, all the Pierce-Arrows and all the incomes in the world compared with a lover!—the one lover, the one mate, to be married to, to toil beside and suffer and joy beside, the one male man lover husband—"

Her voice trailed off, and the sisters sat in soft silence while an ancient crone, staff in hand, twisted, doubled, and shrunken under a hundred years of living, hobbled across the lawn to them. Her eyes, withered to scarcely more than peepholes, were sharp as a mongoose's, and at Bella's feet she first sank down, in pure Hawaiian mumbling and chanting a toothless *mele* of Bella and Bella's ancestry and adding to it an extemporized welcome back to Hawaii after her absence across the great sea to California. And while she chanted her mele, the old crone's shrewd fingers *lomied* or massaged Bella's silk-stockinged legs from ankle and calf to knee and thigh.

Both Bella's and Martha's eyes were luminous-moist, as the old retainer repeated the lomi and the mele to Martha, and as they talked with her in the ancient tongue and asked the immemorial questions about her health and age and great-great-grandchildren—she who had lomied them as babies in the great house at Kilohana, as her ancestresses had lomied their ancestresses back through the unnumbered generations. The brief duty visit over, Martha arose and accompanied her back to the bungalow, putting money into her hand, commanding proud and beautiful Japanese housemaids to wait upon the dilapidated aborigine with *poi,* which is compounded of the roots of the water lily, with *iamaka,* which is raw fish, and with pounded *kukui* nut and *limu,* which latter is seaweed tender to the toothless, digestible and savoury. It was the old feudal tie, the faithfulness of the commoner to the chief, the responsibility of the chief to the commoner; and Martha, three-quarters haole with the Anglo-Saxon blood of New England, was four-quarters Hawaiian in her remembrance and observance of the well-nigh vanished customs of old days.

As she came back across the lawn to the hau tree, Bella's eyes dwelt upon the moving authenticity of her and of the blood of her, and embraced her and loved her. Shorter than Bella was Martha, a trifle, but the merest trifle, less queenly of port; but beautifully and generously proportioned, mellowed rather than dismantled by years, her Polynesian chiefess figure eloquent and glorious under the satisfying lines of a half-fitting, grandly sweeping, black-silk *holoku* trimmed with black lace more costly than a Paris gown.

And as both sisters resumed their talk, an observer would have noted the striking resemblance of their pure, straight profiles, of their broad cheek-bones, of their wide and lofty foreheads, of their iron-grey abundance of hair, of their sweet-lipped mouths set with the carriage of decades of assured and accomplished pride, and of their lovely slender eye-brows arched over equally lovely long brown eyes. The hands of both of them, little altered or defaced by age, were wonderful in their slender, tapering fingertips, love-lomied and love-formed while they were babies by old Hawaiian women like to the one even then eating *poi* and iamaka and limu in the house.

"I had a year of it," Bella resumed, "and, do you know, things were beginning to come right. I was beginning to draw to Husband George. Women are so made, I was such a woman at any rate. For he *was* good. He *was* just. All the old sterling Puritan virtues were his. I was coming to draw to him, to like him, almost, might I say, to love him. And had not Uncle John loaned me that horse, I know that I would have truly loved him and have lived ever happily with him—in a quiet sort of way, of course.

"You see, I knew nothing else, nothing different, nothing better in the way of men. I came gladly to look across the table at him while he read in the brief interval between supper and bed, gladly to listen for and to catch the beat of his horse's hoofs coming home at night from his endless riding over the ranch. And his scant praise was praise indeed, that made me tingle with happiness—yes, Sister Martha, I knew what it was to blush under his precise, just praise for the things I had done right or correctly.

"And all would have been well for the rest of our lives together, except that he had to take steamer to Honolulu. It was business. He was to be gone two weeks or longer, first, for the Glenns in ranch affairs, and next for himself, to arrange the purchase of still more of the upper Nahala lands. Do you know! he bought lots of the wilder and up-and-down lands, worthless for aught save water, and the very heart of the watershed, for as low as five and ten cents an acre. And he suggested I needed a change. I wanted to go with him to Honolulu. But, with an eye to expense, he decided Kilohana for me. Not only would it cost him nothing for me to visit at the old house, but he saved the price of the poor food I should have eaten had I remained alone at Nahala, which meant the purchase price of more Nahala acreage. And at Kilohana Uncle John said yes, and loaned me the horse.

"Oh, it was like heaven, getting back, those first several days. It was difficult to believe at first that there was so much food in all the world. The enormous wastage of the kitchen appalled me. I saw waste everywhere, so well trained had I been by Husband George. Why, out in the servants' quarters the aged relatives and most distant hangers-on of the servants fed better than George and I ever fed. You remember our Kilohana way, same as the Parker way, a bullock killed for every meal, fresh fish by runners from the ponds of Waipio and Kiholo, the best and rarest at all times of everything …

"And love, our family way of loving! You know what Uncle John was. And Brother Walcott was there, and Brother Edward, and all the younger sisters save you and Sally away at school. And Aunt Elizabeth, and Aunt Janet with her husband and all her children on a visit. It was arms around, and perpetual endearings, and all that I had missed for a weary twelvemonth. I was thirsty for it. I was like a survivor from the open boat falling down on the sand and lapping the fresh bubbling springs at the roots of the palms.

"And *they* came, riding up from Kawaihae, where they had landed from the royal yacht, the whole glorious cavalcade of them, two by two, flower-garlanded, young and happy, gay, on the Parker Ranch horses, thirty of them in the party, a hundred Parker Ranch cowboys and as many more of their own retainers—a royal progress. It was Princess Lihue's progress, of course, she flaming and passing as we all knew with the dreadful tuberculosis; but with her were her nephews, Prince Lilolilo, hailed everywhere as the next king, and his brothers, Prince Kahekili and Prince Kamalau. And with the Princess was Ella Higginsworth, who rightly claimed higher chief blood lines through the Kauai descent than belonged to the reigning family, and Dora Niles, and Emily Lowcroft, and … oh, why enumerate them all! Ella Higginsworth and I had been room-mates at the Royal Chief School. And there was a great resting time for an hour—no *luau*, for the luau awaited them at the Parkers'—but beer and stronger drinks for the men, and lemonade, and oranges, and refreshing watermelon for the women.

"And it was arms around with Ella Higginsworth and me, and the Princess, who remembered me, and all the other girls and women, and Ella spoke to the Princess, and the Princess herself invited me to the progress, joining them at Mana whence they would depart two days later. And I was mad, mad with it all—I, from a twelvemonth of imprisonment at grey Nahala. And I was nineteen yet, just turning twenty within the week.

"Oh, I had not thought of what was to happen. So occupied was I with the women that I did not see Lilolilo, except at a distance, hulking large and tall above the other men. But I had never been on a progress. I had seen them entertained at Kilohana and Mana, but I had been too young to be invited along, and after that it had been school and marriage. I know what it would be like—two weeks of paradise, and little enough for another twelve months at Nahala.

"And I asked Uncle John to lend me a horse, which meant three horses of course—one mounted cowboy and a pack horse to accompany me. No roads then. No automobiles. And the horse for myself! It was Hilo. You don't remember him. You were away at school then, and before you came home, the following year, he'd broken his back and his rider's neck wild-cattle-roping up Mauna Kea. You heard about it—that young American naval officer."

"Lieutenant Bowsfield," Martha nodded.

"But Hilo! I was the first woman on his back. He was a three-year-old, almost four-year, and just broken. So black and in such a vigour of coat that the high lights on him clad him in shimmering silver. He was the biggest riding animal on the ranch, descended from the King's Sparklingdew with a range mare for dam, and roped wild only two weeks before. I never have seen so beautiful a horse. He had the round, deep-chested, big-hearted, well-coupled body of the ideal mountain pony, and his head and neck were true thoroughbred, slender, yet full, with lovely alert ears not too small to be vicious nor too large to be stubborn mulish. And his legs and feet were lovely too, unblemished, sure and firm, with long springy pasterns that made him a wonder of ease under the saddle."

"I remember hearing Prince Lilolilo tell Uncle John that you were the best woman rider in all Hawaii," Martha interrupted to say. "That was two years afterward when I was back from school and while you were still living at Nahala."

"Lilolilo said that!" Bella cried. Almost as with a blush, her long, brown eyes were illumined, as she bridged the years to her lover near half a century dead and dust. With the gentleness of modesty so innate in the women of Hawaii, she covered her spontaneous exposure of her heart with added panegyric of Hilo.

"Oh, when he ran with me up the long-grass slopes, and down the long-grass slopes, it was like hurdling in a dream, for he cleared the grass at every bound, leaping like a deer, a rabbit, or a fox-terrier—you know how they do. And cut up, and prance, and high life! He was a mount for a general, for a Napoleon or a Kitchener. And he had, not a wicked eye, but, oh, such a roguish eye, intelligent and looking as if it cherished a joke behind and wanted to laugh or to perpetrate it. And I asked Uncle John for Hilo. And Uncle John looked at me, and I looked at him; and, though he did not say it, I knew he was *feeling* 'Dear Bella,' and I knew, somewhere in his seeing of me, was all his vision of the Princess Naomi. And Uncle John said yes. That is how it happened.

"But he insisted that I should try Hilo out—myself, rather—at private rehearsal. He was a *handful*, a glorious handful. But not vicious, not malicious. He got away from me over and over again, but I never let him know. I was not afraid, and that helped me keep always a *feel* of him that prevented him from thinking that he was even a jump ahead of me.

"I have often wondered if Uncle John dreamed of what possibly might happen. I know I had no thought of it myself, that day I rode across and joined the Princess at Mana. Never was there such festal time. You know the grand way the old Parkers had of entertaining. The pig-sticking and wild-cattle-shooting, the horse-breaking and the branding. The servants' quarters overflowing. Parker cowboys in from everywhere. And all the girls from Waimea up, and the girls from Waipio, and Honokaa, and Paauilo—I can see them yet, sitting in long rows on top the stone walls of the breaking pen and making *leis* for their cowboy lovers. And the nights, the perfumed nights, the chanting of the meles and the dancing of the hulas, and the big Mana grounds with lovers everywhere strolling two by two under the trees.

"And the Prince ..." Bella paused, and for a long minute her small fine teeth, still perfect, showed deep in her underlip as she sought and won control and sent her gaze vacantly out across the far blue horizon. As she relaxed, her eyes came back to her sister.

"He was a prince, Martha. You saw him at Kilohana before ... after you came home from seminary. He filled the eyes of any woman, yes, and of any man. Twenty-five he was, in all-glorious ripeness of man, great and princely in body as he was great and princely in spirit. No matter how wild the fun, how reckless mad the sport, he never seemed to forget that he was royal, and that all his forebears had been high chiefs even to that first one they sang in the genealogies, who had navigated his double-canoes to Tahiti and Raiatea and back again. He was gracious, sweet, kindly, comradely, all friendliness—and severe, and stern, and harsh, if he were crossed too grievously. It is hard to express what I mean. He was all man, man, man, and he was all prince, with a strain of the merry boy in him, and the iron in him that would have made him a good and strong king of Hawaii had he come to the throne.

"I can see him yet, as I saw him that first day and touched his hand and talked with him . . . few words and bashful, and anything but a year-long married woman to a grey haole at grey Nahala. Half a century ago it was, that meeting—you remember how our young men then dressed in white shoes and trousers, white silk shirts, with, slashed around the middle, the gorgeously colourful Spanish sashes—and for half a century that picture of him has not faded in my heart. He was the centre of a group on the lawn, and I was being brought by Ella Higginsworth to be presented. The Princess Lihue had just called some teasing chaff to her which had made her halt to respond and left me halted a pace in front of her.

"His glance chanced to light on me, alone there, perturbed, embarrassed. Oh, how I see him!—his head thrown back a little, with that high, bright, imperious, and utterly carefree poise that was so usual of him. Our eyes met. His head bent forward, or straightened to me, I don't know what happened. Did he command? Did I obey? I do not know. I know only that I was good to look upon, crowned with fragrant *maile*, clad in Princess Naomi's wonderful holoku loaned me by Uncle John from his taboo room; and I know that I advanced alone to him across the Mana lawn, and that he stepped forth from those about him to meet me half-way. We came to each other across the grass, unattended, as if we were coming to each other across our lives.

"Was I very beautiful, Sister Martha, when I was young? I do not know. I don't know. But in that moment, with all his beauty and truly royal-manness crossing to me and penetrating to the heart of me, I felt a sudden sense of beauty in myself—how shall I say?—as if in him and from him perfection were engendered and conjured within myself.

"No word was spoken. But, oh, I know I raised my face in frank answer to the thunder and trumpets of the message unspoken, and that, had it been death for that one look and that one moment I could not have refrained from the gift of myself that must have been in my face and eyes, in the very body of me that breathed so high.

"Was I beautiful, very beautiful, Martha, when I was nineteen, just turning into twenty?"

And Martha, three-score and four, looked upon Bella, three-score and eight, and nodded genuine affirmation, and to herself added the appreciation of the instant in what she beheld—Bella's neck, still full and shapely, longer than the ordinary Hawaiian woman's neck, a pillar that carried regally her high-cheeked, high-browed, high chiefess face and head; Bella's hair, high-piled, intact, sparkling the silver of the years, ringleted still and contrasting definitely and sharply with her clean, slim, black brows and deep brown eyes. And Martha's glance, in modest overwhelming of modesty by what she saw, dropped down the splendid breast of her and generously true lines of body to the feet, silken clad, high-heeled-slippered, small, plump, with an almost Spanish arch and faultlessness of instep.

"When one is young, the one young time!" Bella laughed. "Lilolilo was a prince. I came to know his every feature and their every phase... afterward, in our wonder days and nights by the singing waters, by the slumber-drowsy surfs, and on the mountain ways. I knew his fine, brave eyes, with their straight, black brows, the nose of him that was assuredly a Kamehameha nose, and the last, least, lovable curve of his mouth. There is no mouth more beautiful than the Hawaiian, Martha.

"And his body. He was a king of athletes, from his wicked, wayward hair to his ankles of bronzed steel. Just the other day I heard one of the Wilder grandsons referred to as 'The Prince of Harvard.' Mercy! What would they, what could they have called my Lilolilo could they have matched him against this Wilder lad and all his team at Harvard!"

Bella ceased and breathed deeply, the while she clasped her fine small hands in her ample silken lap. But her pink fairness blushed faintly through her skin and warmed her eyes as she relived her prince-days.

"Well—you have guessed?" Bella said, with defiant shrug of shoulders and a straight gaze into her sister's eyes. "We rode out from gay Mana and continued the gay progress—down the lava trails to Kiholo to the swimming and the fishing and the feasting and the sleeping in the warm sand under the palms; and up to Puuwaawaa, and more pig-sticking, and roping and driving, and wild mutton from the upper pasture-lands; and on through Kona, now *mauka*, now down to the King's palace at Kailua, and to the swimming at Keauhou, and to Kealakekua Bay, and Napoopoo and Honaunau. And everywhere the people turning out, in their hands gifts of flowers, and fruit, and fish, and pig, in their hearts love and song, their heads bowed in obeisance to the royal ones while their lips ejaculated exclamations of amazement or chanted meles of old and unforgotten days.

"What would you, Sister Martha? You know what we Hawaiians are. You know what we were half a hundred years ago. Lilolilo was wonderful. I was reckless. Lilolilo of himself could make any woman reckless. I was twice reckless, for I had cold, grey Nahala to spur me on. I knew. I had never a doubt. Never a hope. Divorces in those days were undreamed. The wife of George Castner could never be queen of Hawaii, even if Uncle Robert's prophesied revolutions were delayed, and if Lilolilo himself became king. But I never thought of the throne. What I wanted would have been the queendom of being Lilolilo's wife and mate. But I made no mistake. What was impossible was impossible, and I dreamed no false dream.

"It was the very atmosphere of love. And Lilolilo was a lover. I was for ever crowned with *leis* by him, and he had his runners bring me leis all the way from the rose-gardens of Mana—you remember them; fifty miles across the lava and the ranges, dewy fresh as the moment they were plucked, in their jewel-cases of banana bark; yard-long they were, the tiny pink buds like threaded beads of Neapolitan coral. And at the *luaus,* the for ever never-ending luaus, I must be seated on Lilo-lilo's Makaloa mat, the Prince's mat, his alone and taboo to any lesser mortal save by his own condescension and desire. And I must dip my fingers into his own *pa wai holoi* where scented flower petals floated in the warm water. Yes, and careless that all should see his extended favour, I must dip into his *pa paakai* for my pinches of red salt, and limu, and kukui nut and chili pepper; and into his *ipu kai* of *kou* wood that the great Kamehameha himself had eaten from on many a similar progress. And it was the same for special delicacies that were for Lilo-lilo and the Princess alone—for his *nelu,* and the *ake,* and the *palu,* and the *alaala.* And his *kahilis* were waved over me, and his attendants were mine, and he was mine; and from my flower-crowned hair to my happy feet I was a woman loved."

Once again Bella's small teeth pressed into her underlip, as she gazed vacantly seaward and won control of herself and her memories.

"It was on, and on, through all Kona, and all Kau, from Hoopuloa and Kapua to Honuapo and Punaluu, a life-time of living compressed into two short weeks. A flower blooms but once. That was my time of bloom—Lilolilo beside me, myself on my wonderful Hilo, a queen, not of Hawaii, but of Lilolilo and Love. He said I was a bubble of colour and beauty on the black back of Leviathan; that I was a fragile dewdrop on the smoking crest of a lava flow; that I was a rainbow riding the thunder cloud ..."

Bella paused for a moment.

"I shall tell you no more of what he said to me," she declared gravely; "save that the things he said were fire of love and essence of beauty, and that he composed hulas to me, and sang them to me, before all, of nights under the stars as we lay on our mats at the feasting; and I on the Makaloa mat of Lilolilo.

"And it was on to Kilauea—the dream so near its ending; and of course we tossed into the pit of sea-surging lava our offerings to *Pele* of maile leis and of fish and hard poi wrapped moist in the *ti* leaves. And we continued down through old Puna, and feasted and danced and sang at Kohoualea and Kamaili and Opihikao, and swam in the clear, sweet-water pools of Kalapana. And in the end came to Hilo by the sea.

"It was the end. We had never spoken. It was the end recognized and unmentioned. The yacht waited. We were days late. Honolulu called, and the news was that the King had gone particularly *pupule*, that there were Catholic and Protestant missionary plottings, and that trouble with France was brewing. As they had landed at Kawaihae two weeks before with laughter and flowers and song, so they departed from Hilo. It was a merry parting, full of fun and frolic and a thousand last messages and reminders and jokes. The anchor was broken out to a song of farewell from Lilolilo's singing boys on the quarterdeck, while we, in the big canoes and whaleboats, saw the first breeze fill the vessel's sails and the distance begin to widen.

"Through all the confusion and excitement, Lilolilo, at the rail, who must say last farewells and quip last jokes to many, looked squarely down at me. On his head he wore my *ilima* lei, which I had made for him and placed there. And into the canoes, to the favoured ones, they on the yacht began tossing their many leis. I had no expectancy of hope … And yet I hoped, in a small wistful way that I know did not show in my face, which was as proud and merry as any there. But Lilolilo did what I knew he would do, what I had known from the first he would do. Still looking me squarely and honestly in the eyes, he took my beautiful ilima lei from his head and tore it across. I saw his lips shape, but not utter aloud, the single word *pau*. Still looking at me, he broke both parts of the lei in two again and tossed the deliberate fragments, not to me, but down overside into the widening water. Pau. It was finished …"

For a long space Bella's vacant gaze rested on the sea horizon. Martha ventured no mere voice expression of the sympathy that moistened her own eyes.

"And I rode on that day, up the old bad trail along the Hamakua coast," Bella resumed, with a voice at first singularly dry and harsh. "That first day was not so hard. I was numb. I was too full with the wonder of all I had to forget to know that I had to forget it. I spent the night at Laupahoehoe. Do you know, I had expected a sleepless night. Instead, weary from the saddle, still numb, I slept the night through as if I had been dead.

"But the next day, in driving wind and drenching rain! How it blew and poured! The trail was really impassable. Again and again our horses went down. At first the cowboy Uncle John had loaned me with the horses protested, then he followed stolidly in the rear, shaking his head, and, I know, muttering over and over that I was pupule. The pack horse was abandoned at Kukuihaele. We almost swam up Mud Lane in a river of mud. At Waimea the cowboy had to exchange for a fresh mount. But Hilo lasted through. From daybreak till midnight I was in the saddle, till Uncle John, at Kilohana, took me off my horse, in his arms, and carried me in, and routed the women from their beds to undress me and lomi me, while he plied me with hot toddies and drugged me to sleep and forgetfulness. I know I must have babbled and raved. Uncle John must have guessed. But never to another, nor even to me, did he ever breathe a whisper. Whatever he guessed he locked away in the taboo room of Naomi.

"I do have fleeting memories of some of that day, all a broken-hearted mad rage against fate—of my hair down and whipped wet and stinging about me in the driving rain; of endless tears of weeping contributed to the general deluge, of passionate outbursts and resentments against a world all twisted and wrong, of beatings of my hands upon my saddle pommel, of asperities to my Kilohana cowboy, of spurs into the ribs of poor magnificent Hilo, with a prayer on my lips, bursting out from my heart, that the spurs would so madden him as to make him rear and fall on me and crush my body for ever out of all beauty for man, or topple me off the trail and finish me at the foot of the *palis*, writing pau at the end of my name as final as the unuttered pau on Lilolilo's lips when he tore across my ilima lei and dropped it in the sea. . . .

"Husband George was delayed in Honolulu. When he came back to Nahala I was there waiting for him. And solemnly he embraced me, perfunctorily kissed my lips, gravely examined my tongue, decried my looks and state of health, and sent me to bed with hot stove-lids and a dosage of castor oil. Like entering into the machinery of a clock and becoming one of the cogs or wheels, inevitably and remorselessly turning around and around, so I entered back into the grey life of Nahala. Out of bed was Husband George at half after four every morning, and out of the house and astride his horse at five. There was the eternal porridge, and the horrible cheap coffee, and the fresh beef and jerky. I cooked, and baked, and scrubbed. I ground around the crazy hand sewing machine and made my cheap holokus. Night after night, through the endless centuries of two years more, I sat across the table from him until eight o'clock, mending his cheap socks and shoddy underwear, while he read the years' old borrowed magazines he was too thrifty to subscribe to. And then it was bed-time—kerosene must be economized—and he wound his watch, entered the weather in his diary, and took off his shoes, the right shoe first, and placed them, just so, side by side, at the foot of the bed on his side.

"But there was no more of my drawing to Husband George, as had been the promise ere the Princess Lihue invited me on the progress and Uncle John loaned me the horse. You see, Sister Martha, nothing would have happened had Uncle John refused me the horse. But I had known love, and I had known Lilolilo; and what chance, after that, had Husband George to win from me heart of esteem or affection? And for two years, at Nahala, I was a dead woman who somehow walked and talked, and baked and scrubbed, and mended socks and saved kerosene. The doctors said it was the shoddy underwear that did for him, pursuing as always the high-mountain Nahala waters in the drenching storms of midwinter.

"When he died, I was not sad. I had been sad too long already. Nor was I glad. Gladness had died at Hilo when Lilolilo dropped my ilima lei into the sea and my feet were never happy again. Lilolilo passed within a month after Husband George. I had never seen him since the parting at Hilo. La, la, suitors a many have I had since; but I was like Uncle John. Mating for me was but once. Uncle John had his Naomi room at Kilohana. I have had my Lilolilo room for fifty years in my heart. You are the first, Sister Martha, whom I have permitted to enter that room ..."

A machine swung the circle of the drive, and from it, across the lawn, approached the husband of Martha. Erect, slender, grey-haired, of graceful military bearing, Roscoe Scandwell was a member of the "Big Five," which, by the interlocking of interests, determined the destinies of all Hawaii. Himself pure haole, New England born, he kissed Bella first, arms around, full-hearty, in the Hawaiian way. His alert eye told him that there had been a woman talk, and, despite the signs of all generousness of emotion, that all was well and placid in the twilight wisdom that was theirs.

"Elsie and the younglings are coming—just got a wireless from their steamer," he announced, after he had kissed his wife. "And they'll be spending several days with us before they go on to Maui."

"I was going to put you in the Rose Room, Sister Bella," Martha Scandwell planned aloud. "But it will be better for her and the children and the nurses and everything there, so you shall have Queen Emma's Room."

"I had it last time, and I prefer it," Bella said.

Roscoe Scandwell, himself well taught of Hawaiian love and love-ways, erect, slender, dignified, between the two nobly proportioned women, an arm around each of their sumptuous waists, proceeded with them toward the house.

Waikiki, Hawaii
June 6, 1916

THE TEARS OF AH KIM

There was a great noise and racket, but no scandal, in Honolulu's
Chinatown. Those within hearing distance merely shrugged their
shoulders and smiled tolerantly at the disturbance as an affair of accustomed usualness. "What is it?" asked Chin Mo, down with a sharp
pleurisy, of his wife, who had paused for a second at the open window
to listen.

"Only Ah Kim," was her reply. "His mother is beating him again."

The fracas was taking place in the garden, behind the living
rooms that were at the back of the store that fronted on the street
with the proud sign above: AH KIM COMPANY, GENERAL MERCHANDISE.
The garden was a miniature domain, twenty feet square, that somehow cunningly seduced the eye into a sense and seeming of illimitable
vastness. There were forests of dwarf pines and oaks, centuries old yet
two or three feet in height, and imported at enormous care and expense. A tiny bridge, a pace across, arched over a miniature river that
flowed with rapids and cataracts from a miniature lake stocked with
myriad-finned, orange-miracled goldfish that in proportion to the lake
and landscape were whales. On every side the many windows of the

several-storied shack-buildings looked down. In the centre of the garden, on the narrow gravelled walk close beside the lake Ah Kim was
noisily receiving his beating.

No Chinese lad of tender and beatable years was Ah Kim. His was
the store of Ah Kim Company, and his was the achievement of building it up through the long years from the shoestring of savings of a
contract coolie labourer to a bank account in four figures and a credit
that was gilt edged. An even half-century of summers and winters had
passed over his head, and, in the passing, fattened him comfortably and
snugly. Short of stature, his full front was as rotund as a water-melon
seed. His face was moon-faced. His garb was dignified and silken, and
his black-silk skull-cap with the red button atop, now, alas! fallen on
the ground, was the skull-cap worn by the successful and dignified
merchants of his race.

But his appearance, in this moment of the present, was anything but
dignified. Dodging and ducking under a rain of blows from a bamboo
cane, he was crouched over in a half-doubled posture. When he was
rapped on the knuckles and elbows, with which he shielded his face
and head, his winces were genuine and involuntary. From the many
surrounding windows the neighbourhood looked down with placid
enjoyment.

And she who wielded the stick so shrewdly from long practice!
Seventy-four years old, she looked every minute of her time. Her thin
legs were encased in straight-lined pants of linen stiff-textured and
shiny-black. Her scraggly grey hair was drawn unrelentingly and flatly
back from a narrow, unrelenting forehead. Eyebrows she had none,
having long since shed them. Her eyes, of pin-hole tininess, were black-
est black. She was shockingly cadaverous. Her shrivelled forearm,
exposed by the loose sleeve, possessed no more of muscle than several taut bowstrings stretched across meagre bone under yellow,
parchment-like skin. Along this mummy arm jade bracelets shot up
and down and clashed with every blow.

"Ah!" she cried out, rhythmically accenting her blows in series of
three to each shrill observation. "I forbade you to talk to Li Faa. To-
day you stopped on the street with her. Not an hour ago. Half an hour
by the clock you talked.—What is that?"

"It was the thrice-accursed telephone," Ah Kim muttered, while she suspended the stick to catch what he said. "Mrs. Chang Lucy told you. I know she did. I saw her see me. I shall have the telephone taken out. It is of the devil."

"It is a device of all the devils," Mrs. Tai Fu agreed, taking a fresh grip on the stick. "Yet shall the telephone remain. I like to talk with Mrs. Chang Lucy over the telephone."

"She has the eyes of ten thousand cats," quoth Ah Kim, ducking and receiving the stick stinging on his knuckles. "And the tongues of ten thousand toads," he supplemented ere his next duck.

"She is an impudent-faced and evil-mannered hussy," Mrs. Tai Fu accented.

"Mrs. Chang Lucy was ever that," Ah Kim murmured like the dutiful son he was.

"I speak of Li Faa," his mother corrected with stick emphasis. "She is only half Chinese, as you know. Her mother was a shameless kanaka. She wears skirts like the degraded haole women—also corsets, as I have seen for myself. Where are her children? Yet has she buried two husbands."

"The one was drowned, the other kicked by a horse," Ah Kim qualified.

"A year of her, unworthy son of a noble father, and you would gladly be going out to get drowned or be kicked by a horse."

Subdued chucklings and laughter from the window audience applauded her point.

"You buried two husbands yourself, revered mother," Ah Kim was stung to retort.

"I had the good taste not to marry a third. Besides, my two husbands died honourably in their beds. They were not kicked by horses nor drowned at sea. What business is it of our neighbours that you should inform them I have had two husbands, or ten, or none? You have made a scandal of me, before all our neighbours, and for that I shall now give you a real beating."

Ah Kim endured the staccato rain of blows, and said when his mother paused, breathless and weary:

"Always have I insisted and pleaded, honourable mother, that you beat me in the house, with the windows and doors closed tight, and not in the open street or the garden open behind the house."

"You have called this unthinkable Li Faa the Silvery Moon Blossom," Mrs. Tai Fu rejoined, quite illogically and femininely, but with utmost success in so far as she deflected her son from continuance of the thrust he had so swiftly driven home.

"Mrs. Chang Lucy told you," he charged.

"I was told over the telephone," his mother evaded. "I do not know all voices that speak to me over that contrivance of all the devils."

Strangely, Ah Kim made no effort to run away from his mother, which he could easily have done. She, on the other hand, found fresh cause for more stick blows.

"Ah! Stubborn one! Why do you not cry? Mule that shameth its ancestors! Never have I made you cry. From the time you were a little boy I have never made you cry. Answer me! Why do you not cry?"

Weak and breathless from her exertions, she dropped the stick and panted and shook as if with a nervous palsy.

"I do not know, except that it is my way," Ah Kim replied, gazing solicitously at his mother. "I shall bring you a chair now, and you will sit down and rest and feel better."

But she flung away from him with a snort and tottered agedly across the garden into the house. Meanwhile recovering his skull-cap and smoothing his disordered attire, Ah Kim rubbed his hurts and gazed after her with eyes of devotion. He even smiled, and almost might it appear that he had enjoyed the beating.

Ah Kim had been so beaten ever since he was a boy, when he lived on the high banks of the eleventh cataract of the Yangtse River. Here his father had been born and toiled all his days from young manhood as a towing coolie. While he died, Ah Kim, in his own young manhood, took up the same honourable profession. Farther back than all remembered annals of the family, had the males of it been towing coolies. At the time of Christ his direct ancestors had been doing the same thing, meeting the precisely similarly modelled junks below the white water at the foot of the canyon, bending the half-mile of rope to each junk, and, according to size, tailing on from a hundred to two hundred coolies of them and by sheer, two-legged man-power, bowed forward and down till their hands touched the ground and their faces were sometimes within a foot of it, dragging the junk up through the white water to the head of the canyon.

Apparently, down all the intervening centuries, the payment of the trade had not picked up. His father, his father's father, and himself, Ah Kim, had received the same invariable remuneration—per junk one-fourteenth of a cent, at the rate he had since learned money was valued in Hawaii. On long lucky summer days when the waters were easy, the junks many, the hours of daylight sixteen, sixteen hours of such heroic toil would earn over a cent. But in a whole year a towing coolie did not earn more than a dollar and a half. People could and did live on such an income. There were women servants who received a yearly wage of a dollar. The net makers of Ti Wi earned between a dollar and two dollars a year. They lived on such wages, or, at least, they did not die on them. But for the towing coolies there were pickings, which were what made the profession honourable and the guild a close and hereditary corporation or labour union. One junk in five that was dragged up through the rapids or lowered down was wrecked. One junk in every ten was a total loss. The coolies of the towing guild knew the freaks and whims of the currents, and grappled, and raked, and netted a wet harvest from the river. They of the guild were looked up to by lesser coolies, for they could afford to drink brick tea and eat number four rice every day.

And Ah Kim had been contented and proud, until, one bitter spring day of driving sleet and hail, he dragged ashore a drowning Cantonese sailor. It was this wanderer, thawing out by his fire, who first named the magic name Hawaii to him. He had himself never been to that labourer's paradise, said the sailor, but many Chinese had gone there from Canton, and he had heard the talk of their letters written back. In Hawaii was never frost nor famine. The very pigs, never fed, were ever fat of the generous offal disdained by man. A Cantonese or Yangtse family could live on the waste of an Hawaii coolie. And wages! In gold dollars, ten a month, or, in trade dollars, two a month, was what the contract Chinese coolie received from the white-devil sugar kings. In a year the coolie received the prodigious sum of two hundred and forty trade dollars—more than a hundred times what a coolie, toiling ten times as hard, received on the eleventh cataract of the Yangtse. In short, all things considered, an Hawaii coolie was one hundred times better off, and, when the amount of labour was estimated, a thousand times better off. In addition was the wonderful climate.

When Ah Kim was twenty-four, despite his mother's pleadings and beatings, he resigned from the ancient and honourable guild of the eleventh cataract towing coolies, left his mother to go into a boss coolie's household as a servant for a dollar a year, and an annual dress to cost not less than thirty cents, and himself departed down the Yangtse to the great sea. Many were his adventures and severe his toils and hardships ere, as a salt-sea junk-sailor, he won to Canton. When he was twenty-six he signed five years of his life and labour away to the Hawaii sugar kings and departed, one of eight hundred contract coolies, for that far island land, on a festering steamer run by a crazy captain and drunken officers and rejected of Lloyds.

Honourable, among labourers, had Ah Kim's rating been as a towing coolie. In Hawaii, receiving a hundred times more pay, he found himself looked down upon as the lowest of the low—a plantation coolie, than which could be nothing lower. But a coolie whose ancestors had towed junks up the eleventh cataract of the Yangtse since before the birth of Christ inevitably inherits one character in large degree, namely, the character of patience. This patience was Ah Kim's. At the end of five years, his compulsory servitude over, thin as ever in body, in bank account he lacked just ten trade dollars of possessing a thousand trade dollars.

On this sum he could have gone back to the Yangtse and retired for life a really wealthy man. He would have possessed a larger sum, had he not, on occasion, conservatively played che fa and fan tan, and had he not, for a twelve-month, toiled among the centipedes and scorpions of the stifling cane-fields in the semi-dream of a continuous opium debauch. Why he had not toiled the whole five years under the spell of opium was the expensiveness of the habit. He had had no moral scruples. The drug had cost too much.

But Ah Kim did not return to China. He had observed the business life of Hawaii and developed a vaulting ambition. For six months, in order to learn business and English at the bottom, he clerked in the plantation store. At the end of this time he knew more about that particular store than did ever plantation manager know about any plantation store. When he resigned his position he was receiving forty gold a month, or eighty trade, and he was beginning to put on flesh. Also, his attitude toward mere contract coolies had become distinctively aristocratic. The manager offered to raise him to sixty fold, which, by the year, would constitute a fabulous fourteen hundred and forty trade, or seven hundred times his annual earning on the Yangtse as a two-legged horse at one-fourteenth of a gold cent per junk.

Instead of accepting, Ah Kim departed to Honolulu, and in the big general merchandise store of Fong & Chow Fong began at the bottom for fifteen gold per month. He worked a year and a half, and resigned when he was thirty-three, despite the seventy-five gold per month his Chinese employers were paying him. Then it was that he put up his own sign: AH KIM COMPANY, GENERAL MERCHANDISE. Also, better fed, there was about his less meagre figure a foreshadowing of the melon-seed rotundity that was to attach to him in future years.

With the years he prospered increasingly, so that, when he was thirty-six, the promise of his figure was fulfilling rapidly, and, himself a member of the exclusive and powerful Hai Gum Tong, and of the Chinese Merchants' Association, he was accustomed to sitting as host at dinners that cost him as much as thirty years of towing on the eleventh cataract would have earned him. Two things he missed: a wife, and his mother to lay the stick on him as of yore.

When he was thirty-seven he consulted his bank balance. It stood him three thousand gold. For twenty-five hundred down and an easy mortgage he could buy the three-story shack-building, and the ground in fee simple on which it stood. But to do this, left only five hundred for a wife. Fu Yee Po had a marriageable, properly small-footed daughter whom he was willing to import from China, and sell to him for eight hundred gold, plus the costs of importation. Further, Fu Yee Po was even willing to take five hundred down and the remainder on note at 6 per cent.

Ah Kim, thirty-seven years of age, fat and a bachelor, really did want a wife, especially a small-footed wife; for, China born and reared, the immemorial small-footed female had been deeply impressed into his fantasy of woman. But more, even more and far more than a small-footed wife, did he want his mother and his mother's delectable beatings. So he declined Fu Yee Po's easy terms, and at much less cost imported his own mother from servant in a boss coolie's house at a yearly wage of a dollar and a thirty-cent dress to be mistress of his Honolulu three-story shack building with two household servants, three clerks, and a porter of all work under her, to say nothing of ten thousand dollars' worth of dress goods on the shelves that ranged from the cheapest cotton crepes to the most expensive hand-embroidered silks. For be it known that even in that early day Ah Kim's emporium was beginning to cater to the tourist trade from the States.

For thirteen years Ah Kim had lived tolerably happily with his mother, and by her been methodically beaten for causes just or unjust, real or fancied; and at the end of it all he knew as strongly as ever the ache of his heart and head for a wife, and of his loins for sons to live after him, and carry on the dynasty of Ah Kim Company. Such the dream that has ever vexed men, from those early ones who first usurped a hunting right, monopolized a sandbar for a fish-trap, or stormed a village and put the males thereof to the sword. Kings, millionaires, and Chinese merchants of Honolulu have this in common, despite that they may praise God for having made them differently and in self-likable images.

And the ideal of woman that Ah Kim at fifty ached for had changed from his ideal at thirty-seven. No small-footed wife did he want now, but a free, natural, out-stepping normal-footed woman that, somehow, appeared to him in his day dreams and haunted his night visions in the form of Li Faa, the Silvery Moon Blossom. What if she were twice widowed, the daughter of a kanaka mother, the wearer of white-devil skirts and corsets and high-heeled slippers! He wanted her. It seemed it was written that she should be joint ancestor with him of the line that would continue the ownership and management through the generations, of Ah Kim Company, General Merchandise.

———

"I will have no half *paké* daughter-in-law," his mother often reiterated to Ah Kim, paké being the Hawaiian word for Chinese. "All paké must my daughter-in-law be, even as you, my son, and as I, your mother. And she must wear trousers, my son, as all the women of our family before her. No woman, in she-devil skirts and corsets, can pay due reverence to our ancestors. Corsets and reverence do not go together. Such a one is this shameless Li Faa. She is impudent and independent, and will be neither obedient to her husband nor her husband's mother. This brazen-faced Li Faa would believe herself the source of life and the first ancestor, recognizing no ancestors before her. She laughs at our joss-sticks, and paper prayers, and family gods, as I have been well told—"

"Mrs. Chang Lucy," Ah Kim groaned.

"Not alone Mrs. Chang Lucy, O son. I have inquired. At least a dozen have heard her say of our joss house that it is all monkey foolishness. The words are hers—she, who eats raw fish, raw squid, and baked dog. Ours is the foolishness of monkeys. Yet would she marry you, a monkey, because of your store that is a palace and of the wealth that makes you a great man. And she would put shame on me, and on your father before you long honourably dead."

And there was no discussing the matter. As things were, Ah Kim knew his mother was right. Not for nothing had Li Faa been born forty years before of a Chinese father, renegade to all tradition, and of a kanaka mother whose immediate forebears had broken the taboos, cast down their own Polynesian gods, and weak-heartedly listened to the preaching about the remote and unimageable god of the Christian missionaries. Li Faa, educated, who could read and write English and Hawaiian and a fair measure of Chinese, claimed to believe in nothing, although in her secret heart she feared the kahunas, who she was certain could charm away ill luck or pray one to death. Li Faa would never come into Ah Kim's house, as he thoroughly knew, and kow-tow to his mother and be slave to her in the immemorial Chinese way. Li Faa, from the Chinese angle, was a new woman, a feminist, who rode horseback astride, disported immodestly garbed at Waikiki on the surf-boards, and at more than one luau had been known to dance the hula with the worst and in excess of the worst, to the scandalous delight of all.

Ah Kim himself, a generation younger than his mother, had been bitten by the acid of modernity. The old order held, in so far as he still felt in his subtlest crypts of being the dusty hand of the past resting on him, residing in him; yet he subscribed to heavy policies of fire and life insurance, acted as treasurer for the local Chinese revolutionists that were for turning the Celestial Empire into a republic, contributed to the funds of the Hawaii-born Chinese baseball nine that excelled the Yankee nines at their own game, talked theosophy with Katso Suguri, the Japanese Buddhist and silk importer, fell for police graft, played and paid his insidious share in the democratic politics of annexed Hawaii, and was thinking of buying an automobile. Ah Kim never dared bare himself to himself and thrash out and winnow out how much of the old he had ceased to believe in. His mother was of the old, yet he revered her and was happy under her bamboo stick. Li Faa, the Silvery Moon Blossom, was of the new, yet he could never be quite completely happy without her.

For he loved Li Faa. Moon-faced, rotund as a water-melon seed, canny business man, wise with half a century of living—nevertheless Ah Kim became an artist when he thought of her. He thought of her in poems of names, as woman transmuted into flower-terms of beauty and philosophic abstractions of achievement and easement. She was, to him, and alone to him of all men in the world, his Plum Blossom, his Tranquillity of Woman, his Flower of Serenity, his Moon Lily, and his Perfect Rest. And as he murmured these love endearments of namings, it seemed to him that in them were the ripplings of running waters, the tinklings of silver wind-bells, and the scents of the oleander and the jasmine. She was his poem of woman, a lyric delight, a three-dimensions of flesh and spirit delicious, a fate and a good fortune written, ere the first man and woman were, by the gods whose whim had been to make all men and women for sorrow and for joy.

But his mother put into his hand the ink-brush and placed under it, on the table, the writing tablet.

"Paint," she said, "the ideograph of *to marry.*"

He obeyed, scarcely wondering, with the deft artistry of his race and training painting the symbolic hieroglyphic.

"Resolve it," commanded his mother.

Ah Kim looked at her, curious, willing to please, unaware of the drift of her intent.

"Of what is it composed?" she persisted. "What are the three originals, the sum of which is it: to marry, marriage, the coming together and wedding of a man and a woman? Paint them, paint them apart, the three originals, unrelated, so that we may know how the wise men of old wisely built up the ideograph of *to marry*."

And Ah Kim, obeying and painting, saw that what he had painted were three picture-signs—the picture-signs of a hand, an ear, and a woman.

"Name them," said his mother; and he named them.

"It is true," said she. "It is a great tale. It is the stuff of the painted pictures of marriage. Such marriage was in the beginning; such shall it always be in my house. The hand of the man takes the woman's ear, and by it leads her away to his house, where she is to be obedient to him and to his mother. I was taken by the ear, so, by your long honourably dead father. I have looked at your hand. It is not like his hand. Also have I looked at the ear of Li Faa. Never will you lead her by the ear. She has not that kind of an ear. I shall live a long time yet, and I will be mistress in my son's house, after our ancient way, until I die."

———

"But she is my revered ancestress," Ah Kim explained to Li Faa.

He was timidly unhappy; for Li Faa, having ascertained that Mrs. Tai Fu was at the temple of the Chinese Æsculapius making a food offering of dried duck and prayers for her declining health, had taken advantage of the opportunity to call upon him in his store.

Li Faa pursed her insolent, unpainted lips into the form of a half-opened rosebud, and replied:

"That will do for China. I do not know China. This is Hawaii, and in Hawaii the customs of all foreigners change."

"She is nevertheless my ancestress," Ah Kim protested, "the mother who gave me birth, whether I am in China or Hawaii, O Silvery Moon Blossom that I want for wife."

"I have had two husbands," Li Faa stated placidly. "One was a paké, one was a Portuguese. I learned much from both. Also am I educated. I have been to High School, and I have played the piano in public. And I learned from my two husbands much. The paké makes the best husband. Never again will I marry anything but a paké. But he must not take me by the ear—"

"How do you know of that?" he broke in suspiciously.

"Mrs. Chang Lucy," was the reply. "Mrs. Chang Lucy tells me every-thing that your mother tells her, and your mother tells her much. So let me tell you that mine is not that kind of an ear."

"Which is what my honoured mother has told me," Ah Kim groaned.

"Which is what your honoured mother told Mrs. Chang Lucy, which is what Mrs. Chang Lucy told me," Li Faa completed equably. "And I now tell you, O Third Husband To Be, that the man is not born who will lead me by the ear. It is not the way in Hawaii. I will go only hand in hand with my man, side by side, fifty-fifty as is the haole slang just now. My Portuguese husband thought different. He tried to beat me. I landed him three times in the police court and each time he worked out his sentence on the reef. After that he got drowned."

"My mother has been my mother for fifty years," Ah Kim declared stoutly.

"And for fifty years has she beaten you," Li Faa giggled. "How my father used to laugh at Yap Ten Shin! Like you, Yap Ten Shin had been born in China, and had brought the China customs with him. His old father was for ever beating him with a stick. He loved his father. But his father beat him harder than ever when he became a missionary paké. Every time he went to the missionary services, his father beat him. And every time the missionary heard of it he was harsh in his language to Yap Ten Shin for allowing his father to beat him. And my father laughed and laughed, for my father was a very liberal paké, who had changed his customs quicker than most foreigners. And all the trouble was because Yap Ten Shin had a loving heart. He loved his honourable father. He loved the God of Love of the Christian missionary. But in the end, in me, he found the greatest love of all, which is the love of woman. In me he forgot his love for his father and his love for the lov-ing Christ.

"And he offered my father six hundred gold, for me—the price was small because my feet were not small. But I was half kanaka. I said that I was not a slave-woman, and that I would be sold to no man. My high-school teacher was a haole old maid who said love of woman was so be-yond price that it must never be sold. Perhaps that is why she was an old maid. She was not beautiful. She could not give herself away. My kanaka mother said it was not the kanaka way to sell their daughters for a money price. They gave their daughters for love, and she would listen to reason if Yap Ten Shin provided luaus in quantity and quality. My paké father, as I have told you, was liberal. He asked me if I wanted Yap Ten Shin for my husband. And I said yes; and freely, of myself, I went to him. He it was who was kicked by a horse; but he was a very good husband before he was kicked by the horse.

"As for you, Ah Kim, you shall always be honourable and lovable for me, and some day, when it is not necessary for you to take me by the ear, I shall marry you and come here and be with you always, and you will be the happiest paké in all Hawaii; for I have had two husbands, and gone to high school, and am most wise in making a husband happy. But that will be when your mother has ceased to beat you. Mrs. Chang Lucy tells me that she beats you very hard."

"She does," Ah Kim affirmed. "Behold!" He thrust back his loose sleeves, exposing to the elbow his smooth and cherubic forearms. They were mantled with black and blue marks that advertised the weight and number of blows so shielded from his head and face.

"But she has never made me cry," Ah Kim disclaimed hastily. "Never, from the time I was a little boy, has she made me cry."

"So Mrs. Chang Lucy says," Li Faa observed. "She says that your honourable mother often complains to her that she has never made you cry."

A sibilant warning from one of his clerks was too late. Having regained the house by way of the back alley, Mrs. Tai Fu emerged right upon them from out of the living apartments. Never had Ah Kim seen his mother's eyes so blazing furious. She ignored Li Faa, as she screamed at him.

"Now will I make you cry. As never before shall I beat you until you do cry."

"Then let us go into the back rooms, honourable mother," Ah Kim suggested. "We will close the windows and the doors, and there may you beat me."

"No. Here shall you be beaten before all the world and this shameless woman who would, with her own hand, take you by the ear and call such sacrilege marriage! Stay, shameless woman."

"I am going to stay anyway," said Li Faa. She favoured the clerks with a truculent stare. "And I'd like to see anything less than the police put me out of here."

"You will never be my daughter-in-law," Mrs. Tai Fu snapped.

Li Faa nodded her head in agreement.

"But just the same," she added, "shall your son be my third husband."

"You mean when I am dead?" the old mother screamed.

"The sun rises each morning," Li Faa said enigmatically. "All my life have I seen it rise—"

"You are forty, and you wear corsets."

"But I do not dye my hair—that will come later," Li Faa calmly retorted. "As to my age you are right. I shall be forty-one next Kamehameha Day. For forty years I have seen the sun rise. My father was an old man. Before he died he told me that he had observed no difference in the rising of the sun since when he was a little boy. The world is round. Confucius did not know that, but you will find it in all the geography books. The world is round. Ever it turns over on itself, over and over and around and around. And the times and seasons of weather and life turn with it. What is, has been before. What has been, will be again. The time of the breadfruit and the mango ever recurs, and man and woman repeat themselves. The robins nest, and in the springtime the plovers come from the north. Every spring is followed by another spring. The coconut palm rises into the air, ripens its fruit, and departs. But always are there more coconut palms. This is not all my own smart talk. Much of it my father told me. Proceed, honourable Mrs. Tai Fu, and beat your son who is my Third Husband To Be. But I shall laugh. I warn you I shall laugh."

Ah Kim dropped down on his knees so as to give his mother every advantage. And while she rained blows upon him with the bamboo stick, Li Faa smiled and giggled, and finally burst into laughter.

"Harder, O honourable Mrs. Tai Fu!" Li Faa urged between paroxysms of mirth.

Mrs. Tai Fu did her best, which was notably weak, until she observed what made her drop the stick by her side in amazement. Ah Kim was crying. Down both cheeks great round tears were coursing. Li Faa was amazed. So were the gaping clerks. Most amazed of all was Ah

Kim, yet he could not help himself; and, although no further blows fell, he cried steadily on.

"But why did you cry?" Li Faa demanded often of Ah Kim. "It was so perfectly foolish a thing to do. She was not even hurting you."

"Wait until we are married," was Ah Kim's invariable reply, "and then, O Moon Lily, will I tell you."

———

Two years later, one afternoon, more like a water-melon seed in configuration than ever, Ah Kim returned home from a meeting of the Chinese Protective Association, to find his mother dead on her couch. Narrower and more unrelenting than ever were the forehead and the brushed back hair. But on her face was a withered smile. The gods had been kind. She had passed without pain.

He telephoned first of all to Li Faa's number but did not find her until he called up Mrs. Chang Lucy. The news given, the marriage was dated ahead with ten times the brevity of the old-line Chinese custom. And if there be anything analogous to a bridesmaid in a Chinese wedding, Mrs. Chang Lucy was just that.

"Why," Li Faa asked Ah Kim when alone with him on their wedding night, "why did you cry when your mother beat you that day in the store? You were so foolish. She was not even hurting you."

"That is why I cried," answered Ah Kim.

Li Faa looked up at him without understanding.

"I cried," he explained, "because I suddenly knew that my mother was nearing her end. There was no weight, no hurt, in her blows. I cried because I knew *she no longer had the strength to hurt me.* That is why I cried, my Flower of Serenity, my Perfect Rest. That is the only reason why I cried."

Waikiki, Honolulu
June 16, 1916

THE BONES OF KAHEKILI

From over the lofty Koolau Mountains, vagrant wisps of the trade wind drifted, faintly swaying the great, unwhipped banana leaves, rustling the palms, and fluttering and setting up a whispering among the lace-leaved algaroba trees. Only intermittently did the atmosphere so breathe—for breathing it was, the suspiring of the languid, Hawaiian afternoon. In the intervals between the soft breathings, the air grew heavy and balmy with the perfume of flowers and the exhalations of fat, living soil.

Of humans about the low bungalow-like house, there were many; but one only of them slept. The rest were on the tense tiptoes of silence. At the rear of the house a tiny babe piped up a thin blatting wail that the quickly thrust breast could not appease. The mother, a slender *hapa-haole*, clad in a loose-flowing holoku of white muslin, hastened away swiftly among the banana and *papaia* trees to remove the babe's noise by distance. Other women, hapa-haole and full native, watched her anxiously as she fled.

At the front of the house, on the grass, squatted a score of Hawaiians. Well-muscled, broad-shouldered, they were all strapping men.

Brown-skinned, with luminous brown eyes and black, their features large and regular, they showed all the signs of being as good-natured, merry-hearted, and soft-tempered as the climate. To all of which a seeming contradiction was given by the ferociousness of their accoutrement. Into the tops of their rough leather leggings were thrust long knives, the handles projecting. On their heels were huge-rowelled Spanish spurs. They had the appearance of banditti, save for the incongruous wreaths of flowers and fragrant maile that encircled the crowns of their flopping cowboy hats. One of them, deliciously and roguishly handsome as a faun, with the eyes of a faun, wore a flaming double-hibiscus bloom coquettishly tucked over his ear. Above them, casting a shelter of shade from the sun, grew a wide-spreading canopy of Ponciana regia, itself a flame of blossoms, out of each of which sprang pompoms of feathery stamens. From far off, muffled by distance, came the faint stamping of their tethered horses. The eyes of all were intently fixed upon the solitary sleeper who lay on his back on a *luuhulu* mat a hundred feet away under the monkey-pod trees.

Large as were the Hawaiian cowboys, the sleeper was larger. Also, as his snow-white hair and beard attested, he was much older. The thickness of his wrist and the greatness of his fingers made authentic the mighty frame of him hidden under loose dungaree pants and cotton shirt, buttonless, open from midriff to Adam's apple, exposing a chest matted with a thatch of hair as white as that of his head and face. The depth and breadth of that chest, its resilience, and its relaxed and plastic muscles, tokened the knotty strength that still resided in him. Further, no bronze and beat of sun and wind availed to hide the testimony of his skin that he was all haole—a white man.

On his back, his great white beard, thrust skyward, untrimmed of barbers, stiffened and subsided with every breath, while with the outblow of every exhalation the white moustache erected perpendicularly like the quills of a porcupine and subsided with each intake. A young girl of fourteen, clad only in a single shift, or *muumuu*, herself a granddaughter of the sleeper, crouched beside him and with a feathered fly-flapper brushed away the flies. In her face were depicted solicitude, and nervousness, and awe, as if she attended on a god.

And truly, Hardman Pool, the sleeping whiskery one, was to her, and to many and sundry, a god—a source of life, a source of food, a fount of wisdom, a giver of law, a smiling beneficence, a blackness of thunder and punishment—in short, a man-master whose record was fourteen living and adult sons and daughters, six great-grandchildren, and more grandchildren than could he in his most lucid moments enumerate.

Fifty-one years before, he had landed from an open boat at Laupahoehoe on the windward coast of Hawaii. The boat was the one surviving one of the whaler *Black Prince* of New Bedford. Himself New Bedford born, twenty years of age, by virtue of his driving strength and ability he had served as second mate on the lost whaleship. Coming to Honolulu and casting about for himself, he had first married Kalama Mamaiopili, next acted as pilot of Honolulu Harbour, after that started a saloon and boarding house, and, finally, on the death of Kalama's father, engaged in cattle ranching on the broad pasture lands she had inherited.

For over half a century he had lived with the Hawaiians, and it was conceded that he knew their language better than did most of them. By marrying Kalama, he had married not merely her land, but her own chief rank, and the fealty owed by the commoners to her by virtue of her genealogy was also accorded him. In addition, he possessed of himself all the natural attributes of chiefship: the gigantic stature, the fearlessness, the pride; and the high hot temper that could brook no impudence nor insult, that could be neither bullied nor awed by an utmost magnificence of power that walked on two legs, and that could compel service of lesser humans, not by any ignoble purchase by bargaining, but by an unspoken but expected condescending of largesse. He knew his Hawaiians from the outside and the in, knew them better than themselves, their Polynesian circumlocutions, faiths, customs, and mysteries.

And at seventy-one, after a morning in the saddle over the ranges that began at four o'clock, he lay under the monkey-pods in his customary and sacred siesta that no retainer dared to break, nor would dare permit any equal of the great one to break. Only to the King was such a right accorded, and, as the King had early learned, to break Hardman Pool's siesta was to gain awake a very irritable and grumpy

Hardman Pool who would talk straight from the shoulder and say unpleasant but true things that no king would care to hear.

The sun blazed down. The horses stamped remotely. The fading trade-wind wisps sighed and rustled between longer intervals of quiescence. The perfume grew heavier. The woman brought back the babe, quiet again, to the rear of the house. The monkey-pods folded their leaves and swooned to a siesta of their own in the soft air above the sleeper. The girl, breathless as ever from the enormous solemnity of her task, still brushed the flies away; and the score of cowboys still intently and silently watched. Hardman Pool awoke. The next outbreath, expected of the long rhythm, did not take place. Neither did the white, long moustache rise up. Instead, the cheeks, under the whiskers, puffed; the eyelids lifted, exposing blue eyes, choleric and fully and immediately conscious; the right hand went out to the half-smoked pipe beside him, while the left hand reached the matches.

"Get me my gin and milk," he ordered, in Hawaiian, of the little maid, who had been startled into a tremble by his awaking.

He lighted the pipe, but gave no sign of awareness of the presence of his waiting retainers until the tumbler of gin and milk had been brought and drunk.

"Well?" he demanded abruptly, and in the pause, while twenty faces wreathed in smiles and twenty pairs of dark eyes glowed luminously with well-wishing pleasure, he wiped the lingering drops of gin and milk from his hairy lips. "What are you hanging around for? What do you want? Come over here."

Twenty giants, most of them young, uprose with a great clanking and jangling of spurs and spur-chains strode over to him. They grouped before him in a semicircle, trying bashfully to wedge their shoulders, one behind another's, their faces a-grin and apologetic, and at the same time expressing a casual and unconscious democraticness. In truth, to them Hardman Pool was more than mere chief. He was elder brother, or father, or patriarch; and to all of them he was related, in one way or another, according to Hawaiian custom, through his wife and through the many marriages of his children and grandchildren. His slightest frown might perturb them, his anger terrify them, his command compel them to certain death; yet, on the other hand, not one of them would have dreamed of addressing him otherwise than intimately by his first name, which name, "Hardman," was transmuted by their tongues into Kanaka Oolea.

At a nod from him, the semicircle seated itself on the *manienie* grass, and with further deprecatory smiles waited his pleasure.

"What do you want?" he demanded, in Hawaiian, with a brusqueness and sternness they knew were put on.

They smiled more broadly, and deliciously squirmed their broad shoulders and great torsos with the appeasingness of so many wriggling puppies. Hardman Pool singled out one of them.

"Well, Iliiopoi, what do *you* want?"

"Ten dollars, Kanaka Oolea."

"Ten dollars!" Pool cried, in apparent shock at mention of so vast a sum. "Does it mean you are going to take a second wife? Remember the missionary teaching. One wife at a time, Iliiopoi; one wife at a time. For he who entertains a plurality of wives will surely go to hell."

Giggles and flashings of laughing eyes from all greeted the joke.

"No, Kanaka Oolea," came the reply. "The devil knows I am hard put to get *kow-kow* for one wife and her several relations."

"Kow-kow?" Pool repeated the Chinese-introduced word for food which the Hawaiians had come to substitute for their own *paina.* "Didn't you boys get kow-kow here this noon?"

"Yes, Kanaka Oolea," volunteered an old, withered native who had just joined the group from the direction of the house. "All of them had kow-kow in the kitchen, and plenty of it. They ate like lost horses brought down from the lava."

"And what do you want, Kumuhana?" Pool diverted to the old one, at the same time motioning to the little maid to flap flies from the other side of him.

"Twelve dollars," said Kumuhana. "I wish to buy a jackass and a second-hand saddle and bridle. I am growing too old for my legs to carry me in walking."

"You wait," his haole lord commanded. "I will talk with you about the matter, and about other things of importance, when I am finished with the rest and they are gone."

The withered old one nodded and proceeded to light his pipe.

"The kow-kow in the kitchen was good," Iliiopoi resumed, licking his lips. "The poi was one-finger, the pig fat, the salmon-belly unstinking, the fish of great freshness and plenty, though the *opihis* had been salty and thereby made tough. Never should the opihis be salted. Often have I told you, Kanaka Oolea, that opihis should never be salted. I am full of good kow-kow. My belly is heavy with it. Yet is my heart not light of it because there is no kow-kow in my own house, where is my wife, who is the aunt of your fourth son's second wife, and where is my baby daughter, and my wife's old mother, and my wife's old mother's feeding child that is a cripple, and my wife's sister who lives likewise with us along with her three children, the father being dead of a wicked dropsy—"

"Will five dollars save all of you from funerals for a day or several?" Pool testily cut the tale short.

"Yes, Kanaka Oolea, and as well it will buy my wife a new comb and some tobacco for myself."

From a gold-sack drawn from the hip-pocket of his dungarees, Hardman Pool drew the gold piece and tossed it accurately into the waiting hand.

To a bachelor who wanted six dollars for new leggings, tobacco, and spurs, three dollars were given; the same to another who needed a hat; and to a third, who modestly asked for two dollars, four were given with a flowery-worded compliment anent his prowess in roping a recent wild bull from the mountains. They knew, as a rule, that he cut their requisitions in half, therefore they doubled the size of their requisitions. And Hardman Pool knew they doubled, and smiled to himself. It was his way, and, further, it was a very good way with his multitudinous relatives, and did not reduce his stature in their esteem.

"And you, Ahuhu?" he demanded of one whose name meant "poison-wood."

"And the price of a pair of dungarees," Ahuhu concluded his list of needs. "I have ridden much and hard after your cattle, Kanaka Oolea, and where my dungarees have pressed against the seat of the saddle there is no seat to my dungarees. It is not well that it be said that a Kanaka Oolea cowboy, who is also a cousin of Kanaka Oolea's wife's half-sister, should be shamed to be seen out of the saddle save that he walks backward from all that behold him.''

"The price of a dozen pairs of dungarees be thine, Ahuhu," Hardman Pool beamed, tossing to him the necessary sum. "I am proud that my family shares my pride. Afterward, Ahuhu, out of the dozen dungarees you will give me one, else shall I be compelled to walk backward, my own and only dungarees being in the like manner well worn and shameful."

And in laughter of love at their haole chief's final sally, all the sweet-child-minded and physically gorgeous company of them departed to their waiting horses, save the old withered one, Kumuhana, who had been bidden to wait.

For a full five minutes they sat in silence. Then Hardman Pool ordered the little maid to fetch a tumbler of gin and milk, which, when she brought it, he nodded her to hand to Kumuhana. The glass did not leave his lips until it was empty, whereon he gave a great audible outbreath of "A-a-ah," and smacked his lips.

"Much *awa* have I drunk in my time," he said reflectively. "Yet is the awa but a common man's drink, while the haole liquor is a drink for chiefs. The awa has not the liquor's hot willingness, its spur in the ribs of feeling, its biting alive of oneself that is very pleasant since it is pleasant to be alive."

Hardman Pool smiled, nodded agreement, and old Kumuhana continued.

"There is a warmingness to it. It warms the belly and the soul. It warms the heart. Even the soul and the heart grow cold when one is old."

"You *are* old," Pool conceded. "Almost as old as I."

Kumuhana shook his head and murmured. "Were I no older than you I would be as young as you."

"I am seventy-one," said Pool.

"I do not know ages that way," was the reply. "What happened when you were born?"

"Let me see," Pool calculated. "This is 1880. Subtract seventy-one, and it leaves nine. I was born in 1809, which is the year Keliimakai died, which is the year the Scotchman, Archibald Campbell, lived in Honolulu."

"Then am I truly older than you, Kanaka Oolea. I remember the Scotchman well, for I was laying among the grass houses of Honolulu at the time, and already riding a surfboard in the *wahine* surf at Waikiki. I can take you now to the spot where was the Scotchman's grass house. The Seaman's Mission stands now on the very ground. Yet do I know when I was born. Often my grandmother and my mother told me of it. I was born when Madame Pele became angry with the people of Paiea because they sacrificed no fish to her from their fish-pool, and she sent down a flow of lava from Huulalai and filled up their pond. For ever was the fish-pond of Paiea filled up. That was when I was born."

"That was in 1801, when James Boyd was building ships for Kame-hameha at Hilo," Pool cast back through the calendar; "which makes you seventy-nine, or eight years older than I. You are very old."

"Yes, Kanaka Oolea," muttered Kumuhana, pathetically attempting to swell his shrunken chest with pride.

"And you are very wise."

"Yes, Kanaka Oolea."

"And you know many of the secret things that are known only to old men."

"Yes, Kanaka Oolea."

"And then you know—" Hardman Pool broke off, the more effectively to impress and hypnotize the other ancient with the set stare of his pale-washed blue eyes. "They say the bones of Kahekili were taken from their hiding-place and lie to-day in the Royal Mausoleum. I have heard it whispered that you alone of all living men truly know."

"I know," was the proud answer. "I alone know."

"Well, do they lie there? Yes or no?"

"Kahekili was an *alii*. It is from this straight line that your wife Kalama came. She is an alii." The old retainer paused and pursed his lean lips in meditation. "I belong to her, as all my people before me belonged to her people before her. She only can command the great secrets of me. She is wise, too wise ever to command me to speak this secret. To you, O Kanaka Oolea, I do not answer yes, I do not answer no. This is a secret of the aliis that even the aliis do not know."

"Very good, Kumuhana," Hardman Pool commanded. "Yet do you

forget that I am an alii, and that what my good Kalama does not dare ask, I command to ask. I can send for her, now, and tell her to command your answer. But such would be a foolishness unless you prove yourself doubly foolish. Tell me the secret, and she will never know. A woman's lips must pour out whatever flows in through her ears, being so made. I am a man, and man is differently made. As you well know, my lips suck tight on secrets as a squid sucks to the salty rock. If you will not tell me alone, then will you tell Kalama and me together, and her lips will talk, her lips will talk, so that the latest *malahini* will shortly know what, otherwise, you and I alone will know."

Long time Kumuhana sat on in silence, debating the argument and finding no way to evade the fact-logic of it.

"Great is your haole wisdom," he conceded at last.

"Yes? or no?" Hardman Pool drove home the point of his steel.

Kumuhana looked about him first, then slowly let his eyes come to rest on the fly-flapping maid.

"Go," Pool commanded her. "And come not back without you hear a clapping of my hands."

Hardman Pool spoke no further, even after the flapper had disappeared into the house; yet his face adamantly looked: "Yes or no?"

Again Kumuhana looked carefully about him, and up into the monkey-pod boughs as if to apprehend a lurking listener. His lips were very dry. With his tongue he moistened them repeatedly. Twice he essayed to speak, but was inarticulately husky. And finally, with bowed head, he whispered, so low and solemnly that Hardman Pool bent his own head to hear: "No."

Pool clapped his hands, and the little maid ran out of the house to him in tremulous, fluttery haste.

"Bring a milk and gin for old Kumuhana, here," Pool commanded; and, to Kumuhana: "Now tell me the whole story."

"Wait," was the answer. "Wait till the little *wahine* has come and gone."

And when the maid was gone, and the gin and milk had travelled the way predestined of gin and milk when mixed together, Hardman Pool waited without further urge for the story. Kumuhana pressed his hand to his chest and coughed hollowly at intervals, bidding for encouragement; but in the end, of himself, spoke out.

"It was a terrible thing in the old days when a great alii died. Kahekili was a great alii. He might have been king had he lived. Who can tell? I was a young man, not yet married. You know, Kanaka Oolea, when Kahekili died, and you can tell me how old I was. He died when Governor Boki ran the Blonde Hotel here in Honolulu. You have heard?"

"I was still on windward Hawaii," Pool answered. "But I have heard. Boki made a distillery, and leased Manoa lands to grow sugar for it, and Kaahumanu, who was regent, cancelled the lease, rooted out the cane, and planted potatoes. And Boki was angry, and prepared to make war, and gathered his fighting men, with a dozen whaleship deserters and five brass six-pounders, out at Waikiki—"

"That was the very time Kahekili died," Kumuhana broke in eagerly. "You are very wise. You know many things of the old days better than we old kanakas."

"It was 1829," Pool continued complacently. "You were twenty-eight years old, and I was twenty, just coming ashore in the open boat after the burning of the *Black Prince*."

"I was twenty-eight," Kumuhana resumed. "It sounds right. I remember well Boki's brass guns at Waikiki. Kahekili died, too, at the time, at Waikiki. The people to this day believe his bones were taken to the *Hale o Keawe* at Honaunau, in Kona—"

"And long afterward were brought to the Royal Mausoleum here in Honolulu," Pool supplemented.

"Also, Kanaka Oolea, there are some who believe to this day that Queen Alice has them stored with the rest of her ancestral bones in the big jars in her taboo room. All are wrong. I know. The sacred bones of Kahekili are gone and for ever gone. They rest nowhere. They have ceased to be. And many kona winds have whitened the surf at Waikiki since the last man looked upon the last of Kahekili. I alone remain alive of those men. I am the last man, and I was not glad to be at the finish.

"For see! I was a young man, and my heart was white-hot lava for Malia, who was in Kahekili's household. So was Anapuni's heart white-

hot for her, though the colour of his heart was black, as you shall
see. We were at a drinking that night—Anapuni and I—the night that
Kahekili died. Anapuni and I were only commoners, as were all of us
kanakas and wahines who were at the drinking with the common
sailors and whaleship men from before the mast. We were drinking on
the mats by the beach at Waikiki, close to the old *heiau* that is not
far from what is now the Wilders' beach place. I learned then and for
ever what quantities of drink haole sailormen can stand. And for us
kanakas, our heads were hot and light and rattly as dry gourds with the
whisky and the rum.

"It was past midnight, I remember well, when I saw Malia, whom
never had I seen at a drinking, come across the wet-hard sand of the
beach. My brain burned like red cinders of hell as I looked upon Anapuni look upon her, he being nearest to her by being across from me in
the drinking circle. Oh, I know it was whisky and rum and youth that
made the heat of me; but there, in that moment, the mad mind of me
resolved, if she spoke to him and yielded to dance with him first, that
I would put both my hands around his throat and throw him down and
under the wahine surf there beside us, and drown and choke out his
life and the obstacle of him that stood between me and her. For know,
that she had never decided between us, and it was because of him that
she was not already and long since mine.

"She was a grand young woman with a body generous as that of a
chiefess and more wonderful, as she came upon us, across the wet sand,
in the shimmer of the moonlight. Even the haole sailormen made
pause of silence, and with open mouths stared upon her. Her walk! I
have heard you talk, O Kanaka Oolea, of the woman Helen who
caused the war of Troy. I say of Malia that more men would have
stormed the walls of hell for her than went against that old-time city of
which it is your custom to talk over much and long when you have
drunk too little milk and too much gin.

"Her walk! In the moonlight there, the soft glow-fire of the jelly-
fishes in the surf like the kerosene-lamp footlights I have seen in the
new haole theatre! It was not the walk of a girl, but a woman. She did
not flutter forward like rippling wavelets on a reef-sheltered, placid
beach. There was that in her manner of walk that was big and queen-

like, like the motion of the forces of nature, like the rhythmic flow of lava down the slopes of Kau to the sea, like the movement of the huge orderly trade-wind seas, like the rise and fall of the four great tides of the year that may be like music in the eternal ear of God, being too slow of occurrence in time to make a tune for ordinary quick-pulsing, brief-living, swift-dying man.

"Anapuni was nearest. But she looked at me. Have you ever heard a call, Kanaka Oolea, that is without sound yet is louder than the conches of God? So called she to me across that circle of the drinking. I half arose, for I was not yet full drunken; but Anapuni's arm caught her and drew her, and I sank back on my elbow and watched and raged. He was for making her sit beside him, and I waited. Did she sit, and, next, dance with him, I knew that ere morning Anapuni would be a dead man, choked and drowned by me in the shallow surf.

"Strange, is it not, Kanaka Oolea, all this heat called 'love'? Yet it is not strange. It must be so in the time of one's youth, else would mankind not go on."

"That is why the desire of woman must be greater than the desire of life, Pool concurred. "Else would there be neither men nor women."

"Yes," said Kumuhana. "But it is many a year now since the last of such heat has gone out of me. I remember it as one remembers an old sunrise—a thing that was. And so one grows old, and cold, and drinks gin, not for madness, but for warmth. And the milk is very nourishing.

"But Malia did not sit beside him. I remember her eyes were wild, her hair down and flying, as she bent over him and whispered in his ear. And her hair covered him about and hid him as she whispered, and the sight of it pounded my heart against my ribs and dizzied my head till scarcely could I half-see. And I willed myself with all the will of me that if, in short minutes, she did not come over to me, I would go across the circle and get her.

"It was one of the things never to be. You remember Chief Konukalani? Himself he strode up to the circle. His face was black with anger. He gripped Malia, not by the arm, but by the hair, and dragged her away behind him and was gone. Of that, even now, can I understand not the half. I, who was for slaying Anapuni because of her, raised neither hand nor voice of protest when Konukalani dragged her away by the hair—nor did Anapuni. Of course, we were common men, and he was a chief. That I know. But why should two common men, mad with desire of woman, with desire of woman stronger in them than desire of life, let any one chief, even the highest in the land, drag the woman away by the hair? Desiring her more than life, why should the two men fear to slay then and immediately the one chief? Here is something stronger than life, stronger than woman, but what is it? and why?"

"I will answer you," said Hardman Pool. "It is so because most men are fools, and therefore must be taken care of by the few men who are wise. Such is the secret of chiefship. In all the world are chiefs over men. In all the world that has been have there ever been chiefs, who must say to many fool men: 'Do this; do not do that. Work, and work as we tell you or your bellies will remain empty and you will perish. Obey the laws we set you or you will be beasts and without place in the world. You would not have been, save for the chiefs before you who ordered and regulated for your fathers. No seed of you will come after you, except that we order and regulate for you now. You must be peace-abiding, and decent, and blow your noses. You must be early to bed of nights, and up early in the morning to work if you would have beds to sleep in and not roost in trees like the silly fowls. This is the season for the yam-planting and you must plant now. We say now, to-day, and not picnicking and hulaing to-day and yam-planting to-morrow or some other day of the many careless days. You must not kill one another, and you must leave your neighbours' wives alone. All this is life for you, because you think but one day at a time, while we, your chiefs, think for you all days and for days ahead.'"

"Like a cloud on the mountain-top that comes down and wraps about you and that you dimly see is a cloud, so is your wisdom to me, Kanaka Oolea," Kumuhana murmured. "Yet it is sad that I should be born a common man and live all my days a common man."

"That is because you were of yourself common," Hardman Pool assured him. "When a man is born common, and is by nature uncommon, he rises up and overthrows the chiefs and makes himself chief over the chiefs. Why do you not run my ranch, with its many thousands of cattle, and shift the pastures by the rain-fall, and pick the bulls, and arrange the bargaining and the selling of the meat to the sailing ships and war vessels and the people who live in the Honolulu houses, and fight with lawyers, and help make laws, and even tell the King what is wise for him to do and what is dangerous? Why does not any man do this that I do? Any man of all the men who work for me, feed out of my hand, and let me do their thinking for them—me, who works harder than any of them, who eats no more than any of them, and who can sleep on no more than one lauhala mat at a time like any of them?"

"I am out of the cloud, Kanaka Oolea," said Kumuhana, with a visible brightening of countenance. "More clearly do I see. All my long years have the aliis I was born under thought for me. Ever, when I was hungry, I came to them for food, as I come to your kitchen now. Many people eat in your kitchen, and the days of feasts when you slay fat steers for all of us are understandable. It is why I come to you this day, an old man whose labour of strength is not worth a shilling a week, and ask of you twelve dollars to buy a jackass and a second-hand saddle and bridle. It is why twice ten fool men of us, under these monkey-pods half an hour ago, asked of you a dollar or two, or four or five, or ten or twelve. We are the careless ones of the careless days who will not plant the yam in season if our alii does not compel us, who will not think one day for ourselves, and who, when we age to worthlessness, know that our alii will think kow kow into our bellies and a grass thatch over our heads.

Hardman Pool bowed his appreciation, and urged:

"But the bones of Kahekili. The Chief Konukalani had just dragged away Malai by the hair of the head, and you and Anapuni sat on without protest in the circle of drinking. What was it Malia whispered in Anapuni's ear, bending over him, her hair hiding the face of him?"

"That Kahekili was dead. That was what she whispered to Anapuni. That Kahekili was dead, just dead, and that the chiefs, ordering all within the house to remain within, were debating the disposal of the bones and meat of him before word of his death should get abroad. That the high priest Eoppo was deciding them, and that she had overheard no less than Anapuni and me chosen as the sacrifices to go the way of Kahekili and his bones and to care for him afterward and for ever in the shadowy other world."

"The *moepuu*, the human sacrifice," Pool commented. "Yet it was nine years since the coming of the missionaries."

"And it was the year before their coming that the idols were cast down and the taboos broken," Kumuhana added. "But the chiefs still practised the old ways, the custom of *hunakele,* and hid the bones of the aliis where no men should find them and make fish-hooks of their jaws or arrow heads of their long bones for the slaying of little mice in sport. Behold, O Kanaka Oolea!"

The old man thrust out his tongue; and, to Pool's amazement, he saw the surface of that sensitive organ, from root to tip, tattooed in intricate designs.

"That was done after the missionaries came, several years afterward, when Keopuolani died. Also, did I knock out four of my front teeth, and half-circles did I burn over my body with blazing bark. And whoever ventured out-of-doors that night was slain by the chiefs. Nor could a light be shown in a house or a whisper of noise be made. Even dogs and hogs that made a noise were slain, nor all that night were the ships' bells of the haoles in the harbour allowed to strike. It was a terrible thing in those days when an alii died.

"But the night that Kahekili died. We sat on in the drinking circle after Konukalani dragged Malia away by the hair. Some of the haole sailors grumbled; they were few in the land in those days and the kanakas many. And never was Malia seen of men again. Konukalani alone knew the manner of her slaying, and he never told. And in after years what common men like Anapuni and me should dare to question him?

"Now she had told Anapuni before she was dragged away. But Anapuni's heart was black. Me he did not tell. Worthy he was of the killing I had intended for him. There was a giant harpooner in the circle, whose singing was like the bellowing of bulls; and, gazing on him in amazement while he roared some song of the sea, when next I looked across the circle to Anapuni, Anapuni was gone. He had fled to the high mountains where he could hide with the bird-catchers a week of moons. This I learned afterward.

"I? I sat on, ashamed of my desire of woman that had not been so strong as my slave-obedience to a chief. And I drowned my shame in large drinks of rum and whisky, till the world went round and round, inside my head and out, and the Southern Cross danced a hula in the sky, and the Koolau Mountains bowed their lofty summits to Waikiki and the surf of Waikiki kissed them on their brows. And the giant harpooner was still roaring, his the last sounds in my ear, as I fell back on the lauhala mat, and was to all things for the time as one dead.

"When I awoke was at the faint first beginning of dawn. I was being kicked by a hard naked heel in the ribs. What of the enormousness of the drink I had consumed, the feelings aroused in me by the heel were not pleasant. The kanakas and wahines of the drinking were gone. I alone remained among the sleeping sailormen, the giant harpooner snoring like a whale, his head upon my feet.

"More heel-kicks, and I sat up and was sick. But the one who kicked was impatient, and demanded to know where was Anapuni. And I did not know, and was kicked, this time from both sides by two impatient men, because I did not know. Nor did I know that Kahekili was dead. Yet did I guess something serious was afoot, for the two men who kicked me were chiefs, and no common men crouched behind them to do their bidding. One was Aimoku, of Kaneche; the other Humuhumu, of Manoa.

"They commanded me to go with them, and they were not kind in their commanding; and as I uprose, the head of the giant harpooner was rolled off my feet, past the edge of the mat, into the sand. He grunted like a pig, his lips opened, and all of his tongue rolled out of his mouth into the sand. Nor did he draw it back. For the first time I knew how long was a man's tongue. The sight of the sand on it made me sick for the second time. It is a terrible thing, the next day after a night of drinking. I was afire, dry afire, all the inside of me like a burnt cinder, like *aa* lava, like the harpooner's tongue dry and gritty with sand. I bent for a half-drunk drinking coconut, but Aimoku kicked it out of my shaking fingers, and Humuhumu smote me with the heel of his hand on my neck.

"They walked before me, side by side, their faces solemn and black, and I walked at their heels. My mouth stank of the drink, and my head was sick with the stale fumes of it, and I would have cut off my right hand for a drink of water, one drink, a mouthful even. And, had I had it, I know it would have sizzled in my belly like water spilled on heated stones for the roasting. It is terrible, the next day after the drinking. All the lifetime of many men who died young has passed by me since the last I was able to do such mad drinking of youth when youth knows not capacity and is undeterred.

"But as we went on, I began to know that some alii was dead. No kanakas lay asleep in the sand, nor stole home from their love-making; and no canoes were abroad after the early fish most catchable then inside the reef at the change of the tide. When we came, past the hoiau to where the Great Kamehameha used to haul out his brigs and schooners, I saw, under the canoe-sheds, that the mat-thatches of Kahekili's great double canoe had been taken off, and that even then, at low tide, many men were launching it down across the sand into the water. But all these men were chiefs. And, though my eyes swam, and the inside of my head went around and around, and the inside of my body was a cinder athirst, I guessed that the alii who was dead was Kahekili. For he was old, and most likely of the aliis to be dead."

"It was his death, as I have heard it, more than the intercession of Kekuanaoa, that spoiled Governor Boki's rebellion," Hardman Pool observed.

"It was Kahekili's death that spoiled it," Kumuhana confirmed. "All commoners, when the word slipped out that night of his death, fled into the shelter of the grass houses, nor lighted fire nor pipes, nor breathed loudly, being therein and thereby taboo from use for sacrifice. And all Governor Boki's commoners of fighting men, as well as the haole deserters from ships, so fled, so that the brass guns lay unserved and his handful of chiefs of themselves could do nothing.

"Aimoku and Humuhumu made me sit on the sand to the side from the launching of the great double-canoe. And when it was afloat all the chiefs were athirst, not being used to such toil; and I was told to climb the palms beside the canoe-sheds and throw down drink-coconuts. They drank and were refreshed, but me they refused to let drink.

"Then they bore Kahekili from his house to the canoe in a haole coffin, oiled and varnished and new. It had been made by a ship's carpenter, who thought he was making a boat that must not leak. It was very tight, and over where the face of Kahekili lay was nothing but thin glass. The chiefs had not screwed on the outside plank to cover the glass. Maybe they did not know the manner of haole coffins; but at any rate I was to be glad they did not know, as you shall see.

" 'There is but one *moepuu*,' said the priest Eoppo, looking at me where I sat on the coffin in the bottom of the canoe. Already the chiefs were paddling out through the reef.

" 'The other has run into hiding,' Aimoku answered. 'This one was all we could get.'

"And then I knew. I knew everything. I was to be sacrificed. Anapuni had been planned for the other sacrifice. That was what Malia had whispered to Anapuni at the drinking. And she had been dragged away before she could tell me. And in his blackness of heart he had not told me.

" 'There should be two,' said Eoppo. 'It is the law.'

"Aimoku stopped paddling and I looked back shoreward as if to return and get a second sacrifice. But several of the chiefs contended no, saying that all commoners were fled to the mountains or were lying taboo in their houses, and that it might take days before they could catch one. In the end Eoppo gave in, though he grumbled from time to time that the law required two moepuus.

"We paddled on, past Diamond Head and abreast of Koko Head, till we were in the midway of the Molokai Channel. There was quite a sea running, though the trade wind was blowing light. The chiefs rested from their paddles, save for the steersmen who kept the canoes bow-on to the wind and swell. And, ere they proceeded further in the matter, they opened more coconuts and drank.

" 'I do not mind so much being the moepuu,' I said to Humuhumu; 'but I should like to have a drink before I am slain.' I got no drink. But I spoke true. I was too sick of the much whisky and rum to be afraid to die. At least my mouth would stink no more, nor my head ache, nor the inside of me be as dry-hot sand. Almost worst of all, I suffered at thought of the harpooner's tongue, as last I had seen it lying on the sand and covered with sand. O Kanaka Oolea, what animals young men are with the drink! Not until they have grown old, like you and me, do they control their wantonness of thirst and drink sparingly, like you and me."

"Because we have to," Hardman Pool rejoined. "Old stomachs are worn thin and tender, and we drink sparingly because we dare not drink more. We are wise, but the wisdom is bitter."

"The priest Eoppo sang a long mele about Kahekili's mother and his mother's mother, and all their mothers all the way back to the beginning of time," Kumuhana resumed. "And it seemed I must die of my sand-hot dryness ere he was done. And he called upon all the gods of the under world, the middle world and the over world, to care for and cherish the dead alii about to be consigned to them, and to carry out the curses—they were terrible curses—he laid upon all living men and men to live after who might tamper with the bones of Kahekili to use them in sport of vermin-slaying.

"Do you know, Kanaka Oolea, the priest talked a language largely different, and I know it was the priest language, the old language. Maui he did not name Maui, but Maui-Tiki-Tiki and Maui-Po-Tiki. And Hina, the goddess-mother of Maui, he named Ina. And Maui's god-father he named sometimes Akalana and sometimes Kanaloa. Strange how one about to die and very thirsty should remember such things! And I remember the priest named Hawaii as Vaii, and Lanai as Ngan-gai."

"Those were the Maori names," Hardman Pool explained, "and the Samoan and Tongan names, that the priests brought with them in their first voyages from the south in the long ago when they found Hawaii and settled to dwell upon it."

"Great is your wisdom, O Kanaka Oolea," the old man accorded solemnly. "Ku, our Supporter of the Heavens, the priest named Tu, and also Ru; and La, our God of the Sun, he named Ra—"

"And Ra was a sun-god in Egypt in the long ago," Pool interrupted with a sparkle of interest. "Truly, you Polynesians have travelled far in time and space since first you began. A far cry it is from Old Egypt, when Atlantis was still afloat, to Young Hawaii in the North Pacific. But proceed, Kumuhana. Do you remember anything also of what the priest Eoppo sang?"

"At the very end," came the confirming nod, "though I was near dead myself, and nearer to die under the priest's knife, he sang what I have remembered every word of. Listen! It was thus."

And in quavering falsetto, with the customary broken-notes, the old man sang.

"A Maori death-chant unmistakable," Pool exclaimed, "sung by an Hawaiian with a tattooed tongue! Repeat it once again, and I shall say it to you in English."

And when it had been repeated, he spoke it slowly in English:

> "But death is nothing new.
> Death is and has been ever since old Maui died.
> Then Pata-tai laughed loud
> And woke the goblin god,
> Who severed him in two, and shut him in,
> So dusk of eve came on."

"And at last," Kumuhana resumed, "I was not slain. Eoppo, the killing knife in hand and ready to lift for the blow, did not lift. And I? How did I feel and think? Often, Kanaka Oolea, have I since laughed at the memory of it. I felt very thirsty. I did not want to die. I wanted a drink of water. I knew I was going to die, and I kept remembering the thousand waterfalls falling to waste down the *palis* of the windward Koolau Mountains. I did not think of Anapuni. I was too thirsty. I did not think of Malia. I was too thirsty. But continually, inside my head, I saw the tongue of the harpooner, covered dry with sand, as I had last seen it, lying in the sand. My tongue was like that, too. And in the bottom of the canoe rolled about many drinking nuts. Yet I did not attempt to drink, for these were chiefs and I was a common man.

" 'No,' said Eoppo, commanding the chiefs to throw overboard the coffin. 'There are not two meopuus, therefore there shall be none.'

" 'Slay the one,' the chiefs cried.

"But Eoppo shook his head, and said: 'We cannot send Kahekili on his way with only the tops of the taro.'

" 'Half a fish is better than none,' Aimoku said the old saying.

" 'Not at the burying of an alii,' was the priest's quick reply. 'It is the law. We cannot be niggard with Kahekili and cut his allotment of sacrifice in half.'

"So, for the moment, while the coffin went overside, I was not slain. And it was strange that I was glad immediately that I was to live. And I began to remember Malia, and to begin to plot a vengeance on Anapuni. And with the blood of life thus freshening in me, my thirst multiplied on itself tenfold and my tongue and mouth and throat seemed as sanded as the tongue of the harpooner. The coffin being overboard, I was sitting in the bottom of the canoe. A coconut rolled between my legs and I closed them on it. But as I picked it up in my hand, Aimoku smote my hand with the paddle-edge. Behold!"

He held up the hand, showing two fingers crooked from never having been set.

"I had no time to vex over my pain, for worse things were upon me. All the chiefs were crying out in horror. The coffin, head-end up, had not sunk. It bobbed up and down in the sea astern of us. And the canoe, without way on it, bow-on to sea and wind, was drifted down by sea and wind upon the coffin. And the glass of it was to us, so that we could see the face and head of Kahekili through the glass; and he grinned at us through the glass and seemed alive already in the other world and angry with us, and, with other-world power, about to wreak his anger upon us. Up and down he bobbed, and the canoe drifted closer upon him.

" 'Kill him!' 'Bleed him!' 'Thrust to the heart of him!' These things the chiefs were crying out to Eoppo in their fear. 'Over with the taro tops!' 'Let the alii have the half of a fish!'

"Eoppo, priest though he was, was likewise afraid, and his reason weakened before the sight of Kahekili in his haole coffin that would not sink. He seized me by the hair, drew me to my feet, and lifted the knife to plunge to my heart. And there was no resistance in me. I knew again only that I was very thirsty, and before my swimming eyes, in mid-air and close up, dangled the sanded tongue of the harpooner.

"But before the knife could fall and drive in, the thing happened that saved me. Akai, half-brother to Governor Boki, as you will remember, was steersman of the canoe, and, therefore, in the stern, was nearest to the coffin and its dead that would not sink. He was wild with fear, and he thrust out with the point of his paddle to fend off the coffined alii that seemed bent to come on board. The point of the paddle struck the glass. The glass broke—"

"And the coffin immediately sank," Hardman Pool broke in; "the air that floated it escaping through the broken glass."

"The coffin immediately sank, being builded by the ship's carpenter like a boat," Kumuhana confirmed. "And I, who was a moepuu, became a man once more. And I lived, though I died a thousand deaths from thirst before we gained back to the beach at Waikiki.

"And so, O Kanaka Oolea, the bones of Kahekili do not lie in the Royal Mausoleum. They are at the bottom of the Molokai Channel, if not, long since, they have become floating dust of slime, or, builded into the bodies of the coral creatures dead and gone, are builded into the coral reef itself. Of men I am the one living who saw the bones of Kahekili sink into the Molokai Channel."

In the pause that followed, wherein Hardman Pool was deep sunk in meditation, Kumuhana licked his dry lips many times. At the last he broke silence:

"The twelve dollars, Kanaka Oolea, for the jackass and the second-hand saddle and bridle?"

"The twelve dollars would be thine," Pool responded, passing to the ancient one six dollars and a half, "save that I have in my stable junk the very bridle and saddle for you which I shall give you. These six dollars and a half will buy you the perfectly suitable jackass of the *pake* at Kokako who told me only yesterday that such was the price."

They sat on, Pool meditating, conning over and over to himself the Maori death-chant he had heard, and especially the line, "So dusk of eve came on," finding in it an intense satisfaction of beauty; Kumuhana licking his lips and tokening that he waited for something more. At last he broke silence.

"I have talked long, O Kanaka Oolea. There is not the enduring moistness in my mouth that was when I was young. It seems that afresh upon me is the thirst that was mine when tormented by the visioned tongue of the harpooner. The gin and milk is very good, O Kanaka Oolea, for a tongue that is like the harpooner's."

A shadow of a smile flickered across Pool's face. He clapped his hands, and the little maid came running.

"Bring one glass of gin and milk for old Kumuhana," commanded Hardman Pool.

Waikiki, Honolulu
June 28, 1916

SHIN-BONES

They have gone down to the pit with their weapons of
war, and they have laid their swords under their heads.

"It was a sad thing to see the old lady revert."

Prince Akuli shot an apprehensive glance sideward to where, under
the shade of a kukui tree, an old wahine was just settling herself to
begin on some work in hand.

"Yes," he nodded half-sadly to me, "in her last years Hiwilani went
back to the old ways, and to the old beliefs—in secret, of course. And,
believe me, she was some collector herself. You should have seen her
bones. She had them all about her bedroom, in big jars, and they constituted most all her relatives, except a half-dozen or so that Kanau
beat her out of by getting to them first. The way the pair of them used
to quarrel about those bones was awe-inspiring. And it gave me the
creeps, when I was a boy, to go into that big, for-ever-twilight room of
hers, and know that in this jar was all that remained of my maternal
grand-aunt, and that in that jar was my great-grandfather, and that in
all the jars were the preserved bone-remnants of the shadowy dust of
the ancestors whose seed had come down and been incorporated in
the living, breathing me. Hiwilani had gone quite native at the last,
sleeping on mats on the hard floor—she'd fired out of the room the

great, royal, canopied four-poster that had been presented to her grandmother by Lord Byron, who was the cousin of the Don Juan Byron and came here in the frigate *Blonde* in 1825.

"She went back to all native, at the last, and I can see her yet, biting a bite out of the raw fish ere she tossed them to her women to eat. And she made them finish her poi, or whatever else she did not finish of herself. She—"

But he broke off abruptly, and by the sensitive dilation of his nostrils and by the expression of his mobile features I saw that he had read in the air and identified the odour that offended him.

"Deuce take it!" he cried to me. "It stinks to heaven. And I shall be doomed to wear it until we're rescued."

There was no mistaking the object of his abhorrence. The ancient crone was making a dearest-loved *lei* of the fruit of the *hala* which is the screw-pine or pandanus of the South Pacific. She was cutting the many sections or nut-envelopes of the fruit into fluted bell-shapes preparatory to stringing them on the twisted and tough inner bark of the hau tree. It certainly smelled to heaven, but, to me, a *malahini*, the smell was wine-woody and fruit-juicy and not unpleasant.

Prince Akuli's limousine had broken an axle a quarter of a mile away, and he and I had sought shelter from the sun in this veritable bowery of a mountain home. Humble and grass-thatched was the house, but it stood in a treasure-garden of begonias that sprayed their delicate blooms a score of feet above our heads, that were like trees, with willowy trunks of trees as thick as a man's arm. Here we refreshed ourselves with drinking-coconuts, while a cowboy rode a dozen miles to the nearest telephone and summoned a machine from town. The town itself we could see, the Lakanaii metropolis of Olokona, a smudge of smoke on the shore-line, as we looked down across the miles of cane-fields, the billow-wreathed reef-lines, and the blue haze of ocean to where the island of Oahu shimmered like a dim opal on the horizon.

Maui is the Valley Isle of Hawaii, and Kauai the Garden Isle; but Lakanaii, lying abreast of Oahu, is recognized in the present, and was known of old and always, as the Jewel Isle of the group. Not the largest, nor merely the smallest, Lakanaii is conceded by all to be the wildest, the most wildly beautiful, and, in its size, the richest of all the islands. Its sugar tonnage per acre is the highest, its mountain beef-cattle the fattest, its rainfall the most generous without ever being disastrous. It resembles Kauai in that it is the first-formed and there-fore the oldest island, so that it had had time sufficient to break down its lava rock into the richest soil, and to erode the canyons between the ancient craters until they are like Grand Canyons of the Colorado, with numberless waterfalls plunging thousands of feet in the sheer or dissipating into veils of vapour, and evanescing in mid-air to descend softly and invisibly through a mirage of rainbows, like so much dew or gentle shower, upon the abyss-floors.

Yet Lakanaii is easy to describe. But how can one describe Prince Akuli? To know him is to know all Lakanaii most thoroughly. In addi-tion, one must know thoroughly a great deal of the rest of the world. In the first place, Prince Akuli has no recognized nor legal right to be called "Prince." Furthermore, "Akuli" means the "squid." So that Prince Squid could scarcely be the dignified title of the straight de-scendant of the oldest and highest aliis of Hawaii—an old and exclu-sive stock, wherein, in the ancient way of the Egyptian Pharaohs, brothers and sisters had even wed on the throne for the reason that they could not marry beneath rank, that in all their known world there was none of higher rank, and that, at every hazard, the dynasty must be perpetuated.

I have heard Prince Akuli's singing historians (inherited from his father) chanting their interminable genealogies, by which they demon-strated that he was the highest alii in all Hawaii. Beginning with Wakea, who is their Adam, and with Papa, their Eve, through as many generations as there are letters in our alphabet they trace down to Nanakaoko, the first ancestor born in Hawaii and whose wife was Kahihiokalani. Later, but always highest, their generations split from the generations of Ua, who was the founder of the two distinct lines of Kauai and Oahu kings.

In the eleventh century A.D., by the Lakanaii historians, at the time brothers and sisters mated because none existed to excel them, their rank received a boost of new blood of rank that was next to heaven's door. One Hoikemaha, steering by the stars and the ancient traditions, arrived in a great double-canoe from Samoa. He married a lesser alii of Lakanaii, and when his three sons were grown, returned with them to Samoa to bring back his own youngest brother. But with him he brought back Kumi, the son of Tui Manua, which latter's rank was highest in all Polynesia, and barely second to that of the demigods and gods. So the estimable seed of Kumi, eight centuries before, had entered into the aliis of Lakanaii, and been passed down by them in the undeviating line to reposit in Prince Akuli.

Him I first met, talking with an Oxford accent, in the officers' mess of the Black Watch in South Africa. This was just before that famous regiment was cut to pieces at Magersfontein. He had as much right to be in that mess as he had to his accent, for he was Oxford-educated and held the Queen's Commission. With him, as his guest, taking a look at the war, was Prince Cupid, so nicknamed, but the true prince of all Hawaii, including Lakanaii, whose real and legal title was Prince Jonah Kuhio Kalanianaole, and who might have been the living King of Hawaii Nei had it not been for the haole Revolution and Annexation—this, despite the fact that Prince Cupid's alii genealogy was lesser to the heaven-boosted genealogy of Prince Akuli. For Prince Akuli might have been King of Lakanaii, and of all Hawaii, perhaps, had not his grandfather been soundly thrashed by the first and greatest of the Kamehamehas.

This had occurred in the year 1810, in the booming days of the sandalwood trade, and in the same year that the King of Kauai came in, and was good, and ate out of Kamehameha's hand. Prince Akuli's grandfather, in that year, had received his trouncing and subjugating because he was "old school." He had not imagined island empire in terms of gunpowder and haole gunners. Kamehameha, farther-visioned, had annexed the service of haoles, including such men as Isaac Davis, mate and sole survivor of the massacred crew of the schooner *Fair American*, and John Young, captured boatswain of the scow *Eleanor*. And Isaac Davis, and John Young, and others of their waywardly adventurous ilk, with six-pounder brass carronades from the captured *Iphigenia* and *Fair American*, had destroyed the war canoes and shattered the morale of the King of Lakanaii's land-fighters, receiving duly in return from Kamehameha, according to agreement: Isaac Davis, six hundred mature and fat hogs; John Young, five hundred of the same described pork on the hoof that was split.

And so, out of all incests and lusts of the primitive cultures and beast-man's gropings toward the stature of manhood, out of all red murders, and brute battlings, and matings with the younger brothers of the demigods, world-polished, Oxford-accented, twentieth century to the tick of the second, comes Prince Akuli, Prince Squid, pure-veined Polynesian, a living bridge across the thousand centuries, comrade, friend, and fellow-traveller out of his wrecked seven-thousand-dollar limousine, marooned with me in a begonia paradise fourteen hundred feet above the sea, and his island metropolis of Olo-kona, to tell me of his mother, who reverted in her old age to ancientness of religious concept and ancestor worship, and collected and surrounded herself with the charnel bones of those who had been her forerunners back in the darkness of time.

"King Kalakaua started this collecting fad, over on Oahu," Prince Akuli continued. "And his queen, Kapiolani, caught the fad from him. They collected everything—old makaloa mats, old *tapas*, old calabashes, old double-canoes, and idols which the priests had saved from the general destruction in 1819. I haven't seen a pearl-shell fish-hook in years, but I swear that Kalakaua accumulated ten thousand of them, to say nothing of human jaw-bone fish-hooks, and feather cloaks, and capes and helmets, and stone adzes, and poi pounders of phallic design. When he and Kapiolani made their royal progresses around the islands, their hosts had to hide away their personal relics. For to the king, in theory, belongs all property of his people; and with Kalakaua, when it came to the old things, theory and practice were one.

"From him my father, Kanau, got the collecting bee in his bonnet, and Hiwilani was likewise infected. But father was modern to his fingertips. He believed neither in the gods of the *kahunas* nor of the missionaries. He didn't believe in anything except sugar stocks, horse-breeding, and that his grandfather had been a fool in not collecting a few Isaac Davises and John Youngs and brass carronades before he went to war with Kamehameha. So he collected curios in the pure collector's spirit; but my mother took it seriously. That was why she went in for bones. I remember, too, she had an ugly old stone-idol she used to yammer to and crawl around on the floor before. It's in the Deacon Museum now. I sent it there after her death, and her collection of bones to the Royal Mausoleum in Olokona.

"I don't know whether you remember her father was Kaaukuu. Well, he was, and he was a giant. When they built the Mausoleum, his bones, nicely cleaned and preserved, were dug out of their hiding-place, and placed in the Mausoleum. Hiwilani had an old retainer, Ahuna. She stole the key from Kanau one night, and made Ahuna go and steal her father's bones out of the Mausoleum. I know. And he must have been a giant. She kept him in one of her big jars. One day, when I was a tidy size of a lad, and curious to know if Kaaukuu was as big as tradition had him, I fished his intact lower jaw out of the jar, and the wrappings, and tried it on. I stuck my head right through it, and it rested around my neck and on my shoulders like a horse collar. And every tooth was in the jaw, whiter than porcelain, without a cavity, the enamel unstained and unchipped. I got the walloping of my life for that offence, although she had to call old Ahuna in to help give it to me. But the incident served me well. It won her confidence in me that I was not afraid of the bones of the dead ones, and it won for me my Oxford education. As you shall see, if that car doesn't arrive first.

"Old Ahuna was one of the real old ones with the hall-mark on him and branded into him of faithful born-slave service. He knew more about my mother's family, and my father's, than did both of them put together. And he knew, what no living other knew, the burial-place of centuries, where were hid the bones of most of her ancestors and of Kanau's. Kanau couldn't worm it out of the old fellow, who looked upon Kanau as an apostate.

"Hiwilani struggled with the old codger for years. How she ever succeeded is beyond me. Of course, on the face of it, she was faithful to the old religion. This might have persuaded Ahuna to loosen up a little. Or she may have jolted fear into him; for she knew a lot of the line of chatter of the old Huni sorcerers, and she could make a noise like being on terms of utmost intimacy with Uli, who is the chiefest god of sorcery of all the sorcerers. She could skin the ordinary *kahuna lapaau* when it came to praying to Lonopuha and Koleamoku; read dreams and visions and signs and omens and indigestions to beat the band; make the practitioners under the medicine god, Maiola, look like thirty cents; pull off a *pule hoe* incantation that would make them dizzy; and she claimed to a practice of *kahuna hoenoho*, which is modern spiritism, second to none. I have myself seen her drink the wind, throw a fit, and prophesy. The *aumakuas* were brothers to her when she slipped offerings to them across the altars of the ruined *heiaus* with a line of prayer that was as unintelligible to me as it was hair-raising. And as for old Ahuna, she could make him get down on the floor and yammer and bite himself when she pulled the real mystery dope on him.

"Nevertheless, my private opinion is that it was the *anaana* stuff that got him. She snipped off a lock of his hair one day with a pair of manicure scissors. This lock of hair was what we call the *muumu*, meaning the bait. And she took jolly good care to let him know she had that bit of his hair. Then she tipped it off to him that she had buried it, and was deeply engaged each night in her offerings and incantations to Uli."

"That was the regular praying-to-death?" I queried in the pause of Prince Akuli's lighting his cigarette.

"Sure thing," he nodded. "And Ahuna fell for it. First he tried to locate the hiding-place of the bait of his hair. Failing that, he hired a *pahiuhiu* sorcerer to find it for him. But Hiwilani queered that game by threatening to the sorcerer to practice *apo leo* on him, which is the art of permanently depriving a person of the power of speech without otherwise injuring him.

"Then it was that Ahuna began to pine away and get more like a corpse every day. In desperation he appealed to Kanau. I happened to be present. You have heard what sort of a man my father was.

"'Pig!' he called Ahuna. 'Swine-brains! Stinking fish! Die and be done with it. You are a fool. It is all nonsense. There is nothing in anything. The drunken haole, Howard, can prove the missionaries wrong. Square-face gin proves Howard wrong. The doctors say he won't last six months. Even square-face gin lies. Life is a liar, too. And here are hard times upon us, and a slump in sugar. Glanders has got into my brood mares. I wish I could lie down and sleep for a hundred years, and wake up to find sugar up a hundred points.'

"Father was something of a philosopher himself, with a bitter wit and a trick of spitting out staccato epigrams. He clapped his hands. 'Bring me a high-ball,' he commanded; 'no, bring me two high-balls.' Then he turned on Ahuna. 'Go and let yourself die, old heathen, survival of darkness, blight of the Pit that you are. But don't die on these premises. I desire merriment and laughter, and the sweet tickling of music, and the beauty of youthful motion, not the croaking of sick toads and googly-eyed corpses about me still afoot on their shaky legs. I'll be that way soon enough if I live long enough. And it will be my everlasting regret if I don't live long enough. Why in hell did I sink that last twenty thousand into Curtis's plantation? Howard warned me the slump was coming, but I thought it was the square-face making him lie. And Curtis has blown his brains out, and his head luna has run away with his daughter, and the sugar chemist has got typhoid, and everything's going to smash.'

"He clapped his hands for his servants, and commanded: 'Bring me my singing boys. And the hula dancers—plenty of them. And send for old Howard. Somebody's got to pay, and I'll shorten his six months of life by a month. But above all, music. Let there be music. It is stronger than drink, and quicker than opium.'

"He with his music druggery! It was his father, the old savage, who was entertained on board a French frigate, and for the first time heard an orchestra. When the little concert was over, the captain, to find which piece he liked best, asked which piece he'd like repeated. Well, when grandfather got done describing, what piece do you think it was?"

I gave up, while the Prince lighted a fresh cigarette.

"Why, it was the first one, of course. Not the real first one, but the tuning up that preceded it."

I nodded, with eyes and face mirthful of appreciation, and Prince Akuli, with another apprehensive glance at the old wahine and her half-made hala lei, returned to his tale of the bones of his ancestors.

"It was somewhere around this stage of the game that old Ahuna gave in to Hiwilani. He didn't exactly give in. He compromised. That's where I come in. If he would bring her the bones of her mother, and of her grandfather (who was the father of Kaaukuu, and who by tradition was rumoured to have been even bigger than his giant son), she would return to Ahuna the bait of his hair she was praying him to death with. He, on the other hand, stipulated that he was not to reveal to her the secret burial-place of all the alii of Lakanaii all the way back. Nevertheless, he was too old to dare the adventure alone, must be helped by some one who of necessity would come to know the secret, and I was that one. I was the highest alii, beside my father and mother, and they were no higher than I.

"So I came upon the scene, being summoned into the twilight room to confront those two dubious old ones who dealt with the dead. They were a pair—mother fat to despair of helplessness, Ahuna thin as a skeleton and as fragile. Of her one had the impression that if she lay down on her back she could not roll over without the aid of block-and-tackle; of Ahuna one's impression was that the tooth-pickedness of him would shatter to splinters if one bumped into him.

"And when they had broached the matter, there was more *pilikia*. My father's attitude stiffened my resolution. I refused to go on the bone-snatching expedition. I said I didn't care a whoop for the bones of all the aliis of my family and race. You see, I had just discovered Jules Verne, loaned me by old Howard, and was reading my head off. Bones? When there were North Poles, and Centres of Earths, and hairy comets to ride across space among the stars! Of course I didn't want to go on any bone-snatching expedition. I said my father was able-bodied, and he could go, splitting equally with her whatever bones he brought back. But she said he was only a blamed collector—or words to that effect, only stronger.

" 'I know him,' she assured me. 'He'd bet his mother's bones on a horse-race or an ace-full.'

"I stood with father when it came to modern scepticism, and I told her the whole thing was rubbish. 'Bones?' I said. 'What are bones? Even field mice, and many rats, and cockroaches have bones, though the roaches wear their bones outside their meat instead of inside. The difference between man and other animals,' I told her, 'is not bones, but brain. Why, a bullock has bigger bones than a man, and more than one fish I've eaten has more bones, while a whale beats creation when it comes to bone.'

"It was frank talk, which is our Hawaiian way, as you have long since learned. In return, equally frank, she regretted she hadn't given me away as a feeding child when I was born. Next she bewailed that she had ever borne me. From that it was only a step to anaana me. She threatened me with it, and I did the bravest thing I have ever done. Old Howard had given me a knife of many blades, and corkscrews, and screw-drivers, and all sorts of contrivances, including a tiny pair of scissors. I proceeded to pare my fingernails.

" 'There,' I said, as I put the parings into her hand. 'Just to show you what I think of it. There's bait and to spare. Go on and anaana me if you can.'

"I have said it was brave. It was. I was only fifteen, and I had lived all my days in the thick of the mystery stuff, while my scepticism, very recently acquired, was only skin-deep. I could be a sceptic out in the open in the sunshine. But I was afraid of the dark. And in that twilight room, the bones of the dead all about me in the big jars, why, the old lady had me scared stiff. As we say to-day, she had my goat. Only I was brave and didn't let on. And I put my bluff across, for my mother flung the parings into my face and burst into tears. Tears in an elderly woman weighing three hundred and twenty pounds are scarcely impressive, and I hardened the brassiness of my bluff.

"She shifted her attack, and proceeded to talk with the dead. Nay, more, she summoned them there, and, though I was all ripe to see but couldn't, Ahuna saw the father of Kaaukuu in the corner and lay down on the floor and yammered. Just the same, although I almost saw the old giant, I didn't quite see him.

" 'Let him talk for himself,' I said. But Hiwilani persisted in doing the talking for him, and in laying upon me his solemn injunction that I must go with Ahuna to the burial-place and bring back the bones desired by my mother. But I argued that if the dead ones could be invoked to kill living men by wasting sicknesses, and that if the dead ones could transport themselves from their burial-crypts into the corner of her room, I couldn't see why they shouldn't leave their bones behind them, there in her room and ready to be jarred, when they said good-bye and departed for the middle world, the over world, or the under world, or wherever they abided when they weren't paying social calls.

"Whereupon mother let loose on poor old Ahuna, or let loose upon him the ghost of Kaaukuu's father, supposed to be crouching there in the corner, who commanded Ahuna to divulge to her the burial-place. I tried to stiffen him up, telling him to let the old ghost divulge the secret himself, than whom nobody else knew it better, seeing that he had resided there upwards of a century. But Ahuna was old school. He possessed no iota of scepticism. The more Hiwilani frightened him, the more he rolled on the floor and the louder he yammered.

"But when he began to bite himself, I gave in. I felt sorry for him; but, over and beyond that, I began to admire him. He was sterling stuff, even if he was a survival of darkness. Here, with the fear of mystery cruelly upon him, believing Hiwilani's dope implicitly, he was caught between two fidelities. She was his living alii, his *alii kapo*. He must be faithful to her, yet more faithful must he be to all the dead and gone aliis of her line who depended solely on him that their bones should not be disturbed.

"I gave in. But I, too, imposed stipulations. Steadfastly had my father, new school, refused to let me go to England for my education. That sugar was slumping was reason sufficient for him. Steadfastly had my mother, old school, refused, her heathen mind too dark to place any value on education, while it was shrewd enough to discern that education led to unbelief in all that was old. I wanted to study, to study science, the arts, philosophy, to study everything old Howard knew, which enabled him, on the edge of the grave, undauntedly to sneer at superstition, and to give me Jules Verne to read. He was an Oxford man before he went wild and wrong, and it was he who had set the Oxford bee buzzing in my noddle.

"In the end Ahuna and I, old school and new school leagued together, won out. Mother promised that she'd make father send me to England, even if she had to pester him into a prolonged drinking that would make his digestion go back on him. Also, Howard was to accompany me, so that I could decently bury him in England. He was a queer one, old Howard, an individual if there ever was one. Let me tell you a little story about him. It was when Kalakaua was starting on his trip around the world. You remember, when Armstrong, and Judd, and the drunken valet of a German baron accompanied him. Kalakaua made the proposition to Howard ..."

But here the long-apprehended calamity fell upon Prince Akuli.

The old wahine had finished her lei hala. Barefooted, with no adornment of femininity, clad in a shapeless shift of much-washed cotton, with age-withered face and labour-gnarled hands, she cringed before him and crooned a mele in his honour, and, still cringing, put the lei around his neck. It is true the hala smelled most freshly strong, yet was the act beautiful to me, and the old woman herself beautiful to me. My mind leapt into the Prince's narrative so that to Ahuna I could not help likening her.

Oh, truly, to be an alii in Hawaii, even in this second decade of the twentieth century, is no light thing. The alii, utterly of the new, must be kindly and kingly to those old ones absolutely of the old. Nor did the Prince without a kingdom, his loved island long since annexed by the United States and incorporated into a territory along with the rest of the Hawaiian Islands—nor did the Prince betray his repugnance for the odour of the hala. He bowed his head graciously; and his royal condescending words of pure Hawaiian I knew would make the old woman's heart warm until she died with remembrance of the wonderful occasion. The wry grimace he stole to me would not have been made had he felt an uncertainty of its escaping her.

"And so," Prince Akuli resumed, after the wahine had tottered away in an ecstasy, "Ahuna and I departed on our grave-robbing adventure. You know the Iron-bound Coast?"

I nodded, knowing full well the spectacle of those lava leagues of weather coast, truly iron-bound so far as landing-places or anchorages were concerned, great forbidding cliff-walls thousands of feet in height, their summits wreathed in cloud and rain squall, their knees hammered by the trade-wind billows into spouting, spuming white, the air, from sea to rain-cloud, spanned by a myriad leaping waterfalls, provocative, in day or night, of countless sun and lunar rainbows. Valleys, so called, but fissures rather, slit the cyclopean walls here and there, and led away into a lofty and madly vertical back country, most of it inaccessible to the foot of man and trod only by the wild goat.

"Precious little you know of it," Prince Akuli retorted, in reply to my nod. "You've seen it only from the decks of steamers. There are valleys there, inhabited valleys, out of which there is no exit by land, and perilously accessible by canoe only on the selected days of two months in the year. When I was twenty-eight I was over there in one of them on a hunting trip. Bad weather, in the auspicious period, marooned us for three weeks. Then five of my party and myself swam for it out through the surf. Three of us made the canoes waiting for us. The other two were flung back on the sand, each with a broken arm. Save for us, the entire party remained there until the next year, ten months afterward. And one of them was Wilson, of Wilson & Wall, the Honolulu sugar factors. And he was engaged to be married.

"I've seen a goat, shot above by a hunter above, land at my feet a thousand yards underneath. *Believe* me, that landscape seemed to rain goats and rocks for ten minutes. One of my canoemen fell off the trail between the two little valleys of Aipio and Luno. He hit first fifteen hundred feet beneath us, and fetched up in a lodge three hundred feet farther down. We didn't bury him. We couldn't get to him, and flying machines had not yet been invented. His bones are there now, and, barring earthquake and volcano, will be there when the Trumps of Judgment sound.

"Goodness me! Only the other day, when our Promotion Committee, trying to compete with Honolulu for the tourist trade, called in the engineers to estimate what it would cost to build a scenic drive around the Iron-bound Coast, the lowest figures were a quarter of a million dollars a mile!

"And Ahuna and I, an old man and a young boy, started for that stern coast in a canoe paddled by old men! The youngest of them, the steersman, was over sixty, while the rest of them averaged seventy at the very least. There were eight of them, and we started in the nighttime, so that none should see us go. Even these old ones, trusted all their lives, knew no more than the fringe of the secret. To the fringe, only, could they take us.

"And the fringe was—I don't mind telling that much—the fringe was Ponuloo Valley. We got there the third afternoon following. The old chaps weren't strong on the paddles. It was a funny expedition, into such wild waters, with now one and now another of our ancient-mariner crew collapsing and even fainting. One of them actually died on the second morning out. We buried him overside. It was positively uncanny, the heathen ceremonies those grey ones pulled off in burying their grey brother. And I was only fifteen, *alii kapo* over them by blood of heathenness and right of hereditary heathen rule, with a penchant for Jules Verne and shortly to sail for England for my education! So one learns. Small wonder my father was a philosopher, in his own lifetime spanning the history of man from human sacrifice and idol worship, through the religions of man's upward striving, to the Medusa of rank atheism at the end of it all. Small wonder that, like old Ecclesiastes, he found vanity in all things and surcease in sugar stocks, singing boys, and hula dancers."

Prince Akuli debated with his soul for an interval.

"Oh, well," he sighed, "I have done some spanning of time myself." He sniffed disgustedly of the odour of the hala lei that stifled him. "It stinks of the ancient!" he vouchsafed. "I? I stink of the modern. My father was right. The sweetest of all is sugar up a hundred points, or four aces in a poker game. If the Big War lasts another year, I shall clean up three-quarters of a million over a million. If peace breaks to-morrow, with the consequent slump, I could enumerate a hundred who will lose my direct bounty, and go into the old natives' homes my father and I long since endowed for them."

He clapped his hands, and the old wahine tottered toward him in an excitement of haste to serve. She cringed before him, as he drew pad and pencil from his breast pocket.

"Each month, old woman of our old race," he addressed her, "will you receive, by rural free delivery, a piece of written paper that you can exchange with any storekeeper anywhere for ten dollars gold. This shall be so for as long as you live. Behold! I write the record and the remembrance of it, here and now, with this pencil on this paper. And this is because you are of my race and service, and because you have honoured me this day with your mats to sit upon and your thrice-blessed and thrice-delicious lei hala."

He turned to me a weary and sceptical eye, saying:

"And if I die to-morrow, not alone will the lawyers contest my disposition of my property, but they will contest my benefactions and my pensions accorded, and the clarity of my mind.

"It was the right weather of the year; but even then, with our old weak ones at the paddles, we did not attempt the landing until we had assembled half the population of Ponuloo Valley down on the steep little beach. Then we counted our waves, selected the best one, and ran in on it. Of course, the canoe was swamped and the outrigger smashed, but the ones on shore dragged us up unharmed beyond the wash.

"Ahuna gave his orders. In the night-time all must remain within their houses, and the dogs be tied up and have their jaws bound so that there should be no barking. And in the night-time Ahuna and I stole out on our journey, no one knowing whether we went to the right or left or up the valley toward its head. We carried jerky, and hard poi and dried *aku*, and from the quantity of the food I knew we were to be gone several days. Such a trail! A Jacob's ladder to the sky, truly, for that first pali, almost straight up, was three thousand feet above the sea. And we did it in the dark!

"At the top, beyond the sight of the valley we had left, we slept until daylight on the hard rock in a hollow nook Ahuna knew, and that was so small that we were squeezed. And the old fellow, for fear that I might move in the heavy restlessness of lad's sleep, lay on the outside with one arm resting across me. At daybreak, I saw why. Between us and the lip of the cliff scarcely a yard intervened. I crawled to the lip and looked, watching the abyss take on immensity in the growing light and trembling from the fear of height that was upon me. At last I made out the sea, over half a mile straight beneath. And we had done this thing in the dark!

"Down in the next valley, which was a very tiny one, we found evidence of the ancient population, but there were no people. The only way was the crazy foot-paths up and down the dizzy valley walls from valley to valley. But lean and aged as Ahuna was, he seemed untirable. In the second valley dwelt an old leper in hiding. He did not know me, and when Ahuna told him who I was, he grovelled at my feet, almost clasping them, and mumbled a mele of all my line out of a lipless mouth.

"The next valley proved to be the valley. It was long and so narrow that its floor had caught not sufficient space of soil to grow taro for a single person. Also, it had no beach, the stream that threaded it leaping a pali of several hundred feet down to the sea. It was a god-forsaken place of naked, eroded lava, to which only rarely could the scant vegetation find root-hold. For miles we followed up that winding fissure through the towering walls, far into the chaos of back country that lies behind the Iron-bound Coast. How far that valley penetrated I do not know, but, from the quantity of water in the stream, I judged it far. We did not go to the valley's head. I could see Ahuna casting glances to all the peaks, and I knew he was taking bearings, known to him alone, from natural objects. When he halted at the last, it was with abrupt certainty. His bearings had crossed. He threw down the portion of food and outfit he had carried. It was the place. I looked on either hand at the hard, implacable walls, naked of vegetation, and could dream of no burial-place possible in such bare adamant.

"We ate, then stripped for work. Only did Ahuna permit me to retain my shoes. He stood beside me at the edge of a deep pool, likewise apparelled and prodigiously skinny.

" 'You will dive down into the pool at this spot,' he said. 'Search the rock with your hands as you descend, and, about a fathom and a half down, you will find a hole. Enter it, head-first, but going slowly, for the lava rock is sharp and may cut your head and body.'

" 'And then?' I queried. 'You will find the hole growing larger,' was his answer. 'When you have gone all of eight fathoms along the passage, come up slowly, and you will find your head in the air, above water, in the dark. Wait there then for me. The water is very cold.'

"It didn't sound good to me. I was thinking, not of the cold water and the dark, but of the bones. 'You go first,' I said. But he claimed he could not. 'You are my alii, my prince,' he said. 'It is impossible that I should go before you into the sacred burial-place of your kingly ancestors.'

"But the prospect did not please. 'Just cut out this prince stuff,' I told him. 'It isn't what it's cracked up to be. You go first, and I'll never tell on you.' 'Not alone the living must we please,' he admonished, 'but, more so, the dead must we please. Nor can we lie to the dead.'

"We argued it out, and for half an hour it was stalemate. I wouldn't, and he simply couldn't. He tried to buck me up by appealing to my pride. He chanted the heroic deeds of my ancestors; and, I remember especially, he sang to me of Mokomoku, my great-grandfather and the gigantic father of the gigantic Kaaukuu, telling how thrice in battle

Mokomoku leaped among his foes, seizing by the neck a warrior in either hand and knocking their heads together until they were dead. But this was not what decided me. I really felt sorry for old Ahuna, he was so beside himself for fear the expedition would come to naught. And I was coming to a great admiration for the old fellow, not least among the reasons being the fact of his lying down to sleep between me and the cliff-lip.

"So, with true alii-authority of command, saying, 'You will immediately follow after me,' I dived in. Everything he had said was correct. I found the entrance to the subterranean passage, swam carefully through it, cutting my shoulder once on the lava-sharp roof, and emerged in the darkness and air. But before I could count thirty, he broke water beside me, rested his hand on my arm to make sure of me, and directed me to swim ahead of him for the matter of a hundred feet or so. Then we touched bottom and climbed out on the rocks. And still no light, and I remember I was glad that our altitude was too high for centipedes.

"He had brought with him a coconut calabash, tightly stoppered, of whale-oil that must have been landed on Lahaina beach thirty years before. From his mouth he took a water-tight arrangement of a matchbox composed of two empty rifle-cartridges fitted snugly together. He lighted the wicking that floated on the oil, and I looked about, and knew disappointment. No burial-chamber was it, but merely a lava tube such as occurs on all the islands.

"He put the calabash of light into my hands and started me ahead of him on the way, which he assured me was long, but not too long. It was long, at least a mile in my sober judgment, though at the time it seemed five miles, and it ascended sharply. When Ahuna, at the last, stopped me, I knew we were close to our goal. He knelt on his lean old knees on the sharp lava rock, and clasped my knees with his skinny arms. My hand that was free of the calabash lamp he placed on his head. He chanted to me, with his old cracked, quavering voice, the line of my descent and my essential high alii-ness. And then he said:

" 'Tell neither Kanau nor Hiwilani aught of what you are about to behold. There is no sacredness in Kanau. His mind is filled with sugar and the breeding of horses. I do know that he sold a feather cloak his grandfather had worn to that English collector for eight thousand dollars, and the money he lost the next day betting on the polo game between Maui and Oahu. Hiwilani, your mother, is filled with sacredness. She is too much filled with sacredness. She grows old, and weak-headed, and she traffics over-much with sorceries.'

" 'No,' I made answer. 'I shall tell no one. If I did, then would I have to return to this place again. And I do not want ever to return to this place. I'll try anything once. This I shall never try twice.'

" 'It is well,' he said, and arose, falling behind so that I should enter first. Also, he said: 'Your mother is old. I shall bring her, as promised, the bones of her mother and of her grandfather. These should content her until she dies; and then, if I die before her, it is you who must see to it that all the bones in her family collection are placed in the Royal Mausoleum.'

"I have given all the Islands' museums the once-over," Prince Akuli lapsed back into slang, "and I must say that the totality of the collections cannot touch what I saw in our Lakanaii burial-cave. Remember, and with reason and history, we trace back the highest and oldest genealogy in the Islands. Everything that I had ever dreamed or heard of, and much more that I had not, was there. The place was wonderful. Ahuna, sepulchrally muttering prayers and meles, moved about, lighting various whale-oil lamp-calabashes. They were all there, the Hawaiian race from the beginning of Hawaiian time. Bundles of bones and bundles of bones, all wrapped decently in tapa, until for all the world it was like the parcels-post department at a post office.

"And everything! Kahalis, which you may know developed out of the fly-flapper into symbols of royalty until they became larger than hearse-plumes with handles a fathom and a half and over two fathoms in length. And such handles! Of the wood of the *kauila*, inlaid with shell and ivory and bone with a cleverness that had died out among our artificers a century before. It was a centuries-old family attic. For the first time I saw things I had only heard of, such as the *pahoas*, fashioned of whale-teeth and suspended by braided human hair, and worn on the breast only by the highest of rank.

"There were tapes and mats of the rarest and oldest; capes and leis and helmets and cloaks, priceless all, except the too-ancient ones, of the feathers of the *mamo,* and of the *iwi* and the *akakano* and the *o-o.* I saw one of the mamo cloaks that was superior to that finest one in the Bishop Museum in Honolulu, and that they value at between half a million and a million dollars. Goodness me, I thought at the time, it was lucky Kanau didn't know about it.

"Such a mess of things! Carved gourds and calabashes, shell-scrapers, nets of *olona* fibre, a junk of *ié-ié* baskets, and fish-hooks of every bone and spoon of shell. Musical instruments of the forgotten days—*ukukes* and nose flutes, and *kiokios* which are likewise played with one unstop-pered nostril. Taboo poi bowls and finger bowls, left-handed adzes of the canoe gods, lava-cup lamps, stone mortars and pestles and poi-pounders. And adzes again, a myriad of them, beautiful ones, from an ounce in weight for the finer carving of idols to fifteen pounds for the felling of trees, and all with the sweetest handles I ever beheld.

"There were the *kuekeekes*—you know, our ancient drums, hollowed sections of the coconut tree, covered one end with shark-skin. The first kaekeeke of all Hawaii Ahuna pointed out to me and told me the tale. It was manifestly most ancient. He was afraid to touch it for fear the age-rotted wood of it would crumble to dust, the ragged tatters of the shark-skin head of it still attached. 'This is the very oldest and father of all our kaekeekes,' Ahuna told me. 'Kila, the son of Moikeha, brought it back from far Raiatea in the South Pacific. And it was Kila's own son, Kahai, who made that same journey, and was gone ten years, and brought back with him from Tahiti the first breadfruit trees that sprouted and grew on Hawaiian soil.'

"And the bones and bones! The parcel-delivery array of them! Be-sides the small bundles of the long bones, there were full skeletons, tapa-wrapped, lying in one-man, and two- and three-man canoes of precious *koa* wood, with curved outriggers of *wiliwili* wood, and proper paddles to hand with the io-projection at the point simulating the con tinuance of the handle, as if, like a skewer, thrust through the flat length of the blade. And their war weapons were laid away by the sides of the lifeless bones that had wielded them—rusty old horse-pistols, derringers, pepper-boxes, five-barrelled fantastiques, Kentucky long rifles, muskets handled in trade by John Company and Hudson's Bay, shark-tooth swords, wooden stabbing-knives, arrows and spears bone-headed of the fish and the pig and of man, and spears and arrows wooden-headed and fire-hardened.

"Ahuna put a spear in my hand, headed and pointed finely with the long skin-bone of a man, and told me the tale of it. But first he unwrapped the long bones, arms, and legs, of two parcels, the bones, under the wrappings, neatly tied like so many faggots. 'This,' said Ahuna, exhibiting the pitiful white contents of one parcel, 'is Laulani. She was the wife of Akaiko, whose bones, now placed in your hands, much larger and male-like as you observe, held up the flesh of a large man, a three-hundred pounder seven-footer, three centuries agone. And this spear-head is made of the shin-bone of Keola, a mighty wrestler and runner of their own time and place. And he loved Laulani, and she fled with him. But in a forgotten battle on the sands of Kalini, Akaiko rushed the lines of the enemy, leading the charge that was successful, and seized upon Keola, his wife's lover, and threw him to the ground, and sawed through his neck to the death with a shark-tooth knife. Thus, in the old days as always, did man combat for woman with man. And Laulani was beautiful; the Keola should be made into a spear-head for her! She was formed like a queen, and her body was a long bowl of sweetness, and her fingers lomi'd to slimness and smallness at her mother's breast. For ten generations have we remembered her beauty. Your father's singing boys to-day sing of her beauty in the hula that is named of her! This is Laulani, whom you hold in your hands.'

"And, Ahuna done, I could but gaze, with imagination at the one time sobered and fired. Old drunken Howard had lent me his Tennyson, and I had mooned long and often over the Idyls of the King. Here were the three, I thought—Arthur, and Launcelot, and Guinevere. This, then, I pondered, was the end of it all, of life and strife and striving and love, the weary spirits of these long-gone ones to be invoked by fat old women and mangy sorcerers, the bones of them to be esteemed of collectors and betted on horse-races and ace-fulls or to be sold for cash and invested in sugar stocks.

"For me it was illumination. I learned there in the burial-cave the great lesson. And to Ahuna I said: 'The spear headed with the long bone of Keola I shall take for my own. Never shall I sell it. I shall keep it always.'

"'And for what purpose?' he demanded. And I replied: 'That the contemplation of it may keep my hand sober and my feet on earth with the knowledge that few men are fortunate enough to have as much of a remnant of themselves as will compose a spearhead when they are three centuries dead.'

"And Ahuna bowed his head, and praised my wisdom of judgment. But at that moment the long-rotted olona-cord broke and the pitiful woman's bones of Laulani shed from my clasp and clattered on the rocky floor. One shin-bone, in some way deflected, fell under the dark shadow of a canoe-bow, and I made up my mind that it should be mine. So I hastened to help him in the picking up of the bones and the tying, so that he did not notice its absence.

"'This,' said Ahuna, introducing me to another of my ancestors, 'is your great-grandfather, Mokomoku, the father of Kaaukuu. Behold the size of his bones. He was a giant. I shall carry him, because of the long spear of Keola that will be difficult for you to carry away. And this is Lelemahoa, your grandmother, the mother of your mother, that you shall carry. And day grows short, and we must still swim up through the waters to the sun ere darkness hides the sun from the world.'

"But Ahuna, putting out the various calabashes of light by drowning the wicks in the whale-oil, did not observe me include the shin-bone of Laulani with the bones of my grandmother."

The honk of the automobile, sent up from Olokona to rescue us, broke off the Prince's narrative. We said good-bye to the ancient and fresh-pensioned wahine, and departed. A half-mile on our way, Prince Akuli resumed.

"So Ahuna and I returned to Hiwilani, and to her happiness, lasting to her death the year following, two more of her ancestors abided about her in the jars of her twilight room. Also, she kept her compact and worried my father into sending me to England. I took old Howard along, and he perked up and confuted the doctors, so that it was three years before I buried him restored to the bosom of my family. Sometimes I think he was the most brilliant man I have ever known. Not until my return from England did Ahuna die, the last custodian of our alii secrets. And at his death-bed he pledged me again never to reveal the location in that nameless valley, and never to go back myself.

"Much else I have forgotten to mention did I see there in the cave that one time. There were the bones of Kumi, the near demigod, son of Tui Manua of Samoa, who, in the long before, married into my line and heaven-boosted my genealogy. And the bones of my great-grandmother who had slept in the four-poster presented her by Lord Byron. And Ahuna hinted tradition that there was reason for that presentation, as well as for the historically known lingering of the *Blonde* in Olokona for so long. And I held her poor bones in my hands—bones once fleshed with sensate beauty, informed with sparkle and spirit, instinct with love and love-warmness of arms around and eyes and lips together, that had begat me in the end of the generations unborn. It was a good experience. I am modern, 'tis true. I believe in no mystery stuff of old time nor of the kahunas. And yet, I saw in that cave things which I dare not name to you, and which I, since old Ahuna died, alone of the living know. I have no children. With me my long line ceases. This is the twentieth century, and we stink of gasoline. Nevertheless these other and nameless things shall die with me. I shall never revisit the burial-place. Nor in all time to come will any man gaze upon it through living eyes unless the quakes of earth rend the mountains asunder and spew forth the secrets contained in the hearts of the mountains."

Prince Akuli ceased from speech. With welcome relief on his face, he removed the lei hala from his neck, and, with a sniff and a sigh, tossed it into concealment in the thick lantana by the side of the road.

"But the shin-bone of Laulani?" I queried softly.

He remained silent while a mile of pasture land flew by us and yielded to caneland.

"I have it now," he at last said. "And beside it is Keola, slain ere his time and made into a spear-head for love of the woman whose shin-bone abides near to him. To them, those poor pathetic bones, I owe more than to aught else. I became possessed of them in the period of my culminating adolescence. I know they changed the entire course of my life and trend of my mind. They gave to me a modesty and a humility in the world, from which my father's fortune has ever failed to seduce me.

"And often, when woman was nigh to winning to the empery of my mind over me, I sought Laulani's shin-bone. And often, when lusty manhood stung me into feeling over-proud and lusty, I consulted the spear-head remnant of Keola, one-time swift runner, and mighty wrestler and lover, and thief of the wife of a king. The contemplation of them has ever been of profound aid to me, and you might well say that I have founded my religion or practice of living upon them."

Waikiki, Honolulu
Hawaiian Islands
July 16, 1916

WHEN ALICE TOLD HER SOUL

This, of Alice Akana, is an affair of Hawaii, not of this day, but of days recent enough, when Abel Ah Yo preached his famous revival in Honolulu and persuaded Alice Akana to tell her soul. But what Alice told concerned itself with the earlier history of the then surviving generation.

For Alice Akana was fifty years old, had begun life early, and, early and late, lived it spaciously. What she knew went back into the roots and foundations of families, businesses, and plantations. She was the one living repository of accurate information that lawyers sought out, whether the information they required related to land-boundaries and land gifts, or to marriages, births, bequests, or scandals. Rarely, because of the tight tongue she kept behind her teeth, did she give them what they asked; and when she did was when only equity was served and no one was hurt.

For Alice had lived, from early in her girlhood, a life of flowers, and song, and wine, and dance; and, in her later years, had herself been mistress of these revels by office of mistress of the hula house. In such atmosphere, where mandates of God and man and caution are inhibited, and where woozled tongues will wag, she acquired her historical knowledge of things never otherwise whispered and rarely guessed. And her tight tongue had served her well, so that, while the old-timers knew she must know, none ever heard her gossip of the times of Kalakaua's boathouse, nor of the high times of officers of visiting warships, nor of the diplomats and ministers and councils of the countries of the world.

So, at fifty, loaded with historical dynamite sufficient, if it were ever exploded, to shake the social and commercial life of the Islands, still tight of tongue, Alice Akana was mistress of the hula house, manageress of the dancing girls who hula'd for royalty, for luaus, house-parties, poi suppers, and curious tourists. And, at fifty, she was not merely buxom, but short and fat in the Polynesian peasant way, with a constitution and lack of organic weakness that promised incalculable years. But it was at fifty that she strayed, quite by chance of time and curiosity, into Abel Ah Yo's revival meeting.

Now Abel Ah Yo, in his theology and word wizardry, was as much mixed a personage as Billy Sunday. In his genealogy he was much more mixed, for he was compounded of one-fourth Portuguese, one-fourth Scotch, one-fourth Hawaiian, and one-fourth Chinese. The Pentecostal fire he flamed forth was hotter and more variegated than could any one of the four races of him alone have flamed forth. For in him were gathered together the cannyness and the cunning, the wit and the wisdom, the subtlety and the rawness, the passion and the philosophy, the agonizing spirit-groping and the legs up to the knees in the dung of reality, of the four radically different breeds that contributed to the sum of him. His, also, was the clever self-deceivement of the entire clever compound.

When it came to word wizardry, he had Billy Sunday, master of slang and argot of one language, skinned by miles. For in Abel Ah Yo were the five verbs, and nouns, and adjectives, and metaphors of four living languages. Intermixed and living promiscuously and vitally together, he possessed in these languages a reservoir of expression in which a myriad Billy Sundays could drown. Of no race, a mongrel par excellence, a heterogeneous scrabble, the genius of the admixture was superlatively Abel Ah Yo's. Like a chameleon, he titubated and scintil-

lated grandly between the diverse parts of him, stunning by frontal attack and surprising and confounding by flanking sweeps the mental
homogeneity of the more simply constituted souls who came in to his
revival to sit under him and flame to his flaming.

Abel Ah Yo believed in himself and his mixedness, as he believed in
the mixedness of his weird concept that God looked as much like him
as like any man, being no mere tribal god, but a world god that must
look equally like all races of all the world, even if it led to piebaldness.
And the concept worked. Chinese, Korean, Japanese, Hawaiian, Porto
Rican, Russian, English, French—members of all races—knelt without friction, side by side, to his revision of deity.

Himself in his tender youth an apostate to the Church of England,
Abel Ah Yo had for years suffered the lively sense of being a Judas sin-
ner. Essentially religious, he had foresworn the Lord. Like Judas therefore he was. Judas was damned. Wherefore he, Abel Ah Yo, was damned;
and he did not want to be damned. So, quite after the manner of humans, he squirmed and twisted to escape damnation. The day came
when he solved his escape. The doctrine that Judas was damned, he
concluded, was a misinterpretation of God, who, above all things, stood
for justice. Judas had been God's servant, specially selected to perform
a particularly nasty job. Therefore Judas, ever faithful, a betrayer only
by divine command, was a saint. Ergo, he, Abel Ah Yo, was a saint by
very virtue of his apostasy to a particular sect, and he could have access with clear grace any time to God.

This theory became one of the major tenets of his preaching, and
was especially efficacious in cleansing the consciences of the backsliders from all other faiths who else, in the secrecy of their subcon-
scious selves, were being crushed by the weight of the Judas sin. To
Abel Ah Yo, God's plan was as clear as if he, Abel Ah Yo, had planned
it himself. All would be saved in the end, although some took longer
than others, and would win only to backseats. Man's place in the ever-
fluxing chaos of the world was definite and pre-ordained—if by no
other token, then by denial that there was any ever-fluxing chaos. This
was a mere bugbear of mankind's addled fancy; and, by stinging au-
dacities of thought and speech, by vivid slang that bit home by sheerest intimacy into his listeners' mental processes, he drove the bugbear

from their brains, showed them the loving clarity of God's design, and, thereby, induced in them spiritual serenity and calm.

What chance had Alice Akana, herself pure and homogeneous Hawaiian, against his subtle, democratic-tinged, four-race-engendered, slang-munitioned attack? He knew, by contact, almost as much as she about the waywardness of living and sinning—having been singing boy on the passenger-ships between Hawaii and California, and, after that, bar boy, afloat and ashore, from the Barbary Coast to Heinie's Tavern. In point of fact, he had left his job of Number One Bar Boy at the University Club to embark on his great preachment revival.

So, when Alice Akana strayed in to scoff, she remained to pray to Abel Ah Yo's god, who struck her hard-headed mind as the most sensible god of which she had ever heard. She gave money into Abel Ah Yo's collection plate, closed up the hula house, and dismissed the hula dancers to more devious ways of earning a livelihood, shed her bright colours and raiments and flower garlands, and bought a Bible.

It was a time of religious excitement in the purlieus of Honolulu. The thing was a democratic movement of the people toward God. Place and caste were invited, but never came. The stupid lowly, and the humble lowly, only, went down on its knees at the penitent form, admitted its pathological weight and hurt of sin, eliminated and purged all its bafflements, and walked forth again upright under the sun, child-like and pure, upborne by Abel Ah Yo's god's arm around it. In short, Abel Ah Yo's revival was a clearing house for sin and sickness of spirit, wherein sinners were relieved of their burdens and made light and bright and spiritually healthy again.

But Alice was not happy. She had not been cleared. She bought and dispersed Bibles, contributed more money to the plate, contralto'd gloriously in all the hymns, but would not tell her soul. In vain Abel Ah Yo wrestled with her. She would not go down on her knees at the penitent form and voice the things of tarnish within her—the ill things of good friends of the old days. "You cannot serve two masters," Abel Ah Yo told her. "Hell is full of those who have tried. Single of heart and pure of heart must you make your peace with God. Not until you tell your soul to God right out in meeting will you be ready for redemption. In the meantime you will suffer the canker of the sin you carry about within you."

Scientifically, though he did not know it and though he continually jeered at science, Abel Ah Yo was right. Not could she be again as a child and become radiantly clad in God's grace, until she had eliminated from her soul, by telling, all the sophistications that had been hers, including those she shared with others. In the Protestant way, she must bare her soul in public, as in the Catholic way it was done in the privacy of the confessional. The result of such baring would be unity, tranquillity, happiness, cleansing, redemption, and immortal life.

"Choose!" Abel Ah Yo thundered. "Loyalty to God, or loyalty to man." And Alice could not choose. Too long had she kept her tongue locked with the honour of man. "I will tell all my soul about myself," she contended. "God knows I am tired of my soul and should like to have it clean and shining once again as when I was a little girl at Kaneohe—"

"But all the corruption of your soul has been with other souls," was Abel Ah Yo's invariable reply. "When you have a burden, lay it down. You cannot bear a burden and be quit of it at the same time."

"I will pray to God each day, and many times each day," she urged. "I will approach God with humility, with sighs and with tears. I will contribute often to the plate, and I will buy Bibles, Bibles, Bibles without end."

"And God will not smile upon you," God's mouthpiece retorted. "And you will remain weary and heavy-laden. For you will not have told all your sin, and not until you have told all will you be rid of any."

"This rebirth is difficult," Alice sighed.

"Rebirth is even more difficult than birth." Abel Ah Yo did anything but comfort her. " 'Not until you become as a little child …' "

"If ever I tell my soul, it will be a big telling," she confided.

"The bigger the reason to tell it then."

And so the situation remained at deadlock, Abel Ah Yo demanding absolute allegiance to God, and Alice Akana flirting on the fringes of paradise.

"You bet it will be a big telling, if Alice ever begins," the beachcombing and disreputable *kamaainas* gleefully told one another over their Palm Tree gin.

In the clubs the possibility of her telling was of more moment. The younger generation of men announced that they had applied for front seats at the telling, while many of the older generation of men joked hollowly about the conversion of Alice. Further, Alice found herself abruptly popular with friends who had forgotten her existence for twenty years.

One afternoon, as Alice, Bible in hand, was taking the electric street car at Hotel and Fort, Cyrus Hodge, sugar factor and magnate, ordered his chauffeur to stop beside her. Willy nilly, in excess of friendliness, he had her into his limousine beside him and went three-quarters of an hour out of his way and time personally to conduct her to her destination.

"Good for sore eyes to see you," he burbled. "How the years fly! You're looking fine. The secret of youth is yours."

Alice smiled and complimented in return in the royal Polynesian way of friendliness.

"My, my," Cyrus Hodge reminisced. "I was such a boy in those days!"

"*Some* boy," she laughed acquiescence.

"But knowing no more than the foolishness of a boy in those long-ago days."

"Remember the night your hack-driver got drunk and left you—"

"S—s—sh!" he cautioned. "That Jap driver is a high-school graduate and knows more English than either of us. Also, I think he is a spy for his Government. So why should we tell him anything? Besides, I was so very young. You remember ..."

"Your cheeks were like the peaches we used to grow before the Mediterranean fruit fly got into them," Alice agreed. "I don't think you shaved more than once a week then. You were a pretty boy. Don't you remember the hula we composed in your honour, the—"

"S-s-sh!" he hushed her. "All that's buried and forgotten. May it remain forgotten."

And she was aware that in his eyes was no longer any of the ingenuousness of youth she remembered. Instead, his eyes were keen and speculative, searching into her for some assurance that she would not resurrect his particular portion of that buried past.

"Religion is a good thing for us as we get along into middle age," another old friend told her. He was building a magnificent house on Pacific Heights, but had recently married a second time, and was even then on his way to the steamer to welcome home his two daughters just graduated from Vassar. "We need religion in our old age, Alice. It softens, makes us more tolerant and forgiving of the weaknesses of others—especially the weaknesses of youth of—of others, when they played high and low and didn't know what they were doing."

He waited anxiously.

"Yes," she said. "We are all born to sin and it is hard to grow out of sin. But I grow, I grow."

"Don't forget, Alice, in those days I always played square. You and I never had a falling out."

"Not even the night you gave that luau when you were twenty-one and insisted on breaking the glassware after every toast. But of course you paid for it."

"Handsomely," he asserted almost pleadingly.

"Handsomely," she agreed. "I replaced more than double the quantity with what you paid me, so that at the next luau I catered one hundred and twenty plates without having to rent or borrow a dish or glass. Lord Mainweather gave that luau—you remember him."

"I was pig-sticking with him at Mana," the other nodded. "We were at a two weeks' house-party there. But say, Alice, as you know, I think this religion stuff is all right and better than all right. But don't let it carry you off your feet. And don't get to telling your soul on me. What would my daughters think of that broken glassware!"

"I always did have an *aloha* for you, Alice," a member of the Senate, fat and bald-headed, assured her.

And another, a lawyer and a grandfather: "We were always friends, Alice. And remember, any legal advice or handling of business you may require, I'll do for you gladly, and without fees, for the sake of our old-time friendship."

Came a banker to her late Christmas Eve, with formidable, legal-looking envelopes in his hand which he presented to her.

"Quite by chance," he explained, "when my people were looking up land-records in Iapio Valley, I found a mortgage of two thousand on your holdings there—that rice land leased to Ah Chin. And my mind drifted back to the past when we were all young together, and wild—a bit wild, to be sure. And my heart warmed with the memory of you, and, so, just as an aloha, here's the whole thing cleared off for you."

Nor was Alice forgotten by her own people. Her house became a Mecca for native men and women, usually performing pilgrimage privily after darkness fell, with presents always in their hands—squid fresh from the reef, opihis and limu, baskets of alligator pears, roasting corn of the earliest from windward Oahu, mangoes and star-apples, taro pink and royal of the finest selection, suckling pigs, banana poi, breadfruit, and crabs caught the very day from Pearl Harbour. Mary Mendana, wife of the Portuguese Consul, remembered her with a five-dollar box of candy and a mandarin coat that would have fetched three-quarters of a hundred dollars at a fire sale. And Elvira Miyahara Makaena Yin Wap, the wife of Yin Wap the wealthy Chinese importer, brought personally to Alice two entire bolts of pina cloth from the Philippines and a dozen pairs of silk stockings.

The time passed, and Abel Ah Yo struggled with Alice for a properly penitent heart, and Alice struggled with herself for her soul, while half of Honolulu wickedly or apprehensively hung on the outcome. Carnival week was over, polo and the races had come and gone, and the celebration of Fourth of July was ripening, ere Abel Ah Yo beat down by brutal psychology the citadel of her reluctance. It was then that he gave his famous exhortation which might be summed up as Abel Ah Yo's definition of eternity. Of course, like Billy Sunday on certain occasions, Abel Ah Yo had cribbed the definition. But no one in the Islands knew it, and his rating as a revivalist uprose a hundred per cent.

So successful was his preaching that night, that he reconverted many of his converts, who fell and moaned about the penitent form and crowded for room amongst scores of new converts burnt by the pentecostal fire, including half a company of negro soldiers from the garrisoned Twenty-Fifth Infantry, a dozen troopers from the Fourth Cavalry on its way to the Philippines, as many drunken man-of-war's men, divers ladies from Iwilei, and half the riff-raff of the beach.

Abel Ah Yo, subtly sympathetic himself by virtue of his racial admixture, knowing human nature like a book and Alice Akana even
more so, knew just what he was doing when he arose that memorable
night and exposited God, hell, and eternity in terms of Alice Akana's
comprehension. For, quite by chance, he had discovered her cardinal
weakness. First of all, like all Polynesians, an ardent lover of nature, he
found that earthquake and volcanic eruption were the things of which
Alice lived in terror. She had been, in the past, on the Big Island,
through cataclysms that had slacken grass houses down upon her while
she slept, and she had beheld Madame Pele fling red-fluxing lava down
the long slopes of Mauna Loa, destroying fish-ponds on the sea-brim
and licking up droves of beef cattle, villages, and humans on her fiery
way.

The night before, a slight earthquake had shaken Honolulu and
given Alice Akana insomnia. And the morning papers had stated
that Mauna Kea had broken into eruption, while the lava was rising
rapidly in the great pit of Kilauea. So, at the meeting, her mind vexed
between the terrors of this world and the delights of the eternal world
to come, Alice sat down in a front seat in a very definite state of the
"jumps."

And Abel Ah Yo arose and put his finger on the sorest part of her
soul. Sketching the nature of God in the stereotyped way, but making
the stereotyped alive again with his gift of tongues in Pidgin-English
and Pidgin-Hawaiian, Abel Ah Yo described the day when the Lord,
even His infinite patience at an end, would tell Peter to close his day
book and ledgers, command Gabriel to summon all souls to Judgment,
and cry out with a voice of thunder: "Welakahao!"

This anthromorphic deity of Abel Ah Yo thundering the modern
Hawaiian-English slang of *welakahao* at the end of the world, is a fair
sample of the revivalist's speech-tools of discourse. *Welakahao* means
literally "hot iron." It was coined in the Honolulu Iron Works by the
hundreds of Hawaiian men there employed, who meant by it "to hus-
tle," "to get a move on," the iron being hot meaning that the time had
come to strike.

"And the Lord cried 'Welakahao,' and the Day of Judgment began
and was over *wiki-wiki* just like that; for Peter was a better bookkeeper

than any on the Waterhouse' Trust Company Limited, and, further, Peter's books were true."

Swiftly Abel Ah Yo divided the sheep from the goats, and hastened the latter down into hell.

"And now," he demanded, perforce his language on these pages being properly Englished, "what is hell like? Oh, my friends, let me describe to you, in a little way, what I have beheld with my own eyes on earth of the possibilities of hell. I was a young man, a boy, and I was at Hilo. Morning began with earthquakes. Throughout the day the mighty land continued to shake and tremble, till strong men became seasick, and women clung to trees to escape falling, and cattle were thrown down off their feet. I beheld myself a young calf so thrown. A night of terror indescribable followed. The land was in motion like a canoe in a Kona gale. There was an infant crushed to death by its fond mother stepping upon it whilst fleeing her falling house.

"The heavens were on fire above us. We read our Bibles by the light of the heavens, and the print was fine, even for young eyes. Those missionary Bibles were always too small of print. Forty miles away from us, the heart of hell burst from the lofty mountains and gushed red-blood of fire-melted rock toward the sea. With the heavens in vast conflagration and the earth hulaing beneath our feet, was a scene too awful and too majestic to be enjoyed. We could think only of the thin bubble-skin of earth between us and the everlasting lake of fire and brimstone, and of God to whom we prayed to save us. There were earnest and devout souls who there and then promised their pastors to give not their shaved tithes, but five-tenths of their all to the church, if only the Lord would let them live to contribute.

"Oh, my friends, God saved us. But first he showed us a foretaste of that hell that will yawn for us on the last day, when he cries 'Welaka-hao!' in a voice of thunder. When the iron is hot! Think of it! When the iron is hot for sinners!

"By the third day, things being much quieter, my friend the preacher and I, being calm in the hand of God, journeyed up Mauna Loa and gazed into the awful pit of Kilauea. We gazed down into the fathomless abyss to the lake of fire far below, roaring and dashing its fiery spray into billows and fountaining hundreds of feet into the air like Fourth of July fireworks you have all seen, and all the while we were suffocating and made dizzy by the immense volumes of smoke and brimstone ascending.

"And I say unto you, no pious person could gaze down upon that scene without recognizing fully the Bible picture of the Pit of Hell. Believe me, the writers of the New Testament had nothing on us. As for me, my eyes were fixed upon the exhibition before me, and I stood mute and trembling under a sense never before so fully realized of the power, the majesty, and terror of Almighty God—the resources of His wrath, and the untold horrors of the finally impenitent who do not tell their souls and make their peace with the Creator.*

"But oh, my friends, think you our guides, our native attendants, deep-sunk in heathenism, were affected by such a scene? No. The devil's hand was upon them. Utterly regardless and unimpressed, they were only careful about their supper, chatted about their raw fish, and stretched themselves upon their mats to sleep. Children of the devil they were, insensible to the beauties, the sublimities, and the awful terror of God's works. But you are not heathen I now address. What is a heathen? He is one who betrays a stupid insensibility to every elevated idea and to every elevated emotion. If you wish to awaken his attention, do not bid him to look down into the Pit of Hell. But present him with a calabash of poi, a raw fish, or invite him to some low, grovelling, and sensuous sport. Oh, my friends, how lost are they to all that elevates the immortal soul! But the preacher and I, sad and sick at heart for them, gazed down into hell. Oh, my friends, it *was* hell, the hell of the Scriptures, the hell of eternal torment for the undeserving ..."

Alice Akana was in an ecstasy or hysteria of terror. She was mumbling incoherently: "O Lord, I will give nine-tenths of my all. I will give all. I will give even the two bolts of pina cloth, the mandarin coat, and the entire dozen silk stockings ..."

By the time she could lend ear again, Abel Ah Yo was launching out on his famous definition of eternity.

"Eternity is a long time, my friends. God lives, and, therefore, God lives inside eternity. And God is very old. The fires of hell are as old

---

* See Dibble's *A History of the Sandwich Islands.*

and as everlasting as God. How else could there be everlasting torment for those sinners cast down by God into the Pit on the Last Day to burn for ever and for ever through all eternity? Oh, my friends, your minds are small—too small to grasp eternity. Yet is it given to me, by God's grace, to convey to you an understanding of a tiny bit of eternity.

"The grains of sand on the beach of Waikiki are as many as the stars, and more. No man may count them. Did he have a million lives in which to count them, he would have to ask for more time. Now let us consider a little, dinky, old minah bird with one broken wing that cannot fly. At Waikiki the minah bird that cannot fly takes one grain of sand in its beak and hops, hops, all day long and for many days, all the way to Pearl Harbour and drops that one grain of sand into the harbour. Then it hops, hops, all day and for many days, all the way back to Waikiki for another grain of sand. And again it hops, hops all the way back to Pearl Harbour. And it continues to do this through the years and centuries, and the thousands and thousands of centuries, until, at last, there remains not one grain of sand at Waikiki and Pearl Harbour is filled up with land and growing coconuts and pine-apples. And then, oh my friends, even then, *it would not yet be sunrise in Hell!*"

Here, at the smashing impact of so abrupt a climax, unable to withstand the sheer simplicity and objectivity of such artful measurement of a trifle of eternity, Alice Akana's mind broke down and blew up. She uprose, reeled blindly, and stumbled to her knees at the penitent form. Abel Ah Yo had not finished his preaching, but it was his gift to know crowd psychology, and to feel the heat of the pentecostal conflagration that scorched his audience. He called for a rousing revival hymn from his singers, and stepped down to wade among the hallelujah-shouting negro soldiers to Alice Akana. And, ere the excitement began to ebb, nine-tenths of his congregation and all his converts were down on knees and praying and shouting aloud an immensity of contriteness and sin.

———

Word came, via telephone, almost simultaneously to the Pacific and University Clubs, that at last Alice was telling her soul in meeting; and, by private machine and taxi-cab, for the first time Abel Ah Yo's revival was invaded by those of caste and place. The first comers beheld the curious sight of Hawaiian, Chinese, and all variegated racial mixtures of the smelting-pot of Hawaii, men and women, fading out and slinking away through the exits of Abel Ah Yo's tabernacle. But those who were sneaking out were mostly men, while those who remained were avid-faced as they hung on Alice's utterance.

Never was a more fearful and damning community narrative enunciated in the entire Pacific, north and south, than that enunciated by Alice Akana, the penitent Phryne of Honolulu.

"Huh!" the first comers heard her saying, having already disposed of most of the venial sins of the lesser ones of her memory. "You think this man, Stephen Makekau, is the son of Moses Makekau and Minnie Ah Ling, and has a legal right to the two hundred and eight dollars he draws down each month from Parke Richards Limited, for the lease of the fish-pond to Bill Kong at Amana. Not so. Stephen Makekau is not the son of Moses. He is the son of Aaron Kama and Tillie Naone. He was given as a present, as a feeding child, to Moses and Minnie, by Aaron and Tillie. I know. Moses and Minnie and Aaron and Tillie are dead. Yet I know and can prove it. Old Mrs. Poepoe is still alive. I was present when Stephen was born, and in the night-time, when he was two months old, I myself carried him as a present to Moses and Minnie, and old Mrs. Poepoe carried the lantern. This secret has been one of my sins. It has kept me from God. Now I am free of it. Young Archie Makekau, who collects bills for the Gas Company and plays baseball in the afternoons, and drinks too much gin, should get that two hundred and eight dollars the first of each month from Parke Richards Limited. He will blow it in on gin and a Ford automobile. Stephen is a good man. Archie is no good. Also he is a liar, and he has served two sentences on the reef, and was in reform school before that. Yet God demands the truth, and Archie will get the money and make a bad use of it."

And in such fashion Alice rambled on through the experiences of her long and full-packed life. And women forgot they were in the tabernacle, and men too, and faces darkened with passion as they learned for the first time the long-buried secrets of their other halves.

"The lawyers' offices will be crowded to-morrow morning," Mac-

Ilwaine, chief of detectives, paused long enough from storing away useful information to lean and mutter in Colonel Stilton's ear.

Colonel Stilton grinned affirmation, although the chief of detectives could not fail to note the ghastliness of the grin.

"There is a banker in Honolulu. You all know his name. He is 'way up, swell society because of his wife. He owns much stock in General Plantations and Inter-Island."

MacIlwaine recognized the growing portrait and forbore to chuckle.

"His name is Colonel Stilton. Last Christmas Eve he came to my house with big aloha and gave me mortgages on my land in Iapio Valley, all cancelled, for two thousand dollars' worth. Now why did he have such big cash aloha for me? I will tell you ..."

And tell she did, throwing the searchlight on ancient business transactions and political deals which from their inception had lurked in the dark.

"This," Alice concluded the episode, "has long been a sin upon my conscience, and kept my heart from God.

"And Harold Miles was that time President of the Senate, and next week he bought three town lots at Pearl Harbour, and painted his Honolulu house, and paid up his back dues in his clubs. Also the Ramsay home at Honokiki was left by will to the people if the Government would keep it up. But if the Government, after two years, did not begin to keep it up, then would it go to the Ramsay heirs, whom old Ramsay hated like poison. Well, it went to the heirs all right. Their lawyer was Charley Middleton, and he had me help fix it with the Government men. And their names were ..." Six names, from both branches of the Legislature, Alice recited, and added: "Maybe they all painted their houses after that. For the first time have I spoken. My heart is much lighter and softer. It has been coated with an armour of house-paint against the Lord. And there is Harry Werther. He was in the Senate that time. Everybody said bad things about him, and he was never re-elected. Yet his house was not painted. He was honest. To this day his house is not painted, as everybody knows.

"There is Jim Lokendamper. He has a bad heart. I heard him, only last week, right here before you all, tell his soul. He did not tell all his soul, and he lied to God. I am not lying to God. It is a big telling, but I am telling everything. Now Azalea Akau, sitting right over there, is his wife. But Lizzie Lokendamper is his married wife. A long time ago he had the great aloha for Azalea. You think her uncle, who went to California and died, left her by will that two thousand five hundred dollars she got. Her uncle did not. I know. Her uncle died broke in California, and Jim Lokendamper sent eighty dollars to California to bury him. Jim Lokendamper had a piece of land in Kohala he got from his mother's aunt. Lizzie, his married wife, did not know this. So he sold it to the Kohala Ditch Company and gave the twenty-five hundred to Azalea Akau—"

Here, Lizzie, the married wife, upstood like a fury long-thwarted, and, in lieu of her husband, already fled, flung herself tooth and nail on Azalea.

"Wait, Lizzie Lokendamper!" Alice cried out. "I have much weight of you on my heart and some house-paint too ..."

And when she had finished her disclosure of how Lizzie had painted her house, Azalea was up and raging.

"Wait, Azalea Akau. I shall now lighten my heart about you. And it is not house-paint. Jim always paid that. It is your new bath-tub and modern plumbing that is heavy on me ..."

Worse, much worse, about many and sundry, did Alice Akana have to say, cutting high in business, financial, and social life, as well as low. None was too high nor too low to escape, and not until two in the morning, before an entranced audience that packed the tabernacle to the doors, did she complete her recital of the personal and detailed iniquities she knew of the community in which she had lived intimately all her days. Just as she was finishing, she remembered more.

"Huh!" she sniffed. "I gave last week one lot worth eight hundred dollars cash market price to Abel Ah Yo to pay running expenses and add up in Peter's books in heaven. Where did I get that lot? You all think Mr. Fleming Jason is a good man. He is more crooked than the entrance was to Pearl Lochs before the United States Government straightened the channel. He has liver disease now; but his sickness is a judgment of God, and he will die crooked. Mr. Fleming Jason gave me that lot twenty-two years ago, when its cash market price was thirty-five dollars. Because his aloha for me was big? No. He never had aloha inside of him except for dollars.

"You listen. Mr. Fleming Jason put a great sin upon me. When Frank Lomiloli was at my house, full of gin, for which gin Mr. Fleming Jason paid me in advance five times over. I got Frank Lomiloli to sign his name to the sale paper of his town land for one hundred dollars. It was worth six hundred then. It is worth twenty thousand now. Maybe you want to know where that town land is. I will tell you and remove it off my heart. It is on King Street, where is now the Come Again Saloon, the Japanese Taxicab Company garage, the Smith & Wilson plumbing shop, and the Ambrosia Ice Cream Parlours, with the two more stories big Addison Lodging House overhead. And it is all wood, and always has been well painted. Yesterday they started painting it again. But that paint will not stand between me and God. There are no more paint pots between me and my path to heaven."

The morning and evening papers of the day following held an unholy hush on the greatest news story of years; but Honolulu was half a-giggle and half aghast at the whispered reports, not always basely exaggerated, that circulated wherever two Honoluluans chanced to meet.

"Our mistake," said Colonel Chilton, at the club, "was that we did not, at the very first, appoint a committee of safety to keep track of Alice's soul."

Bob Cristy, one of the younger islanders, burst into laughter, so pointed and so loud that the meaning of it was demanded.

"Oh, nothing much," was his reply. "But I heard, on my way here, that old John Ward had just been run in for drunken and disorderly conduct and for resisting an officer. Now Abel Ah Yo fine-tooth combs the police court. He loves nothing better than soul-snatching a chronic drunkard."

Colonel Chilton looked at Lask Finneston, and both looked at Gary Wilkinson. He returned to them a similar look.

"The old beachcomber!" Lask Finneston cried. "The drunken old reprobate! I'd forgotten he was alive. Wonderful constitution. Never drew a sober breath except when he was shipwrecked, and, when I remember him, into every deviltry afloat. He must be going on eighty."

"He isn't far away from it," Bob Cristy nodded. "Still beach-combs, drinks when he gets the price, and keeps all his senses, though he's not spry and has to use glasses when he reads. And his memory is perfect. Now if Abel Ah Yo catches him ..."

Gary Wilkinson cleared his throat preliminary to speech.

"Now there's a grand old man," he said. "A left-over from a forgotten age. Few of his type remain. A pioneer. A true kamaaina. Helpless and in the hands of the police in his old age! We should do something for him in recognition of his yeoman work in Hawaii. His old home, I happen to know, is Sag Harbour. He hasn't seen it for over half a century. Now why shouldn't he be surprised to-morrow morning by having his fine paid, and by being presented with return tickets to Sag Harbour, and, say, expenses for a year's trip? I move a committee. I appoint Colonel Chilton, Lask Finneston, and ... and myself. As for chairman, who more appropriate than Lask Finneston, who knew the old gentleman so well in the early days? Since there is no objection, I hereby appoint Lask Finneston chairman of the committee for the purpose of raising and donating money to pay the police-court fine and the expenses of a year's travel for that noble pioneer, John Ward, in recognition of a lifetime of devotion of energy to the upbuilding of Hawaii."

There was no dissent.

"The committee will now go into secret session," said Lask Finneston, arising and indicating the way to the library.

Glen Ellen, California
August 30, 1916

FROM THE RED ONE

THE RED ONE

There it was! The abrupt liberation of sound! As he timed it with his watch, Bassett likened it to the trump of an archangel. Walls of cities, he meditated, might well fall down before so vast and compelling a summons. For the thousandth time vainly he tried to analyse the tone-quality of that enormous peal that dominated the land far into the strong-holds of the surrounding tribes. The mountain gorge which was its source rang to the rising tide of it until it brimmed over and flooded earth and sky and air. With the wantonness of a sick man's fancy, he likened it to the mighty cry of some Titan of the Elder World vexed with misery or wrath. Higher and higher it arose, challenging and demanding in such profounds of volume that it seemed intended for ears beyond the narrow confines of the solar system. There was in it, too, the clamour of protest in that there were no ears to hear and comprehend its utterance.

—Such the sick man's fancy. Still he strove to analyse the sound. Sonorous as thunder was it, mellow as a golden bell, thin and sweet as a thrummed taut cord of silver—no; it was none of these, nor a blend of these. There were no words nor semblances in his vocabulary and experience with which to describe the totality of that sound.

Time passed. Minutes merged into quarters of hours, and quarters of hours into half-hours, and still the sound persisted, ever changing from its initial vocal impulse yet never receiving fresh impulse—fading, dimming, dying as enormously as it had sprung into being. It became a confusion of troubled mutterings and babblings and colossal whisperings. Slowly it withdrew, sob by sob, into whatever great bosom had birthed it, until it whimpered deadly whispers of wrath and as equally seductive whispers of delight, striving still to be heard, to convey some cosmic secret, some understanding of infinite import and value. It dwindled to a ghost of sound that had lost its menace and promise, and became a thing that pulsed on in the sick man's consciousness for minutes after it had ceased. When he could hear it no longer, Bassett glanced at his watch. An hour had elapsed ere that archangel's trump had subsided into tonal nothingness.

Was this, then, *his* dark tower?—Bassett pondered, remembering his Browning and gazing at his skeleton-like and fever-wasted hands. And the fancy made him smile—of Childe Roland bearing a slug-horn to his lips with an arm as feeble as his was. Was it months, or years, he asked himself, since he first heard that mysterious call on the beach at Ringmanu? To save himself he could not tell. The long sickness had been most long. In conscious count of time he knew of months, many of them; but he had no way of estimating the long intervals of delirium and stupor. And how fared Captain Bateman of the blackbirder *Nari*? he wondered; and had Captain Bateman's drunken mate died of delirium tremens yet?

From which vain speculations, Bassett turned idly to review all that had occurred since that day on the beach of Ringmanu when he first heard the sound and plunged into the jungle after it. Sagawa had protested. He could see him yet, his queer little monkeyish face eloquent with fear, his back burdened with specimen cases, in his hands Bassett's butterfly net and naturalist's shot-gun, as he quavered, in Beche-de-mer English: "Me fella too much fright along bush. Bad fella boy, too much stop'm along bush."

Bassett smiled sadly at the recollection. The little New Hanover boy had been frightened, but had proved faithful, following him without hesitancy into the bush in the quest after the source of the wonderful sound. No fire-hollowed tree-trunk, that, throbbing war through the jungle depths, had been Bassett's conclusion. Erroneous had been his next conclusion, namely, that the source or cause could not be more distant than an hour's walk, and that he would easily be back by mid-afternoon to be picked up by the *Nari's* whale-boat.

"That big fella noise no good, all the same devil-devil," Sagawa had adjudged. And Sagawa had been right. Had he not had his head hacked off within the day? Bassett shuddered. Without doubt Sagawa had been eaten as well by the "bad fella boys too much" that stopped along the bush. He could see him, as he had last seen him, stripped of the shot-gun and all the naturalist's gear of his master, lying on the narrow trail where he had been decapitated barely the moment before. Yes, within a minute the thing had happened. Within a minute, looking back, Bassett had seen him trudging patiently along under his burdens. Then Bassett's own trouble had come upon him. He looked at the cruelly healed stumps of the first and second fingers of his left hand, then rubbed them softly into the indentation in the back of his skull. Quick as had been the flash of the long-handled tomahawk, he had been quick enough to duck away his head and partially to deflect the stroke with his up-flung hand. Two fingers and a hasty scalp-wound had been the price he paid for his life. With one barrel of his ten-gauge shot-gun he had blown the life out of the bushman who had so nearly got him; with the other barrel he had peppered the bushmen bending over Sagawa, and had the pleasure of knowing that the major portion of the charge had gone into the one who leaped away with Sagawa's head. Everything had occurred in a flash. Only himself, the slain bush-man, and what remained of Sagawa, were in the narrow, wild-pig run of a path. From the dark jungle on either side came no rustle of move-ment or sound of life. And he had suffered distinct and dreadful shock. For the first time in his life he had killed a human being, and he knew nausea as he contemplated the mess of his handiwork.

Then had begun the chase. He retreated up the pig-run before his hunters, who were between him and the beach. How many there were, he could not guess. There might have been one, or a hundred, for aught he saw of them. That some of them took to the trees and trav-elled along through the jungle roof he was certain; but at the most he never glimpsed more than an occasional flitting of shadows. No bow-strings twanged that he could hear; but every little while, whence dis-charged he knew not, tiny arrows whispered past him or stuck tree-boles and fluttered to the ground beside him. They were bone-tipped and feather shafted, and the feathers, torn from the breasts of humming-birds, iridesced like jewels.

Once—and now, after the long lapse of time, he chuckled gleefully at the recollection—he had detected a shadow above him that came to instant rest as he turned his gaze upward. He could make out nothing, but, deciding to chance it, had fired at it a heavy charge of number five shot. Squalling like an infuriated cat, the shadow crashed down through tree-ferns and orchids and thudded upon the earth as his feet, and, still squalling its rage and pain, had sunk its human teeth into the ankle of his stout tramping boot. He, on the other hand, was not idle, and with his free foot had done what reduced the squalling to silence. So inured to savagery had Bassett since become, that he chuckled again with the glee of the recollection.

What a night had followed! Small wonder that he had accumulated such a virulence and variety of fevers, he thought, as he recalled that sleepless night of torment, when the throb of his wounds was as noth-ing compared with the myriad stings of the mosquitoes. There had been no escaping them, and he had not dared to light a fire. They had literally pumped his body full of poison, so that, with the coming of day, eyes swollen almost shut, he had stumbled blindly on, not caring much when his head should be hacked off and his carcass started on the way of Sagawa's to the cooking fire. Twenty-four hours had made a wreck of him—of mind as well as body. He had scarcely retained his wits at all, so maddened was he by the tremendous inoculation of poi-son he had received. Several times he fired his shot-gun with effect into the shadows that dogged him. Stinging day insects and gnats added to his torment, while his bloody wounds attracted hosts of loathsome flies that clung sluggishly to his flesh and had to be brushed off and crushed off.

Once, in that day, he heard again the wonderful sound, seemingly more distant, but rising imperiously above the nearer war-drums in the bush. Right there was where he had made his mistake. Thinking that he had passed beyond it and that, therefore, it was between him and the beach of Ringmanu, he had worked back toward it when in reality he was penetrating deeper and deeper into the mysterious heart of the unexplored island. That night, crawling in among the twisted roots of a banyan tree, he had slept from exhaustion while the mosquitoes had had their will of him.

Followed days and nights that were vague as nightmares in his memory. One clear vision he remembered was of suddenly finding himself in the midst of a bush village and watching the old men and children fleeing into the jungle. All had fled but one. From close at hand and above him, a whimpering as of some animal in pain and terror had startled him. And looking up he had seen her—a girl, or young woman rather, suspended by one arm in the cooking sun. Perhaps for days she had so hung. Her swollen, protruding tongue spoke as much. Still alive, she gazed at him with eyes of terror. Past help, he decided, as he noted the swellings of her legs which advertised that the joints had been crushed and the great bones broken. He resolved to shoot her, and there the vision terminated. He could not remember whether he had or not, any more than could he remember how he chanced to be in that village, or how he succeeded in getting away from it.

Many pictures, unrelated, came and went in Bassett's mind as he reviewed that period of his terrible wanderings. He remembered invading another village of a dozen houses and driving all before him with his shot-gun save for one old man, too feeble to flee, who spat at him and whined and snarled as he dug open a ground-oven and from amid the hot stones dragged forth a roasted pig that steamed its essence deliciously through its green-leaf wrappings. It was at this place that a wantonness of savagery had seized upon him. Having feasted, ready to depart with a hind-quarter of the pig in his hand, he deliberately fired the grass thatch of a house with his burning glass.

But seared deepest of all in Bassett's brain, was the dank and noisome jungle. It actually stank with evil, and it was always twilight. Rarely did a shaft of sunlight penetrate its matted roof a hundred feet overhead. And beneath that roof was an aerial ooze of vegetation, a monstrous, parasitic dripping of decadent life-forms that rooted in death and lived on death. And through all this he drifted, ever pursued by the flitting shadows of the anthropophagi, themselves ghosts of evil that dared not face him in battle but that knew that, soon or late, they would feed on him. Bassett remembered that at the time, in lucid moments, he had likened himself to a wounded bull pursued by plains' coyotes too cowardly to battle with him for the meat of him, yet certain of the inevitable end of him when they would be full gorged. As the bull's horns and stamping hoofs kept off the coyotes, so his shotgun kept off these Solomon Islanders, these twilight shades of bushmen of the island of Guadalcanal.

Came the day of the grass lands. Abruptly, as if cloven by the sword of God in the hand of God, the jungle terminated. The edge of it, perpendicular and as black as the infamy of it, was a hundred feet up and down. And, beginning at the edge of it, grew the grass—sweet, soft, tender, pasture grass that would have delighted the eyes and beasts of any husbandman and that extended, on and on, for leagues and leagues of velvet verdure, to the backbone of the great island, the towering mountain range flung up by some ancient earth-cataclysm, serrated and gullied but not yet erased by the erosive tropic rains. But the grass! He had crawled into it a dozen yards, buried his face in it, smelled it, and broken down in a fit of involuntary weeping.

And, while he wept, the wonderful sound had pealed forth—if by *Peal*, he had often thought since, an adequate description could be given of the enunciation of so vast a sound melting sweet. Sweet it was, as no sound ever heard. Vast it was, of so mighty a resonance that it might have proceeded from some brazen-throated monster. And yet it called to him across that leagues-wide savannah, and was like a benediction to his long-suffering, pain-racked spirit.

He remembered how he lay there in the grass, wet-cheeked but no longer sobbing, listening to the sound and wondering that he had been able to hear it on the beach of Ringmanu. Some freak of air pressures and air currents, he reflected, had made it possible for the sound to carry so far. Such conditions might not happen again in a thousand days or ten thousand days, but the one day it had happened had been the day he landed from the *Nari* for several hours' collecting. Especially had he been in quest of the famed jungle butterfly, a foot across from wing-tip to wing-tip, as velvet-dusky of lack of colour as was the gloom of the roof, of such lofty arboreal habits that it resorted only to the jungle roof and could be brought down only by a dose of shot. It was for this purpose that Sagawa had carried the ten-gauge shot-gun. Two days and nights he had spent crawling across that belt of grass land. He had suffered much, but pursuit had ceased at the jungle-edge. And he would have died of thirst had not a heavy thunderstorm revived him on the second day.

And then had come Balatta. In the first shade, where the savannah yielded to the dense mountain jungle, he had collapsed to die. At first she had squealed with delight at sight of his helplessness, and was for beating his brain out with a stout forest branch. Perhaps it was his very utter helplessness that had appealed to her, and perhaps it was her human curiosity that made her refrain. At any rate, she had refrained, for he opened his eyes again under the impending blow, and saw her studying him intently. What especially struck her about him were his blue eyes and white skin. Coolly she had squatted on her hams, spat on his arm, and with her finger tips scrubbed away the dirt of days and nights of muck and jungle that sullied the pristine whiteness of his skin.

And everything about her had struck him especially, although there was nothing conventional about her at all. He laughed weakly at the recollection, for she had been as innocent of garb as Eve before the fig-leaf adventure. Squat and lean at the same time, asymmetrically limbed, string-muscled as if with lengths of cordage, dirt-caked from infancy save for casual showers, she was as unbeautiful a prototype of woman as he, with a scientist's eye, had ever gazed upon. Her breasts advertised at the one time her maturity and youth; and, if by nothing else, her sex was advertised by the one article of finery with which she was adorned, namely a pig's tail, thrust through a hole in her left ear-lobe. So lately had the tail been severed, that its raw end still oozed blood that dried upon her shoulder like so much candle-droppings. And her face! A twisted and wizened complex of apish features, perforated by upturned, sky-open, Mongolian nostrils, by a mouth that sagged from a huge upper-lip and faded precipitately into a retreating chin, by peering querulous eyes that blinked as blink the eyes of denizens of monkey-cages.

Not even the water she brought him in a forest-leaf, and the ancient and half-putrid chunk of roast pig, could redeem in the slightest the grotesque hideousness of her. When he had eaten weakly for a space, he closed his eyes in order not to see her, although again and again she poked them open to peer at the blue of them. Then had come the sound. Nearer, much nearer, he knew it to be; and he knew equally well, despite the weary way he had come, that it was still many hours distant. The effect of it on her had been startling. She cringed under it, with averted face, moaning and chattering with fear. But after it had lived its full life of an hour, he closed his eyes and fell asleep with Balatta brushing the flies from him.

When he awoke it was night, and she was gone. But he was aware of renewed strength, and, by then too thoroughly inoculated by the mosquito poison to suffer further inflammation, he closed his eyes and slept an unbroken stretch till sun-up. A little later Balatta had returned, bringing with her a half-dozen women who, unbeautiful as they were, were patently not so unbeautiful as she. She evidenced by her conduct that she considered him her find, her property, and the pride she took in showing him off would have been ludicrous had his situation not been so desperate.

Later, after what had been to him a terrible journey of miles, when he collapsed in front of the devil-devil house in the shadow of the breadfruit tree, she had shown very lively ideas on the matter of retaining possession of him. Ngurn, whom Bassett was to know afterward as the devil-devil doctor, priest, or medicine man of the village, had wanted his head. Others of the grinning and chattering monkey-men, all as stark of clothes and bestial of appearance as Balatta, had wanted his body for the roasting oven. At that time he had not understood their language, if by *language* might be dignified the uncouth sounds they made to represent ideas. But Bassett had thoroughly understood the matter of debate, especially when the men pressed and prodded and felt of the flesh of him as if he were so much commodity in a butcher's stall.

Balatta had been losing the debate rapidly, when the accident happened. One of the men, curiously examining Bassett's shot-gun, managed to cock and pull a trigger. The recoil of the butt into the pit of the man's stomach had not been the most sanguinary result, for the charge

of shot, at a distance of a yard, had blown the head of one of the de-
baters into nothingness.

Even Balatta joined the others in flight, and, ere they returned, his
senses already reeling from the oncoming fever-attack, Bassett had regained possession of the gun. Whereupon, although his teeth chattered with the ague and his swimming eyes could scarcely see, he held
on to his fading consciousness until he could intimidate the bushmen
with the simple magics of compass, watch, burning glass, and matches.
At the last, with due emphasis, of solemnity and awfulness, he had
killed a young pig with his shot-gun and promptly fainted.

Bassett flexed his arm-muscles in quest of what possible strength
might reside in such weakness, and dragged himself slowly and totter-
ingly to his feet. He was shockingly emaciated, yet, during the various
convalescences of the many months of his long sickness, he had never
regained quite the same degree of strength as this time. What he
feared was another relapse such as he had already frequently experienced. Without drugs, without even quinine, he had managed so far to
live through a combination of the most pernicious and most malignant
of malarial and black-water fevers. But could he continue to endure?
Such was his everlasting query. For, like the genuine scientist he was,
he would not be content to die until he had solved the secret of the
sound.

Supported by a staff, he staggered the few steps to the devil-devil
house where death and Ngurn reigned in gloom. Almost as infamously
dark and evil-stinking as the jungle was the devil-devil house—in Bassett's opinion. Yet therein was usually to be found his favourite crony
and gossip, Ngurn, always willing for a yarn or a discussion, the while
he sat in the ashes of death and in a slow smoke shrewdly revolved curing human heads suspended from the rafters. For, through the months'
interval of consciousness of his long sickness, Bassett had mastered the
psychological simplicities and lingual difficulties of the language of the
tribe of Ngurn and Balatta and Vngngn—the latter the addle-headed
young chief who was ruled by Ngurn, and who, whispered intrigue had
it, was the son of Ngurn.

"Will the Red One speak to-day?" Bassett asked, by this time so accustomed to the old man's gruesome occupation as to take even an interest in the progress of the smoke-curing.

With the eye of an expert Ngurn examined the particular head he was at work upon.

"It will be ten days before I can say 'finish,' " he said. "Never has any man fixed heads like these."

Bassett smiled inwardly at the old fellow's reluctance to talk with him of the Red One. It had always been so. Never, by any chance, had Ngurn or any other member of the weird tribe divulged the slightest hint of any physical characteristic of the Red One. Physical the Red One must be, to emit the wonderful sound, and though it was called the Red One, Bassett could not be sure that red represented the colour of it. Red enough were the deeds and powers of it, from what abstract clues he had gleaned. Not alone, had Ngurn informed him, was the Red One more bestial powerful than the neighbour tribal gods, ever athirst for the red blood of living human sacrifices, but the neighbour gods themselves were sacrificed and tormented before him. He was the god of a dozen allied villages similar to this one, which was the central and commanding village of the federation. By virtue of the Red One many alien villages had been devastated and even wiped out, the prisoners sacrificed to the Red One. This was true to-day, and it extended back into old history carried down by word of mouth through the generations. When he, Ngurn, had been a young man, the tribes beyond the grass lands had made a war raid. In the counter raid, Ngurn and his fighting folk had made many prisoners. Of children alone over five score living had been bled white before the Red One, and many, many more men and women.

The Thunderer was another of Ngurn's names for the mysterious deity. Also at times was he called The Loud Shouter, The God-Voiced, The Bird-Throated, The One with the Throat Sweet as the Throat of the Honey-Bird, The Sun Singer, and The Star-Born.

Why The Star-Born? In vain Bassett interrogated Ngurn. According to that old devil-devil doctor, the Red One had always been, just where he was at present, for ever singing and thundering his will over men. But Ngurn's father, wrapped in decaying grass-matting and hanging even then over their heads among the smoky rafters of the devil-devil house, had held otherwise. That departed wise one had believed that the Red One came from out of the starry night, else why—

so his argument had run—had the old and forgotten ones passed his name down as the Star-Born? Bassett could not but recognize something cogent in such argument. But Ngurn affirmed the long years of his long life, wherein he had gazed upon many starry nights, yet never had he found a star on grass land or in jungle depth—and he had looked for them. True, he had beheld shooting stars (this in reply to Bassett's contention); but likewise had he beheld the phosphorescence of fungoid growths and rotten meat and fireflies on dark nights, and the flames of wood-fires and of blazing candle-nuts; yet what were flame and blaze and glow when they had flamed and blazed and glowed? Answer: memories, memories only, of things which had ceased to be, like memories of matings accomplished, of feasts forgotten, of desires that were the ghosts of desires, flaring, flaming, burning, yet unrealized in achievement of easement and satisfaction. Where was the appetite of yesterday? the roasted flesh of the wild pig the hunter's arrow failed to slay? the maid, unwed and dead ere the young man knew her?

A memory was not a star, was Ngurn's contention. How could a memory be a star? Further, after all his long life he still observed the starry night-sky unaltered. Never had he noted the absence of a single star from its accustomed place. Besides, stars were fire, and the Red One was not fire—which last involuntary betrayal told Bassett nothing.

"Will the Red One speak to-morrow?" he queried.

Ngurn shrugged his shoulders as who should say.

"And the day after?—and the day after that?" Bassett persisted.

"I would like to have the curing of your head," Ngurn changed the subject. "It is different from any other head. No devil-devil has a head like it. Besides, I would cure it well. I would take months and months. The moons would come and the moons would go, and the smoke would be very slow, and I should myself gather the materials for the curing smoke. The skin would not wrinkle. It would be as smooth as your skin now."

He stood up, and from the dim rafters, grimed with the smoking of countless heads, where day was no more than a gloom, took down a matting-wrapped parcel and began to open it.

"It is a head like yours," he said, "but it is poorly cured."

Bassett had pricked up his ears at the suggestion that it was a white man's head; for he had long since come to accept that these jungle-dwellers, in the midmost centre of the great island, had never had intercourse with white men. Certainly he had found them without the almost universal beche-de-mer English of the west South Pacific. Nor had they knowledge of tobacco, nor of gunpowder. Their few precious knives, made from lengths of hoop-iron, and their few and more precious tomahawks from cheap trade hatchets, he had surmised they had captured in war from the bushmen of the jungle beyond the grass lands, and that they, in turn, had similarly gained them from the salt-water men who fringed the coral beaches of the shore and had contact with the occasional white men.

"The folk in the out beyond do not know how to cure heads," old Ngurn explained, as he drew forth from the filthy matting and placed in Bassett's hands an indubitable white man's head.

Ancient it was beyond question; white it was as the blond hair attested. He could have sworn it once belonged to an Englishman, and to an Englishman of long before by token of the heavy gold circlets still threaded in the withered ear-lobes.

"Now your head ..." the devil-devil doctor began on his favourite topic.

"I'll tell you what," Bassett interrupted, stuck by a new idea. "When I die I'll let you have my head to cure, if, first, you take me to look upon the Red One."

"I will have your head anyway when you are dead," Ngurn rejected the proposition. He added, with the brutal frankness of the savage: "Besides, you have not long to live. You are almost a dead man now. You will grow less strong. In not many months I shall have you here turning and turning in the smoke. It is pleasant, through the long afternoons, to turn the head of one you have known as well as I know you. And I shall talk to you and tell you the many secrets you want to know. Which will not matter, for you will be dead."

"Ngurn," Bassett threatened in sudden anger. "You know the Baby Thunder in the Iron that is mine." (This was in reference to his all-potent and all-awful shotgun.) "I can kill you any time, and then you will not get my head."

"Just the same, will Vngngn, or some one else of my folk get it," Ngurn complacently assured him. "And just the same will it turn and turn here in the devil-devil house in the smoke. The quicker you slay me with your Baby Thunder, the quicker will your head turn in the smoke."

And Bassett knew he was beaten in the discussion.

What was the Red One?—Bassett asked himself a thousand times in the succeeding week, while he seemed to grow stronger. What was the source of the wonderful sound? What was this Sun Singer, this Star-Born One, this mysterious deity, as bestial-conducted as the black and kinky-headed and monkey-like human beasts who worshipped it, and whose silver-sweet, bull-mouthed singing and commanding he had heard at the taboo distance for so long?

Ngurn had he failed to bribe with the inevitable curing of his head when he was dead. Vngngn, imbecile and chief that he was, was too imbecilic, too much under the sway of Ngurn, to be considered. Remained Balatta, who, from the time she found him and poked his blue eyes open to recrudescence of her grotesque female hideousness, had continued his adorer. Woman she was, and he had long known that the only way to win from her treason of her tribe was through the woman's heart of her.

Bassett was a fastidious man. He had never recovered from the initial horror caused by Balatta's female awfulness. Back in England, even at best the charm of woman, to him, had never been robust. Yet now, resolutely, as only a man can do who is capable of martyring himself for the cause of science, he proceeded to violate all the fineness and delicacy of his nature by making love to the unthinkably disgusting bushwoman.

He shuddered, but with averted face hid his grimaces and swallowed his gorge as he put his arm around her dirt-crusted shoulders and felt the contact of her rancid-oily and kinky hair with his neck and chin. But he nearly screamed when she succumbed to that caress so at the very first of the courtship and mowed and gibbered and squealed little, queer, pig-like gurgly noises of delight. It was too much. And the next he did in the singular courtship was to take her down to the stream and give her a vigorous scrubbing.

From then on he devoted himself to her like a true swain as frequently and for as long at a time as his will could override his repugnance. But marriage, which she ardently suggested, with due observance of tribal custom, he balked at. Fortunately, taboo rule was strong in the tribe. Thus, Ngurn could never touch bone, or flesh, or hide of crocodile. This had been ordained at his birth. Vngngn was denied ever the touch of woman. Such pollution, did it chance to occur, could be purged only by the death of the offending female. It had happened once, since Bassett's arrival, when a girl of nine, running in play, stumbled and fell against the sacred chief. And the girl-child was seen no more. In whispers, Balatta told Bassett that she had been three days and nights in dying before the Red One. As for Balatta, the breadfruit was taboo to her. For which Bassett was thankful. The taboo might have been water.

For himself, he fabricated a special taboo. Only could he marry, he explained, when the Southern Cross rode highest in the sky. Knowing his astronomy, he thus gained a reprieve of nearly nine months; and he was confident that within that time he would either be dead or escaped to the coast with full knowledge of the Red One and of the source of the Red One's wonderful voice. At first he had fancied the Red One to be some colossal statue, like Memnon, rendered vocal under certain temperature conditions of sunlight. But when, after a war raid, a batch of prisoners was brought in and the sacrifice made at night, in the midst of rain, when the sun could play no part, the Red One had been more vocal than usual, Bassett discarded that hypothesis.

In company with Balatta, sometimes with men and parties of women, the freedom of the jungle was his for three quadrants of the compass. But the fourth quadrant, which contained the Red One's abiding place, was taboo. He made more thorough love to Balatta—also saw to it that she scrubbed herself more frequently. Eternal female she was, capable of any treason for the sake of love. And, though the sight of her was provocative of nausea and the contact of her provocative of despair, although he could not escape her awfulness in his dream-haunted nightmares of her, he nevertheless was aware of the cosmic verity of sex that animated her and that made her own life of less value than the happiness of her lover with whom she hoped to mate. Juliet or Balatta? Where was the intrinsic difference? The soft and tender product of ultra-civilization, or her bestial prototype of a hundred thousand years before her?—there was no difference.

Bassett was a scientist first, a humanist afterward. In the jungle-heart of Guadalcanal he put the affair to the test, as in the laboratory he would have put to the test any chemical reaction. He increased his feigned ardour for the bushwoman, at the same time increasing the imperiousness of his will of desire over her to be led to look upon the Red One face to face. It was the old story, he recognized, that the woman must pay, and it occurred when the two of them, one day, were catching the unclassified and unnamed little black fish, an inch long, half-eel and half-scaled, rotund with salmon-golden roe, that frequented the fresh water, and that were esteemed, raw and whole, fresh or putrid, a perfect delicacy. Prone in the muck of the decaying jungle-floor, Balatta threw herself, clutching his ankles with her hands, kissing his feet and making slubbery noises that chilled his backbone up and down again. She begged him to kill her rather than exact this ultimate love-payment. She told him of the penalty of breaking the taboo of the Red One—a week of torture, living, the details of which she yammered out from her face in the mire until he realized that he was yet a tyro in knowledge of the frightfulness the human was capable of wreaking on the human.

Yet did Bassett insist on having his man's will satisfied, at the woman's risk, that he might solve the mystery of the Red One's singing, though she should die long and horribly and screaming. And Balatta, being mere woman, yielded. She led him into the forbidden quadrant. An abrupt mountain, shouldering in from the north to meet a similar intrusion from the south, tormented the stream in which they had fished into a deep and gloomy gorge. After a mile along the gorge, the way plunged sharply upward until they crossed a saddle of raw limestone which attracted his geologist's eye. Still climbing, although he paused often from sheer physical weakness, they scaled forest-clad heights until they emerged on a naked mesa or tableland. Bassett recognized the stuff of its composition as black volcanic sand, and knew that a pocket magnet could have captured a full load of the sharply angular grains he trod upon.

And then holding Balatta by the hand and leading her onward, he came to it—a tremendous pit, obviously artificial, in the heart of the plateau. Old history, the South Seas Sailing Directions, scores of remembered data and connotations swift and furious, surged through his brain. It was Mendana who had discovered the islands and named them Solomon's, believing that he had found that monarch's fabled mines. They had laughed at the old navigator's child-like credulity; and yet here stood himself, Bassett, on the rim of an excavation for all the world like the diamond pits of South Africa.

But no diamond this that he gazed down upon. Rather was it a pearl, with the depth of iridescence of a pearl; but of a size all pearls of earth and time, welded into one, could not have totalled; and of a colour undreamed of in any pearl, or of anything else, for that matter, for it was the colour of the Red One. And the Red One himself Bassett knew it to be on the instant. A perfect sphere, full two hundred feet in diameter, the top of it was a hundred feet below the level of the rim. He likened the colour quality of it to lacquer. Indeed, he took it to be some sort of lacquer, applied by man, but a lacquer too marvellously clever to have been manufactured by the bush-folk. Brighter than bright cherry-red, its richness of colour was as if it were red builded upon red. It glowed and iridesced in the sunlight as if gleaming up from underlay under underlay of red.

In vain Balatta strove to dissuade him from descending. She threw herself in the dirt; but, when he continued down the trail that spiralled the pit-wall, she followed, cringing and whimpering her terror. That the red sphere had been dug out as a precious thing, was patent. Considering the paucity of members of the federated twelve villages and their primitive tools and methods, Bassett knew that the toil of myriad generations could scarcely have made that enormous excavation.

He found the pit bottom carpeted with human bones, among which, battered and defaced, lay village gods of wood and stone. Some, covered with obscene totemic figures and designs, were carved from solid tree trunks forty or fifty feet in length. He noted the absence of the shark and turtle gods, so common among the shore villages, and was amazed at the constant recurrence of the helmet motive. What did these jungle savages of the dark heart of Guadalcanal know of helmets? Had Mendana's men-at-arms worn helmets and penetrated here centuries before? And if not, then whence had the bush-folk caught the motive?

Advancing over the litter of gods and bones, Balatta whimpering at his heels, Bassett entered the shadow of the Red One and passed on under its gigantic overhang until he touched it with his finger-tips. No lacquer that. Nor was the surface smooth as it should have been in the case of lacquer. On the contrary, it was corrugated and pitted, with here and there patches that showed signs of heat and fusing. Also, the substance of it was metal, though unlike any metal, or combination of metals, he had ever known. As for the colour itself, he decided it to be no application. It was the intrinsic colour of the metal itself.

He moved his finger-tips, which up to that had merely rested, along the surface, and felt the whole gigantic sphere quicken and live and respond. It was incredible! So light a touch on so vast a mass! Yet did it quiver under the finger-tip caress in rhythmic vibrations that became whisperings and rustlings and mutterings of sound—but of sound so different; so elusively thin that it was shimmeringly sibilant; so mellow that it was maddening sweet, piping like an elfin horn, which last was just what Bassett decided would be like a peal from some bell of the gods reaching earthward from across space.

He looked at Balatta with swift questioning; but the voice of the Red One he had evoked had flung her face downward and moaning among the bones. He returned to contemplation of the prodigy. Hollow it was, and of no metal known on earth, was his conclusion. It was right-named by the ones of old-time as the Star-Born. Only from the stars could it have come, and no thing of chance was it. It was a creation of artifice and mind. Such perfection of form, such hollowness that it certainly possessed, could not be the result of mere fortuitousness. A child of intelligences, remote and unguessable, working corporally in metals, it indubitably was. He stared at it in amaze, his brain a racing wild-fire of hypotheses to account for this far-journeyer who had adventured the night of space, threaded the stars, and now rose before him and above him, exhumed by patient anthropophagi, pitted and lacquered by its fiery bath in two atmospheres.

But was the colour a lacquer of heat upon some familiar metal? Or was it an intrinsic quality of the metal itself? He thrust in the blue-point of his pocket-knife to test the constitution of the stuff. Instantly the entire sphere burst into a mighty whispering, sharp with protest, almost twanging goldenly, if a whisper could possibly be considered to twang, rising higher, sinking deeper, the two extremes of the registry of sound threatening to complete the circle and coalesce into the bull-mouthed thundering he had so often heard beyond the taboo distance.

Forgetful of safety, of his own life itself, entranced by the wonder of the unthinkable and unguessable thing, he raised his knife to strike heavily from a long stroke, but was prevented by Balatta. She upreared on her own knees in an agony of terror, clasping his knees and suppli-cating him to desist. In the intensity of her desire to impress him, she put her forearm between her teeth and sank them to the bone.

He scarcely observed her act, although he yielded automatically to his gentler instincts and withheld the knife-hack. To him, human life had dwarfed to microscopic proportions before this colossal portent of higher life from within the distances of the sidereal universe. As had she been a dog, he kicked the ugly little bushwoman to her feet and compelled her to start with him on an encirclement of the base. Part way around, he encountered horrors. Even, among the others, did he recognize the sun-shrivelled remnant of the nine-years girl who had accidentally broken Chief Vngngn's personality taboo. And, among what was left of these that had passed, he encountered what was left of one who had not yet passed. Truly had the bush-folk named them-selves into the name of the Red One, seeing in him their own image which they strove to placate and please with such red offerings.

Farther around, always treading the bones and images of humans and gods that constituted the floor of this ancient charnel-house of sacrifice, he came upon the device by which the Red One was made to send his call singing thunderingly across the jungle-belts and grass-lands to the far beach of Ringmanu. Simple and primitive was it as was the Red One's consummate artifice. A great king-post, half a hundred feet in length, seasoned by centuries of superstitious care, carven into dynasties of gods, each superimposed, each helmeted, each seated in the open mouth of a crocodile, was slung by ropes, twisted of climb-ing vegetable parasites, from the apex of a tripod of three great forest trunks, themselves carved into grinning and grotesque adumbrations of man's modern concepts of art and god. From the striker king-post, were suspended ropes of climbers to which men could apply their strength and direction. Like a battering ram, this king-post could be driven end-onward against the mighty red-iridescent sphere.

Here was where Ngurn officiated and functioned religiously for himself and the twelve tribes under him. Bassett laughed aloud, almost with madness, at the thought of this wonderful messenger, winged with intelligence across space, to fall into a bushman strong-hold and be worshipped by ape-like, man-eating and head-hunting savages. It was as if God's World had fallen into the muck mire of the abyss underlying the bottom of hell; as if Jehovah's Commandments had been presented on carved stone to the monkeys of the monkey cage at the Zoo; as if the Sermon on the Mount had been preached in a roaring bedlam of lunatics.

The slow weeks passed. The nights, by election, Bassett spent on the ashen floor of the devil-devil house, beneath the ever-swinging, slow-curing heads. His reason for this was that it was taboo to the lesser sex of woman, and therefore, a refuge for him from Balatta, who grew more persecutingly and perilously loverly as the Southern Cross rode higher in the sky and marked the imminence of her nuptials. His days Bassett spent in a hammock swung under the shade of the great breadfruit tree before the devil-devil house. There were breaks in this programme, when, in the comas of his devastating fever-attacks, he lay for days and nights in the house of heads. Ever he struggled to combat the fever, to live, to continue to live, to grow strong and stronger against the day when he would be strong enough to dare the grass-lands and the belted jungle beyond, and win to the beach, and to some labour-recruiting, black-birding ketch or schooner, and on to civiliza-tion and the men of civilization, to whom he could give news of the message from other worlds that lay, darkly worshipped by beastmen, in the black heart of Guadalcanal's midmost centre.

On the other nights, lying late under the breadfruit tree, Bassett spent long hours watching the slow setting of the western stars beyond the black wall of jungle where it had been thrust back by the clearing for the village. Possessed of more than a cursory knowledge of as-tronomy, he took a sick man's pleasure in speculating as to the dwellers on the unseen worlds of those incredibly remote suns, to haunt whose houses of light, life came forth, a shy visitant, from the rayless crypts of matter. He could no more apprehend limits to time than bounds to space. No subversive radium speculations had shaken his steady scientific faith in the conservation of energy and the indestructibility of matter. Always and forever must there have been stars. And surely, in that cosmic ferment, all must be comparatively alike, comparatively of the same substance, or substances, save for the freaks of the ferment. All must obey, or compose, the same laws that ran without infraction through the entire experience of man. Therefore, he argued and agreed, must worlds and life be appanages to all the suns as they were appanages to the particular of his own solar system.

Even as he lay here, under the breadfruit tree, an intelligence that stared across the starry gulfs, so must all the universe be exposed to the ceaseless scrutiny of innumerable eyes, like his, though grantedly different, with behind them, by the same token, intelligences that questioned and sought the meaning and the construction of the whole. So reasoning, he felt his soul go forth in kinship with that august company, that multitude whose gaze was forever upon the arras of infinity.

Who were they, what were they, those far distant and superior ones who had bridged the sky with their gigantic, red-iridescent, heaven-singing message? Surely, and long since, had they, too, trod the path on which man had so recently, by the calendar of the cosmos, set his feet. And to be able to send a message across the pit of space, surely they had reached those heights to which man, in tears and travail and bloody sweat, in darkness and confusion of many counsels, was so slowly struggling. And what were they on their heights? Had they won Brotherhood? Or had they learned that the law of love imposed the penalty of weakness and decay? Was strife, life? Was the rule of all the universe the pitiless rule of natural selection? And, and most immediately and poignantly, were their far conclusions, their long-won wisdoms, shut even then in the huge, metallic heart of the Red One, waiting for the first earth-man to read? Of one thing he was certain: No drop of red dew shaken from the lion-mane of some sun in torment, was the sounding sphere. It was of design, not chance, and it contained the speech and wisdom of the stars.

What engines and elements and mastered forces, what lore and mysteries and destiny-controls, might be there! Undoubtedly, since so much could be enclosed in so little a thing as the foundation stone of a public building, this enormous sphere should contain vast histories, profounds of research achieved beyond man's wildest guesses, laws and formulae that, easily mastered, would make man's life on earth, individual and collective, spring up from its present mire to inconceivable heights of purity and power. It was Time's greatest gift to blindfold, insatiable, and sky-aspiring man. And to him, Bassett, had been vouchsafed the lordly fortune to be the first to receive this message from man's interstellar kin!

No white man, much less no outland man of the other bush-tribes, had gazed upon the Red One and lived. Such the law expounded by Ngurn to Bassett. There was such a thing as blood brotherhood. Bassett, in return, had often argued in the past. But Ngurn had stated solemnly no. Even the blood brotherhood was outside the favour of the Red One. Only a man born within the tribe could look upon the Red One and live. But now, his guilty secret known only to Balatta, whose fear of immolation before the Red One fast-sealed her lips, the situation was different. What he had to do was to recover from the abominable fevers that weakened him, and gain to civilization. Then would he lead an expedition back, and, although the entire population of Guadalcanal be destroyed, extract from the heart of the Red One the message of the world from other worlds.

But Bassett's relapses grew more frequent, his brief convalescences less and less vigorous, his periods of coma longer, until he came to know, beyond the last promptings of the optimism inherent in so tremendous a constitution as his own, that he would never live to cross the grass lands, perforate the perilous coast jungle, and reach the sea. He faded as the Southern Cross rose higher in the sky, till even Balatta knew that he would be dead ere the nuptial date determined by his taboo. Ngurn made pilgrimage personally and gathered the smoke materials for the curing of Bassett's head, and to him made proud announcement and exhibition of the artistic perfectness of his intention when Bassett should be dead. As for himself, Bassett was not shocked. Too long and too deeply had life ebbed down in him to bite him with fear of its impending extinction. He continued to persist, alternating periods of unconsciousness with periods of semi-consciousness, dreamy and unreal, in which he idly wondered whether he had ever truly beheld the Red One or whether it was a nightmare fancy of delirium.

Came the day when all mists and cob-webs dissolved, when he found his brain clear as a bell, and took just appraisement of his body's weakness. Neither hand nor foot could he lift. So little control of his body did he have, that he was scarcely aware of possessing one. Lightly indeed his flesh sat upon his soul, and his soul, in its briefness of clarity, knew by its very clarity that the black of cessation was near. He knew the end was close; knew that in all truth he had with his eyes beheld the Red One, the messenger between the worlds; knew that he would never live to carry that message to the world—that message, for aught to the contrary, which might already have waited man's hearing in the heart of Guadalcanal for ten thousand years. And Bassett stirred with resolve, calling Ngurn to him, out under the shade of the bread-fruit tree, and with the old devil-devil doctor discussing the terms and arrangements of his last life effort, his final adventure in the quick of the flesh.

"I know the law, O Ngurn," he concluded the matter. "Whoso is not of the folk may not look upon the Red One and live. I shall not live anyway. Your young men shall carry me before the face of the Red One, and I shall look upon him, and hear his voice, and thereupon die, under your hand, O Ngurn. Thus will the three things be satisfied: the law, my desire, and your quicker possession of my head for which all your preparations wait."

To which Ngurn consented, adding:

"It is better so. A sick man who cannot get well is foolish to live on for so little a while. Also is it better for the living that he should go. You have been much in the way of late. Not but what it was good for me to talk to such a wise one. But for moons of days we have held little talk. Instead, you have taken up room in the house of heads, making noises like a dying pig, or talking much and loudly in your own language which I do not understand. This has been a confusion to me, for I like to think on the great things of the light and dark as I turn the heads in the smoke. Your much noise has thus been a disturbance to the long-learning and hatching of the final wisdom that will be mine before I die. As for you, upon whom the dark has already brooded, it is well that you die now. And I promise you, in the long days to come when I turn your head in the smoke, no man of the tribe shall come in to disturb us. And I will tell you many secrets, for I am an old man and very wise, and I shall be adding wisdom to wisdom as I turn your head in the smoke."

So a litter was made, and, borne on the shoulders of half a dozen of the men, Bassett departed on the last little adventure that was to cap the total adventure, for him, of living. With a body of which he was scarcely aware, for even the pain had been exhausted out of it, and with a bright clear brain that accommodated him to a quiet ecstasy of sheer lucidness of thought, he lay back on the lurching litter and watched the fading of the passing world, beholding for the last time the breadfruit tree before the devil-devil house, the dim day beneath the matted jungle roof, the gloomy gorge between the shouldering mountains, the saddle of raw limestone, and the mesa of black volcanic sand.

Down the spiral path of the pit they bore him, encircling the sheening, glowing Red One that seemed ever imminent to iridesce from colour and light into sweet singing and thunder. And over bones and logs of immolated men and gods they bore him, past the horrors of other immolated ones that yet lived, to the three-king-post tripod and the huge king-post striker.

Here Bassett, helped by Ngurn and Balatta, weakly sat up, swaying weakly from the hips, and with clear, unfaltering, all-seeing eyes gazed upon the Red One.

"Once, O Ngurn," he said, not taking his eyes from the sheening, vibrating surface whereon and wherein all the shades of cherry-red played unceasingly, ever a-quiver to change into sound, to become silken rustlings, silvery whisperings, golden thrummings of cords, velvet pipings of elfland, mellow distances of thunderings.

"I wait," Ngurn prompted after a long pause, the long-handled tomahawk unassumingly ready in his hand.

"Once, O Ngurn," Bassett repeated, "let the Red One speak so that I may see it speak as well as hear it. Then strike, thus, when I raise my hand; for, when I raise my hand, I shall drop my head forward and make place for the stroke at the base of my neck. But, O Ngurn, I, who am about to pass out of the light of day for ever, would like to pass with the wonder-voice of the Red One singing greatly in my ears."

"And I promise you that never will a head be so well cured as yours," Ngurn assured him, at the same time signalling the tribesmen to man the propelling ropes suspended from the king-post striker. "Your head shall be my greatest piece of work in the curing of heads."

Bassett smiled quietly to the old one's conceit, as the great carved log, drawn back through two-score feet of space, was released. The next moment he was lost in ecstasy at the abrupt and thunderous liberation of sound. But such thunder! Mellow it was with preciousness of all sounding metals. Archangels spoke in it; it was magnificently beautiful before all other sounds; it was invested with the intelligence of supermen of planets of other suns; it was the voice of God, seducing and commanding to be heard. And—the everlasting miracle of that interstellar metal! Bassett, with his own eyes, saw colour and colours transform into sound till the whole visible surface of the vast sphere was a-crawl and titillant and vaporous with what he could not tell was colour or was sound. In that moment the interstices of matter were his, and the interfusings and intermating transfusings of matter and force.

Time passed. At the last Bassett was brought back from his ecstasy by an impatient movement of Ngurn. He had quite forgotten the old devil-devil one. A quick flash of fancy brought a husky chuckle into Bassett's throat. His shot-gun lay beside him in the litter. All he had to do, muzzle to head, was to press the trigger and blow his head into nothingness.

But why cheat him? was Bassett's next thought. Head-hunting, cannibal beast of a human that was as much ape as human, nevertheless Old Ngurn had, according to his lights, played squarer than square. Ngurn was in himself a forerunner of ethics and contract, of consideration, and gentleness in man. No, Bassett decided; it would be a ghastly pity and an act of dishonour to cheat the old fellow at the last. His head was Ngurn's, and Ngurn's head to cure it would be.

And Bassett, raising his hand in signal, bending forward his head as agreed so as to expose cleanly the articulation to his taut spinal cord, forgot Balatta, who was merely a woman, a woman merely and only and undesired. He knew, without seeing, when the razor-edged hatchet rose in the air behind him. And for that instant, ere the end, there fell upon Bassett the shadows of the Unknown, a sense of impending marvel of the rending of walls before the imaginable. Almost, when he knew the blow had started and just ere the edge of steel bit the flesh and nerves it seemed that he gazed upon the serene face of the Medusa, Truth—And, simultaneous with the bite of the steel on the onrush of the dark, in a flashing instant of fancy, he saw the vision of his head turning slowly, always turning, in the devil-devil house beside the breadfruit tree.

Waikiki, Honolulu
May 22, 1916

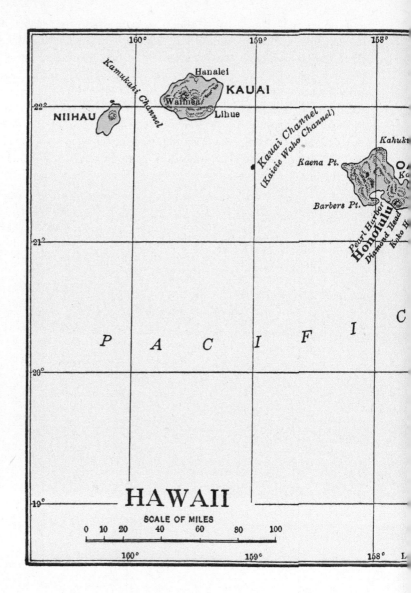

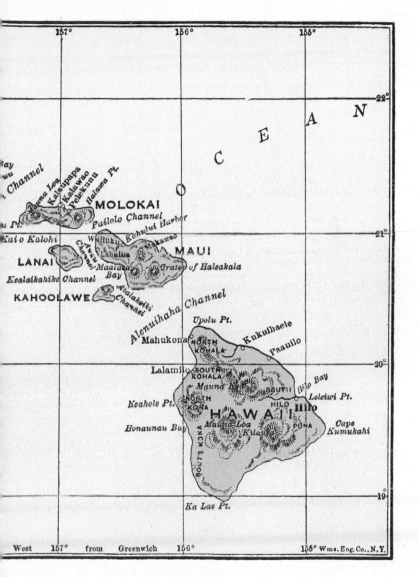

THE HAWAIIAN ISLANDS

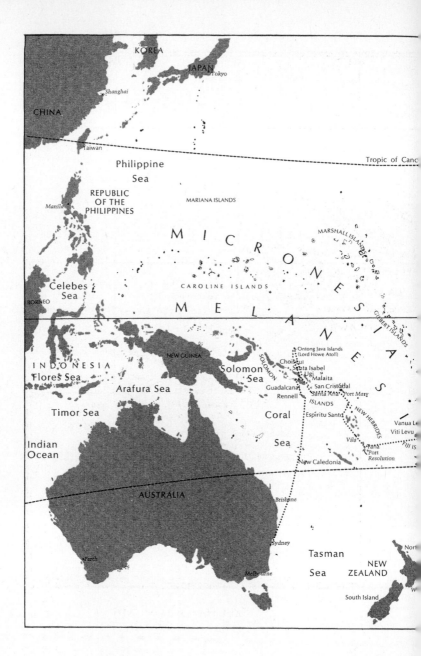

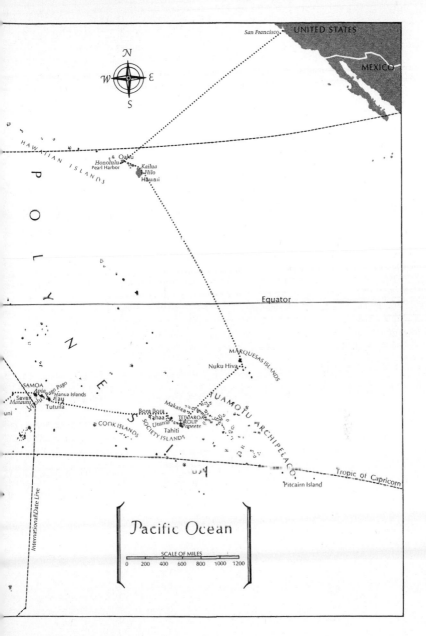

THE SOUTH SEAS

NOTES

FROM *HOUSE OF PRIDE AND OTHER TALES OF HAWAII*

THE HOUSE OF PRIDE

p. 3 *lanai*   porch

p. 4 *algaroba trees*   Spruce trees that commonly grow to about twenty feet in height.

p. 6 *Kamehameha I*   Monarch credited with uniting the eight major islands of Hawaii under one rule (c. 1758–1819).

p. 7 *luna*   boss

p. 8 *ukase*   decree

p. 9 *Kanaka*   A Hawaiian or other South Sea islander.

p. 9 *anchorite*   religious recluse or hermit

p. 10 *taro*   A perennial herb that has been a staple of Hawaiian diet from early times to the present day.

p. 13 *holokus*   A loose, seamed dress, modeled on those worn by the missionaries.

KOOLAU THE LEPER

p. 18 *Molokai*   Fifth largest of the Hawaiian islands. The leper colony at Kalaupapa on the north coast was established in 1866.

p. 22 *ti-plant*   A member of the lily family. The plant is an emblem of high rank. The roots can be boiled into a potent drink known as *okolehao*.

p. 23 *haoles*   white men

GOOD-BYE, JACK

p. 40 *malahini*   newcomer

p. 41 *Henley's lines*   William Ernest Henley (1849–1903), English poet, critic, and editor. The lines are from "Waiting," poem two of *In Hospital* (1873–75).

p. 42 *Olga Nethersole*   A well-known English actress, writer, and director (1870–1951).

FROM *SOUTH SEA TALES*

THE SEED OF McCOY

p. 49 *the Bounty . . . Pitcairn*   On April 28, 1789, following ongoing tyrannical conduct by their commander, Lieutenant William Bligh, the crew of H.M.S. *Bounty* mutinied while a few days' sail from Tahiti. Most of the mutineers settled in Tahiti, but nine sailed for Pitcairn Island accompanied by some native women. Their fate remained unknown until 1808, when an American vessel discovered the children of the mutineers, ruled by John Adams, the last surviving British sailor.

p. 60 *Acteon Islands*   The Actaeon Group is in the Tuamotu Archipelago, to the east of Tahiti.

p. 62 *Sumner method*   T. H. Sumner, an American sea captain, invented a new method for finding a ship's position at sea in 1837.

THE HOUSE OF MAPUHI

p. 78 *pandanus tree*   Known in English as the "screw pine." Its leaves are used for weaving, and its roots and fruit are eaten.

p. 79 *octagon-drop-clock*   A popular American clock that required winding only every eight days.

THE HEATHEN

p. 103 *vahine*   woman, especially Hawaiian woman (also spelled *wahine*)

p. 106 *"Païen noir!"*   "Black pagan!"

p. 106 *Bora Bora . . . Society Group*   The Society Islands are an archipelago, mostly of volcanic origin, in the South Seas. The principal island is Tahiti. They were annexed by France in 1880.

p. 109 *beche de mer*   The sea cucumber, reputed to be an aphrodisiac.

p. 110 *guano*   A natural fertilizer, made from bird droppings, and highly prized in the nineteenth century.

p. 111 *blackbirding*   Kidnapping of Africans or Polynesians for slavery or, as here, recruiting natives of the Solomons to work for several years for little reward.

p. 112 *Berserker rage*   A Berserker was a Norse warrior who fought with desperate courage and rage.

p. 114 *Savaii ... Upolu*   Samoan islands. Savaii is the largest island in Polynesia outside of Hawaii and New Zealand. Upolu lies to its southwest across the Apolima Strait.

p. 114 *lava-lava*   loincloth

MAUKI

p. 119 *Malaita*   One of the Solomon Islands, then reputed to be inhabited by headhunters and cannibals.

p. 123 *bêche-de-mer English*   London devotes a chapter of *The Cruise of the "Snark"* (1911), his account of his voyage through the South Seas, to a summary of *bêche-de-mer* English. The language was developed by traders to communicate with the many different tribes who had innumerable languages and dialects that were encountered in the region.

FROM *A SON OF THE SUN*

p. 148 *the Line*   The equator.

THE DEVILS OF FUATINO

p. 158 *Raiatea*   In the Society Islands.

p. 160 *talofa*   hello; greetings

p. 165 *Iorana*   greetings

THE FEATHERS OF THE SUN

p. 198 *Kai-kanak*   man-eater

FROM *ON THE MAKALOA MAT*

ON THE MAKALOA MAT

p. 209 *meles*   poems or vocal music

p. 212 *opihis*   limpets

p. 212 *Emerson*   Ralph Waldo Emerson (1803–82). American critic, philosopher, lecturer, and poet, most famous for his Transcendentalist essays, such as "Nature," "Self-Reliance," and "The American Scholar," who advocated moral individualism and a mistrust of convention.

p. 212 *mauka*   mountainward

p. 220 *luau*   feast

p. 222 *Kitchener*   British Field Marshal Horatio Herbert Kitchener (1850–1916). He brought the Boer War to an end, was commander in chief in India (1902–09), consul general in Egypt (1911), and secretary for war (1914).

p. 222 *leis*   flower garlands

p. 223 *maile*   A native shrub (*Alyxia olivaeformis*) used as a decoration.

p. 226 *pa wai holoi*   finger bowl

p. 226 *pa paakai*   salt dish

p. 226 *ipu kai*   fish-sauce dish

p. 226 *kahilis*   elaborately designed and decorated fans, signifying high social status

p. 226 *Pele*   fire goddess or volcano goddess

p. 227 *pupule*   insane

p. 227 *pau*   finish

p. 228 *palis*   precipices

THE TEARS OF AH KIM

p. 235 *brick tea*   a long-lasting and compact tea, pressed into cubes. It has been used in China since the tenth century, and has a harsh, tobacco-like odor.

p. 236 *Lloyds*   London association of underwriters, engages in insuring ships and their cargoes.

p. 239 *kahunas*   Hawaiian witch doctors or priests

THE BONES OF KAHEKILI

p. 246 *hapa-haole*   half white

p. 247 *lauhala mat*   A mat made by plaiting the pandanus leaf.

p. 253 *alii*   high chief

p. 255 *Hale o Keawe*   mausoleum

p. 256 *heiau*   temple

p. 260 *hunakele*   concealment

p. 262 *hoiau*   temple

p. 267 *pake*   Chinese

SHIN-BONES

p. 269 *"They ... heads"*   Ezekiel 32.27.

p. 272 *Black Watch ... Magersfontein*   The Black Watch, or Royal Highlanders, were among British troops under Lord Methuen, who were met by a Boer army at Magersfontein near the Modder River on December 10, 1899. The Black Watch were beaten back, suffering heavy losses.

p. 274 *kahuna lapaau*   medicine man

p. 275 *aumakuas*   family gods or deified ancestral spirits

p. 275 *heiaus*   temples or shrines

p. 277 *pilikia*   trouble

p. 277 *Jules Verne*   French writer (1828–1905) most famous for his travel tales, such as *Around the World in Eighty Days* and *Twenty Thousand Leagues Under the Sea.*

p. 279 *alii kapo*   sacred chiefess

p. 282 *Medusa*   In Greek mythology, one of the three winged female monsters known as gorgons. They turned all who looked on them to stone and had snakes for hair. Medusa was slain by Perseus, who watched her using his shield as a mirror, so as not to gaze at her directly.

p. 282 *Ecclesiastes*   Book of the Old Testament, in which ruminations on the transitory nature of life culminate in the assertion that "all is vanity."

p. 286 *pahoas*   daggers

p. 288 *lomi'd*   massaged

p. 288 *Tennyson* ... "Idyls of the King"   Alfred, Lord Tennyson (1809–92). English poet, who succeeded Wordsworth as poet laureate in 1850. *The Idylls of the King* appeared in installments in 1859, 1870, 1872, and 1885.

WHEN ALICE TOLD HER SOUL

p. 293 *Billy Sunday*   William Ashley "Billy" Sunday (1862–1935) played professional baseball for the Chicago White Stockings, before becoming a born-again Christian in 1886. His revivalist preaching was hugely popular and condemned the "sins" of modern life.

p. 297 *kamaainas*   native-born, especially old-timers

p. 298 *aloha*   greeting; also warm regard or love

p. 300 *wiki-wiki*   quickly

p. 302 *Dibble's "A ... Islands"*   The author Sheldon Dibble (1809–45), whose *History of the Sandwich Islands* was published in 1843.

FROM *THE RED ONE*

THE RED ONE

p. 312 *dark tower* ... *Browning* ... *Childe Roland*   The English poet Robert Browning (1812–89), whose "Childe Roland to the Dark Tower Came" was published in 1855.

p. 324 *Memnon*   In Greek mythology the son of Tithonus and Eos. He helped the Greeks in the Trojan war and was killed by Achilles.

p. 326 *Mendana*   The Solomon Islands were discovered by the Spanish explorer Alvaro de Mendaña in the sixteenth century.

READING GROUP GUIDE

1. Discuss Jack London's characterizations and descriptions of the South Seas and its islands. What is his overarching opinion of this territory, if any? In what way(s) does London diverge from the popularized romantic view of the South Seas? Or does he?

2. How does London depict the colonists, and how does he depict the natives, generally speaking? In what ways do you find that his views on colonialism and the clash of cultures illuminate the period? Do you find his positions contrary to contemporary opinion on the subject? On the other hand, in what ways does London conform to modern thought?

3. In his introduction, Tony Horwitz notes that "the dark tone of many of these stories reflects, in part, London's disturbed state of mind and health." How does this assertion inform your reading of the stories? Did you find any of London's stories in any way unbelievable? Why or why not?

4. Discuss the different kinds of risks London describes in this tropical environment. How do the threats posed by other humans stack up next to those

present in mother nature, whether in the form of storm, illness, or beast? How do London's protagonists generally fare in this challenging environment?

5. How does the recurring character David Grief embody white identity in these stories? Is Grief's character a realistic one, in your opinion? Is he typical of the other white characters London depicts on the islands, or not? Does London have an agenda in his depiction of Grief?

6. Nature and the physical world occupy a dichotomous territory in many of London's tales. The islands of the South Seas require tremendous physical endurance of their inhabitants and present much bodily threat, but at the same time London attributes significant health benefits to life in the wilderness. Does London attempt to resolve or explain this conflict, in your opinion?

7. In his preface, Christopher Gair discusses London's later tales, primarily published posthumously and in some ways a seeming departure from the tone of the earlier stories. In what ways did you find this to be true, if at all? How conflicted is London with regard to his American values?

A NOTE ON THE TYPE

The principal text of this Modern Library edition
was set in a digitized version of Janson, a typeface that
dates from about 1690 and was cut by Nicholas Kis,
a Hungarian working in Amsterdam. The original matrices have
survived and are held by the Stempel foundry in Germany.
Hermann Zapf redesigned some of the weights and sizes for
Stempel, basing his revisions on the original design.